Praise for
Watermark

"Authoritative and evocative in its use of historical detail, this stunning debut novel will transport readers to medieval France where evil lurks in unlikely places and love endures. Like the river Auda, for which the novel's unforgettable heroine is named, this story flows deep and dark and swift from its beginning to its powerful end."

—Brenda Vantrease

"*Watermark* is a powerful novel about the destructive forces unleashed by ignorance and superstition. Readers will care deeply for the courageous Auda who finds love where she least expects it, in the shadow of the Inquisition."

—*New York Times* bestselling author Sharon Kay Penman

"*Watermark* is a stunning debut—moving, compelling, and illuminating. Vanitha Sankaran has magically captured the lost world of medieval France in all its social, religious, and philosophical complexity, and done so with an admirable verve. Peopled with a wide array of compelling characters, *Watermark* is historical fiction at its best."

—David Liss, author of
The Devil's Company and *The Whiskey Rebels*

"An addictively engaging novel set at a time when reading and writing bloomed—the dawn of papermaking. What book lover could resist?"

—Nicole Mones, author of
The Last Chinese Chef and *Lost in Translation*

"A beautiful look at the dangers of an intolerant yesterday . . . whose battles are still fought today."

—Erika Mailman, author of *The Witch's Trinity*

"This engaging, clearly written novel pulls readers into a corner of the Middle Ages not often seen. . . . In recounting one woman's journey to discover her literary voice, Vanitha Sankaran evokes a distant era with startling parallels to our time."

—Sarah Johnson, book review editor,
The Historical Novels Review and
author of *Historical Fiction II: A Guide to the Genre*

Watermark

Vanitha Sankaran

AVON

An Imprint of HarperCollins*Publishers*

Map of Narbonne courtesy of the author.

WATERMARK. Copyright © 2010 by Vanitha Sankaran. All rights reserved. Printed in the United States of America. No part of this book may be used or reproduced in any manner whatsoever without written permission except in the case of brief quotations embodied in critical articles and reviews. For information address HarperCollins Publishers, 10 East 53rd Street, New York, NY 10022.

HarperCollins books may be purchased for educational, business, or sales promotional use. For information please write: Special Markets Department, HarperCollins Publishers, 10 East 53rd Street, New York, NY 10022.

FIRST EDITION

Designed by Diahann Sturge

Library of Congress Cataloging-in-Publication Data is available upon request.

ISBN 978-0-06-184927-5

10   11   12   13   14   OV/RRD   10 9 8 7 6 5 4 3 2 1

For my sister, Suja,
Who always believed this day would come.

With the Lord's help, the Inquisitor can,
with an obstetrician's hand, bring the twisting
snake out of the sink and abyss of error.

—Bernardo Gui,
Practica inquisitionis heretice pravitatis

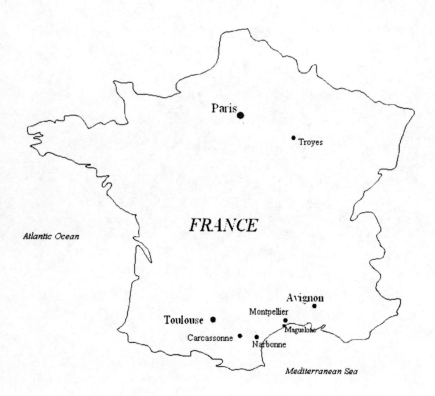

Paris

Troyes

FRANCE

Atlantic Ocean

Avignon

Montpellier

Toulouse

Maguelone

Carcassonne

Narbonne

Mediterranean Sea

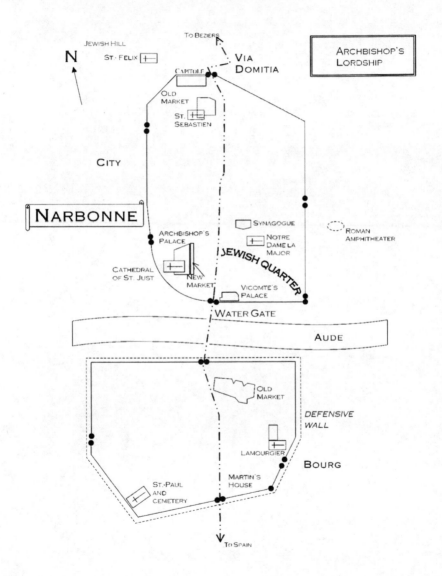

Watermark

Chapter One

Elena clutched her distended belly and tried not to cry out. A cold winter draft blew through crevices in the cottage's half-timbered walls. Yet rivulets of sweat still ran down the sides of her face. Propped in a corner, straddling a hay bale, she crossed her arms over the life growing inside her.

"Not y-yet," she hiccupped amid the fierce pain cramping her belly. She tilted her head back to stop her tears from falling and the salty moisture dripped into her throat. Her gaze rested on the wildflowers drying upside down in the corner. An old tune flitted through her head, a folksong her own mother had taught her, the lyrics long forgotten. In a broken voice, she hummed the melody.

Another sharp pang shot through her and she doubled over with a low cry. Warm liquid surged between her legs. She reached to feel the sticky wetness: thick dark blood. She looked across the room, over the floor of withered rushes and past the hearth to the single plank of wood that served as supper table, kitchen lath, and her husband Martin's workbench. A near-empty flagon of wine rested beside his paper vat.

Knocking her head back against the wall, she cried out for him. He had left hours earlier with their daughter, Poncia, to find the midwife. Why hadn't they returned?

Suddenly, the door flung open and an elderly woman stumbled through on thick legs and swollen knees. Not the midwife but someone else. Biatris, the healer. Had Martin brought her? She'd lost track of everything but the pain.

The woman directed her assistant, Onors, to build up the dwindled fire, then hovered over Elena. The healer looked like a leathery vegetable, weathered and withered, with a head of white wiry curls.

Elena whimpered and searched for her husband. She found him standing in the shadows, holding their daughter. Fear shone in his dark eyes. She tried to smile. He shook his head only once. Onors trundled him outside.

Elena keened a low cry after him. Another wave of birthing blood coursed onto the linen blanket tucked between her legs. The bleeding had to stop, but how? She curled her head over her stomach.

"Rest easy," Biatris said. She reached out to steady Elena, then glanced at her apprentice. "We need a compress of cinque-foil root to slow the bleeding. Look in the kitchen garden."

The young girl cast Biatris a grateful look and slipped outside. A cold winter gust blew through the rickety cottage and the door slammed shut. Elena gasped again, arms encircling her belly. Her body pushed out globs of half-clotted blood.

The healer shoved a cup of wine at Elena. She choked on the bitter poppy-laced drink.

Its warmth slid down her throat and seeped into her veins,

limbs, belly, and head. Soon a slow drowse tugged at her mind. The upsurge of pain receded into a dull ache and then into nothing. Her fingers relaxed and dropped the cup. She blinked, her vision murky, her eyelids weighted down.

Biatris stumbled among the stools and barrels cluttering the dim one-room home. Elena tossed her head back and forth. Oh, Martin would be angry, the way the woman pushed aside his tools, quills, and ink that lay scattered on the supper board.

Another jolt of pain knifed through her belly. Elena stifled a gasp and breathed in and out to calm herself.

"That's it, loosen the muscles," the healer said, picking up Elena's cup. She waddled to the table and washed her hands in the basin of river water, then dried each finger.

A low moan escaped Elena's lips. Pangs of homesickness and pain mingled together. *"Mare,"* she sobbed. But her mother wasn't there. Elena was alone, without mother, aunts, or cousins who could see her through this birth. Surely there would have been work enough for Martin in the family paper mill back home. Why had they ever left? A forlorn sadness gurgled through her lips. Her limbs slackened.

Biatris passed a full cup of the drugged wine back to her, then lowered herself beside the makeshift seat of hay.

Elena blinked back tears and swallowed the draught. She felt cold, too cold, her only remaining warmth focused in the lump of her belly. The metallic stench of blood gagged in her throat. She wheezed. Why was it so hard to breathe?

"My child. My babe," she said in a fading whisper. She dropped the cup. Dry tongue licked dry lips. Would her babe survive? How, motherless in this world? She focused on the healer, who reached to touch her clammy forehead and smooth her sweat-soaked hair. "Please."

Biatris gripped her hand and leaned in. "The Church permits

us only to cut babes from dead wombs." Her gaze darted to the door through which the young assistant had disappeared. "By then it may be too late." She stared into Elena's eyes.

What had she said—dead wombs, dead babes? Elena stared back, comprehension dawning. She placed her hands on either side of her belly and felt the receding warmth.

"Cut my babe free," she said in a whisper. Her breath burbled into a sob. Who would look out for her children, both of them? She struggled to remember what her daughter looked like.

The healer looked at her. "No time to call for a priest, but I bless you in God's name. He will understand."

Struggling to her feet, the healer reached for her bag and uncorked a clay bottle. She poured a thick white salve on Elena's belly and rubbed the numbing balm in circles into her cold skin.

"Prepare yourself," she said and shoved a wooden stick between Elena's teeth. Her hand curved around the haft of her large knife. She placed the tip of the blade on Elena's pregnant bulge and drew in her breath. Exhaling, she pushed the knife in hard.

Elena screamed, a shrill cry that split the bare room. The stick slipped from her mouth and fell onto the straw. The woman was killing her—the babe too? The healer pulled the blade through her thick flesh. Elena screamed again. Her stomach tore apart like a split gourd. She kicked, trying to escape the agony.

The healer broke through her belly and reached into her womb. Elena thrashed, shrieking. Biatris pressed on her abdomen and drew the child out, guiding its head and shoulders into the cold air. The infant's scream rang out.

Elena sobbed. Her babe lived.

In the background, the healer fussed over the child, cleaning the mucous from its eyes, nose, and mouth. Elena closed her eyes and drew in ragged breaths.

But then Biatris gasped. "My God."

Elena turned her pain-swollen gaze to her babe. Another girl? A boy? "Alive?"

"Your babe has will to live," the healer said, though Elena heard reluctance in her voice.

Biatris brought the infant close but Elena couldn't see, could only feel its slimy skin stick to hers. She tried to smile, but her lips felt heavy and curved downward.

"My babe," she said. Her fingers swiped at the air and fell. The room grew dimmer. A tune—her babe needed a tune. Again her mother's song ran through her head; with cracked sobs, Elena tried to hum along. A few words surfaced in her hazy memory.

> *Love, my love, how can a mortal be*
> *So pure, and innocent as is she.*
> *Dressed in beauty, will and God's grace*
> *What wonders will she see?*

Such wonders you will see, she thought to her child, and closed her eyes.

Chapter Two

The lady Elena was dead.

Onors, the healer's apprentice, dropped her muddy clump of roots and leaves and rushed to Elena's side. Seeing a child kick beside its mother's eviscerated body, she crossed herself. Had the old healer butchered the poor mother and cut the child from the dead corpse? She looked more closely at the infant and gasped. This thing was no child at all but a sickly creature, ivory-colored in skin and hair, white as bone. Even its eyes were so light, the translucent pink of a worm.

It had come too soon, undercooked, with no color yet baked into its skin and hair, so silent that she wondered for a moment if it still lived. But then it blinked.

"Demon," she said in a whisper and crossed herself again. The healer swaddled it in a rough woolen blanket and thrust it toward her. Onors jumped back, warding the white creature away. Biatris stepped closer and shoved it into her arms.

"Nonsense," she said. "Take the babe to her father." Her gaze lingered on the mother's peaceful face, then dropped to the bloody tear that gaped from Elena's deflated stomach. "I have work yet."

Onors mouthed a quick prayer. She held the creature at arm's length and shuddered in revulsion. What a small thing, weak, like an animal that had been born in a barn, doomed to be crushed under its mother's feet—as this witch-child ought to have been. The healer turned her back on them. Onors shifted the babe's weight onto one hip and grabbed the blood-ied knife.

She tucked the blade into her sash and pushed open the door. Father and daughter rushed to her with fearful questions writ large in their eyes.

"She's dead," Onors said, turning as their faces crumpled. They stumbled past her into the house. The door shut behind them and she bolted with the babe.

She ran blindly, sliding between brush and garigue all the way downhill until she ended at the river Aude. Fed by glacial runoff from the Pyrenees, the water ran black save for white eddies laced with shards of floating ice. She placed the witch-child on the rocky ground and stared at its too-white flesh and watery eyes, and the blood-specked white fuzz that covered its head. What kind of child could be born without color?

No, not a child, but a creature cut from dead flesh and born bedeviled. She'd heard about wretched abominations like this before, born in other towns. Cursed omens, they heralded ill fortune and despair. Maybe this one would bring bad crops, drought, even the dying sickness.

"*Roumèque,*" she whispered at it with a tremble. She should dump the creature in the river and watch it drown.

But she couldn't do it.

An idea was born in her head. Dipping her hand into the river, she crossed herself and traced a cold, wet cross on the child's forehead. Shouts sounded, not far in the distance. She withdrew the knife. "Born badly. But still I can save you."

She shoved three fingers into the child's mouth and pinched

its tongue. With her free hand, she brought the knife under the pink flap of flesh. In a single tug she slashed the blade through. Bright red blood spurted from the wound and splattered against Onors's face. The child opened her mouth into a wide, perfect circle and screamed.

"O Lord," Onors said, not flinching at the girl's cries. She raised her eyes to the cloudy sky. "We give this unto You to protect the babe from the devilment." She flung the piece of flesh into the dark river. It swirled into an eddy and disappeared.

She stared at the shrieking child. If the wound healed and the babe lived . . . No ifs. This babe would live. Determination burned bright in her pink eyes. Yet at least now the curse of her birth would bleed from her soul, and then the babe would be safe.

Just as the child launched into another wail, her father burst through the copse of trees, holding his other daughter. He dropped the girl and rushed toward Onors. Snatching the babe, he slapped Onors hard across the face. She fell to the ground.

Scuttling away from his fury, she gaped at him with unblinking eyes filled with tears. Didn't he understand?

"What have you done?" he demanded. His eyes darted over the babe's pale face, then moved down the length of her body. His fingers rested on her lips and came away crimson with blood. He wrenched loose a corner of the child's blanket and held the bunched up cloth against her mouth. A vibrant red seeped across the brown material. He let out a low cry.

"Nothing wrong, I've not done anything wrong," Onors insisted. The words tumbled from her lips.

The man pried his older daughter off of his leg and placed the infant on the dirt beside her.

"Papa?" the girl cried.

"Just sit." He advanced toward Onors.

"I've not done anything wrong," she said again. "I've saved her." She backed up on her hands and rear. "The babe won't never speak, won't never have the chance to spread the devil's lies."

Biatris crashed through the brush in front of them, sweating and struggling to recover her breath. Her gaze roved from Onors to the father, then rested on the young girl and the babe. She rushed to them with a cry.

Forgotten for a moment, Onors pulled back along the riverbank.

"The babe lives. She may yet be saved," Biatris said, taking the injured child in her arms. She lurched toward the path that led uphill back to the house. "If we move fast."

The man swallowed and clenched his fists. He stared hard at Onors, then followed the old woman. Onors watched until the pale-white babe disappeared from her view. Had she saved it? Would it live?

Only God knew.

It is too difficult to detect heretics when they do not openly admit their error but hide it, or when there is not certain and sufficient evidence against them.

—Bernardo Gui,
Practica inquisitionis heretice pravitatis

Part I
Spring 1320

Chapter Three

A clap of thunder startled Auda awake. Bolting upright on her pallet of hay, she pushed aside the oilcloth flap covering the square outlook by her bed. Storm clouds darkened the predawn sky. She huddled in her blanket and breathed against the furious thump of her heart. Closing her eyes, she tried to drowse to the rumble of her father's snores from the loft above, but it was no use. She couldn't fall back asleep.

By habit, she reached across the pallet for her sister, Poncia, to ask her to sing a tune, a love song or a hymn from church. Sometimes, after a nightmare, her sister would hold Auda's hand and hum an old lullaby of their mother's. But Poncia, only six months ago, had married and moved away.

Auda slid out of her pallet and pulled a woolen dress on over her shift, her bare toes scrunching against the cold winter ground. Thin ice shards had formed in the basin of rainwater that stood outside the larder where she slept. She picked them out and washed her face, then stole into the hearth room. Dried rushes and alder leaves crunched under her feet, their sweet woody fragrance rising up.

The fire had dwindled low under the cook pot. Auda fanned the embers, then opened the shutters over the outlook and rolled up the oilcloth flap to let in some air. The rain had started again. Little wonder: it had rained every day for the past four months in Narbonne. Each morning, the downpour arrived with the salty breeze of the *marin* off the Mediterranean. Normally, the dry gusts of the evening *cers* would chase the rain away, but not these days. These days the rain was constant.

"The inquisitors are circling Narbonne like hawks," her father had told her with a dark look, "while the priests claim the rain is all the work of the devil." He snorted. "Pure nonsense."

But the Church had added extra masses at Matins and Prime just to accommodate all the newfound piety.

Auda fed the fire sticks of wood. Orange shadows flickered over the sparsely furnished room. In one corner, a table and two benches stood alongside a shelf that held a pair of empty wine flagons and a green wax tablet with a wooden stylus. Two sackcloth cloaks hung on hooks nailed into the door.

Fanning away the acrid smoke that rose from the burning pine kindling, Auda tiptoed down the corridor that led to her father's studio. A familiar sense of anticipation prickled her spine.

This was where she and her father made paper, reams of blank sheets to be filled with words from all manner of people—rich lords, learned priests.

Even her.

The workshop was centered around a large vat holding the

linen mixture that made up the paper pulp. Fashioned from an old wine barrel, the vat sat on a plinth over a low fire and next to a drainage gulley cut into the rough brick floor. Auda crossed the channel by way of a wooden duckboard and lit a torch. The flame's reflection danced on the vat's black liquid surface. Today her father would beat the macerated linen into a pulp; when he was done, the actual papermaking would begin.

Auda dropped the torch in a sconce over a row of smaller barrels, where the degrading cloth that would go into the next batch of pulp was kept. The wet linen rags, balled up inside, were already moldy and fermenting. She breathed in, picking out nuances in the ripe odor, the sweetness and the acidic undertone that lingered in her nostrils. Another week and they'd be ready.

She sat down at the corner desk. Its surface was cluttered with a miscellaneous ruck: quills, blades, brushes, old bits of paper, older pieces of parchment, pots of ink and sand, and an empty flagon of wine. In the middle sat a large book that her father, Martin, had rented from the stationer.

He rented books as often as he could from Tomas, even when the men had no work to discuss. A shopkeeper with strong ties to the Church and the Parchmenter's Guild, Tomas was loath to speak in public about Martin's paper, but for a few discreet coins would approach the papermaker with some side work.

"Cheap men need cheap copies," Tomas would say, sniffing as he handed her father a thick wrapped package containing a book made of parchment.

It was almost always a text for a university, though occasionally a colorful romance or collection of verse made an appearance. Martin would make sheets of paper in an identical size and number to the parchmented work and copy the text in his careful hand. A binder would sew the work up into gatherings of eight pages, then stitch the gatherings together and bind them with cloth-board covers. The resulting book would be far less grand than a parchmented work with colorful illuminations and a tooled leather cover, and would fetch small coin for all the effort. Still, Martin jumped at every chance to copy a parchmented book on paper.

"Someday people will flock to us directly, eh, Auda?" he said often. "They will seek us out to have their words captured in a dozen books spread all over Christendom."

Auda quelled a shiver of excitement and tried not to dream, as she often did, that the first original book Martin made would be written by her. Surely that was his dream, too—why else would he go through such effort to bring books home to share with her? She could picture it, a leather-bound volume containing pages and pages of her writing, maybe even decorated with bright illuminations. If Poncia knew of her ambitions, she would scoff at them both, asking what kind of woman wanted to write books? Few could even read.

Poncia might well be right. But what if she wasn't?

"The Lord saved you for a reason, my special child," Auda had heard her father mumble once. "If only I knew why."

She caressed the dark book on the desk, her fingers trailing over the fat black script on the book's cloth-board cover. *Liber compositae medicinae.* She'd told her father she wanted to make a booklet of simples and herbal cures for her sister, on the occasion of Poncia's saint's day. Her sister was ever at a loss to remember which herbs fought melancholy, which soothed distemper, and which chilled a fever. The week after Auda had shared her plan with her father, he had brought her this book on physicking. The volume was due to go back to the stationer's today.

She flipped it open. The first page, as usual, bore the book's curse.

He who thieves this Book
May he die the death of pain,
May he be frizzled in a pan.
Says the servant of the Lord:
Steal not this Book, stranger or friend
Or fearing the Gallows will be your end.
And when you die the Lord will say
Where is my Book that you stole away?

The curse should have scared her but Auda only felt a kinship with the writer who'd authored the warning not to mistreat his book.

Reaching into a desk drawer, she pulled out the paper booklet she was making for Poncia. She'd already sketched in the symbols for wind, earth, fire, and water over a drawing on the human body, copied from a Greek codex she'd read months before. On the front page she had drawn a pelican, which had been a favorite of their mother's. On the back page she'd written herbal wisdom on getting a babe secured in the womb.

She flipped to the blank middle now and chose a last few simples to copy. Humming while she worked, she wrote each recipe like a verse to be sung, crafting it into a rhyme that her sister could remember.

For soothing sleep, slumber sublime
Lemon and lavender's the cure.
If frights and fears in dreams disturb,
Add chamomile, to be sure.

She read the words over, pleased. It was only in moments like this when she thought she heard her own voice.

A loud snore interrupted her tune and she glanced up at the loft. Her father had returned home late last night from the tavern, drunker than a sheep's head soused in ale. His snores rumbled, deep and regular. Dawn would soon break. If he didn't wake soon, he would miss the morning market. Three times a week, on market days, Tomas allowed Martin to set up in a corner of his stall to serve as a scribe, a reader and writer of letters for those who could not do for themselves. The work earned Martin a few pennies, and Tomas even more for supplying the parchment and ink.

Auda laid down her quill, intending to wake her father. Yet as if on cue, he groused himself awake and a few moments later, lumbered into the workshop. The months of dampness had stiffened his joints and he walked with a slight limp. The rains had waterlogged the crops and thinned the stock of birds and beast sent to the butchers. Martin's once ample paunch had receded into mere chubbiness, though his shoulders were still strongly muscled.

Martin climbed the steps to the vat and loosed a stream of urine into the murky water to help the soaking linens degrade. He leaned in and plunged a hand into the pulpy water. Gray strands stuck to his fingers.

Sitting back, Auda focused on her father as light from the torch caught him in profile. On the surface he looked like any other man, stout with swarthy skin, thick limbs, and cropped hair. But to her his brown eyes spoke of his true character, of risk and passion.

She loved watching him work in the quiet moments of the morning. Somehow, when he held his long-handled paddle and churned the pulp, his awkward gait grew into grace, his reserved manner into an expression of devotion.

Today, however, he didn't pick up his tools. Instead, he rubbed his wet fingers against his smock and sought his daughter in the shadows.

"Ah, *ma filla*," he said, his thin lips curving into a wide smile, "one week more and this batch will be ready to sell. And just in time! This is going to be the batch that changes everything for us."

Auda lifted her head to meet his merry eyes. What did he mean?

"We have order for paper, Auda. A real order! Not this piddling work of scribing dull letters or copying books for the cheapest bidder. No, this request is for blank sheets, not just a few but four whole reams. And here's the best part." Martin leaned in. "The order comes straight from the palace!"

Chapter Four

Auda blinked, trying to understand. Someone from the palace wanted his paper? Who could it be? Where had this person found Martin? Had he said what the paper would be used for? Her father had been trying for years—since before she was born—to get anyone of worth to notice his paper. She wanted to know every detail.

Martin mistook her confusion for wonder. "I know, it's an amazing fortune for us. But there'll be time enough to discuss it later. Come, we'll be late to meet Tomas."

He hurried her out of the room before she could ask any questions, reminding her to take the physicking book with them. While he packed a sack of the tools he needed for scribing—Tomas provided nothing but a corner of the stall and a small table and stool—Auda busied herself with the ritual of getting dressed to go outdoors. She tied her bone white hair into a knot at the nape of her neck, covering it with a square of tan cloth and a cap over that. Wrapping herself in a thick sackcloth cloak, she drew the hood around her face.

Out of habit, she patted her nose, lips, and cold cheeks, feeling the tiny pockmarks where ash from the hearth and vat had singed her cheeks. Skinny and pale, with the straight body of a boy, she was certainly no beauty. But as long as she tucked her hair under layers of fabric and her white skin stayed hidden under her dress and cloak, she would look no different than any other girl swaddled against the cold rain.

She wrapped the book in a sackcloth cover and waited for her father outside. The air smelled of drenched earth and loam. Auda raised her face to the drizzle, breathing in the cold wetness until her chest felt full to bursting.

"Come along, Auda," her father said, clapping a hand on her shoulder. "Let's be off."

She followed him down the long dirt path that led to the main road. Her father set a brisk pace today, his step quickened with happiness. Well, why not? An order for four reams would keep them fed for months. And if the customer liked the paper, that could change everything for them. She smiled, feeling a lightness in her step also.

"Such a fine day, Auda," Martin said, looking back at her. "No matter what the priests say, with all the rains, the town looks like it's born anew."

The rain had brought a certain lushness to town: the flowers and trees and the thriving vineyards that carpeted the fields outside of Narbonne. The grapes ended at the rocky hills of La Clape, which stood as a barrier between the precious fruit and the salty marshes that led out to sea beyond. To the west, the hazy silhouette of the Corbières blended into the gray sky. A long ribbon of storm clouds nestled in the valley of the mountains.

Whatever else the rains heralded, for Auda they brought clarity of sight. Her pale eyes hurt in the open daylight, burned in the full sun. Even with her hand shaded over her lids, she could scarcely see in the brightness of a normal summer day.

But in the dimness of first light, especially under a cloudy sky like this, she could almost discern detail beyond the usual shabby blurs.

The church bells rang for Matins and peasants dressed in dirty work clothes began emerging from the huts lining the road. Full on a breakfast of bread and watered beer, they headed toward the fields to plough the land for the spring sowing. Auda smiled at each of them as she passed, but received scant acknowledgment in return.

She frowned. Normally, when she went out with her sister, people nodded with a greeting. Had the rains visited so much ill will on town that people had forgotten how to smile?

Priests settled in pairs along the road, calling out sermons to the few people passing by.

"The Second Flood is Coming: God will Save the Faithful," one of them yelled. "Repent now and be forgiven of your sins! The Church will save your souls."

"The only thing the Church is going to do," her father muttered in a low tone, "is to bring in the inquisitors. Idiots."

Auda closed her mouth against the thick nubbin of her tongue. The threat of inquisitors had been with her for her entire life. Her father had even built a hiding place in the kitchen to secret her away in case of danger, a small hole behind the wall, barely large enough to hold one person.

Well, rain or no, this town was her home and she felt safe here. Anywhere else, she might have been killed because of her appearance, or at least walled away in a convent. Yet even among the conflagrations of heresy that had burned whole towns to ashes in the last century, Narbonne prospered. It wasn't for lack of heresy. Forbidden churches spouting a myriad of philosophies had once lived side by side in town. People might gripe about their neighbors' doings to themselves, but to the outside world and the Church they would say nothing. Narbonne guarded her own.

The rain grew thicker, flooding the numerous puddles. They picked up their pace, turning onto the cobblestone Via Domitia, an old Roman merchant road, toward Auda's namesake, the river Aude. The rising waters flowed alongside the houses and shops, beyond the docks where the butchers dumped their offal every morning, past the new cathedral construction, and eventually out to sea. The Aude bisected Narbonne into two districts, the rich city of the nobles and the poorer, working-man's bourg, where her father's cottage stood.

Swollen with weeks of rain, the river was reckless and feck-less with abandon. Its roar seemed like the melody of a hundred discordant voices. Had these very voices clamored for the piece of her that now rested in frigid waters? Auda wondered, as she had so many times before, whether her father had named her after the river as a reminder or a caution. She knew only the bare facts of her birth and mutilation, and very little about her mother. Neither her father nor her sister liked to speak of that time.

"Come along, Auda, no time to dally," Martin interrupted, hurrying her away.

Auda kept her eyes on her feet as they strode along the path to Parchmenter's Lane, until at last they reached the stationer's shop. Sitting in the middle of the line of shops, the tiny building housed sheer wizardry: here one could buy all the ingredients to make someone smile, laugh, fall in love, even hate.

Martin ushered her inside. The shop was arranged in precise order, each wall lined with shelves crammed with items. The lower sills held the inexpensive and bulky articles: copper vessels and clay pots; thongs, cords, and cloth boards for binding; glue made of gum, fish, and sometimes even cheese; wax tablets in red and green; bottles of chalk, ash, powdered bore, and pumice; clothlets; scraps of leather; old lengths of twice-used palimpsest; and a rack of thin needles. Auda trailed her fingers over a pair of rolled hemp balls and onto a stack of wooden boards—oak and smoothed pine.

The higher shelves (in plain sight of Monsieur Tomas) stored the more expensive, exotic merchandise. Here lay the burnishing tools for smoothing parchment; quills, reed pens, and metal tips; bone points; gall ink and inkhorns; dyes of every color (red ochre, terre verte, saffron, red brazil, vegetable green pigments, azurite and tumsole seeds, even cinnabar and lapis lazuli); ivory tablets; knives of fine steel; creamy rolls of parchment and thinner sheets of vellum; and boxes whose treasures she had not yet had the chance to discover.

Tomas himself guarded her favorite shelf, a thick plank of iron-studded wood bearing chains that hung in heavy loops behind his desk. Anchored into these chains were the books the stationer ordered from faraway scriptoriums, usually at the behest of a nobleman.

Martin hurried to the counter.

"You're late," Tomas said in frank disapproval. A thin man with a stingy frown that seemed fixed on his face, he always looked down on Martin, and even more so on Auda.

"There's a customer waiting for you to pen his words. And that dirty Jew came by looking for you again. Tell him he's not to come around here anymore. If you want to consort with the likes of him, do it on your own time."

Jew—he must have meant Shmuel, an old friend of her father's.

Martin offered a smile as he reached into the pouch on his belt and drew out two pennies. "Ah, but I brought you your fee, for this week and the next."

Tomas's frown softened as he picked the coins from Martin's palm. "Hm. Well, at least I was able to sell a few items to the man while he waited. Nothing spectacular, only some twine and old leather I'd meant to dispose of anyway."

He nodded toward the back of the store, which opened up into a small stall facing the market. "See to this man who wants to write a message to his two bickering sons." He jerked his chin at Auda. "And tell the girl to sit on a stool in the back, if she must."

Martin shrugged an apology to Auda and disappeared behind the linen curtain that separated the shop from the stall. She shook her head and searched for a stool. Even though she'd been accompanying her father for months—ever since her sister had married—still the stationer couldn't accept that, while Auda could not speak, she could hear just fine. He'd raised a fuss when she had first started handling his books, like the physicking book she'd brought back with her. But when he saw that she was more careful than her father with the pages, he grudgingly let her be.

Breathing in the musty scents of pigment and charcoal, Auda took a seat toward the back of the shop, just near the curtain that separated her from her father. Here she could work in peace, copying the last of the simples into the booklet for Poncia while she listened to her father talk to his customers, and tried to catch an occasional glimpse of the market crowds.

She had just finished another verse when the door to the shop opened. Craning her neck, she saw a short, round fellow with dark skin and tattered clothes, patched in different shades of green and gray, tottering toward the counter. A Gypsy! She had seen them before, in the Great Fair. Martin had made friends with one called Donino, and every summer he took Auda personally to see Donino and the treasures the Gypsies brought in from different corners of the world.

Reaching Tomas, the gypsy unrolled a cloth bundle and spread its contents over the counter.

"What is this junk?" Tomas protested. "Get this garbage out of here!"

The gypsy bowed. His stringy gray hair fell in rancid braids about his face. "*Dominus*! I only bring you some worldly goods to add to your excellent range of merchandise. Please, just have a look."

Tomas glowered. "If you don't leave now, I'll call the street guard for you," he said, waving the peddler off. "I've work to do, and a customer, don't you see?" He gestured at Auda.

"All the more reason to consider my wares, *dominus*," the Gypsy said. He clacked a pair of illustrated wooden squares together. "Perhaps some fortune cards? Or a pen made from the finger bone of St. Adolphus himself?" His tone was a mixture of encouragement and servility.

Auda drew near. The Gypsy smelled of minty spices. He was also filthy, with grease and dirt caked into his clothes and skin. She scanned the jumble of articles he'd scattered over the counter. Most looked like rubbish: wooden chits, old jars, a handful of dried seeds.

"I'll not tell you again. Get this garbage out of my shop," Tomas ordered, his voice rising.

"You have a look, *domna*." A note of despair entered the Gypsy's voice. "Maybe a bottle of liquid fire? Or a watermark from the papermakers in Italy?"

Auda, about to turn away in disappointment, paused. The papermakers in Italy? Her father talked about them often. The Italian papermakers were at the forefront of innovation. Supported by the needs of seven universities, compared to the two in France and one in Spain, the Italians were kept busy copying textbooks for the scores of students who passed through over the years.

If the Italians saw fit to mark their paper as their own, per-haps her father needed too as well– especially now that he was supplying a patron in the palace itself.

The Gypsy nodded. "Yes, see." He picked out a piece of twisted wire from the assorted litter on the counter that was crudely crafted into the shape of a bull. He held the device up to the weak light filtering in through the window. "The finest papermakers are using them. It's yours, for mere pennies."

Auda tilted her head. How did it work?

"No, no, no," Tomas cried, sweeping the cloth roll with all of its articles onto the ground. "I won't have anyone saying I con-sort with Gypsies and Jews, not in my shop! Get out of here."

"Please, *dominus*, just a moment. *Domna*." Their eyes met. The gypsy drew back for a second, then grabbed at her skirt. "Just a look."

Auda moved away and hid her face. She edged back toward the curtain and the comforting sound of her father's deep voice.

"Get out!" Tomas pushed the man out of the store, barely allowing him to gather his belongings. He slammed the door shut.

"Damned rain," he swore, more to himself than to Auda, "brings all the cursed wretches out like rats from the gutter. Best be wary of them. That wire of his was probably some fraud. I've heard about these tricks with paper before, clever ways for those like him to send messages to one another. Some say even the Good Men used them." He muttered something more on the damnation of heretics as he walked away.

Auda shook her head as she watched his retreating back. Foolishness and superstition. Did the bakers use their dough marks to communicate dark deeds to one another? Did leatherworkers use their brands? Marking one's work was hardly testament to believing in heresies.

Yet her father was forever on the lookout for new ways to promote his paper. Perhaps he could make use of this device—if he could figure out how to use it. She would ask him later. Or maybe she would surprise him with a gift when the Gypsies came to town for the fair that summer.

Chapter Five

Martin didn't linger when the bells rang for Terce, signaling noon and the end of his shift at the stall. He waved a hasty farewell to Tomas.

"I'll see you midweek."

When they were out on the street, he turned to Auda. "What a bore that customer was, talked my ear into a drowse on how his two sons have fallen in love with the same woman and were threatening to fight a duel over her hand. In the end he didn't even send them separate letters, just one forbidding either to marry the girl!"

Auda didn't answer, staring instead through the heavy patter. Two black-cloaked clergymen had just turned the corner, not twenty feet from them.

Despite herself, she tensed with fear. Jacobins, in this town? Large and hefty, they moved like a pair of fearless rats. It was said that the Dominicans, as some called them, had the skill to see into a person's soul and root out its evil. Had they come on account of the rains?

"Save your Soul!" one yelled at the passing carts and pedestrians.

"Hear the Lord! He will absolve you," the other said. His gaze turned toward them.

Martin sucked in his breath. "This way."

Grasping Auda by the arm, he veered onto a side street and pulled her along a crooked path that led out of town. Through the rain, Auda couldn't see if the men were following them. Trying not to make any noise, she clamped her mouth shut and listened, hearing nothing but the patter of water on dirt and stone. Her breath burst out in a cough. Finally, their house came into view.

"Go inside," Martin said in a terse voice, nodding at the door. "I'll see to the animals."

Pushing through the gate, Auda came to the front door and slipped off her hood, when suddenly she paused. The door was ajar—hadn't she closed it before she left? Tightening her hold on her basket, Auda edged backward. Had someone come looking for her father?

The door flung open and a familiar face peered out. Poncia, her sister, called to her. "Auda! Where in the world have you been?"

Auda rushed to embrace her sister. Poncia, wearing a worried frown, kept stiff for a moment, but then relaxed and returned the hug. Pulling back at last, Auda held her sister at arm's length. Poncia looked nothing like her, flushed rosy where Auda grew pale, moved sleekly where Auda stumbled. Her sister had grown into the type of woman all girls sought to be, with round hips meant for bearing children, blond hair braided and tucked under a handkerchief, and soft skin oiled with pork fat. Even her speech sounded superior, crisp and sharp, unlike their father's muddy mixture of Catalan, Occitan, and Spanish.

Hard to believe this finely dressed blue-eyed beauty was related to her at all.

"You look well," Poncia said, fluffing her deep blue skirts. She sat on the bench. Her six-month trip to help her new husband acquire stock for his spice trade had taken her all through the country—even to Paris itself.

Auda hadn't known when her sister would return, had secretly feared that Poncia wouldn't leave merry Paris at all. Why would she? Her life now was so different from the drab routine she had had here at home, stuck taking care of a sister who lived in the dark.

No, that wasn't fair. Poncia had never once complained about the burden. But it was clear to all who knew her that the fair girl wanted fine clothes and a rich life. She had stayed at home longer than she should have, to take care of Auda. Any other girl her age might not have found a man to marry. But Poncia had undertaken the task with vigor, doing favors for old women in church and taking advice from matronly mothers wishing to pass on their wisdom. It was not long before one of them introduced Poncia to the handsome Jehan. Months later, they were married.

Auda dropped her basket, wiped her face dry, and hung up her sackcloth cloak beside her sister's new surcoat. She fingered the soft blue cloth that matched Poncia's laced kirtle—so this is what marriage to a fine merchant brought! She pushed away a pang of envy and sat next to her sister. Lifting her hands, she rolled them around each other in imitation of wagon wheels and pointed to her mouth.

Your trip. Tell me. She smiled and touched her sister's arm for a response.

Poncia shook her head. "Pull up your sleeves, Auda," she said. "I can't see your fingers."

The sisters had developed the crude sign language long ago. Her father had picked it up too, despite grumbling that he'd gone through the effort of teaching the girls their letters. Wax tablets hung in every room, but pressing words into the wax with a stylus took too much time to accommodate real conversation.

Auda smiled at the memory of learning her letters. Reading and writing were common enough among nobles, and Narbonne boasted a small school where boys could learn the basics of grammar even if they were not destined for the clergy. Of course girls were not admitted, not that Martin could have afforded the hefty fee. Instead he had taught her and Poncia how to read and write himself.

"It will be our secret language," he'd said to the both of them, though his eyes met Auda's.

She had mastered reading and writing with ease, and was soon poring over books borrowed from the stationer on physicking and philosophy while Poncia still struggled to spell common words. Auda never gloated over her ability, but secretly was glad she was skilled at something that eluded her pretty sister.

Auda rolled up her sleeves and mimed the motion of rolling wheels again.

"Oh, the trip." Poncia waved the request away. "Later. First I want to know what you were doing out by yourself. Don't tell me it was to buy bread." Her voice grew apprehensive. "It's not safe out there now."

Auda shook her head in exasperation. Like their father, her sister worried too much.

Poncia frowned at her. "Where's Papa?"

Feeding the animals. Just back from scribing. She signed the image of a goat with her left hand and fed it with her right, then mimed the motion of writing.

"He took you to the stationer's with him?"

Auda crossed her arms over her chest. *It's safe.*

Poncia pursed her lips. "Well, while both of you were out, I pulled greens from the kitchen garden, and brought in the eggs from the barn—only two mind you." She nodded at the basket on the table. "You have to learn these things, Auda. You can't just shrug them off anymore, follow in Papa's shadow."

Auda touched her sister's cheek. After the loneliness of the past months, she was glad to have Poncia back. Even her sister's strict words brought a smile to Auda's face.

Poncia relented and leaned over to kiss Auda's brow. "It's high time I returned," she admitted. "I worried the entire time I was away about you." Ignoring Auda's frown, she passed her the vegetable basket. "And the north bred such a chill in my bones."

While Poncia chattered about the glorious scenery and the opulence of Paris shops, Auda sorted through the greens. She dumped a handful of peas on the table. The garden had grown lean in the recent deluge; yesterday she had found only a couple of withered carrots among the rotting vegetation. Even with the ham bone, today's pottage would taste thin. At least there were eggs.

"Word at the king's court is that rose is the scent to be smelled this season," Poncia said, shelling the peas. "I suppose I'll be drying petals for months." She pushed aside a pile of pods to feed to the animals later.

Music? Auda signed, strumming an imaginary fiddle.

"Song and dance on every road," her sister said and sang a witty verse about a courtier fooling his lord over an affair with the lord's wife.

Auda smiled in appreciation. She'd always fancied clever tales and the rhythm of words set to song, often humming her favorites when she was alone. It was the only time her voice sounded normal, sounded real. She rarely spoke, even at home. Her stump tongue could produce some sounds. Growing up, Poncia had encouraged her to try different syllables.

Na. Ma. Pa. But the noises always sounded harsh to Auda, underscored her inability to speak normally. Nothing like her voice on paper.

"Papa would do well to put aside this business of making paper and scribe instead, in a real city, somewhere with more coin," her sister said.

Auda sighed and turned so as not to answer. She fanned the hearth flames and poured a jug of water into the pot of grease and oats from last night's meal. An old apple core floated to the top.

"Surely even here he can turn to a better trade than peddling paper to the masses—perhaps scribing for the abbey up in Fontfroide. It's a foolhardy risk to be associated with an invention discovered by Moors and infidels."

Poncia warmed to her subject. "What need do simple folk have of knowing letters anyway? What would they know to write? The names of their lord's sheep and the number of needles in a stack of hay? For pity's sake."

Auda grit her teeth and chopped the savory, her knife knocking against the table. Poncia made this argument often, usually to their father. Scribing could be a lucrative profession, if managed well. And papermaking, well it was a risk. What was the use in making cheap paper when the only ones who knew their letters—noblemen and priests—could afford the more costly parchment rolls?

Still, the price of parchment went up every year; animal hide was increasingly scarce. Tomas explained it was on account of death in the cattle herds, lack of feed, and better uses for the skins.

"Now that I'm married, I'll ask Jehan to find a better living for Papa," Poncia continued. "Maybe as a scribe for a fine house. And you should have a thought for yourself. It's well past time to start searching for a man to wed you." She looked at Auda sidelong. "All the women in town are surely talking, and you can ill afford that."

Auda squared her jaw and huffed at her sister's lecture.

Women, sour and old. Gossip more than whores. She didn't let on how much the comments hurt—not that she was plain or even a fright, but that she was a burden on their father.

"Auda!"

Always talk when I'm there. She templed her hands into the sign of a house, and made a cross with her fingers. *Send her to the convent!*

"Who said that?" Poncia asked in a sharp tone.

Auda tossed the peas and herbs into the pot and fanned the flames. She shrugged. *I can tell tales too.* She took the oversized tablet from the shelf and scratched into the green wax with a stylus. The words played a rhythm in her head. If she'd had time, she would have written the words like verse to a song, with cadence and flair. But Poncia was an impatient reader and scanned the words over Auda's shoulder as she wrote.

Lady Margaret, the cloth-maker's wife.
Whose servant wench is always saying when the Master
will be gone.
So the lady can rush to see the widower chandler.
Who is always looking to couple.
And when the deed is done, the lady will go home,
To find someone else polishing her husband's pole.
Who?
None other than the servant wench,
Who earns two pennies for every tumble.

Poncia's flattened lips gave way to a muffled giggle. "You shouldn't tease about such things."

Smirking, Auda took the eggs from the basket.

"Best not to write such things either," Poncia said, serious again. She carried the tablet to the hearth fire and tilted it back and forth near the flames until the wax melted and ran level. "Nothing that would make a stranger look twice at you."

Auda frowned and gave the pottage a quick stir. Her sister never knew how to have fun. She dropped the eggs into it whole. The scent of garlic and ham rose from the almost bubbling soup.

"I know you think I fret overly," Poncia sighed. "But there are madmen out there who would easily trade your soul to safeguard their own. In a single blink of the eye, they would descend upon you."

For? Auda didn't look up as she crooked her finger in question.

Poncia bit her lip. "A sign. Of error in thought. In words. Heresy or witchery. Auda, you haven't seen what I have. You don't understand how the heretics can bewitch you. They'll come to you with honeyed words, saying they accept all men and all women as the same, that everyone is equal in the eyes of God." She shook her head. "As if a pauper can equal a lord."

Auda tilted her head over the strange mixture of fear and contempt in her sister's voice. How had Poncia learned this? She raised her hands to ask.

The door swung open and their father walked in.

"Papa!" Poncia ran to him.

"Ah, Poncia! You're looking well," Martin said. He struggled to take off his sackcloth cloak. "It's a garbage grave out there," he said, shaking the rough material. He hung it on the wall and raked water out of his hair with one hand. "Rain mixed with animals mixed with shit mixed with people."

Auda retreated. She set three scratched wooden plates on the table, lined them with trenchers, and ladled spoons of pottage onto the stale bread. Their father liked a stout breakfast, but since he had missed his this morning, this dinner, usually lighter fare, would have to take its place.

She ducked into the larder and brought back two cups of beer, watching her father and sister talk in easy conversation. A familiar knot of envy lodged in her chest. She pushed it down and listened. Her sister's tone had returned to its normal merriness.

"The country air did you good," Martin was saying as he embraced Poncia.

"Paris is no country town, Papa." She laughed. "You think the king wishes to live in the burg with the peasants?"

His wrinkled face creased into a smile. "Come, give us a story about this big city of yours." He straddled the bench and reached for his beer. "What news?"

"News? Nothing but the king's taxes." Poncia sat across from him. "I'd rather know what passes here. I return home to a town of madness." Her voice sounded light. Auda recognized it as a ploy her sister used to disarm their father.

"At church, they tell us to pray as we never have, and on street corners and in the markets, they preach en masse that we'll be drowned in the flood of our sins." Poncia picked at her plate of pottage, then pushed it aside and wiped the grease from her fingers.

Auda turned a worried gaze on her sister. She'd assumed the rains were like this all through the land. Was something different in Narbonne?

"Madness is the word," Martin said, arching his brow at Auda. He drained his mug of beer. "The rain has addled their heads."

Auda fished the eggs, now boiled, from the pottage. Setting them on the table, she sat beside her father.

"Madness or ill thoughts," Poncia agreed, reaching for an egg. "They say the pope has given permission to the inquisitors in Carcassonne and Toulouse to arrest those suspected of witchcraft, anyone who's made a 'pact with hell.' Carcassonne! It's just on our doorstep." She shuddered. "They're speaking of it even in Paris."

Auda swallowed. A tremble underscored Poncia's words. What was her sister hiding?

"The inquisitor in Toulouse writes a manuscript," Poncia continued. She shelled the egg and split it into quarters with her thumbs. "A treatise on the questioning of heretics. Parts of it have already passed through many hands, is the talk of kings and priests alike. This inquisitor rides south as we speak, on a mission to seek out examples for his writing."

Martin frowned. So the tales were true? Auda wondered, accepting the egg from her sister. The inquisitors *were* about?

Poncia gathered the discarded eggshells into a pile. "It's said he may yet stop nearby, or in Narbonne itself."

Fidgeting, Auda looked at her father, but Martin shrugged and ate his pottage. "The inquisitors will find nothing in Narbonne," he said. "They'll move on, as they always do."

Auda remembered the Jacobins on the bridge that morning and shivered. She ate the yolk of the egg first, savoring its richness.

Martin placed a warm hand over Auda's. "It has nothing to do with us. We brook no heresy."

Poncia raised grave eyes to him. "If only it were so simple." She rose and rummaged through her surcoat, returning with a piece of parchment. "Listen." She read aloud, stumbling over the words.

> *On the interrogation of witches and demonists*
> *Seek them where crops fail, where weather turns bad, and men*
>   *resort to eating other men. Ask them what they know, or have*
>   *known, of:*

Lost or damned souls
Making fertile fields barren and barren women fertile
Feeding on dead skin, nails and hair
The condition of dead souls
Conjuring with song
And spells cast on infants and the unborn.
The pale witch of heresy roams about and tempts our men to the
   devilry.

Auda's breath caught in her throat. Who had written this, and given it to her sister?

Martin took the page and scanned it. His lips stretched thin, and white spots pulsed above his reddened cheeks. Jaw clenched, he tossed the writing back toward Poncia.

"Rubbish."

"What if it's not?" Poncia stood to face him. "Do we dare take the chance?"

Auda looked back and forth between them.

Martin swallowed a mouthful of egg and stood. "What choice do we have? There's aught we can do about it."

Poncia flashed him a triumphant smile. "But there is. We can arrange for Auda's safety. It's already done." Her voice grew solid with confidence. She turned to her sister.

"It's time you got married. And I have just the man for you."

Chapter Six

Auda stared at her sister in confusion.

What? she signed. *Marry?*

Martin frowned. "Who is this man and what is this talk of marriage?"

Poncia waved the questions away. "I'll tell you all about him, Papa. But first we must decide how to move forward with this. I've already spoken to him—"

Auda slammed her fists on the table with a bang, rattling the dishes and cups. The others flinched. *Ask me? No!*

Martin nodded. "We'll hear the whole of this from your sister now." He turned a stern look on Poncia. "You had best begin at the start."

Poncia let out an exaggerated sigh and rolled the inquisitor's scroll back up. "Auda, I thought you'd be pleased. He's a good man, a friend of Jehan's who is looking for a wife. A miller, very wealthy."

What foolery had her sister concocted? *Why marry me?*

"He's an older man, looking for a girl to bear him a family. He's been married twice already, and is twice the widower."

Poncia met Auda's glare. "All he wants is a quiet girl who'll mind home and hearth."

Martin made a rumbling noise deep in his throat. "What he wants is no concern of mine. I'm not sending my girl off to live with some stranger."

"He'll be no stranger if they marry," Poncia countered.

Ugly, fat, stupid? Auda signed in rapid succession. What manner of man would consent to marry a girl he had never even seen? Especially one like her?

Poncia ignored her and spoke to Martin. "It's the best plan we have, to keep Auda safe—"

"The best plan we had," Martin cut in, "was for her to stay here with me. She's safe outside of the town's notice. Besides, we are on our way to prosperity even as we speak. We've just received an order for paper from the palace itself!"

Poncia narrowed her eyes. "From the palace? Who placed the order?"

Martin shrugged. "I don't yet know, but it doesn't matter. Once they see our paper is as good as parchment, we'll have our pick of whom Auda marries. *If* she chooses to marry."

Glancing back and forth between them, Auda blushed. They'd never talked about her marrying before—she'd never even thought it was a possibility.

Poncia shook her head. "Maybe so. But with this tripe from the inquisitor, we should look after every option. Any chance we can give her of a life of normalcy—"

Auda frowned.

Poncia turned to her, softening. "I didn't mean it that way. But being a wife and mother will go far to show people that you are like everyone else."

But she wasn't like everyone else. Hadn't her father and sister always told her that?

I'll stay here. She clasped her father's arm.

"When Papa's gone and you're alone, what will you do then?" Poncia's voice was kind. "How will you fend for yourself?"

Paper. Scribe. Yet even as she mimed the motion, the improbability of scribing for a living was obvious to her.

"When something goes awry, you'll be the first person they hunt," Poncia said in a soft tone. "You of all people should know that. A woman living alone, with no man to guide her. The white witch."

Auda shook her head, stubborn despite her fear.

"I was fortunate to hear about the miller early. We can arrange this before others come forward with their suits." Poncia fixed a resolute gaze on her sister. "I am hosting a supper for some men of importance in a few days. You can meet him then."

And what of Papa? she signed, gesturing at their father. Did Poncia mean to leave him alone while his daughters both sought better fortunes? She tried to catch her father's gaze, but he only looked down.

"He can care for himself, Auda. The miller knows about your . . . condition, and says it matters not a whit to him."

Auda shook her head and reached for her father's arm again, this time more desperately.

He looked reluctant. "It leaves me ill at ease, the thought of Auda so far from home. I need her here."

"The miller lives in town, not far at all," Poncia said in the same patient tone. "Papa, be reasonable. You didn't think Auda would stay at home forever?"

Why not, Auda asked, *not safe?* She sat back and crossed her arms over her chest. Her father's mouth turned down.

"Safer than this," Poncia said, addressing Martin again. "Marriage and a normal life is better protection than anything else you can give her. The things that I have seen—" Her voice faltered.

Martin's gaze grew troubled. "The madness of men . . . we know it well. But that Auda should marry—it's something that bears more thought. I don't want to keep her from having something she might want."

Auda clenched her jaw. *Don't want to marry.*

"It's what Maman would want," Poncia said in a soft voice.

Martin flinched. He pressed his hands against his temples and bowed his head. Auda glowered at her sister.

"Things are changing, Papa, for all of us," Poncia said, a light sadness lacing her voice. "Think on that when you decide what to do." She grabbed her cloak from the wall and stopped to squeeze her sister around her shoulders, but Auda shrugged her off.

Poncia's hand hovered over Auda for a moment. She dropped it and left, looking back only once. The scent of rose and citrus lingered in her wake.

Without a word, Martin retreated into his studio and slammed the door behind him. Auda stayed at the table, tears pricking at her eyes.

It's what Maman would want.

Yes, their mother would no doubt have wanted what safety she could give her children, what good fortune. And it *was* a good chance that Poncia had arranged for her. But surely fate had something else in mind; she had only to see her reflection to know.

An image of herself working side by side with her father flashed in Auda's mind. They were poised to do great things together, she was sure of it. She sighed in bitterness. As if what she wanted mattered in the face of such terror as the inquisitor could bring upon them.

She swallowed, suddenly finding it difficult to breathe.

Mind reeling, she rose to scrape Poncia's uneaten meal back into the pot, and took the dishes to wash in the barrel of rainwater out back. She was just returning inside when she caught sight of the woman who sold old rags ambling up the road. The door to her father's workshop remained shut. She'd have to take care of the woman herself.

The ragpicker stood on the doorstep until Auda waved her in. Glancing askance at her, the woman dumped a basket of old linens at her feet. Most of the women who came to see her father—the wine seller, the fur seller, and the lady chandler— were used to her silent presence, even smiled at her. This woman was new, had moved to town only a year ago. She had come by a few times to make eyes at Martin and unload her remnants, torn cloth fit for little else but the paper pulp. It made a living, but probably only just. The woman's husband had taken the cross and joined the war, she told everyone, but others whispered that he had run off with the kitchen maid. Her story would make for good song.

"Five deniers for the lot," the woman said in a loud voice. She stepped back as Auda moved near.

Auda bent to sort through the pile. Most of the rags were torn and dirty, and sported holes ringed with bare threads. A few might be salvaged for bandage dressings. She would wash and darn them later to sell to the physickers in town for a denier.

The ragpicker rubbed a thick finger inside her mouth. The click of her nail against her teeth was erratic. Auda stood and held up three fingers; the woman countered with four.

"Your father?" the woman said without looking at her.

Auda dropped the pennies onto the ragpicker's dirt-lined palm. She shrugged and pointed at the closed door to the workshop.

The woman clacked her teeth and picked up her empty basket. Casting a last scornful look at Auda, she headed out.

"*Masco*." Her accusation was no louder than a whisper.

Auda stared in shock at the ragpicker's retreating back. Had she heard correctly? The woman had called her a witch, an omen of darkness.

She slammed the door shut and carried the rags into the workshop. She dropped the cloths on the ground in front of the vat, where Martin stood stirring the pulp.

Seeing her come in, Martin laid down his mallet. "You shouldn't be imprisoned here, in this room and this house," he began. "You should have the life your sister has."

Auda let out a sigh. *I don't want*, she signed, shaking her head, all the while wondering if that were true.

It wasn't like her to smile as brightly as Poncia, to bat her eyes and speak in coy tones, to catch a man at the height of love. Maybe if there were a man who knew her, who could understand her as well as her family did. She banished the thought. No such man existed in her world, certainly not this old miller. Why should she trade the joy of working with her father for life with a stranger?

Her father watched her but said nothing. She walked to him and laid a kiss on his sweaty head.

Stay here, Papa, she signed, staring into his eyes.

Martin's shoulders drooped. "If this inquisitor does turn his eye on Narbonne . . ."

Auda touched his cheek but he moved away.

"Wife of a miller could bring good fortune. You would have wealth, at least. And with wealth you can do many other things. Perhaps this is the chance we waited for."

It didn't seem like any good chance at all. Auda scowled, trying not to give in to tears.

Make my own chance.

Martin's voice grew gravelly. He laid a heavy hand on Auda's shoulder. "I don't know what to advise. But your sister was right about one thing." He dropped his hand and turned away. "It's what your mother would want."

Chapter Seven

Auda climbed the ladder to the loft where her father slept and let herself sink into the hay bed beside the window. Loneliness solidified into a lump between her shoulders.

The impressions she had of her mother were few, either imagined or given to her by Poncia. Had she lived, how would Elena look today? Martin rarely spoke of his beautiful wife who had died so young. Auda imagined that she must have looked just like Poncia.

Would things have been different had she lived? What had her mother's last thoughts been? Were they for the baby she carried, a prayer for the life she might have taken to the grave? Or perhaps she'd been angry at this mewling 'it' that clawed inside her, blamed it for tearing through her. Perhaps she'd held her breath and shut her legs, had never wanted Auda to be born, died to keep it from happening.

Uncharitable thoughts, Auda realized. She should be blaming herself for taking her mother from her sister and father. She wondered, not for the first time, on the circumstances of her birth. Neither father nor sister would speak of it, except to say her mother loved her.

Yet whoever she'd been, whatever she'd thought, Elena had taken a piece of her daughter with her. Not just the lack of color that had left Auda an unsightly specter, nor the flesh cut from her living body. Something deeper. Tears collected in the corners of Auda's eyes.

Maman, help me if you can, she prayed. She meant to ask for her mother's guidance: was Poncia right to insist Auda should move to a strange home with a strange man away from her family? Who would take care of her father? Yet other thoughts invaded instead.

Please, Maman, am I to find someone who loves me as Papa loved you? Will he want to know me, know what I think and what I write? A darker thought surfaced—would he even let her write?

Her father and sister had never talked to her about such things. Martin only spoke of books and writing, and gossip he learned while scribing. Poncia had not spoken much of love to Auda either, never shared dreams of the future. She just worried over Auda's safety.

So how then was Auda to know what to hope for?

Sighing, she drifted back down to the studio. Martin had brought out his mould and deckle, the basic tools of his trade, for cleaning. Each mould consisted of a wire sieve mounted in a wooden frame that would be dipped into the paper vat to filter the pulp slurry. A larger wooden rim, the deckle, fit on top of the mould, creating a tray that both kept the pulp from sliding back into the vat and defined the edges of the sheet. The fibers left after the water dripped through the wire screen would be pressed and dried, and cut into pages.

Her father usually used his favored mould and deckle set, acquired from his apprenticeship in Spain, but over the years he'd collected many others. There was the large set for making receipt books for the moneylenders, the long, narrow set meant to duplicate the feel of scrolls, and another for palm-leaf books. Stacked to the side were the lesser used sets—the one made of stitched bamboo reeds bought from an Oriental at the fair in Barcelona, another made from thin strips of flattened wood shavings that her uncle Guerau had given him, even one made of grass and animal hair.

Martin took out a small hammer and began tapping at his deckle, fixing it so it would fit more flatly atop its companion mould. He glanced at her for a moment but said nothing.

Walking over to him, she picked up one of the moulds and drifted her fingers over the screen. How would that watermark the Gypsy spoke of fit into the process of papermaking? Was the wire supposed to be attached to the mould? Or pressed into the paper after it had dried?

What did it matter? She dropped the mould back on the table. In a few weeks, at the most a month, she'd be steeped in another family's matters with nothing to connect her to reading, writing, or paper.

"Best cut some quills," her father said, still watching her, "so we can test the paper properly. This new batch has to be perfect. Nothing but the best for the palace."

Auda nodded. She rummaged through her basket of quills sitting on the desk and picked out the broken shafts to burn later.

She spread the bedraggled feathers saved from yesterday's chicken across the desk. It had been hard for her and Martin to get any meat at all from the butcher, despite the fact Poncia had bought from him every week for years. Under the torrent that had waterlogged the whole town, every last scrap of fat and remnant suddenly had a price. They had taken the smallest chicken to get these feathers—eight deniers for a scrawny carcass that shouldn't have cost more than six. When they'd stopped the butcher from plucking the bird, he hesitated like a gambler told to tithe his winnings.

"T'were for the abbey," he said. "On account of the rains."

Martin had clenched his jaw and added another penny to the pile. The butcher mumbled about the goodwill of priests. A penny more.

Auda picked up the feathers, wiping blood and dirt off each one. She dumped them in a tall pail of rainwater, nibs down. The feathers clung together in a bundle. Stowing the pail under the workbench, she took out another bucket holding feathers that had been soaking for a full day. Their shafts, clear when dry, swelled milky white and flexible now. She dried each with a soft cloth and picked up her knife.

"Heat those before you cut them," her father said. "We've nothing to waste, so take care." He took a bucket of sand from the shelf and placed it on the fire where the vat of pulp had stood before. Ten score sheets would be sieved with the mould and deckle, then pressed and dried in the barn. It would be another week before the fermenting linens in the barrels would be ready to be made into the next batch of pulp. In the meantime, the finished sheets had to be smoothed and tested. Most would be boxed loose into quires of fifty, but some would be sewn into folios.

Martin plunged his fingers into the sand. "Wait till it's warm to the touch."

Prepare quills. Know how. She twitched her lips.

He said nothing.

She crouched by the bucket, checking the temperature of the sand. When it grew lukewarm, she took the bucket off the fire and propped the quills inside. Minutes later, when they'd cooled, their shafts had returned to their original transparency, tougher, smaller, and tempered.

She cut tips on each of the quills, shavings from the shaft curling on the floor. How many more times would she cut quills for her father before they sent her away? How often would she see her father? When would she ever work in his studio again?

Martin cleared his throat, still watching her.

"Those will be fine for our regular work. But we need thicker nibs for the new ink. Goose feathers will do us better. Could be we'll find some in Carcassonne tomorrow."

She whipped her head around. *We?*

He shrugged, voice still nonchalant. "I've business to attend, if you want to join me."

Is it safe?

"Safe enough, I should think. And I want to keep you with me." His smile was laced with sadness.

Her only reply was to jump up and embrace him.

They left the next morning, renting passage on a merchant cart heading west across a carpet of green grass and vineyards. Auda huddled in her cloak and peered into the misty rain, but seeing only blurs of color, she settled back in the wet straw. Despite the muddy ruts in the roads that made their wheels stick, she dozed until they arrived, early in the evening.

Carcassonne was surrounded by a stone wall lined with turrets and arrow loops for archers. Seven large towers stood on the front side of the walls. The tops of further towers loomed behind the city like a studded crown atop the knoll.

"Narbonne looks like a bunch of huts from here," her father said, but Auda couldn't discern the town from the vineyards far on the horizon.

Martin pointed to their right. "The old Roman amphitheater. And beyond that, the Aude."

Squinting through the drizzle, she searched for the fat snake of gray that was her namesake. Their cart wound up the hill and stopped at the double drawbridge lowered over a full moat. Martin nudged her.

Gathering her sack, which contained a heel of bread and a flagon of wine, she jumped off the cart and followed him across a set of bridges. She stepped quickly through wooden doors in the outer and inner walls and ducked under the hanging iron portcullis.

Martin motioned for her to keep moving. "Stay near."

Larger than Narbonne and built on a hill to separate the nobles on high from their poorer neighbors, Carcassonne was still peopled with the usual vendors, Gypsies, and noblemen jostling each other in mutual chaos. Painted signs with colorful pictures hung above the shops, the odd torch burning inside some, hinting at an inner vivacity. But mostly the city's luster was dampened by the same gloom that shrouded Narbonne, the same patter of rain.

As at home, the clergy perched on trestles, chanting prayers to passersby amidst the heavy clanging of bells. A pair of priests shepherded chained penitents past Auda and Martin, followed by a column of self-flagellants carrying thick whips they used against their own bloodied flesh. Nearby cries heralded the sight of more prisoners, naked save for their loincloths and reeking of fear, prodded forward by guards with sharpened pikes.

Auda turned her head. This was nothing like she'd expected. She heard the cruel snap of a switch hitting bare skin and hid her face.

"It's never been like this before," Martin said, grim. He picked up the pace and led her along the narrow promenades, pointing out various artisan streets and the giant well where the lower city inhabitants drew their water. Prayer tokens and crosses hung on nearly every door.

They arrived at a house squeezed between two others on

Parchmenter's Lane. Through the milky animal skin covering the window, a bulky figure moved.

Martin knocked. "Arnaud," he called out, knocking again. A slot in the door opened and a pair of large eyes, rheumy with suspicion, appeared in the crack.

"Martin!" The gray eyes softened and the door swung wide. A large man clasped hands with her father and showed them in. The house was small, not much larger than their own hearth room, but cozy and warm, exuding the faint scent of cooked meat.

The man looked her over. His gaze lingered on her eyes, but he said nothing.

Auda returned his look with sadness. Was this how it would always be for her, even among friends? Would anything change if she did marry the miller? Maybe she'd be better accepted then, if only for the wealth she married into.

"Arnaud," Martin said, "this is my youngest daughter, Auda. Auda, Arnaud and I have been friends for many years."

Arnaud dipped his head in greeting. His face was kind and craggy, crowned with thick white hair that shot out in all directions. He held out a wrinkled hand. "Come, sit by the fire. It's a cold beast that hunts this evening."

They hung their cloaks to dry near the fire. Martin pulled the wineskin and brown bread from their bag while Arnaud added water to the pot on the hearth and spooned out the broth into coarse wooden bowls. He garnished it with shavings of bacon.

"Not much, but it fills the belly," Arnaud said between sips. "Prices have gone up everywhere and people hoard what they have." He snorted. "The only one doing well these rain-infested days is the Church. She has her mercenaries on every corner, preaching to the poor on what their sins have visited upon us all."

Martin tore off a chunk of bread and handed it to Auda. "It's the same in Narbonne."

Arnaud shook his head. "No, it can't be. Surely you've seen the penitents and prisoners suffering on the road. Narbonne will never resort to such ugly displays."

Auda had read in one of Tomas's history books that back in the days of heresy, the days of the Good Men, all of south France had burned except for Narbonne. The one time the town had been threatened with destruction on account of her heretics, her guardians—the archbishop and the *vicomte*— had sold all of the town's gold in exchange for the safety of the people. Rumors suggested that perhaps some within the Church—not to mention the old *vicomte*—had succumbed to the allure of heresy themselves.

What was this heresy that scared the Church so? she wondered. She knew that the heretics shunned all physical things, including their own bodies, as evil creations of the devil. Only the soul was pure, they said, created by God. Her sister once said that the heretics defiled their own bodies with buggery and mortification.

Yet whatever this heresy was, it gave its people uncommon will to survive. They seemed indefatigable.

"Narbonne is no longer the haven it once was," Martin said and looked at Auda.

"Maybe," Arnaud allowed. "But if it's that bad in Narbonne, imagine how much worse it must be everywhere else."

Martin's mouth turned down in worry. "Perhaps it was not the best time to come here. I had thought it might be better than at home."

Arnaud shrugged. "Madness is afoot. The worst is the Inquisition. The bastards have brought out two score of condemned in the past month. The only thing keeping them from burning is this wretched rain." He spat out a piece of chewed fat and examined it. "If you listen to the priests, all the heretics in the whole of France have flocked here. The inquisitors won't be satisfied until half the town is drowned or burned to cinders and ashes."

Better this town than her own, Auda thought, then flushed at her lack of charity. She mouthed a short prayer for the penitents they'd passed on the road.

"Well then." Arnaud turned to Martin. "Have you come to tell me you've given up this nonsense with paper?"

Martin snorted. "And what, turn to parchment? I've no call to be the Church's whore. At least they still let me sell my paper, even if they won't give me a stall of my own in the market."

"Why struggle so hard? Parchmenters make a living same as you."

"Aaarch." Martin set his cup down. "Many trades make a living. In fact, I've come to meet with a bookseller who says he may have need of paper books."

Auda looked up. Why hadn't he told her of this customer?

"I've brought the best of my papers to show to him," Martin continued. "You've a fine hand and a good eye for colors, Arnaud. Come, illustrate my paper for me. We'll make books for the people and split the profits as brothers, half to each."

Auda shot her father a look of betrayal. She'd not yet even gone from his home and already he was conspiring to work with another.

But Arnaud only looked askance at Martin. "And whose whore will we be then? You fool yourself." He waved a hand as Martin started to speak. "Paper will be no different."

"It will be the great equalizer, surely you see that. If learning and letters are no longer the province of the Church and nobles alone—"

"You assume that people wish to learn, Martin." Arnaud

leaned in. "Sometimes the seed falls upon the path and is trampled under the feet of ignorance."

"Then, old friend, we shall drag up the depths of our society, lurking as they are in their hovels and their own shit. I've seen it in my own hometown—works of genius committed to paper by men who might not otherwise have a means to share their words."

Auda nodded, feeling a familiar thrill, and Martin gave her a sidelong glance.

Arnaud followed his gaze. "You've heard what the inquisitors write on heresy and witchery?" he asked.

Martin did not answer. Auda tensed beside him, remembering the frightening words Poncia had shared with them.

Arnaud sighed. "When fools learn to care about reading and writing, it will be the hope and the bane of us all."

The next morning, Martin left Auda at the door to the Basilica of St. Nazaire.

"Heed Arnaud's words," he told Auda. "Stay in the church, in the back."

Touching her cap, she nodded.

Martin clutched his case and slipped into the flow of pedestrians, carts, and animals on the street.

Watching him disappear into the crowd, Auda drew her arms close about her. The sky was gray and melancholy this dawn. A fat raindrop splattered against the ground in front of her, followed by several more that turned into a steady patter. She heard the plucking of notes nearby and smiled. It wouldn't hurt to hear a bit of music. Not for a few moments.

She sought out the sound, focusing on the clear notes. A musician had set up not far from her, a flutist with a thick wooden pipe that he unwrapped from layers of cloth. Laying the dark fabric out for coins, he stood under the rafters of a closed stand and began to play.

The musician piped a familiar melody, an old troubadour song about troubled love. She remembered the lyrics.

> *Plunged into great distress am I,*
> *More than the knight who woos me.*
> *Handsome and earnest, perfect, in truth,*
> *He loves but does not see me.*

Auda nodded her head in time. The piper was a thin man with wet, patched clothes. He seemed young, though his face bore wrinkles of worry and his shoulders were weighted down by weariness. Yet as he played, his fatigue seemed to lift, carrying with it the city's sunken spirit.

A group of guards passed them, splashing through the puddles. Auda moved closer to the piper and he resumed playing, as though especially to her. Crowds passed, but she noticed only one other person listening: a tall olive-skinned man who lingered nearby. He dropped a coin onto the flutist's cloth and stayed close to the piper, but his gray eyes were fixed on the crowd gathering near a large stage in the center of the square. The damning words of priests and preachers rose above the city prattle, drowning out the piper's melody.

She had better get inside.

But before she could withdraw the bells rang for Prime, and Martin appeared suddenly, his cloak flapping about him. He blinked when he caught sight of her. Why had he come back so soon? He'd barely been gone an hour. The audience by the stage had grown thicker even though the rain had grown stronger.

"What are you doing outside? Never mind. We must leave

now," her father said, pulling her away from the square. His face looked ruddy and worn, and sweat stained the sides of his tunic.

The vestiges of the piercing melody melted away. Behind her father, the growing crowd engulfed the piper. Tension creased the corners of her father's eyes and mouth. Had his meeting gone awry?

What happened?

He grabbed her with one hand, gripping his case with the other. "It was a mistake to come here. We must leave."

He tried to lead her out of the square, but the people streaming out of the basilica crowded the square from all directions. Father and daughter were pushed back with the masses jeering at the stage.

"The hour of the heretics is at hand," someone yelled.

Auda sucked in her breath and strained to look around. A small group of penitents huddled together on the tall stage, surrounded by guards. Their heads were shaven and their faces were dirty. People were throwing rocks and rotten vegetables at their bodies, and Auda winced as the hard clumps smacked their bruised flesh.

Behind them, a tall black-robed priest nodded in approval. An inquisitor? She tried to breathe but the flesh of her tongue stump caught in her mouth.

"Eyes to the ground and move forward." Her father's voice was low and close to her ear.

Auda forced her feet to move as the crowd jostled around her. A man wrapped in sackcloth stumbled into her side. Pain shot through her. Crushed between strangers, she struggled to regain her balance but slipped on the wet cobblestones.

"Damned crowds," the man said, twisting his head. Their eyes connected, a handspan from each other. Auda smelled his sour breath on her face.

He pushed her away with both hands. "God save us!" he blurted out.

Martin pulled her up, but the man had already begun screaming.

"It's a witch!" he yelled, making a sign of the cross. He waved his arms at the crowd. "She's one of them. Right here!"

He reached toward her, still shouting. Someone else pulled her arm; another grabbed at her head and shoulders. Her wimple was torn away and her long white hair tumbled free, exposed. On the dais, the inquisitor turned toward the commotion.

"Ahherr," she tried to say.

Someone screamed. "The devil walks among us, we have a witch!" More hands tugged at her clothing. Someone tripped; others fell. Suddenly she felt herself scooped up under someone's cloak and pulled forward by strong arms.

"The devil, hideous devil!"

"Ahhh," she moaned and struggled, but she couldn't break away.

"Let her go," her father yelled.

Yet the man carrying her away only held her closer to his chest. "Be quiet," he hissed. "Just follow."

Auda twisted to get out of the man's grasp. She could only see a blur of hands and faces as the man spirited her through crooked alleys. She thrashed against his hold, but the man only clenched her with a tighter grip.

"Shh! I'm trying to help you." His voice was a warm whisper in her ear. She smelled meat and vinegar on his breath.

She listened for her father, a heavy breath or grunt to know he was close, but she was pulled so quickly that she couldn't even look behind her. Where was this man taking her?

Finally the voices of the crowd grew distant and the man

stopped running. He let her down gently. Auda pulled away, ducking her head. They were in a cemetery behind an old church. She had only regained her bearing when Martin ran up to her, and, sobbing, Auda let herself fall into his embrace. Martin squeezed her back, and then they both turned to address the stranger.

It was the man from the square, the same man whom she had noticed listening to the piper. He stood tall and lean, dark-haired and dark-eyed, garbed in fraying clothes.

"My thanks, sir," her father said, dipping his head. "You saved us both." Through her shaky tears, Auda tried to smile at this handsome stranger who'd saved her.

But the stranger only held up a hand. "The crowds can be rough. And the Church is quick to condemn, slow to protect." His voice grew bitter. "Best hide here for a while, till the mob finds another prey." Letting out a mirthless chuckle, he dipped his head and disappeared down the street.

From the town, the voices in the crowd grew louder. Martin and Auda sprinted across the shaded grounds, until at last they hid themselves behind a large wooden cross by the church door.

Bringing her knees to her chest, Auda huddled next to her father. She tried not to think of the corpses whose graves they trod upon. Closing her eyes, she mouthed the Lord's Prayer, and her mother's face came to mind, Elena's smile soothing her daughter's nerves.

Shouts of warning cut through the rainfall.

"Over here!"

"No, I saw them head this way!"

Slowly, the voices grew distant.

Martin and Auda hid in the cemetery until the bells for afternoon prayer sounded. Only after Mass was sounded and the crowds in nearby streets thinned out did they sneak through the driving rain to the town gates to await the cart that would take them home.

In the wagon, neither made a sound as they settled among three other passengers shrouded in damp cloaks. But even as they rattled farther away from Carcassonne, Auda couldn't calm her terror. She huddled into her cloak and tried to slow her breathing. It wasn't until their companions had fallen asleep much later that Auda noticed her father's empty hands. She nudged him with her elbow.

She drew a rectangle in the air and mimed gripping the handle. *Where is the case?*

His eyes were tired. "Lost in the square."

Months of painstaking work, gone in an instant.

But Martin's voice sounded of relief.

"I'd thought Poncia was wrong, that maybe she'd just seen something on her trip that had scared her. But she knows the truth of it. And thank God we weren't too late to see it too."

She shook her head vehemently, but he'd already closed his eyes.

The wagon left them at their home late that night. Auda looked around, nervous that someone would have tracked them to the house and be waiting in the shadows. Even after her father lit a torch and opened up the house, she couldn't breathe. She remembered the strange man's warm arms around her and relaxed a fraction.

Heading for the stairs, Martin reached into his cloak and pulled out a parcel wrapped in cloth. He threw it on the table and ascended to the loft.

She waited until his footsteps subsided before she picked the parcel up. Untying the twine, she pulled back the cloth. Inside was a bundle of a dozen large goose feathers, each of them stiff and spotted with dried blood.

Chapter Eight

The inquisitor reached with a gloved hand for the woman strapped in the chair. He caressed her cheek. She whimpered and knuckled her hands atop the pregnant belly bulging through her billowing white gown. Auda ran toward the black-clad man standing over his prisoner under a charcoal tree in the darkened valley of the woods. She sprinted across the clearing under the starless night sky. Twigs and rocks bruised the soles of her feet. Spying the face of the prisoner, she skidded to a stop.

It was her mother. Elena's pale face gleamed with a ghostly glow.

She swung her arm and pointed at her daughter. "A wife! A mother! You?" Her laughter was bitter.

Seething, the inquisitor turned toward Auda. He held up a thick silver cross and began advancing toward her.

Auda screamed and bolted upright in her pallet, knocking over the pitcher of water by her bed. Her entire body was filmed in sweat. Just a dream, only a dream. Her mother's harsh voice still rang in her ears. No, not her mother—her mother had been kind and doting, not this specter of fright. She clenched her fists to stop the tremble in her hands.

Martin hurried downstairs. "What was it?" he asked in alarm.

Inquisitor, Mother, was all she could sign with shaking fingers.

Her father sat beside her. "Only a dream, no doubt on account of your sister's supper," he said.

Auda set her jaw. Poncia had sent word that her supper was that evening.

Not going, she signed.

Martin rose and picked up the shattered pottery. "It's not for you to decide."

Auda flinched at his cold voice.

Martin escorted Auda to Poncia's house himself. Garbed in a thick linen dress with her sackcloth cloak wrapped over it, she wore both a cap to cover her hair and a wimple to shroud her face. No doubt she looked for all the world like a leper binding her body parts so they would not fall off. Well, better a leper than a witch, she thought bitterly, following her silent father through the misty rain. At least lepers had the protection of the Church.

Poncia's new house stood on the north side of the river, in the prosperous quarter of the merchant dwellings. Auda paused on the bridge, surprised to see her father stop as well. He looked down at the river, whose waters ran gray and chaotic under the drizzle. He bowed his head for a mere moment and resumed walking. Auda let out a heavy breath and followed.

They passed the ornate water gate into the city center, where Narbonne hid its ancient Roman heart, buried under the roads. A torch blazed near the unfinished cathedral, which was covered in a grid of scaffolding. Behind the building, carts of mud and debris protected a circle of roughly hewn sculptures—biblical scenes, demons, and allegories. It was the perfect backdrop for the priests and peddlers who scurried through the square, proffering harbor against the devil.

"A prayer for your soul!" one yelled at the people jostling each other on the busy road.

Martin hurried Auda past the man.

"A charm for your salvation!" another followed.

Such a funereal song blanketed the town now, a cacophony of Latin hymns sung to the incessant ringing of prayer bells, hand bells, even the church bells. Who could smile, even breathe, under a dirge such as this?

They slipped out of the main traffic and hastened along the side of the road until the loud voices of piety faded and Poncia's house came into sight. The stone behemoth stood a full story above neighboring post-and-beam dwellings, the largest on its road in the northwest quarter of the city. At its sight, moisture welled in Auda's eyes.

"Go on," Martin said, nudging her toward the door. He wiped the tears that rolled down her face with one thumb and pushed her again.

Steeling herself, Auda knocked on her sister's door, but no one answered. She rubbed her chilled hands together and waited. The rain picked up strength, pelting her wet face with sharp drops. She looked back at her father.

"Knock again."

She knocked twice more, but still no one came. Finally, she tested the handle and the door opened by itself. With a final reluctant nod to her father, she stepped inside. Where were the servants? She'd only visited the immense house once, before the wedding. A single hallway led away from the anteroom, probably to some sort of workshop or office. Jehan kept living quarters on an upper level, if she remembered correctly.

Shaking the rain from her cloak, Auda ascended the steep flight until she arrived at the solar. A fire blazed under the hood of the chimney and oil lamps hung from the ceiling over a long wooden table. Fresh rushes covered the floor, while hanging embroidered tapestries kept the warmth from dissipating into the walls. Auda walked past the table and the cupboard holding the silverware and fine plates, maneuvering around the low buffet that held the pewter utensils for everyday use.

Muffled shouts sounded from the nearby kitchen. Auda peeked in. The large room was crowded with spoons and hanging foodstuffs, and a cook with a troupe of servants who bustled in between. A rack bearing a dozen kettles and pots stood beside a great vat of rainwater and a shelf that held spoons, scoops, pincers, spits, skewers, and a long-handled fork. A thick stew bubbled on a fire near a large fish tank that lined the back wall.

The cook took one, two, then three spices from a cupboard jammed with pots and dried herbs. He threw a liberal amount of the medley into the kettle and the sweet scents of rosemary and marjoram filled the room.

"*Oc,*" he said and nodded, licking a taste of stew off his fingers. He sprinkled more of the blend into the meal. Looking up, he spied Auda.

"Girl, did Fabrisse send you up with the bacon from the larder? Don't just stand there like the dunce's bride. Where is it?"

The dunce's bride. The label stuck in her craw.

Faltering, Auda shook her head and retreated to the hall. Seeing a door cracked ajar on the other side of the staircase, she moved closer. Voices echoed within. She peered through the slit of the doorjamb.

Jehan stood inside with two men dressed in plain brown

cloaks and bearing cropped hair. Sewn to the cloak of the shorter man were two large yellow crosses, one on the front and the other wide across his back. The three men huddled over a patched leather satchel opened across the table.

She drew an anxious breath. Who were these men who spoke in whispers to her brother-in-law? Priests? Had Jehan summoned them on account of her? He must know Poncia was arranging a marriage with one of his friends. Was he angry her sister traded on his fortune for her own family? The suspicious looks she'd gotten the last few days stood stark in her mind.

Yet these men seemed poor and weary with stained, threadbare clothes and fingers bereft of fine jewels. Nothing at all like the priest at St. Paul's. What did her sister's new husband want with these impoverished men of the cloth? She strained to hear their speech.

"My thanks for helping my parents journey inland," Jehan said with a light laugh, stroking his beard. "It's for the best, until this lunacy is over, you understand." His forehead creased and his smile disappeared. "You haven't come with news about them?"

His parents? Jehan's parents had looked as plain as these two, spoke little at the wedding, and cast disapproving frowns at Poncia, the fine cloth, food and wine—everything displayed in full abundance. They left soon after on a long pilgrimage they took every year, Jehan explained, and said nothing more about them.

"No, there's much else to be discussed," the shorter one said, sitting at the table. He rubbed a hand over his balding head.

Jehan lowered his voice. "Do you need food? Other provisions? It must be days since you've eaten."

"We'll take some with us when we leave," the man said. "Fish, if you can spare it. And watered wine."

The tall man shook his head. "Leave it for later. We came to ask you for aid."

Was it her imagination or did fear just flash through Jehan's black eyes?

"Now is not the best time," Jehan said. "I need a few months."

"It's never a good time," the thin man said. "Particularly for us, among all this superstition. There are many who need to be taught. We need new folios."

Folios? Auda bent in to hear better. Was Jehan courting business for her father? Poncia hadn't spoken of it. Who were these two men? Brothers from some small monastery? Monks seeking wisdom as cheaply as it could be had?

She tried to lean closer, but just then footsteps sounded on the stairs and a short maidservant descended from the third floor. Auda scurried away from the door, looking around as if lost.

The maid sniffed. "You must be *domna*'s sister. What are you doing up here? Come with me." She continued down the stairs.

Auda lagged, throwing a last glance at the small room. She turned away from the mysterious conversation and followed the servant girl to find her sister.

Na Maria, Poncia's personal maid, fussed over Auda.

"You've grown like the king's own rosebush, girl!" she said, pulling a long shift over Auda's head. Maria had been Auda's wet nurse years ago, even though the injured babe could barely take suck. Over time, Martin had paid the woman a few coins to care for his girls whenever he traveled, though not in many years.

Maria clucked at her. "And into a body to look at, no less."

Blushing, Auda turned her head. No one had seen her naked since she was a child, much less thought to pay her appearance a compliment. What would the miller think when he saw her on their wedding night? The thought made her uneasy.

"Almost ready. Though you're pale as a ghost." Maria pinched Auda's cheeks. "No matter. We'll dress you as a lady, though not one so fine as to give herself airs."

She held up a pale linen dress embroidered with lace at the sleeves and hem. The cuffs were ringed with dirt and the bodice stained with grease. Still, it was finer than anything Auda, an artisan's daughter consigned by law to wear only drab browns and grays in public, had ever owned.

Maria gestured at her niece Rubea, whom she'd summoned for help. A short girl as wide as her aunt, Rubea had curly brown hair and eyes sharp like a vulture's on a fresh carcass.

"Go back and get some mint. Out in the verge."

After Rubea returned with two large stems from the kitchen garden, Maria rubbed a sprig on the inside of the yellow dress and handed another to Auda, who wadded it in her mouth.

"What d'you work here for anymore?" Rubea said to her aunt, glancing sidelong at Auda. "You ain't had enough of this odd folk?"

Auda sucked in her breath and turned to glare at Rubea.

Yet Maria only patted her auburn mane, which had escaped its braid into a crow's nest about her head. She smiled, wrinkles ridging up at her lips, eyes, and forehead.

"She's nothing to fear at. Her and her sister, they ain't bad girls. Her papa's a fine man, and fine lookin' too. Pity he never got over that wife of his. Must have been some beauty, that one." She laughed again and applied a liberal amount of red salve to Auda's cheeks and lips.

Auda's pulse quickened at the mention of her mother. But Maria hadn't known her, couldn't tell Auda what her mother had been like, why Elena had married her father.

She took a sprig of mint from Maria and chewed it, trying

to hide her sadness and worry by focusing on the taste of the herb. Maria brushed out Auda's white hair and bound it tightly under a yellow cap, then sniffed at Auda's neck.

"Pity there's no orange water for sprinklin'. Be still, child. It's a queen's work getting you ready for a meal such as this."

Did everyone know what was in store for her this evening but her? A sudden alarm twinged in her mind. This life Poncia had married into was finer than anything they'd had as children. Well enough for her sister, who had always coveted such wealth and had pursued Jehan with sweet words and learned manners. From what Auda saw, the two were besotted with each other and the fine life they luxuriated in.

Not so for Auda. Whatever she was to do in her life, surely it would not come in the guise of wifery and motherhood. And now it seemed to all depend on the nature of this miller. Perhaps he was of a sort like her father, who would support Martin's dreams to see paper become a common household good, reading and writing a common skill. She and this miller could teach their own children letters and fund a school to instruct others. And she could still write. Perhaps, as her sister believed, it would turn out just fine.

Maria kissed the top of Auda's head and ushered Rubea out to finish their chores. The church bells chimed Vespers. Auda shifted from one foot to the other. Her dress held too tight in the front and the lace carried bits of wire that itched worse than sackcloth.

The bells rang again and Poncia appeared, breathless, at the door. She embraced Auda, and then pulled back, looking her sister up and down in approval.

"Maria did well. It's a fancy supper this evening, but only for other merchants and guildsmen," she said, fluffing her fur-trimmed gown. Auda cast her an uncertain glance and her sister frowned.

"Don't fret, Auda. It gives you an ill look." Her tone softened. "I know you worry over what will happen tonight. But don't fear." She gave Auda's hand a quick squeeze. "I'll be right there with you."

Auda tried to quell the anxiety that fluttered in her stomach. For the hundredth time, she wished Poncia had just let her be, a quiet girl living a quiet life with her father. Reading, writing, and staying out of notice. She closed her eyes, remembering their trip to Carcassonne. Staying out of notice was only going to get harder.

Her sister led her into the hallway to a pair of dark wooden doors where Jehan strode up to them. He was a sizeable man, both wide in girth and taller than most. He'd trimmed his thick black beard and moustache to match the short cut of his straight black hair in the current fashion of the nobles. His eyes flickered at Auda, and she stared back in frank curiosity. Was his meeting over? Would he tell them about it?

He drew Poncia aside. "It's not a good time for this," he said, echoing his earlier words to the strange monks.

"Nonsense," Poncia said. "We can't back away now." Jehan stared for a moment, then clenched his jaw and walked past them.

Auda frowned. Jehan was usually outspoken, effusive even, and never without a smile. Was he angry on account of her?

"Pay him no mind," Poncia said in a low tone as Jehan threw back the door and disappeared into the supper hall. "He worries easily."

Auda crooked her finger into a hook. *Why?*

Her sister pulled her forward. "God only knows what drives men and their ambitions. Come."

Safe?

What if Jehan *had* summoned those churchmen to question her? Maybe he planned to give her to them. What did she know of this man, with his wealth and worldly concerns? What did Poncia really know of him either?

"It's safe, Auda, I promise you." Poncia sighed and touched Auda's cheek. "Remember what I told you, about Maman's wish for us? She said to me, when you were still a lump in her belly, that what fortunes waited for you waited for me too. And what grace I was given should be shared with you."

So Poncia said, but what would their mother really have wanted had she known she would birth a witch-child?

Her sister's voice dropped. "My prosperity is yours, as your happiness is mine." She laid a kiss on Auda's head. "I don't want you ever to forget it."

Chapter Nine

The sisters entered the supper hall hand in hand. Auda gasped. The room loomed twice the size of their father's entire plot of land—house and barn. Dark wooden benches fitted with red cushions lined one wall, and a long table with twelve chairs stood next to a fire burning high in the hearth. Costly candles flickered on the walls, dripping light and wax onto the ground.

Poncia tugged her forward and smiled at her guests. Her eyes widened when she spied a tall man standing in the back of the room. Auda followed her sister's gaze. The stranger was dressed in a rich blue tunic and seemed to be holding a miniature court in the back of her sister's supper hall. Not far from him stood a woman in a gleaming green gown. Regal and bejeweled, the woman was speaking to an older dame and ignoring the three men clustered around them.

Jehan stepped in between the sisters, bobbing his head at Auda even as he turned to her sister.

"I tried to warn you," he murmured. His face and lips stayed flat, but his tense voice carried a hint of sympathy.

Auda tried to look around for the miller. All she knew of

the man was that he was mature and wealthy. Poncia nudged her forward and led her toward the tall stranger in the back of the room, where Jehan was already headed. As old as her father, the stranger had pocked skin and straight gray hair, with an angular brown face and thin lips that curved into a smile. Handsome, despite his age and thin frame, he moved with vigor, holding his head high and casting an indulgent smile over her sister in her own home. In his rich-scented presence, even Poncia and Jehan's matching woolen finery seemed mediocre.

Surely this wasn't the miller? Auda swallowed, unsure whether it was anxiety or thrill that coursed through her blood. Perhaps a little of both.

Poncia pulled her into a deep curtsy.

"My lord," Jehan began with a bow. "We are honored you've come to our humble home."

"You do us much favor attending our supper," Poncia said, her voice shy. Auda glanced up at the uncharacteristic deference but Poncia squeezed her hand.

"I am fortunate to be able to do so." He gave Auda an indulgent smile. "You must be Lady Poncia. But who is this fair maiden?"

Auda curtsied again. Feeling the man's eyes upon her covered head, she touched a hand to her laced cap.

Poncia tugged on Auda's sleeve. "My sister, Auda, my lord. She cannot speak, an incident as a babe."

"Not at all the curse it would seem," the man said with aplomb. "After all, a silent wife . . ."

Poncia's laughter was immediate. Auda whipped her head up at the crude but common joke, and the man's eyes, seeing her face, widened for a mere second. Poncia gave her a light frown and Auda dropped her head, but not before she caught a look of curiosity pass across the lord's face.

Jehan stepped in. "My Lord Vicomte, if you please, there is someone I'd like you to meet."

"If you'll excuse me." He bowed.

My Lord Vicomte? Auda put her hands to her reddening cheeks. This was the town's lord? Amaury the Second, heir to a dynasty of *vicomtes*, wedded for centuries to Narbonne and her people? No wonder Jehan hadn't wanted her at the meal!

Auda had seen the lord only once before, from the back of a large crowd at a town celebration. He'd gleamed like a gilded painting, standing with his wife, Jeanne de L'Isle-Jourdain. Dressed in their family colors of green and black, they had presided over a brightly dressed troupe that mummed around the city's fir tree, decorating it with apples and red berries.

"You should watch your manners," Poncia said in a low voice, still smiling in the direction of the retreating men. "I'd not expected him to come, nor his lady wife." She nodded at the regal woman dressed in matching green.

Nervous shame surged once more across Auda's cheeks. How was she to know the *vicomte* himself would attend her sister's supper? She'd thought he was the miller! Her flush deepened. No doubt she was the only one here naïve enough not to know who the tall lord was.

She swallowed, aware of how different she was from everyone else in this room. These were people used to going about the world with business in mind—not like her, a lowly girl who'd barely left the confines of her father's house on the outskirts of town. Would this miller be as worldly as the rest of Poncia's guests? Would he encourage her to attend events like this, to learn and write and share?

How had Poncia managed? Somewhere along the way, her sister had found her way into a world beyond their father's life. Maybe the miller would be just like them. Poncia had done well for herself; maybe this was Auda's chance too.

"Come," Poncia said, looking around at the guests. "I'll introduce you to Edouard, the miller."

A plain, doughy-faced man was wandering toward them. "My lady," he said with an awkward bow. "My ladies."

A feeling of dread sank into Auda's gut. So this was the miller. He had to be. He was everything she had feared: a large man with a belly that hung over his belt, lackluster brown hair that barely covered his skull, ears that stuck out too large, and a tendency to bob his head when he spoke. Fat and old, but more plain than ugly—and she, of all people, knew the perils of judging on looks alone.

Poncia smiled. "Ah, my lord Edouard, I am so glad you were able to come tonight. I know you don't often come to these engagements. Please, come and meet my sister. I've told her much about you."

The man returned her smile, though the curve of his thick lips seemed an odd expression on his wrinkled face. "Lady Poncia. It's true I don't often get out. Fine suppers are a frivolity I've little time for. But I understand it is an important thing for ladies." He nodded at Auda, who forced herself not to droop under his words.

"Isn't it, though?" Poncia beamed at him. "I'll leave you two alone to get acquainted," she said, squeezing Auda's shoulder. Auda couldn't look at her.

The miller surveyed her up and down, nodding. "You are as your sister says. No obvious blemish, except for your hair and your tongue, I suppose." He gave a half shrug of his thick shoulders. "You don't have need of either, really."

Auda clenched her fists. What had he just said?

"I won't need a dowry," he continued, tugging at an ear, "and our courtship will be short. Jewels and rich clothes will do you no good anyway as I rarely have time to attend fancies like this." He gestured at the minstrels.

Auda schooled her face into a mask. She didn't need jewels or rich clothes either, nor anything more than his approval to do what she loved most—work with her father and write for herself. She would be marrying for safety, she reminded herself, for a home to call her own. Not the gilded fortune that Poncia had built for herself.

The miller must have sensed her disappointment. "You'll have everything you'll need to run a good household, I can promise you that. I've enough to build a second story atop my house by the river. Construction starts next week. We need not wait until the formal marriage to keep house together either. Best to get familiar with the routine, and start on getting heirs." He nodded and spoke in a lower tone, as if talking to himself. "I've wasted too many years already, with no sons to show for it."

Auda trembled at the thought, bearing this stranger's children, keeping his house, tending to his needs. Would she too come to think of it as a life wasted? Surely it would be better to dream of finer things than to settle for this. Had Poncia really thought Auda could be happy with him? Safety is better than happiness, her sister would probably say. At least her mother died bearing a child out of love. Would childbirth serve her so well?

Too many questions when she really only wanted to know one thing about him, only had one type of creation she'd ever dreamed of. Reaching into a pouch that hung on the belt of her dress, she pulled out a tiny scrap of paper she had brought with her to Poncia's house. She unfolded it, thinking of the single question she had written upon it: what form of story do you like best?

Fingers shaking, she smoothed the page out and held it out to the miller.

Edouard frowned, surprised, and accepted the scrap. He turned it over in his hands. "What is it?"

Auda edged closer to him and pointed at the words.

"Hm. I can't read." With an air of dismissal, he handed her the page. The scrap fluttered to the ground before she could take it.

"We'll talk again soon," he said, then with a bob of his head, left.

Auda scrambled for her note, swallowing against tears. She wouldn't marry this man, couldn't. There had to be another way.

A horn sounded the meal and Poncia extricated herself from a nearby knot of guests to find her. "You will have to tell me all about Edouard after the meal. Please, Auda, this is a good chance—use it to your advantage!"

Auda bit her lip and turned her face from her sister's expectant looks, grateful for once that she couldn't speak.

Poncia sat her near the middle of the board and settled beside her, across from her husband, a finger's length above the dish of salt. Auda stared around with her with dull confusion. Her gaze fixed on the salt. Growing up, they had never had such a valuable spice. The *vicomte* and his wife were ensconced at the head, at the warm end of the board, also in reach of the salt.

Across from Auda, a large man with his nose buried in his ale cup ignored his suppermates. Next to him, an old dame with drooping lips was conversing with her younger husband. The others present, all persons of importance within the Artisan and Trade Guilds, sat below the salt along the remaining length of the board, each dressed in bright cloth and jewels. The miller sat near the other end, despite Poncia's entreaties to sit closer to them.

Hiding her exasperation with a false smile, Poncia sat at her place. She bent her head toward Auda's and guided her eyes toward the guests.

"See the sleepy one? That's Prades," Poncia whispered. "He heads the craft guilds. The fleur-de-lys under his seal means he's a consul. And that one there"—Poncia nodded toward the man married to the old dame—"he heads the Draper's Guild, and you won't find one richer."

Auda nodded without listening, unable to comprehend anything but the horror that would be marriage to the miller.

At last Jehan stood and lifted his cup of wine.

"We are pleased you've joined us this evening, despite the rain and portents that we may be doomed shortly," his voice boomed. "It is a fine night to be gathered together in warmth. And we are honored to be graced by the presence of our good lord, the Vicomte—"

"No, no," the *vicomte* interrupted, raising his cup higher. His deep voice drowned out Jehan's toast. "It is a fine enough thing that you hold such a cheery supper in these dreary times. I trust you were able to get past the archbishop's tiresome priests, and the obscenity that is to be his next offering to God? I must apologize for the muck and rubbish he has cast all about my town."

Frowning, Jehan swallowed his wine, and Poncia shifted in her seat. Was it because the lord had preempted his toast, or because he maligned the men of God? The *vicomte* had to be a bold man to speak out against the Church. One never knew who might be listening. Auda refused to look at the miller, to see what his reaction was.

The *vicomte* refilled his host's cup. "Let us drink to happier things. To cheer and health. *A la vòstra,*" he said, raising his own glazed goblet, and his wife held up her own.

Auda struggled not to choke on the unwatered wine, a red

vintage that burned her throat. When would this evening end? Around her, conversation settled into two groups, one on either side.

"If the Vicomte is so concerned with the cheer of his people," the draper said in a low tone, "he might show it a little more public concern. Perhaps ease the anxiety in people's hearts with a speech to counteract the fear the Church spreads around." He dipped his fingers in the water.

"*Oc*, but the Vicomte has his own anxieties," the man seated next to the draper said. He glanced at the tall lord, who was conversing with Jehan, and leaned in. "A bad bit of business, this *pariage* that gives Narbonne the Crown's protection, unasked, and for a fee no less. We'll see if he finds time away from his concerns to keep out the inquisitors as he says."

So the rumors were true—the inquisitors *had* cast their eyes toward Narbonne. A surge of fear resurfaced in her mind.

"Not that he's done anything to stop this half-witted hysteria over the rains," the draper continued.

The man sitting across from Auda shrugged over his wine. "As long as he keeps the inquisitors out of Narbonne, what do we care?"

"Well," the dame observed, "at least the Crown's touch will bring a bit of fashion back to the city." She smiled at Lady Jeanne and raised her voice. "Surely, you must miss the court, *domna*?"

The *vicomtesse* shrugged and arched a thin brow. Auda lowered her head, wondering whether the well-coiffed woman's powdered face and rouged lips attracted her husband's gaze. Was that the way one found love? The lady didn't seem like a retiring maiden. Did the *vicomte* mind?

The servants entered with plates and bowls of steaming food. First came sugared almonds, white bread with fat drippings, and a nutty yellow cheese. A game stew with venison

and herbs dressed in verjuice and mint followed, along with a
pork roast prepared in sweet fat and parsley. A large platter of
smoked fish—smelt and trout—served with mustard appeared
at Auda's elbow, and fish jelly with figs and wafers not far
from that. Such a feast in her sister's home! The warm odors
of meat, fat, and syrup mingled in the air.

Auda took a smaller sip of wine and, letting its drowsy
warmth calm her nerves, positioned herself so the miller was
not in her view. She concentrated on the *vicomte*'s words.

"Ever the complaint is the taxes," the consul Prades was
saying to him.

"*Oc, oc,* lower the taxes on this, eliminate the surcharge on
that," the *vicomte* replied, speaking over Poncia's head. He
selected a sugared almond and popped it into his mouth. "The
absurdity of the masses—they quibble over pennies and never
realize those pennies add up to pave the roads their caravans
travel, and to pay the *banderii* who guard them."

"Not to mention the market space you arranged in town,"
Jehan agreed.

The *vicomte* shook his head. "Just this afternoon, some
trader imprisoned by the Church petitioned me. The man sold
artifacts from the Levant, some more genuine than others, I
gather, though who am I to care? If a fool wants to buy infidel
relics from a dishonest merchant, why should I point out his
idiocy? Though this trader's the true idiot. He set up shop
right under the archbishop's nose and neglected to pay the tax
on religious items. Now the halfwit finds himself in prison
and calls to me for help! Horse's ass."

But who else could he go to? Auda wondered, intrigued by
their talk.

Jehan coughed on his meat and took a deep drink of his
wine, trading a terse look with his wife. "Threats against
money, threats against soul, and still these people keep deal-

ing with the Moors. Just punishment would be to have this trader take the cross."

Poncia stiffened, but said nothing.

The *vicomte* shrugged. "For him. But I need the trade to pay off the king's *pariage*. Between the Church and the Crown, they're squeezing me like shit from a dog. Already I have to raise taxes in the Old Market."

"My lord!" Prades said, turning raised eyebrows upon him.

The *vicomte* raised a hand. "And without a tax, where will the money for the new scriptorium come from? The archbishop's allotted a poor share for it, and the Old Market pays far less in taxes than the archbishop charges in his own market. At least now everyone can curse over the same rates," he added with a bitter laugh.

Auda cast an excited look at Poncia. A scriptorium—now this was fine news! Small rooms set up with desks and easels for scribes to copy books and scrolls, scriptoriums were usually only attached to libraries or monasteries, reserved for rich towns or those with large abbeys. Poncia had forever told their father to seek employment as a scribe up at the abbey's scriptorium in Fontfroide, a half-day's walk from Narbonne.

Still aside from those wanting copies of textbooks or religious documents, who would need a scriptorium here? Perhaps one built by a nobleman might go in other directions entirely. All manners of documents might need to be copied, deeds and writs arranged for easy access. Maybe even verse. Auda felt her heart beat faster at the thought.

And who would be the *armarius*, directing tasks, distributing materials and overseeing the work? A churchman? Or someone who would look past parchment, and cast an approving eye over her father's cheaper paper? A man such as that might order whole reams at a time. Auda couldn't stop herself from smiling. Perhaps her father could quit scribing and devote himself fulltime to making paper. She could help him—no time to get married.

The old dame entered the conversation. "I've never heard of a scriptorium outside of an abbey," she pronounced in a loud voice. "Though it'd be no bad thing to have an abbey here." She shook her head, her hoary wattle swinging back and forth. "What with all this talk of heretics in town. I'd thought that with the burning of the Authié brothers, we'd finished this nonsense. But now, all these years later, two dozen friars are summoned to the king's palace on charges of ministering to the Good Men! Do all the priests in town warn against their heresy?" Her icy glare settled on Auda.

Auda froze, conscious of the sudden attention. Yet what did she know of heretics and the Good Men? Suspicion of merely knowing a heretic could condemn a man to death.

Poncia leaned over her sister. "Father Michel has ministered to us for years at the Basilica of St. Paul-Serge," she said, a trace of fear edging her voice. "Though I look forward to hearing Mass in the new cathedral, perhaps as early as next year, they say."

The dame frowned at Auda. "Well, girl?" Her voice grew loud. "Speak. Or has the devil got your tongue?"

The conversation around them halted and the sound of spoons hitting against the silver-rimmed wooden bowls slowed. The *vicomte* turned his gaze to the ladies.

Drawing up her courage, Auda forced herself to meet the dame's stare. "Nohh," she said, struggling to push the sound out through her lips. It came out loud, a disfigured noise even to her ears.

The dame moved back a fraction but didn't say anything. No one at the supper table moved. Even the miller, with his plain face and simple demeanor, seemed shocked.

Only the *vicomtesse*, and her husband, looked more thoughtful than appalled. "Of course not, girl," the lady said, not unkindly. "Narbonne is God's own town. You say you attend the Basilica, in the bourg?"

"Our entire lives," Poncia answered. "My sister is mute. She lives with our father."

"Ah, yes, the scribe," the *vicomte* said, snapping his fingers, though his gaze was fixed on Auda. "I remember, from when Jehan said he was marrying." He gave Poncia's husband an exaggerated wink. "A thousand hearts broke over the news. But the scribe's daughter has made a good match for you."

Auda blushed under the *vicomte*'s look. He was appraising her, but for what? Her flush darkened with worry. Attention by a powerful man could only lead to trouble. Luckily, the *vicomtesse* spoke.

"I don't suppose your father also makes a type of cloth parchment?" Her voice sounded light.

"*Oc*, that's what some call it," Poncia said and flashed Auda an uncertain look.

The *vicomtesse* didn't seem to notice the reluctance in Poncia's voice. "So he's the one." She turned to her husband. "Remember that I told you of the papermaker I found?"

"Hmmm," was all the lord replied, his eyes returning to Auda. His scrutiny brought a blush to her face.

Auda only looked down, embarrassment competing with excitement. The order from the palace had come from the *vicomtesse* herself. What luck! She could only imagine her father's reaction when he found out. Suddenly, the problems of the miller, the Jacobins, and even the inquisitor seemed far away.

Chapter Ten

Auda sat by the hearth in her sister's solar. Rain pattered against the roof like an avalanche of pebbles. At the end of last night's supper, Poncia had sent a maid to escort Auda to the guest hall. The others still had much to discuss on matters of trade and town, and Auda was not invited to attend.

Yet she did want to talk to Poncia. In the cold dawn of morning, Auda was certain of her decision not to marry the miller, glad he had left the supper right after the meal. Her father would support her, especially if he knew of the dismissiveness with which the man had dropped his paper to the floor. Anyway, they had more important matters to consider, like the lady's interest in his work. Despite Poncia's reservation, surely the lady's attention could only bring good things? And why should their father not reach for the same sort of prosperity Poncia enjoyed?

She sat back and watched the flicker of the hearth fire. Well, if Poncia would not find her, she would have to find her sister. No doubt by this late in the morning Poncia was already in the marketplace, tending Jehan's stall.

Donning her cloak and a tight wimple over her head, Auda slipped out of her sister's home into the rain. In the market, the streets were lined with stalls full of hanging chickens, bloody cuts of beef, and baskets of waterlogged apples. Itinerant merchants jostled each other along the narrow road as they yelled out their wares:

"Mushrooms, freshly picked! Garlic! Onions for your pottage!"

"Pies! Meat pies! Goose and pork! Hot and tasty! Pies! Hot pies!"

"Cheese! Fresh cheese! *Pelardon! Du cabre! Amé notz!*"

Auda felt a pang of hunger at the warm scents. Although the bourg boasted a larger market, its space overflowing with merchants and farmers calling out to customers over loaded tables, the city was Narbonne's true metropolis. The coinage gleamed brighter here, the fruits and vegetables smelled fresher and looked more colorful.

Jehan's stall was the largest of the tables, marked by a blue cloth cover among surrounding stalls swathed in reds and browns. Sackcloth bags of peppercorns, gingerroot, cardamom pods, brown sea salt, and lemon peels lay spread across the counter, their colors a blazing spectrum. Scents rose into the damp air, an angry mixture of tang and heat, but dominated by fresh lemon. Additional bags lay on the floor, stacked in piles and waiting to fill the bare shelves.

Auda hurried inside and peeled off her drenched cloak.

Poncia was the only one working the stall this morning, her fingers busy unwrapping bundles tied tight with twine. As Auda approached, she glanced up. "What are you doing out? I would have sent the maid for you later."

Auda shook her head at her sister's distant voice. Poncia was frustrated by the miller's early departure last night, suspicious of what Auda had done to scare him. Well, they'd have to talk about it soon enough. She nodded around at the stall. *Everyone. Where?*

Her sister pursed her mouth. "Late. The maid is nearing her time. Her mother hovers and the cook frets. The house-boy has disappeared." Her lower lip softened. "This stall is all a mess and I've only just started learning how to work it."

Putting a hand under Poncia's chin, Auda forced her sister to look at her.

"It didn't go at all the way it was supposed to," Poncia blurted with sudden tears. "The miller decided things were not . . . so clear as they were before. A mute girl shouldn't be able to cause so much commotion! And now the *vicomte* and *vicomtesse* ask questions, about Papa and about you. If only that damned old lady hadn't fixed on you."

What did the *vicomte* want to know of her?

She slid around her sister and faced her. *Good for Papa.*

Poncia glared at her with red-rimmed eyes. "I would have helped Papa," she said in a watery voice. "After I arranged things for you."

Auda snorted. *Dull man.* With no vision, no passion, no zeal except for his would-be heirs. She shook her head. The *vicomtesse*'s patronage would bring far more choices, far better chances.

Poncia's nostrils flared. "Yes, everything is too dull for you, everything but these fantasies Papa feeds you. Can't you see now is not a good time to bring the Church's eyes upon us? How do you think the archbishop will feel, knowing the *vicomte* is building a scriptorium? And here you are, already thinking our father will give his paper to stock it!"

Why not? Auda shrugged.

Poncia turned away, dabbing her tears with the hem of her sleeve. "You are naïve if you really mean to ask that."

Auda pushed away a pang of hurt. She watched in silence for Poncia to continue, but her sister said nothing more. A pair of customers slowed near the stall, then walked away.

Question for you, Auda signed after a moment. Rolling up her wet cloak, she stuffed it behind her basket and faced her sister. *Men last night, met with Jehan. Know them?*

Her sister rubbed her tired eyes. "There were many men at supper last night, Auda."

Auda took out her wax tablet and began to describe the men she'd seen, their clothes and the yellow cross one wore.

Poncia read over her shoulder as she wrote, but before Auda had finished she grabbed her wrist in midstroke.

"Auda!" Pulling the tablet away, Poncia rubbed at it with a piece of old sacking until the words disappeared. "Where did you see them? Never mind. Their business is none of yours. Put them from your mind."

Auda stared, taken aback. What did these men speak of that had frightened her? She watched Poncia scrub at the tablet until nearly half the wax had peeled onto the rag.

Auda put out her arm. *Stop.* She looked around the stall. *Help you.* She'd ask again later, when her sister was calmer.

At last Poncia put down the rag and nodded.

"Jehan has many associates. Their business can be sensitive, and he angers even when I ask about them. Sometimes, Auda, it's best not to know."

Auda nodded without understanding.

Stepping away, Poncia pointed her toward a tall shelf in the back of the stall and unwrapped the scales stored beneath the counter. Her voice grew solid. "The spices are there. You'll have to measure what we need onto one of those trays." She gestured at a stack of polished lacquered squares. "Be careful with the balance. We bought it new in Paris."

Poncia demonstrated how to measure a hand weight of

pepper using metal weights and made Auda repeat the exercise, cautioning all the while.

"Don't press on the trays."

Auda fingered each of the weights, measuring them against each other. Poncia sighed and moved to speak with a customer who'd paused by the entrance of the stall.

Auda pulled a sackcloth bag smelling of anise out of the nearest pile. An oval seed was drawn on the dirty linen label. She picked up another: the label bore a picture of red paprika. The next bag contained saffron, and the one after that, cumin. She shook her head. What a mess.

"This is how the servants arrange it every day," Poncia said, reaching around her to measure a heap of yellow ginger. "They have their own method with the pictures."

You can read and write. Auda twitched her lips and fished a charcoal pencil from her basket to scratch letters on the cumin label.

Refusing to answer, her sister turned to another shelf.

Auda opened the next bag and sniffed a deep citrus scent. Orange peel. She lettered the label.

A customer appeared at the counter, a servant girl who recited a list from memory as Poncia struggled to keep up. Another girl and two older ladies followed. They all knew Poncia, smiled at her and chatted, lingering when their business was done. Poncia didn't seem to mind, encouraging their talk with smiles and trivial chatter.

Was it only Auda's imagination, or did the girls look askance at her with fear?

"Auda, some spices," Poncia called out. "A dram of cloves—long with a clawed end; another of cinnamon—curled brown stick; and a scruple of mace—it looks like orange-dyed lace. Oh, and an ounce of gingerroot." Then, in a lower tone, "Yes, your mistress will need that. No doubt she makes a mince-meat pie. *Oc*, you'll want some anise too."

Auda watched wistfully. Their mother had grown up in a merchant's household. Had she worked a stall as Poncia did now? If Elena had lived, would she be directing Poncia, dispensing wisdom before her girl could even think to ask? Mother and daughter, side by side, all while Auda watched, mute in the shadows?

The wooden shelves creaked and bags of spices fell from the counter onto Auda's feet, startling her into a cry. Seeing the commotion, Poncia stepped away from her customer and returned to help Auda sort through the jumbled pile of bags.

"We can still fix things with the miller," she murmured, kneeling by the fallen spices. "I'm sure of it."

Auda doubted it. The look on his face when she'd been questioned by the *vicomtesse* was not a happy one. That man could never grow accustomed to the attention Auda always drew. Especially not if she continued to work with her father, continued to read and write and learn.

"Let him speak to Papa about you," Poncia said, trying to group the spice bags on the counter. "He asks for no dowry and he would be a good husband. He keeps busy with work and only wants a modest family." She turned and met Auda's gaze. "Yes, he is old, and large, and more than a little dull. But at least you wouldn't be alone. You'd be taken care of when Father no longer can. Sometimes you have to sacrifice what you have to get something you want more."

Yes, sometimes you did, Auda agreed. But to sacrifice what she loved for imprisonment was not a sentence she could bear. Couldn't her sister see that?

"Well! It seems I have two beautiful women working for me today!"

Auda turned at the boom of her brother-in-law's voice. Jehan was smiling. So, he was in a better mood today. What had changed his fortune?

Stepping into the stall, Jehan took his wife's arm and kissed her fingers, though she looked distracted at the interruption.

Auda stepped around the couple, scrutinizing them from the side. Jehan smiled at Poncia, caressing her fingers and hands.

Her sister only said one word, though she looked at neither of them.

"Please." Still gazing at Auda, Poncia led Jehan aside and spoke to him in soft tones.

Closing her eyes, Auda let out a heavy breath. She thought again of her mother. Had marriage, even life, been this hard for her?

"A moment, if I could," a crisp male voice said.

Her eyes flashed open.

"My pardon." A man stood at the counter, raindrops falling off his eyelashes and from the tip of his crooked nose. He cleared his throat and spoke in a lower tone. "A fistful of grape shoots, please."

Auda stepped back, aghast. It was the stranger from Carcassonne, the one who had saved her from the mob. She was sure of it.

"It's you," he said in the same soft voice.

Auda shook her head, meeting his eyes. How had he found her? Why was he looking?

"God's grace!" The words slipped out of his mouth. "Your eyes."

Auda forced herself to keep her expression still. With all the varied colors of eyes—blues and blacks and greens—why did they always flinch when they looked at hers, neither red nor yellow nor any other dastardly color? The color of death, someone had called her tan watery eyes. Did they truly think her a *roumèque*, as the peasant children playing in the fields called her, avoiding her like some hideous ghost sent to frighten the babes? Had the inquisitor sent this man to find her?

But no, he'd saved her once.

He held out his hand. "A second pardon. I've never seen anyone like you."

She stepped back. Poncia was busy with another customer. Should she call her sister anyway?

The stranger kept staring. "Truly, I didn't mean to scare or offend you. I only came to buy supplies and saw you. I never thought I would see you again, but I'm glad to see you are safe."

Despite herself, Auda felt herself softening. There was something about this man that seemed so harmless, almost lost. A foreigner, undoubtedly—with olive skin and large gray eyes, he spoke in a hurried, oily accent. His cloth was threadbare, patched in many places and smeared with dabs of paint. Most likely an itinerant artist in search of work.

Noticing the conversation at last, Poncia hurried over with an arched brow.

"May I get something for you?" she asked the man, sending Auda a puzzled glance.

"A fistful of grape shoots will do," he said politely, though he addressed his words to Auda.

Poncia made a low reply and nudged Auda with her foot. "Stay in the back, Auda. I'll see to the customers," she said and rushed back to the other counter.

"Just a fist of dried grape shoots and I promise to be off. I don't mean to trouble you any further," the man repeated.

Auda regarded him. He was a handsome man, to be sure, though not in any traditional way. His eyes held a faraway glint, as though searching for something he couldn't quite recognize. A mystery to puzzle out, she thought, then scolded herself for the whimsy.

Turning back to the shelf, she searched for a bag of dried shoots. She'd seen them before in Tomas's shop, small twigs used to make charcoal for drawing and painting. Tomas baked his own and sold them in bundles. The sticks could be used as pencils or ground up and mixed with water or oil to make a dark black paint. She fingered the contents of a dozen bags until finally she found the correct one. These shoots were cheap stock, made for inferior browns and grays rather than the black the painter probably searched for. Tomas kept these in his shop also.

Selecting a fistful from the bag, she wrapped the package and tied it with twine, then held up three fingers.

He handed her the coins with a dusty black hand. "Aah, this ink and charcoal get everywhere," he apologized, wiping his fingers on his tunic.

So she'd been right. Feeling emboldened, she mimed the motion of painting.

He tilted his head at her and blinked. "Oh. Yes." He smiled. "Color and gilded miniatures, mostly, though I've done some illumination. I just arrived in town, came here looking for a space to sell my work. Not an easy thing."

It didn't surprise her. Portraitures commanded a good deal of money and though Narbonne acted like a rich city, people still preferred simpler tastes and practical wealth. This man would have done better to search for a patron in the northern cities. But the mention of illumination piqued her curiosity. Illuminators typically trained at monasteries. Was he a monk like the ones at Jehan's house? He certainly looked poor enough. What manner of works had he illustrated?

She nodded toward his box, and the corners of his eyes lifted. Smiling, he untied the cords that bound his case shut to reveal a clutter inside: quills, pieces of charcoal, chalk pencils, and lumps of wax in various colors. Pulling out a cloth bundle, he unwrapped a stack of parchments and stiffened linen and shuffled through the collection: bright renditions of saints and manger scenes, dogs on the hunt and drawings of nobles in feast.

He had skill, she supposed, though she knew nothing about the taste of artistic patrons. There was something about the shading that made it seem like there was more to his subjects than what first caught the eye.

When he reached a section of drawings, he began to flip past, but she slipped her hand in the box.

The man tilted his head. "Oh, those are only some sketches. Just people who catch my eye, things I'm trying, to get better . . ." His voice grew shy.

She took out the collection—simple line drawings of daily life on the streets, in the markets, on the docks. She had never seen such work before—normal people, not kings nor saints nor heavenly creatures, but people like her or Poncia, living their common lives. He'd inked them in various colors, blues and reds and greens.

She stopped on a brown ink sketch of a woman cutting the head off a fish. The woman's flesh spilled out of her smock into puddles on the counter where she worked. Her wiry hair escaped in grimy wisps from her bun, and her entire face, tired and angry, was tied into a scowl that looked like a wet cloth that had been wrung to dry. The drawing centered on the woman's lips, large and fleshy, puckered as if she had tasted something foul or was gathering a wet glob of spit. The woman was hideous.

"She's beautiful, isn't she?"

Auda tore herself from the picture and stared at the artist, heart racing. She looked again at the drawing, trying to see what he saw.

Something about the woman stood out—her determination? Perhaps. Her anger? Maybe that she had a purpose. It was the same expression her father wore when he was working. The feeling was familiar.

"I like her lips in particular," he said. "The ripeness of them, like two pieces of a plum, succulent and sweet."

She caressed the edge of the drawing.

"I don't suppose you'd want her? It would be my first sale in town." His words came out in a tumble.

Her heart plunged. She owned no wealth of her own.

"Or perhaps a trade? The picture for the shoots?"

A tempting offer. The picture was worth far more than a hand weight of old twigs, even if you took only the cost of the parchment into account. But the branch wasn't hers to give. She glanced at Poncia; the thought of asking the favor somehow cheapened the drawing. She shook her head with reluctance.

"Well," he said, a smile quick on his lips and a sudden glibness to his voice, "let's hope my luck improves."

She lowered her head in apology. Before she could think twice, she reached into her basket to pull out her tablet. Quickly, she pressed on the wax and pushed it toward him.

Auda.

She pointed to herself.

He searched her face, from eyes to lips, chin, forehead and ears, and head covered by a thick cap. His entire face lit up in a smile and he gave her a flourished bow.

"So you can write? I am surprised, I admit. I am Jaime." He took her fingers in his for a kiss.

She felt herself shiver as his lips grazed her fingers, his breath hot on her cold skin. Blushing, she snatched her fingers away before her sister could see. He bowed again and, with a wink, disappeared into the crowd.

Chapter Eleven

Martin arrived at the stall just after the bells sounded for midday. Poncia had left the wares in charge of the pregnant maid, who had finally shown up, and returned home with Jehan. Auda was glad to see her father. The maid had been darting fretful looks at her, drawing back every time Auda moved or made a sound.

He greeted her with a wide smile. "It was a fine morning, *ma filla*. One of the cobblers came by with a message from his son. Turns out the son's wife had her first child. A boy! The cobbler made me write the news out to three people right then."

Ducking out of the stall with a nod to the maid, Auda herded him toward the edge of the market, away from the town center with its priests and Jacobins. Impatient, she handed him her tablet. She had been waiting all day to see him, had already written a few sentences to explain last night's dinner. She reiterated with her fingers, miming first a sheet of paper, then a crown atop a lady's head. *Paper ordered by vicomtesse.*

Martin stopped in the middle of the road and asked Auda to sign again.

"The *vicomtesse*? I knew my patron had to be someone wealthy, but I never expected this. And a scriptorium in town? Now *this* is the chance we've been waiting for!" Clapping his hands, he laughed out loud. People surrounding them stared.

Auda remembered the bloodied demonstrator in the square and shuddered. Taking her father's hand, she forced him to keep walking. The rains had broken for the moment, but there was no point in lingering and getting drenched. And there were other things she wanted to discuss.

Miller, she started to sign, but Martin interrupted.

"Never mind the fat miller," her father said, waving the thought away. "As my fortunes rise, so do yours. We'll find you a man far more worthy than the miller."

Auda thought of the painter and flushed.

Her father took a sharp turn to the left. "Come, Auda, I almost forgot. Remember what Tomas said, about Shmuel looking for me? Let's stop and see what he has to say. I've a good feeling about this day."

The Jew. Her sister had warned her about them, said they killed innocent gentile children in the gray moments just before a ruby sky dawned. Of course Poncia told her so many rumors that Auda wasn't sure when to believe her. Shmuel had always been courteous when he stopped at Tomas's shop to see her father. But then why did the stationer view him with such suspicion?

They turned eastward at the synagogue. A pair of darkly dressed men, with their hair in ringlets topped by inky black hats, walked on the opposite side of the street. Auda tried to look discreetly. She had never seen any Jews, other than her father's friend Shmuel, before. The quarter was well marked, to ward away innocents and to keep in the many Jews who were fugitives from the French expulsion some fifteen years back. Eventually they had returned, albeit with heavy fines and restrictions on their movements. And always there was some vague threat of reprisal hanging over them.

"They dance with the devil on their Sabbath days," Auda had heard said of them. "To celebrate their killing of Christ, the Lord."

What did those same people say of her?

She glanced at the men again, but still they paid her no mind. Wrapping her wet cloak around her, she tried not to shiver. Shmuel's house was a small building squeezed between identical houses on either side. The front door was closed and the windows were shuttered.

Martin motioned for her to stay by the gate while he stepped onto the verandah and knocked. A flurry of whispers hissed through the thin walls. The door cracked open to let out a sliver of light, a sweet, warm smell emanating from inside.

"I'm looking for Shmuel," her father said. "Tell him Martin, the papermaker, wishes to speak with him."

"Wait." The voice was female, the accent harsh and unfamiliar.

Auda looked at her father. Why had they not invited him inside?

"It's better to conduct business out where people can see," Martin said, a rueful note lining his voice. "There are many who would see a Christian enter a Jew's house and condemn him for that alone."

The door opened again and a small man with a graying beard appeared in the doorway. He was dressed in a warm brown robe, a pair of thin spectacles perched on his nose. Auda had seen this contraption before, at the Gypsy's tables in the fair. She wondered if their friend Donino had sold it to him.

"Martin! I have been looking for you." His voice, though low, sounded warm.

"Yes, Tomas told me. He was not so pleased to see you."

Shmuel shrugged. "That's all you can expect from a man such as he. But we have other matters to discuss. Your business is going well, I take it? You have decent stock?"

"I just finished a new batch," Martin replied, before adding in a happier tone, "Some of it will even go to the palace!"

"Good news indeed," Shmuel said, his eyebrows lifting. "Well, I have more happy news for you. I have another customer, a man who comes to me from time to time. He has need of folios, ten to start, perhaps more later. Can you handle this, my friend?"

Auda craned her neck to listen more clearly. Ten folios? That was a bigger order than even the palace had placed! Who had the money, and the knowledge, to go to her father with such aspirations?

She peeked around him to see what she could of the inside of the Jew's house. It was a crowded space, stuffed with scrolls and books lining the shelves all around the room. An older man sat at a desk next to a glowing plate of coals, his face buried behind a stack of parchments. Two young boys wearing dark robes with the yellow patch of a wheel sewn on the front sat behind him, scratching on wax tablets.

"When do you need the folios?" her father asked, only a slight tremble in his voice hinting at his excitement.

"Midsummer," he said. "Sooner if you can."

The men leaned in and dropped their voices beneath Auda's hearing—no doubt discussing the matter of payment and delivery. The door closed and Martin turned to her with a smile wider than any she'd seen on his face before.

"I told you this day would be special," he exclaimed. "This batch of paper I made is just the beginning."

Auda nodded. But who needed the folios? Someone had seen the utility of paper. What were they writing on it?

Martin didn't stop smiling the entire time as they journeyed home to prepare supper. He even bought another chicken at the market, a fitting extravagance to mark their new fortune and to welcome a visit from her uncle Guerau. A tradesman who'd left the paper business for a more lucrative trade in cloths and furs, her uncle still maintained an interest in his old career and stopped to see Martin every few months. He'd sent word ahead that he was on his way.

"Auda!" her uncle cried as soon as he arrived, opening his large arms to envelop her in an embrace. His beard smelled of smoked fish, his breath of fresh wine. "You've grown, girl. The time to search for a husband for you can't be far off. Eh, Martin? Then you and your extra pair of hands can start your own paper mill."

Auda twitched her lips and ducked her head, but her uncle laughed, drawing a large bottle of wine and a bundle of dried fish from his sack.

"Come, have a drink with your old uncle. It's the *Rioja*, no? From your homeland. Your real homeland," he said, poking at her father. "Martin, you need some too."

"*Una mica*," her father said. Guerau overfilled his cup.

Auda listened to the two men as they gossiped of family and politics. Though related only by marriage, they both had dark hair and ruddy skin, except that her uncle's was hidden behind a thick beard and moustache while her father was clean-shaven. They had the same stoutness, ample and strong, their bodies used to hard work.

Even their mannerisms were similar, the way their fingers explored what they touched, examining surfaces and textures. Subtle, like the feel of the artist's soft lips on her fingers.

"I went back to the old mill last month," her uncle said. "Master Símon was still at the vats, voice as loud as a bull's." Guerau laughed and swigged his wine. "Yelling at the boys as always. I felt like I had returned to my youth."

"I can still feel the pain of his screams, and mine, that time he boxed my ears. Do you remember when he caught us playing maces with our mallets? I thought he would take a strap to us."

"He should have," Guerau chuckled, pouring more wine. "Tell me, then, how does business go?"

Martin grinned. "For years it has crept and crawled like a babe on its first legs. But finally the winds are changing."

"Ah, the French are catching up," Guerau said. "Once you convince these peasants . . ."

"Bah, forget about the peasants!" Martin rubbed his hands. "What if I get the eye of the nobles?" He relayed Auda's news about the *vicomtesse*.

"Good fortune, good fortune!" Guerau cried in approval and raised his cup again. "Let's drink to it."

Auda picked up a piece of smoked trout from the table and bit in, happy to be listening to her uncle's rich voice. When she was a child, her father had often told her how much her uncle resembled his sister, her mother. They were subtle features—the shine of their dark eyes, the wave in their black hair, the nimbleness of their fingers, long and tapered. Auda had inherited those fingers. She looked down, curling and uncurling her fists.

"If only these damned rains would stop," Martin said. "Or at least if the Church would stop preaching over it."

Guerau shrugged. "I think sometimes we have forgotten how to live simply. We become bored and look for trouble." He sighed. "In the meantime, it's all in the hands of God and His Church."

"Most men are men of conscience in their hearts, I think," her father said after a moment, clearing his throat. "It's only when they judge one another that their own purpose falters."

"I am glad to hear you say that," Guerau said, his sudden

melancholy lifting. He reached into his leather satchel and withdrew a stack of folded papers. "I have news. Not far from here, I met a man who sought me out to give me these. Here. They are from the Good Men. There is a town nearby where they gather. They are papermakers, Martin! Like us! And they need help to make the quantities they need for their writings."

"The Good Men?" Martin repeated. He pushed the pamphlets away. "You come here at a bad time, bringing things that should not be read!"

Auda straightened. The Good Men? Again she wondered why the Church hated them so, but she knew enough not to ask. Things had changed—people had changed. Narbonne's old tolerance was vanishing.

"They are men of God," Guerau said in a light tone. "They believe in His teachings. They say the Church has corrupted the message of how we are to find Heaven."

"It doesn't matter what they say, what they believe," Martin snapped. "They are heretics. And it has nothing to do with us. Unless you've fallen for their words?"

"Come, Martin, you know me. I'm not one to listen too hard to what men say of God. Can you see me giving up sex, meat, and drink?" Guerau laughed and leaned in closer. "But did you hear me? They make paper, and it is very fine. Here, feel this, its smoothness." He pushed a pamphlet into Martin's hands. "You can write on it and the ink doesn't bleed through. Surely you're interested in learning more of their craft, maybe to better interest this *vicomtesse* of yours?"

Martin stroked the sheet, then pushed it away. "No, no, it is lunacy. Auda, take them to the fire."

"There's no need to go that far," Guerau said, holding up a hand. "It's only a few pamphlets, Martin. Look over them this evening. Tomorrow, you can burn them."

"Either these burn tonight," Martin insisted, "or take them with you now. I'll not bring this danger into our home." He glanced at Auda. "Not for anything."

Guerau followed his gaze. Dropping his hand, he shrugged. "As you wish. I only brought it for your benefit."

Martin passed the bundle of sheets to Auda and she carried them over to the fire. So these were the pages that bore the words of heretics! Some were written by hand, but most bore the measured script of a woodcut, words carved in reverse into a block that could be stamped on paper many times over with little effort. She squinted to make out their words.

"Have done and burn them," her father interrupted before she could read anything.

One by one under Martin's intent gaze, she fed the pages into the flames, watching each sheet curl into embers and ash. She held one up to the flame and caught the shadow of an image buried into the paper, lines like a ladder. A watermark? It had to be. Again, she squinted to make out its details.

"Burn them all, Auda," her father repeated. "Their words are not for you."

A reckless courage flared up inside her. Maybe her father didn't want to know more of these people and their work, but she did. And what of these marks they left on their paper?

Turning her back toward Martin, she burned the pages slowly, squinting to see if any of the others bore the trace of a watermark. She could see none. But the memory of the ladder stayed with her.

Somehow, she would find a way to learn more.

Chapter Twelve

Two days later, Martin loaded a rented donkey cart with stacks of paper he'd chosen to take to the palace. Auda lingered around him in the misty drizzle, wondering if she could come along.

"Of course." He seemed surprised. "*Ma filla*, you are my lucky star. If not for you, I would never even know who my grand patron is." He winked. "Better not tell her we also have another."

As they made their way to the palace, neither father nor daughter spoke, each absorbed in private thoughts. Auda's mind raced to plot the future of their business. Between the lady's interest and the order for ten folios, it certainly looked like their luck was changing. Maybe, if enough coin came from the sale, she could ask her father to buy the painter's drawing, the one of the fisherwoman. Surely Martin would want to help the man who had so selflessly helped them?

Once inside the palace gates, they were admitted to a large room where the *vicomtesse* sat waiting with her attendants. Martin and Auda bowed low before her. Seeing Martin freeze at the finery on the walls, Auda took her father's hand, sweaty like hers, and squeezed. She knew what questions raced through his mind: did he have enough variety, was the paper fine enough? He had fretted over his choices all night.

The *vicomtesse* ordered a long board be brought out. "Well?" she said, gesturing at the board. "Lay your goods out for me."

Martin hurried to unpack his boxes. As he fussed alongside the servants, Auda looked around the hall. At one corner of the luxurious solar, she noticed a table holding a slim book cased in soft leather. She squinted to see better. It was a Book of Hours, a prayer book with liturgy written in Latin for each hour. Most prosperous families owned such a book, complete with a calendar marking the holy days and special prayers. The illumination of the words would be masterful, vivid letters and fanciful creatures drawn in bright colors and edged in gold. How much would such a volume cost? Could it be done on paper? The thought made her tremble.

"Girl, stop your agitation," the *vicomtesse* said in a firm voice. She turned to Martin. "Her mother ought not send her about without a shawl, what with that thin dress. It's an ill look."

Martin dipped his head, but the smile pasted on his face did not waver. He clasped his hands behind his back and spread his stance wider.

Auda evaluated the woman. What did the *vicomte* see in this haughty woman with high cheeks, a fine nose, and eyes that held judgment over everything? Maybe it was her power, the authority she seemed to command with a single look. Strength to match his.

Certainly the miller wanted a wife with needs as simple as he required for himself. Auda flushed, thinking of the painter's kiss on her wrist. What did he see when he looked at her?

The *vicomtesse* turned to Martin. "Explain what you've brought."

They had packed two boxes full of cloth-wrapped papers. Martin spread them in piles across the board.

"We have papers of all sizes here. I've brought them loose as you requested, but we can sew these up into folios, if you prefer."

"Hmm." She went through each pile, picking up pages to finger. Her fingers lingered over one sheet in particular, a delicate stationery Martin had designed for noblemen's wives, scented with rose petals.

"A good thought." The *vicomtesse* sniffed the page. "But I'll wager you've not had much luck. The men of this town scantly know their letters, let alone the women."

"Yet."

The lady turned a shrewd gaze on him, and Martin colored. Tapping a finger against her cheek, she inspected the rest of the bundles. "I've seen paper before," the lady said. "But it was coarse stuff, nothing like this. Tell me, do you command special cloths for this?"

"No, *domna*," Martin replied. "I need only the poorest of linens, cloth worthy for neither wear nor use. It takes patience to blend the pulp fine, but I have much, being a simple man with simple concerns."

"I see. And how does your paper compare to parchment?"

Martin's smile deepened. "Let us show you."

The lady commanded a servant to fetch a quill, ink, and a section of fresh parchment. When she handed the inked feather to Martin, he passed it to Auda. Surprise glinted in the *vicomtesse*'s eyes.

Auda held her gaze for a moment without flinching. The lady looked away, selecting a sheet of paper and pushing it across the table. Auda regarded the plain sheet before her. Was it a wise idea to show the lady she could write? Perhaps she should just draw a simple design. Pride warred with good sense.

At last, she squared her shoulders and wrote her name in bold strokes, one line at the top of the page, another in the middle, and a final line at the bottom. She repeated with the flat section of parchment.

"So, girl, you are not as simple as you look," the *vicomtesse* murmured while they waited for the words to dry.

Auda flushed, blowing on the wet ink. She picked up both pages, holding them to the light to show the lady that the lettering on both was fine and uniform, and that the dark ink hadn't bled greatly through the paper. Out of habit, her fingers played over the paper's surface; she felt for lumps of pulp that hadn't been beaten out or dimples that might suggest carelessness. But there were none.

"It's a comparison of the paper to the parchment," Martin explained.

In a swift movement, Auda brought the page to her ear and crumpled it in her fist. The lady gasped. Auda repeated the process with the parchment. The sound was the same, light and crisp. Unfolding the crushed pages, she spat on them. The moisture didn't show through the parchment, and just barely bled through the paper.

Stepping away, Auda waited for the lady to speak. The *vicomtesse* took the crumpled paper from her and examined it front and back.

"It's a pretty routine, that I'll swear," she said. "I can't pretend it means anything."

"You see, their textures are the same," Martin said. "We've gotten better at making certain the ink doesn't bleed through the page, although if I were to be an honest man, I'd have to admit that, in this, parchment can be superior."

The lady tilted her head at him, considering.

"I will take the four reams we discussed, plus an additional two," she said, drawing herself up tall. "I'll send my chamberlain for the extra when it's ready. No doubt I will order more after my husband has seen this."

Auda stifled a tremble, remembering the *vicomte*'s thoughtful gaze upon her. The warmth of the memory mingled with the painter's kiss.

Not noticing her tense beside him, Martin bowed and began packing up the remainder of his wares.

If they had a watermark, Auda thought, they could design paper specially for the lady, with her own design upon it. A woman of such pride would relish the idea. She'd have to tell her father later.

Before they were dismissed to leave, the *vicomtesse* spoke again. "I do, also," she said, "have need of a scribe. If this paper holds up, as you say, it will mean months, perhaps years, of work. Will a regular scribe, maybe an apprentice from the abbey, be able to work with this paper?"

Auda's eyes widened. To think that Martin could scribe for the lady—could write for the nobility, instead of at the stationer's cramped stall!

Martin bowed again. "There is no special trick to scribing on paper, my lady, though it takes time to grow accustomed to the surface. I'd scribe for you myself, but I know someone who could do it better."

Auda gaped at him, not understanding. Why was he not jumping at this chance?

The *vicomtesse* shook her head. "I've a tight budget, good man. If you think to help a friend, I'd best tell you now I can afford no Church scribe."

"Not a Church scribe." Her father shook her head. "A girl. My daughter."

Auda reeled back. What was he doing?

The *vicomtesse* regarded her, uncertain. "A girl as a scribe?"

"She is no normal girl." Her father gave Auda a pointed look and she bowed her head.

The *vicomtesse* slowly nodded. "Yes, she does have a fine hand. Well then, what wages will you have me set?"

"If you keep her here with room and board," Martin said after a moment, "I'll take three deniers each week, with Sunday free as a holy day."

Auda bit back a gasp. He was setting terms with the lady?

"Done." The lady sounded satisfied. "I'll send for her when I am ready. When the rains are over."

Auda kept her eyes averted as she helped Martin pack the rest of his wares, excitement and confusion working themselves out in her head. The servants showed them out into the yard. Only once they were out of the palace did she turn to face her father.

Why me? Why don't you scribe? He'd given away the best opportunity he'd ever had, to her!

Martin was silent for a moment. Auda could see he was trembling. "Better the safety of the *vicomtesse* than to trust in a stranger whose motives we don't know. Anyway, this chance was made for you. You're smarter than I, quicker in wit. You'll do great things. Just promise me," he added in a sad tone, "that you'll share them with me when you return home."

Auda took her father's hand in both of hers and held on tight. Lifting her face to the sky, she waited for the rain to wash away her budding tears. But all she saw was the sun's emerging light and its warmth, so long forgotten, wide across her face.

As the heretics cannot defend themselves against the truth of faith by strength, reason or authorities, they quickly resort to sophistries, deceit and verbal trickery to avoid detection.

—Bernardo Gui,
Practica inquisitionis heretice pravitatis

Part II
Summer 1320

Chapter Thirteen

In Narbonne, summer came on with a vengeance.

Since the rains had ended, weeks ago, the sun had come out every day, baking the moisture from the waterlogged town. Priests in town called it a miracle and Narbonne fêted its fortune for days.

As the villagers celebrated their turn in luck, summons came from the palace that Auda was to report to the *vicomtesse* in one week. She looked again at the creamy roll of parchment bearing the lady's writ and seal, still amazed at her fortune. She wished he could speak to her sister about it. Auda hadn't seen her since the morning after her ill-fated meeting with Edouard, but Martin had gone to tell Poncia in person that Auda would be taking employment with the lady and was not free for marriage. Auda didn't know what words passed between them, but Martin came home that evening with a grim set about his mouth. He drank an entire flagon of wine without so much as uttering a word.

Now her father followed her gaze to the lady's summons. He nodded, pleased. "It looks like we're just in time, *ma filla*," he said, winking at Auda. "The Gypsies arrived this morning so we'll have a chance to see them before you leave."

Auda smiled. Her father had gone to the market every day to check for the Gypsies. The caravans came early and left early, depending on the success of their sales. Some years, when they had other, bigger fairs to attend, they would only stay in town for a week. But the fair this year was the largest Narbonne had ever held.

Now Martin smiled at his daughter. "I've already told Tomas I will be late tomorrow. We can go in the morning."

She nodded, eager to see if the Gypsies could tell her anything more of watermarks.

Auda woke well before the break of dawn. It would be a bright day today. She hadn't been outside since the rains had ended, and the burgeoning sunlight was already hurting her eyes. After she had finished dressing, she returned to her room for a final piece of cloth hanging on the wall. It was a covering Poncia had designed for her, a headcap with extra cloth that hung on the sides and over her forehead to be used as a shield against the sun. Auda tied it over a tighter wimple that hid her pale hair. Opening the door, she winced against the bright sunlight.

They left just after the bells rang for Matins. The whole town was stirring as if just brought back to life. Lifting her face into the warm breeze, Auda smelled the scents of threshed grass and baked dung in the streets. All of Narbonne was immersed in the business of sowing crops, seeding gardens, and making cheese and bread. The work would last through the Great Fair, which would arrive the following week and last through the harvest.

Auda thought about the Gypsy she'd seen in Tomas's shop this past winter. Such a servile creature, dirty and cringing— nothing like the Gypsies she and Martin had befriended at the fair. Still, the shabby man had introduced the watermark to her. Hopefully she would learn more about it today.

As they neared the market, traffic along the Via Domitia grew heavy with merchants transporting their wares into the stalls. A skinny boy stood in the center of the bustle, crying out the day's news. He rapped on a thick drum suspended around his neck.

"*Oyez! Oyez!* Market spaces to be extended for duration of the fair. See the Consul's Office to apply." He drummed again. "Bridge tolls to be raised on the new week! Penitents attending the masses exempt!"

A band of young children darted between the mules and peddlers on the road. One small boy, running to catch a ball, bumped into her. Auda turned away her face, not wanting the child to see her pale face and watery eyes.

Martin reached for her hand. "Just the folly of a child. The priests have been silenced. The Jacobins have left. It was as I told you. They found nothing here."

Yet Auda couldn't forget the terror of the past months, the feel of strange hands trying to carry her away, condemning her as a witch. It seemed to her that a darkness still lingered. And she hadn't forgotten about the inquisitor who wrote about witches and heresy.

They headed toward the center of the Bourg, where merchants and artisans were readying for the Great Fair with a frenzied pitch. Auda ducked between the strangers crowd-

ing every cranny of the marketplace. Part of her thrilled at
the idea of finding her artist among them. She glanced at her
father. What would she do if she *did* find Jaime?

The scent of meat pies, sweet and spicy, wafted over the
tangy smell of sweat and ale. Martin smiled and hailed the
itinerant vendor. Giving the man two pennies, he passed a
beef pie soaked in wine and mixed with nuts and currants to
Auda. The spiced meat, kept hot by glowing coals in the vendor's cart, seared her tongue-stump and slid down her throat,
warm and filling.

Martin finished his pie in quick swallows. "Ahh, nothing
like the first bite of fair food!"

He led her to the outskirts of the market, where a small
shabby tent had been pitched just outside the fairgrounds.
Patches of orange and brown cloth had been sewn over the
opening like a curtain and two small tables stood in front
of the tent. A dozen men and women hovered around them,
piling their wares for display. They barked at a gang of young
boys who hung by the tent, laughing and chatting.

Someone carted a wagon full of brass lamps in front of her,
nearly trodding on her feet. Auda stepped back, eyeing the
tables. Miracles abounded here, stoppered in jars or hidden
under dark cloths. There was the south-pointing spoon for
lost travelers, glass that reflected like shined metal, even a
game of kings and armies played on a checkered board with a
handful of carved chits. But she only had an eye for one thing,
and she hadn't found it yet.

Martin spotted an old friend setting up in the back, a Gypsy
who often brought paper tracts and pamphlets for Martin.

"Auda, don't go far. I'll be right back."

She nodded and wandered around to the front of the table.
Donino, the man in charge of the stall, flashed her a smile
of bright white teeth against sun-darkened skin. She nodded

shyly. As long as she could remember, Donino had brought his caravans to the fair. She'd thought him a magician once, and in a way, still did. At his invitation, she moved closer to the table, seeing many more items crowded on the wooden board. Some, like the seeing-eye glass and cakes of carved soap, she'd seen before.

A stout man wearing a lopsided red cross on his tunic called out to passersby:

"Join the Shepherds' Crusade! Fight for the Holy Spirit against Jews and infidels, and be forgiven your sins, forgiven your debts."

Auda frowned, edging closer to Donino's table to get away from the man's righteous harangue.

Her gaze fixed upon a piece of wire bent into the pattern of a stylized cross edged with hooks on the four corners. She smiled.

"You've a good eye, *domna*," the Gypsy said, pulling out of his conversation with another customer. "That piece is all the fashion in Italy. It's called a watermark, perfect for your trade. It makes a pattern in the paper, like this."

He drew out a sheet from under the table and held it near a torch. "Do you see?"

She squinted against the bright flame. There was a faint design in the paper, just like the wandering Gypsy had said there would be. Just like the heretic's tract her uncle had brought with him bore. She took the page and inspected both sides, then examined the wire device. Frowning, she placed the watermark against the paper and held them up.

Donino laughed. "You attach it to the screen of your mould before you dip it in the pulp, like this." Reaching under the table again, he drew out a small scrap of screen. He hooked the watermark onto the thin metal grid and handed it to her.

"*Voilà,*" he said with a flourish of his thick hands. "The

pattern dries into the paper just like that." He winked. "And a superior sheet of paper it is, yes?"

Auda caressed the faint mark on the paper. So that was how it worked. The heavier wire of the watermark would emboss its design into the wet paper pulp. When the paper dried, it seemed the watermark would show through. She nodded, appreciating the cleverness of the idea.

"It's only three pennies for that one. But I have others." He opened a wooden box filled with a dozen different wire pieces.

Auda put the page down and picked through the box, examining each piece. Donino had collected many intricate designs of other crosses, crowns, keys, even some with complex heraldry. Her father would be enchanted with such an item, but nothing here spoke of him.

"You want something else? We can make a new pattern." He cleared a space on the table and placed an inked quill in her hand. "Show me."

Gripping the quill, she pondered for a moment. What symbol could capture her father? What could define his trade? After a moment, she sketched a clumsy drawing of lines and curves on his sheet of paper.

"Ah," Donino nodded, "the famed bridge of Narbonne, yes. I can do this for you." He turned and barked in a foreign tongue to someone in the back.

Auda fingered the paper. The watermark was certainly a wonder, but even the Gypsy's paper was different. Shinier. Smoother. Donino had been selling paper for years, as others in the fair did, but his wares had always been coarse, and unfinished. Nothing like this. Where had he gotten it?

"There's a trick to it," a voice said to her.

Auda stepped back, reaching to pull her wimple closer to her face. It was the customer Donino had been speaking with earlier. Auda squinted at him. He was a tall man with a round ruddy face that matched his plain brown tunic, and he looked familiar. Reaching for the paper, he pointed at her crude sketch, then flipped it to the backside. "The ink doesn't bleed. The page has been sized, you see."

She shook her head, wrinkling her brow.

"Stiffened, coated, if you will, dipped in a jelly made of hide cuttings, hoof shavings, powdered bones and the like." The stranger gave her a conspiratorial wink.

Auda tilted her head. He spoke with a local accent, though she didn't recognize him. How did he know this? She jerked her chin toward his smiling face, but when he said no more, she took the paper from him and picked up the quill to ask.

The man shook his head and spoke in a lowered voice.

"Not here."

Auda dropped the quill and stared at him. She recalled the peculiar conversation she'd overheard between two men and Jehan weeks back. They had been an odd pair, both dressed in tattered brown cloaks. This stranger looked like one of those men. Yes, that's where she had seen him before.

Donino returned. "You are fortunate, *domna*, to be our first customer. I can have the device for you in a week. Now for the cost—"

The stranger wandered behind the tables and disappeared into Donino's tent.

"*Domna?*"

Tearing her gaze from the stranger, she fished for her coin pouch. She picked out three pennies and laid them on the table. Donino laughed.

"Ah, *domna*, the price for a custom design is over thrice that."

She put down another penny and they haggled for a few moments, settling on the price of five deniers, of which she paid two. She gestured at her father, who was still talking to his friend. Placing a finger over her lips, she shook his head.

The Gypsy laughed. "It's to be a surprise then?"

Auda nodded.

Donino bowed his head. "Don't fret. We are known for our ability to keep secrets."

Chapter Fourteen

Martin escorted Auda to the palace the next day.

"I'll meet you here at week's end, after my shift at the stall is over." He kissed the top of her head. "You'll do well, *ma filla*. We will celebrate when you return home in a week."

Auda blinked away sudden tears. She'd never been separated from her father, not for long. How would her days be without his larger-than-life talk, his wild dreams and cheer?

An ache settled in her chest, but she nodded at him and turned to the large stone palace standing across from the skeleton of the archbishop's new cathedral. Green flags fluttered high on the standard and twin stone cherubs, flanked by glass-encased candles, smiled at her from above the palace doorway. One cast a hopeful smile, while the other leered.

She approached the heavy oak door with some trepidation. The guard standing beside it sized her up.

"What is your business?"

She handed him the wooden chit the *vicomtesse* had sent with her summons. Eyeing her with some suspicion, he muttered something under his breath and motioned her to walk ahead of him. He directed her along a set of long passageways marked by plain walls and flickering torches. In quick succession, he pointed out the kitchens and the room she was to live in. She struggled to keep pace. He left her in front of a large room in the lady's wing.

Listening to his receding footsteps, Auda stood alone in the hallway and tried to calm her mounting anxiety. She'd been so relieved to not have to marry the miller that she hadn't worried about what a life here would be like. Until now.

The *vicomtesse*'s voice spilled from the room into the corridor, crescendoing into a tirade.

Swallowing, Auda forced herself to step forward toward the entrance and peered inside. The room itself seemed plain by castle standards, though it was richer than Auda's entire home, with a large table bearing stacks of parchment and paper and two benches. Blue-and-yellow flowered tapestries hung on the walls, beside a painting of a vineyard framed in gilded metal. Rich yellow curtains were draped over two large windows and a trio of candles burned on each wall.

The lady was scolding two stiff-backed maids, younger than Auda, the shorter one cowering against the taller.

"Look at what lurks here!" The lady glared at the maids and spread a handful of the rushes from the ground across the table; mixed with the wilted foliage were bones, rocks, and dried balls of cat dung.

"And under this yet is beer, grease, and spittle—all that is and smells foul in the world."

Auda trembled under the lady's withering voice.

The lady clapped her hands. "Off with you, then! Fresh rushes every week! And if I catch another room in a state as deplorable as this, Cook will put apples in your mouths and roast you on the spit for dinner! Now, go!"

The girls scrambled out, rushing past Auda in the doorway

as she tried to avoid attention. But the lady spied Auda and waved her in. Looking her up and down, the *vicomtesse* let out an explosive breath.

"Have you not anything else to wear, girl? Or at least thought to clean this dress?"

Auda flushed. The yellow gown Poncia had given her needed washing, reeked of sweat, but she'd worried about ruining the fabric by cleaning something so fine. Would the lady dismiss her for it?

"Stop by the kitchen and speak to Amélie, the housekeeper..." The *vicomtesse* paused and frowned. "No, of course not. I'll have one of the maids inquire. Amélie always frets that her girls cast off their costumes faster than her boys. She will have something."

Auda bowed in gratitude.

The lady harrumphed. "No, just sit. Let us see how you wear this new uniform before we claim to be pleased about it." She smoothed her gown. The lines in her pale, unpowdered skin eased for a moment. With her hair uncovered and tied in a loose braid, she looked younger, pretty in her simplicity.

"Tell me, girl, why have you not been sent to the convent, or taken a maid's job?" She pursed her lips, frowning. "Plenty would pay well for a maid who can't talk back nor spread their household business. I daresay it would be difficult to find you a husband, but even that has to be a possibility among some, no?"

It was a reasonable question, yet it rankled. Reluctantly, Auda pressed her stylus into one of her tablets.

I work with my father, making paper.

The *vicomtesse* raised her eyebrows. "It's an ill work that takes the hands of a girl from her house. Surely your mother doesn't consent?"

Auda stiffened. Why did everyone assume a woman had to marry and keep house? Surely one so fine as the *vicomtesse* had more lofty dreams for herself.

Lifting her chin, she wrote again.

She died of childbed fever.

The lady's gaze didn't waver, though the corners of her blue-edged eyes softened. She sat at the table and drummed her fingers on the wood.

"Not many girls have the luck to learn their letters. Your father has vision."

Auda ducked her head, suddenly unsure. Did the lady mean to compliment, or criticize?

"No, don't look away." The lady's voice cracked like a switch on bare flesh. "It's nothing to hide, knowing one's letters. My husband has brought wise men from all over the world to this town. He's even given money to that school for the Jews. If the Jews can learn, why not our own women?"

Auda nodded in spite of herself.

"It can be a dangerous world for women. Like your mother, my only sister died in childbirth. The babe died too and her husband married again." She cleared her throat. "Let us begin. You can share now in the experience of a mother writing to her child."

Though the words sounded harsh, Auda heard the telltale softness in the lady's voice when she spoke of her sister. It was exactly like the tremble in her father's hands and eyes when her mother was mentioned.

She bit her lip and pulled out a pair of quills and a small pot of ink from her basket. Her father had made the ink especially for her, soaking crushed gallnuts in water laced with verjuice and adding gum and iron salts. He swore the verjuice made the ink blacker, almost the color of midnight.

She put ink and quills to the side, next to the twin stacks of parchment and paper, and took out a pair of large tablets.

The lady clasped her hands behind and nodded at the tablet. "Address to Guillaume de Narbonne, Seigneur de Montagnac."

Auda pressed the letters into the red wax and waited. The lady resumed pacing, mulling over her words.

> *My dearest son,*
>
> *It has been near to one year since we last heard word from you. We received news of your marriage to the daughter of Montbrun's baron. Your father is pleased. It distresses me that you did not think to inform us, better to invite us. No doubt the fête was enjoyed.*
>
> *Have a thought for your old mother, who frets for her second son.*
>
> > *On this day, in the grace of the Lord,*
> > *Your mother, Jeanne*

The lady took the tablet. She digested the words but changed nothing.

Such a curt letter, Auda wondered. Was that how a mother spoke to her child?

The lady began the next message.

> *Dear brother,*
>
> *I am certain you have heard Narbonne thrives.*
>
> *The fair has come and the scriptorium is under construction, to be complete by Martinmas. Outside of Narbonne, however, the conflict rages.*
>
> *Inquisitors control much —*

The stylus slipped from Auda's hand, clattering to the ground.

The lady paused and sighed at the consternated frown on the girl's face. "You worry at the mention of inquisitors." Her voice was flat.

Auda bowed her head, feeling the top of her ears burn.

"Good." She nodded her approval. "Most everyone else in town believes the inquisitors and their scrutiny have vanished with the rains." The wrinkles around her mouth creased. "No, the inquisitors have not left, nor turned their eyes from our town. Even now one writes a treatise on how to ferret out the heretics who most surely have gone into hiding."

Auda blinked. The inquisitor Poncia had warned her of was still about? Had he released more of his writing on how to search for heretics and witches? She crossed herself, shuddering.

The lady cast a shrewd glance at her. "They will strike when the town least expects it, I suppose. If they wait for a lull, people may get careless. We will see."

The fear returned to the pit of Auda's stomach.

Instructing Auda to pick up her stylus, the lady continued her narration.

> *Outside of Narbonne, however, the conflict rages.*
> *Inquisitors control much and too many flee*
> *to Narbonne for safety. Their care costs*
> *a good deal. Pages smuggled from a nearby*
> *abbey speak of a guide to root out heretics.*
> *The words are harsh and ugly.*
> *Your position at the abbey may be of use in keeping*
> *our town intact. Please advise us what to do.*
>
> *In God's Love,*
> *Your sister*

The *vicomtesse* read the message and nodded, gesturing back at the desk.

"Make two copies, if you will. The parchment rolls are for the letters to be sent. My copies can be written on paper." She arched a brow. "We shall see how this material of yours fares. There will be more letters to pen tomorrow." Without another word, she swept out of the room.

Auda sat at the desk to copy out the messages. It took longer than she expected to script them on the creamy parchment. Used to writing on paper, she had to slow her movements and press deeper with her quill. But her excitement at hearing about the scriptorium couldn't be tamped—such news to tell her father! She spread a handful of light sand across the page when she finished to absorb any excess ink—an inconvenience avoided with the more absorbent paper.

Massaging her cramped hand, Auda stowed her tools in her basket and looked around the palace corridor. How was she to find her room? She chose a random path, taking only right turns as she floundered for a familiar sight. Instead she found herself at a dead end, in a small musty room lit only by a narrow row of candles. The stained pattern of the glass window stayed dark against a dark sky. Reds and blues winked among the shadows, mute without the sun. A chill in the room covered the faded scent of incense, and dust filmed the three dark wooden pews. They faced a bay in the wall that held a statue of the blessed Mary cradling the baby Jesus. *La Vierge de Fontfroide.*

Auda knelt. Though she had never felt comfortable in church, with the priest accusing everyone of sin, she'd always felt a special warmth for the Virgin Mother who had birthed the Lord. She had seen paintings of the famed statue in the market, the lady Mary who sat amidst her voluminous robes while clasping her babe on one knee. Mary's hand rested on her paunch, the bulge so ample it might have belonged to an old drunkard. Auda recalled the Virgin's peaceful smile from the paintings, though she couldn't discern the statue's details with her hazy eyesight. She squinted at the statue and mouthed the words of the Lord's Prayer in gratitude for their changes in fortune.

As she finished the prayer, footsteps sounded behind her. Auda crossed herself and stood, suddenly wondering if she was not allowed in here. She turned around, expecting a servant to hurry her away, and came face-to-face with the *vicomte*.

He nodded at her, unsurprised to see her. "So you prayed for the grace of the Lady." She stayed still as he walked up to the statue and reached to touch its cheeks, then brought his fingers to Auda's chin.

Blinking, she tried not to squirm, nor to meet his gaze. His fingers felt hot on her skin.

"She's a bleak woman, no? Such sorrow. How much different she would look with the hint of life painted on her cheeks and lips. My sister and I used to talk of it when we were young. Sacrilege to touch the Lady, though we didn't know it then, with hands that grasp in sex and lust, that hurt and kill. But we did it." His voice turned flat.

Auda caught her breath and eyed him.

"Red for her cheeks, black for her lips. We left her eyes blank." A tic began throbbing at his left temple. "My father was furious, of course. He paid reparations to the abbey, and beat me himself. From then on, the tutors came here. I never returned." He dropped his hand. "Come with me."

Auda let out her breath. The back of her neck tingled but she didn't look back, not even at the Virgin. What did the *vicomte* want with her?

The hallways seemed a maze, confined and cold with dark

corners and a warren of narrow corridors. Torches illuminated short sections of the passage with their flickering orange light, leaving a signature of soot and grime on the walls.

The *vicomte* ushered her into a small room that looked like an office. The air smelled like stale breath, even with the open window that faced the rushing river. The room was furnished with a cushioned chair that sat behind a desk covered in rolls of parchment, a thin rug on the stone floor, and a wooden bench lining the longest wall. A white greyhound lay on its back in front of a strong fire, its paws twitching.

The *vicomte* motioned toward the bench and sat next to her, close but not touching. He followed her gaze to the stacks of parchment littering the floor by his desk. Such wealth in this room, measured in books and scrolls.

"It's a never-ending business, protecting this town from itself," he said.

She nodded. What power this man commanded, writs and decrees that he could issue from this small room. His path had been decided at birth. A nobleman, an eldest son, a *vicomte*'s heir. Perhaps everyone's fate was decided at birth, before birth even.

Had anyone decided a fate for her?

The *vicomte* reached for a large canvas roll. It was a map of Narbonne, city and bourg, bisected by the Aude. Half of the city and most of the bourg were inked in red, province of the Lord Archbishop.

"This town is mine," he remarked. "Did you know we held it all at one time? Church and palace. For decades, this land has been in my family—my kin, *comtes* of Toulouse and Foix, held court in this backwater. They held on to it, didn't trade it for riches, or give it away in dowry. Why?"

She shivered at the passion in his tone. Why was he telling her this? Had he brought her here for a history lesson?

And yet she couldn't turn away from the seductiveness of his voice.

The *vicomte* rose, tapping his polished fingernail on the Roman roads that led to and from Narbonne, and to the path out to the sea. "This town, she's poised to be something big, something great. But now the Church takes over like a pestilence. I would restore the glory my family brought to Narbonne. If only I could."

She found herself nodding again, entranced. To create a thing of beauty—was that not what everyone wanted? Poncia with hopes for a child, Martin with his paper. And Auda? All she had ever wanted was to find her voice.

The *vicomte*'s lips curved and his voice turned soft. "These are difficult times. You've traded for your fortune well. Under my roof, in my home," he said. His breath wafted over her. "At least here you are safe from the inquisitors. They search for those such as you."

Her eyes widened at the implied threat.

"The papermaker's fragile daughter. Yes, fragile. The white witch."

She started at the mention of the phrase the inquisitor had used in his treatise.

"Safety comes at a price, my dear."

Auda's heart quickened. What did this man want, this powerful, dangerous man, who could suffocate her life on a whim?

"You are so unlike the others. Any other." He leaned in. "A starling poised for full flight. Any other born like you might have withered. But you, you thrive."

His thigh brushed against hers and she shivered, jerking back. What did he want? A quick tumble with a white witch? Unlikely, for this man. He could have a virgin every night, if that was his taste.

Their eyes connected and he stretched out a single finger to caress her neck. Her cheeks burned again.

"You are beautiful, I don't suppose you know. Has anyone ever told you, little bird?"

She trembled.

"Such a puzzle, the voiceless daughter of a man who works a trade of letters and words." He dropped his hand. "Yes, the pope himself would be pleased to know of one such as you. Such favor I could curry, delivering you into the care of his favorite inquisitor."

Auda shut her eyes, imagining the dark face of a black-robed inquisitor watching her from within the depths of his cowl. He raised his hand, in her mind's eye, in judgment over her and her father. She whimpered.

"But I won't," the *vicomte* said.

Her eyes flew open.

"Discovery of a witch, even an imagined one, will only bring the inspection of the Church further into town. I will not have my people harassed for the delight of the archbishop. Bide your job and stay out of notice, understand, little bird?"

Auda nodded, heart still racing.

The *vicomte* smiled, a smile that didn't seem entirely unkind. "You will be safe here. As safe as any of us."

Chapter Fifteen

Each day at the palace started well before dawn. The bustle outside Auda's door came in spurts: first the hurried step of the maidservants off to build the hearths up in the large building, then the cooks' assistants scrambling to the kitchen to bake the bread needed to feed the palace inhabitants. Just as the bells rang for Matins, the guards would change shift. Auda rose to the measured rhythm of their march in the hallways.

The privy for the servants was often crowded in the morning, so she made a habit of taking her breakfast in the servants' kitchen immediately after she dressed. The dress the *vicomtesse* had arranged for her arrived, a gown of pale linen, the softest thing she had ever worn. It hung loose on her frame, but still she felt grand walking through the hallways with the skirt swishing about her ankles.

Everyone in the palace was required to attend a morning Mass. The palace priest was a kind man, who spoke in a warm tone and kept the prayers to a minimum. As soon as he rang the bell to dismiss them, Auda headed into the courtyard for her only chance to catch the morning air. The sun was shielded by the large guard tower to the east, so in these early hours she could raise her face to the sky and feel the summer warmth.

The courtyard bustled with activity. At one end, the smith worked at his massive forge while his apprentices labored beside him to smooth out horseshoes and shape nails. At the other end, the palace laundress washed and hung buckets full of sheets, tablecloths, and towels, forever scolding her troupe of maids in her strident voice.

"Be quick now! There's still an army to clothe!"

Grooms passed by carrying hay into the stables, while maids emptied chamber pots into a gutter that ran into the river.

Auda felt bewildered among such commotion. Each day, she hurried through the courtyard to the lady's wing of the palace. With her head down to avoid the crowds, she couldn't tell if people stared at her.

The *vicomtesse* met Auda in the study every morning at the second bell. The lady had Auda compose a lengthy message on her wax tablet, and for the next few days Auda made dozens of copies of the missive to the *vicomtesse*'s family and friends. It was a plea for help requesting extra rolls of parchment for the new scriptorium. The rains had decimated the cattle and the price of hides had gone up by a full silver. The Church hoarded its own shares of rolls, offering only a fraction for sale and then at twice the regular cost.

Each night, Auda hurried from the drawing room to her own bed, eyes down, hoping not to be caught by the Lord Vicomte, whose odd interest troubled her. She spent her evenings alone, eschewing the evening prayer when she could, sometimes even supper. Her room became her haven. It was scarcely larger than her own pallet under the loft at home, decorated only by a small wooden crucifix on the wall, but the bed was firm and the blankets clean. By habit, Auda kept her papers, and an extra wax tablet, hidden under the hay.

Most nights she went to bed thinking about her father, worrying about how he was managing on his own. Or sometimes, as she prepared to sleep, she remembered the artist and his sketches, wondering what he'd thought when he'd made them. She took out her tablet and wrote about his fisherwoman. Though her fingers cramped, unused to writing so much and with such care, she could not help but be moved by memory of his sketch. The eyes of the hideous woman had tales to tell.

That first week seemed to last an eternity. The morning her father was supposed to take her home, Auda woke before sunrise. She still had a few hours before Martin had planned to meet her. Though he meant for her to wait in the palace, Auda couldn't resist her first chance to go out in the town alone. With her first wages in her pocket, she had something she wanted to do.

Auda slipped out of the palace early. The morning air was fresh and new, but activity was already high in the streets. The fair would officially open today, and the roads were crammed with vendors hawking services and performers singing and acting with flamboyant gestures. She turned away from the main grounds, heading instead toward the river. On her first day back home to her father, she wanted to bring him something special.

She walked toward the eastern end of the river, where a series of docks were anchored to the riverbank and fishmongers were busy offloading their catch for the market day. The river was running high today. People said the hot summer was melting snow in the mountains; they worked hard to build heaps of sand and dirt into an embankment to protect the town. Every year the river seemed to grow higher, but this year the difference was larger than Auda had ever seen.

What should she buy? she wondered. Eel pie was one of Martin's favorites. Talk in the palace said all manners of fish were showing up in the nets these days, coming in by boatloads and closer to shore, perhaps on account of the rains.

Drawing her wimple closer to her face, Auda looked around. Fisherman's Alley was crowded with long tables heaped with fillets and finless bodies of different colors and flavors, all mingling in a slight rotten stench. Leaning in to inspect one table, Auda just missed being hit across the cheek by the flat side of a large brown fish. Wiping watery drops of brine from her face, she dared to raise her head and glare at him.

"Out of the way then!" he yelled at her, not even looking at her.

She shook her fist at him and turned to another table. Across the way, one vendor was speaking to a group of potential customers. "This here's a fish from far north. Very, very popular in England, most 'specially at court. Herring—the white ones are salted, the red ones cured. Strong fish with a strong taste."

Another merchant creaked his cart past them. "Barbels and mullets for Fish Day!"

Still another vendor sold sea eel, corb, and rockfish, followed by one selling whiting and porpoise. "Pudding of porpoise," he was saying to his customers. "Take his blood and grease, mix into oatmeal with salt and pepper, ginger if y'have it. Gut 'im and stuff 'im full of it, then boil a good while. Lay him on the fire, if ye've a quick hand. Till he blisters, no more. Cut him to the plate with onions and verjuice. Mmmmm." He held up a generous cut.

Finally Auda made her pick, and the merchant wrapped

the fish in oilcloth. Her father would be pleased. One errand done—another to go.

Leaving the fish market behind, she walked across to the far side of the market: the artisan's corner. She passed covered stalls stacked with helmets and swords brought back from the never-ending war with the Moslems, tables heaped with handwoven rugs and tapestries, and scores of stacked candle lamps. Finally, she caught sight of what she was looking for.

Drawing up her courage, she pushed back the drape of her wimple and entered a cramped tent filled with drawings and paintings. Sketches of fisher folk and peasants were stacked alongside bright paintings of angelic Madonnas.

"Come in, *domna*. Take a good look, enjoy what you see, and leave with what you like."

She turned toward the drawling voice, surprised to see a thin, grease-spotted man standing in the corner, watching her. He bit into a half-eaten chicken leg, his gaze roving over her clean dress and new round-toed shoes. He drew back when he saw her face. Fear flitted in his eyes before they filmed over in pretended boredom.

"Frightful one, aren't you?" he shrugged, wiping his fingers on his blue doublet. "Well, if you can pay, I can sell. Looking for something special?"

She looked around. Where was the painter Jaime?

The stranger took another bite. "Look well then. I've sold portraitures to the consuls' families themselves. I've a great selection of ready-made works as well, from our own churches in Narbonne to a lovely one of our Mother Mary in the Holy Papal City." He chuckled. "Whichever city you like."

"Mmmm," she managed, ignoring the tired barb at their French pope. Conscious of the man's eyes upon her, she made a show of looking through the paintings. Even among walls of bright scenes featuring angels and saints, she could tell which had been painted by her artist. He tended to add minor details—a smile lurking at the corner of a shepherd's mouth, or the reflection of a blooming flower in a cherub's eye, like prizes for the discerning viewer. But what truly interested her were his sketches of commoners. In the tent, he'd displayed only two, of children playing in the mud.

"Ugly pieces, no?" the man remarked, coming up behind her. "They're not mine, thanks be to God. My partner does them. I can't figure on why the man picks sour women and dirty children to draw." The man laughed, spreading his arms wide. "If we wanted to see the ugliness in the world, I say just look around." His gaze lingered on her, before he continued. "Strange man with strange tastes. It was his idea to share the stall. Said there wasn't a point to paying twice for the same lousy bit of market." He picked at his scraggly brown beard. "Only thing he's been right about so far."

She walked past a series of paintings depicting Christ in the manger and nodded toward the empty stool by the drawings.

"Oh, you're looking for him?" Now the painter smirked. "Who knows where he is? Maybe the church. Maybe the privy. Maybe the room he's rented in the whorehouse. You know, drink a little ale, rub a little skin, find his inspiration." He leered. "So no manger fresco for you then, *domna*?"

Auda fidgeted, drawing the hanging cloth of her wimple back over her face. It had been a mistake to come, and now she only wanted to get away from this coarse man. She nodded farewell and turned, bumping straight into Jaime.

He wore the same short black tunic with the patched brown trousers, and the same crooked smile. His leanness brought out the darkness in his high cheekbones, the sleepy circles under his dark eyes.

"You've come," was all he said.

The sound of his voice thrilled her.

The painter, seated in his corner, took another bite of his chicken and watched. With a frown in his direction, Jaime took Auda by the arm and escorted her out of the stall.

"Follow me," he said, leading her alongside a procession of goats and children into the main square. He paused near a shuttered shop along the crowded Via Domitia. Carts rattled past them, one close after another.

Auda cast her eyes down, the sun's brightness bleeding through her wimple. Her mouth went dry.

"I was hoping to see you again," he admitted, his voice warm and low. "I went back to the spice stall the day after we met."

Auda shook her head, as though unable to believe him, and he laughed.

"I went there every morning for five days straight. I finally found the courage to ask about you, but they would tell me nothing." He bowed. "So it is my good fortune that you found me."

Nodding, she rubbed her damp palms against her dress. She'd planned this meeting in her head, but now that she was here she remembered nothing. She fingered the folded sheet of paper in her belt pouch. Looking up into his encouraging smile, she pulled the paper out and offered it to him.

His eyebrows arched in surprise. Taking the page, he unwrapped it and read aloud.

> *Down at the docks, not far from here,*
> *There toils a tired fisherwoman,*
> *Who, dawn to dusk, sits a stool*
> *In her poor husband's home.*
>
> *Clutching cleaver to his lean catch*
> *She chop-chop-chops meat from bone,*
> *And remembers memories of old*

When both were so much in love.

His flow'rs, now dead flow'rs, saved and dried
Hang the wall near wooden Cross,
Sad tokens of a life once lived,
Sad tokens of a life once loved.

"This warn't the life I wanted!
This warn't the life he promised!"
She screams and cuts, screams and then cuts,
Her curses screech out like a song.

She takes up her once-prized cleaver
Tosses it down and stomps it dead.
"I shan't cut me no fish no more,"
She says, and goes to lie in her bed.

"O Wife! Come close!" her husband cries.
"Behold this Bounty we're given!"
She sees him with two bags a'full,
Two more on the dock are wrigglin'.

"Thanks, all our thanks, O Lord," he weeps.
She kneels and weeps 'longside too.
Not for him, his fish, or their life
But for her dead dented blade.

Her poor dead dented blade.

His voice trailed off at the last.

Auda bit her lip, watching him for a further reaction. Drops of sweat collected at her neck. She'd spent her evenings agonizing over the verse. Had she missed something in the rhythm?

Should she have included another detail? Discarded bits of verse ran through her mind. He hadn't said a word yet, was still staring at the page. She should never have given it to him.

At last Jaime looked up, blinking. "You move me with your work. You give life to my lady." Not disdain at all in his voice, but appreciation.

A smile tugged at the corners of her lips. She grinned, giddy, as if she had just traded a naughty joke with her sister.

He drew closer, as if to embrace her, and lowered his head to hers. She swallowed, unable to breathe as his lips came near to hers. What was she to do? Could she kiss a man without her tongue?

Jaime stiffened, his gaze suddenly unsure, and dropped his arms. In that moment, Auda glimpsed the blue sky and the sun-dappled pattern on his cheeks. She smelled the dust from the nearby bustle, the warmth of nearby pastry shops, the honest fragrance of wildflowers and fresh fruit above the warm scent of garlic pork lingering on the artist's lips. What was the purpose of life if not to grab at beautiful moments like this?

She brought her hands to his neck, pulling him back until their lips connected. For a moment, she felt nothing at all except the happiness that lifted her lips and spread inside her. It would never have been like this with the miller.

After a moment, the artist pulled back and held her at arm's length. "I have a wedding to attend at month's end. Please tell me you'll be my companion?"

Without a moment of hesitation, she nodded, and kissed the artist once more.

Chapter Sixteen

Auda barely made it back to the gate of the palace in time to meet her father. He was already walking up the road, looking for her, when she ran forward to greet him.

Martin's face split into a smile. "Auda! You look well, quite well!" He drew her into an embrace. "Come, tell me about your week while we walk home."

She nodded, smiling back, and passed him her basket to free up her hands. *Good week.* Miming the motion of writing, she spread her hands wide. *Many letters.*

"Personal or matters of court?"

Both. Hiding the blush that crept up her neck as she thought of her own personal matter with the artist, she told him about the progress on the scriptorium, the shortage in parchment, and the letters the lady sent to all of her relatives and former ladies-in-waiting, asking them to send what rolls they could.

"At least she keeps copies of her letters on our paper," her father said. "It's a start."

Auda nodded and flexed her hand against the cramping from her scribe work. Again she thought of Jaime, his pleasure over the verse she'd written for him. The blush returned.

Martin didn't seem to notice. "Yes, scribing does take a toll." He held up his right hand, showing her how his fingers had swelled from years of work. "We'll get you a salve for that."

They walked in silence the rest of the way, Auda sneaking glances into the bright daylight to look around. Everything seemed sharper, brighter, suffused with color compared to the gray stone of the palace, even to her weak eyes. Was this the filter of love, as one song she'd heard put it?

Martin nudged her as they approached their house. "Go see to the animals. I'll be in the studio."

Happy to be alone with her joy, Auda fed the chickens and the goats, taking eggs from one, milking the other. From the yard, she could see smoke piping into white curls from their chimney. The only time her father grew the hearth to full strength in the summer was when he was drying paper. Auda smiled as she pushed through the kitchen door.

She breathed in, taking in the sweet smell of thyme. Martin always threw a fresh bouquet of the herb on the flames when he set his papers to dry. Her mother used to do that, he'd told her, to mask the soggy odor that permeated the house. Ever since, Auda had associated the delicate fragrance with Elena.

In the week that had passed, Martin had rearranged his studio to better suit the needs of one person. The desk had been pushed aside, replaced by a table where he kept all the tools he needed at a moment's notice. Auda sighed, saddened for a moment, and took the wrapped fish from her basket. Without her there to help him, the workshop was already in disarray.

From the doorway, she watched her father work. Dipping his mould horizontally into the pulp, Martin steadied his hand, letting the light from an overhead torch cast a shadow of the mould on the liquid's surface. When he pulled it again, equally level, the screen of the mould was covered with wet fibers. He reached to his side with one hand and felt for the deckle, which he slipped on top of the mould, and gave the set a shake to help the fibers felt and intermingle.

Auda thought of the watermark she'd designed for him, suddenly impatient for the gift to be ready. She felt suffused with love and wanted to share it with the whole world, in thought, in action, and most importantly, in verse.

Instead, she brought the cut of porpoise to him.

Martin looked up and smiled.

"What is this?" He unwrapped the oilcloth and beamed in pleasure. "Ah, it's been so long since I've had a bite of fish. You do me well, girl! I've this last batch to make for Shmuel. We'll stop after this set for the night to enjoy this bounty, and tomorrow I'll get started on the order for the folios. The *vicomtesse* received her two extra reams?"

Auda nodded, pleased she had made her father smile.

Martin jerked his chin toward the table. "Come help me then."

A pile of rough cloths had been stacked on the ground and she picked one up, smoothing it on the table. On the other side of the room, Martin shook the mould and deckle over the vat until no more water dripped from it. Then, sliding off the deckle, he rolled the matted wet fibers off the screen and unrolled it onto the cloth to absorb any excess water.

He nodded for Auda to hand him the fabric. He placed it on top of a stack of wet pages, each separated by a similar piece of cloth. "Just like normal, eh?" he said, transferring the stack, nearly half his own height, onto a flat wooden board on the floor and placing a similar board on top. He grinned at her. "Tell me, now, how was life in the palace?"

Auda bit her lip, considering. She reached for the tablet hanging on the wall and pressed a few lines into the wax.

Busy. Many people doing varied things.
The palace is like its own city.

Her father nodded. "I've heard it's so." He leaned his weight into the top board and a few more beads of water ballooned on the side of the stack. When he moved back, the height of the stack had shrunk, maybe by a thumb's width. It would take him another hour to squeeze the water out, and then he'd peel each page from its cloth and hang it on drying lines.

"Your sister sent word. She wants to see you next Sunday. Meet her at St. Paul's for your mother's saint's day. I reckon you've grown enough in these days to get there from the palace by yourself." His voice was flat. No doubt Poncia was still angry over the miller.

"Your old nurse, Maria, sent word too, that her niece is marrying the same day."

At month's end, on Sunday, Auda had promised to go to a wedding with Jaime, probably the same one. Only nobles held weddings for one couple, most people not having the time or luxury of making too large of a fuss over such a common event. Auda would just tell her father she lingered late with Poncia over prayers for their mother. Ashamed already by the lie, she sat at the desk and massaged her fingers.

Martin rummaged through his shelves and brought out a pot with a salve of knapweed. "You made this yourself for me, remember? He rubbed the balm into each of her fingers. "You'll get used to it in time. Just this morning I had a missive to write for the wooler, Michel. He sends to his cousin to inquire on the trade roads all the way to Paris. Seems the rains have moved north. Whole crops have been ruined. No one can afford his cloth." He shook his fingers. "His lament went on and on."

Auda snorted, and her father shared the other bits of gossip he'd gleaned from scribing. Most of it was useless, family matters of who had been born, who had died, who had inherited what. Martin saved the worst news for last.

"I read one letter yesterday," he said, "from an uncle to his nephew, who hopes to join the abbey as a novice. Seems they've been having problems at home, in Albi and Toulouse.

"Heretics and burnings." His voice grew grim. "The people have started rioting, and the churchmen hide in their houses of God."

"The inquisitor Poncia told us of has released another page on his treatise on heretics and witches. He rides to Carcassonne, it's said."

Auda met his fearful look and remembered the *vicomte's* caution.

"At least we can be thankful you are safe in the palace."

Chapter Seventeen

Auda returned to the palace the next morning, pausing at the bridge to stare at the river. Swollen with the spate of rains and runoff from melted snow, the Aude looked like it might well overflow. Unlike the gray hue it bore all winter under an overcast sky, now the river surged brown and white, bearing sticks and rocks and bramble to the sea. She hurried past the cool breeze that wafted from its surface and tried not to think of the power of the rushing water.

When she arrived at the lady's study, Auda found the entire table covered with documents. Two wooden boxes holding rolls and books were stacked along the wall. She waited for the *vicomtesse* to arrive, but after a few minutes alone couldn't resist the temptation to rummage through the pile. All manners of documents had been collected here, from faded letters to dense contracts, liturgical writings, even some verse. Some were written in Occitan, which she knew well, others in Latin, which was harder to understand.

The rolls of parchment showed signs of disrepair. They had been stored badly, some torn and damaged by insect bites. A few had been repaired, but most would only get worse with time. Some even showed water damage, were left discolored, brittle, and wrinkled with blurred writing that Auda could barely read.

She fingered the edge of a book. The Church objected to the fragility of paper, yet parchment stored without care could disintegrate just as easily.

The *vicomtesse* walked into the room, her steps brisk. "I kept the letters you copied for me on paper out in the sun for a week," she said without greeting. "Several days of full sunlight, and the material has neither bleached nor the ink faded." She tapped her cheek with one finger. "It seems your father was right about the potential of this paper he makes. At least, it will be good enough for what I need."

Auda nodded, eager, and the lady continued.

"I found these writings in an old storage hall. Some hail from the time of Lady Ermengarde. Verse and scripts, those are the real gems, I'm certain."

Auda gazed at the lady, astonished. The Lady Ermengarde, a *vicomtesse* from two centuries ago, had been a strong patron of music, calling troubadours and jongleurs from all over the county to perform for her. Auda had read of her in a book that Tomas had wanted copied for a Narbonnaise noble. She hadn't imagined documents from those times could survive to this day.

"I want you to start copying these, on your father's paper. These documents are to go into the scriptorium, when it's time, but I want my own copies. Much of Narbonne's history is recorded here." Her gaze was thoughtful.

Auda bowed, trying to quell her excitement. Where would she begin?

"There are scores more crates to sort," the lady said. "I'll have my manservant bring them up."

Left alone again, Auda resumed her survey of the writings. It would take years just to copy these documents, much less the additional boxes the *vicomtesse* promised. Surely the lady would be happier if Auda scribed the more interesting documents first—perhaps the verses from Lady Ermengarde's time. She unrolled a few scrolls and read their contents. It was all written in some formal language, words she couldn't fully understand. Still she could tell, from the style of each document, whether the writing spoke of business, with numbers and lists, or were matters of correspondence. Some bore denser writing, with a few words she recognized: love, sadness, beauty.

She sorted the parchment into four piles: lists of numbers, like some sort of accounts; court documents; documents bearing the seal of a cross or other Church sign; and everything else, whose purpose seemed less clear.

It took her several days to organize the first of the dozen boxes that accumulated in the drawing room. She requested twine and a long length of oilcloth, which she cut into pieces to fit each manuscript. After she cleaned each roll or book, she wrapped the document in the cloth and bound it, hoping to save it from further harm. The lady surely would not mind if she took pains to salvage what documents she could.

Once the sorting was done, she pushed aside the court writings, religious texts, and the lists of numbers, and concentrated on the fourth group: those rolls of text whose provenance she wasn't fully certain of.

She picked up the first one. It seemed to be some sort of verse written by one Bernart de Ventadorn. The words took time to puzzle out, but they bore a certain rhythm that made them easier to decipher.

> *Domna, I ask for nothing*
> *But the chance to be your good servant*

And to serve my love as lowly lord
Please relieve me of this torment.

She raised her eyebrows, intrigued by the song. She'd heard verse like this set to song in the market. Narbonne had once supported an abundance of music, minstrels, and jongleurs with their colorful, bawdy tunes alongside the more lyrical troubadours, whose poems succored both heart and head.

Not anymore; the era of the troubadours had passed, a book she'd borrowed from Tomas had said. Fearful of the Inquisition's fires that spread throughout Occitania, the poets had taken their witty lyrics to safer havens. Their memory still persisted, though, along with snippets of their verse sung in the market. But never had Auda seen such words captured in writing.

She read the verse again. Did people truly speak like this, men of high station wooing their ladies? Had Jehan murmured such promises to her sister? Surely the *vicomte* hadn't to his lady. She could well imagine the artist Jaime saying this to someone. Maybe even to her.

Auda put the verse aside and looked for other similar documents. Soon she had collected a small pile, each a vaunted tribute to the virtues of courtly love. Affection seemed to blossom most often between a highborn lady and a commoner, an impossible love made all the more noble for its implausibility. The love was a sensual one, somewhere between lust and chastity, a spirit that could move the body, give purpose to a life that otherwise seemed lusterless.

She read through them again and again, excited. Such tales of pure love enchanted her, so few in her world were lucky to find it. What a fine thing it would be to share this discovery with someone, but whom? Her father? Sister? She thought of Jaime and blushed.

The second week passed, each day a blur. Auda looked forward to her work when she awoke, spending sunrise to sunset among the words of strangers. During the day, she took care to start copying the official documents on paper, beginning with the court documents, whose words she did not understand. At night, she smuggled the verse to her room and made copies for herself on scraps of wrinkled paper she'd brought with her from home. Her mind ran through the fanciful words that showed how a man spoke to his lover, how his lover spoke back to him.

> *My love, happiness is the world's nature*
> *When two friends are brought together*
> *In grief and in joy, they share*
> *Whatever they felt with one 'nother.*

Was this what she would say if she could speak to Jaime? The thought made her heart quicken.

By the end of the week, Auda had amassed a small stack of copies to show the *vicomtesse*. The lady looked through the piles she had sorted, nodding until she came to the last one—containing the verses.

Auda stood before her, arms clasped behind her back so the lady wouldn't see her tremble.

"I am frankly surprised," the lady said. "I had not expected this. I had thought you'd copy half a dozen documents, maybe more if you were motivated. But this, you've surpassed my expectations. You've found the very treasures of Narbonne's history—her music."

Auda flushed, aware that the lady's words were a mixture of praise and suspicion. She wrote on her wax tablet, looking the lady in the eyes.

Beautiful words. Beautiful rhythm.

The *vicomtesse* nodded. "Yes, that is so. You are a clever one." She tapped her chin. "Continue as you have. But leave these to me." She swept up the pile of verses.

Auda was glad she'd made her own copies. Would the *vicomtesse* be as enthralled with the verses as she was?

"Aha," a baritone voice cut in. "I've found you."

Auda swiveled at the sound of footsteps entering the hall, watching as the *vicomtesse* glided over to her husband.

"You've returned sooner than I expected," she said, dipping her body in a graceful curtsy. "I thought you were holding court."

The *vicomte* gave her a sardonic smile. "Again, we veered off into discussions on the Church. The inquisitor in Toulouse released more of his manuscript, rails against the Good Men again. He travels back to Carcassonne this month."

Auda swallowed. So her father had been right! She wished she could slip out, uncomfortable so near to this strange lord, but the only path out of the room took her right past him.

"The rest of the world sends ships to discover new lands, builds new devices, learns new things," he remarked, his voice laced with venom, "and we hover with stingers poised like swords and gad about, condemning our own with these accusations of heresy." He closed his eyes for a moment and the lines on his pocked face smoothed. "Enough. Tell me what you are doing here. What are you and your ladies hatching?"

"The most fantastic of discoveries within our old records," she said, looking at Auda with approval. "We've made quite the find here."

Something sparked in the *vicomte*'s eyes as he turned his attention to Auda.

"And what is this?" the *vicomte* said, giving her a complicit look. "A child tinier than a bird, ready to fly?"

The lady waved him off. "My scribe. She copies documents for me, the most interesting of lyrics."

"Ah, I remember this one. A mute girl, no?" the *vicomte* said. The flatness of his tone was belied by the coy sparkle in his eyes. "A girl who writes? Now that is an oddity."

The intensity of his gaze made her flush. Auda realized with a start that he desired her. She lowered her face.

The *vicomtesse*'s eyes narrowed for a moment. "The girl is mute, not deaf. Don't trouble her," she sniffed, and turned back to the table to pick up the verses.

While his wife looked away, the *vicomte* moved closer to Auda, reaching out to stroke her left cheek. She shivered, his touch demanding—but as a lover or an accuser, she wasn't sure.

The lady turned back to them. "Return to your work, girl," she said. "We'll discuss this later."

Auda bowed, her mind reeling with relief and confusion. She heard the *vicomte*'s whisper behind her: "I look forward to it."

Chapter Eighteen

The next morning, Auda left early to meet her sister at the Basilica of St. Paul-Serge. She had slept poorly, dreaming of the handsome artist she was to meet, and the *vicomte* whom she wished she could get away from. But today was their mother's saint day, and the girls always went to the church at dawn to say their prayers for Elena's soul. It would be another beautiful day, bright and warm with a light breeze that smelled of the sea and of the promise of summer. Yet on the horizon, near Carcassonne, a thick greasy smoke lingered. What was burning? Surely the grass was not dry enough yet to catch fire.

She walked down the main road from city to bourg, past hungover revelers and early-bird merchants. The church looked dark and abandoned this morning. People attended sermons less often in the summer, when the fair and the harvest took most of their attention. The priests constantly threatened hellfire and damnation to anyone avoiding the Lord's words, but few paid attention these days.

Auda made a hasty genuflection at the font and hurried

toward her sister, who was already perched on her knees in the nave. Poncia didn't open her eyes when Auda knelt beside her.

The floors of the church, made of stone quarried from nearby mountains, felt cold under Auda's flesh. She struggled to suppress the image of the bones beneath them, ancient priests interred in their dark crypts.

"Amen," Poncia murmured, opening her eyes. "You're late."

Auda lowered her head in apology. Poncia, as always, had bought masses for their mother.

"This time I bought double the prayers," her sister said without preamble. "Not just for Maman, but for the wretched souls still awaiting judgment by the inquisitor. May God forgive them and move them to repent." Poncia swallowed. "May He also hear our piety."

Auda glanced up at her sister. *Who?*

Poncia looked at her in sad surprise. "Surely you heard. They're burning heretics in Carcassonne."

Auda swallowed her nausea. So that was the smoke she had seen. The inquisitors had come back. She shuddered, wondering how the condemned prisoners felt as they burned. Could they smell the stench of their own hair and flesh melted by the flames? Did their eyes water, their screams echo? Such terrible pains that humans could devise for each other, and some would still say it was a mercy compared to the wrath of God. Auda didn't know what to believe.

She shivered, frigid in this basilica. The priest, a young man she didn't know, walked down the aisle with a gold ciborium covered in pristine white silk, followed by an acolyte bearing a vessel puffing incense. Auda twisted her head so the spicy smoke wouldn't settle upon her, holding her breath as the white swirls rose up. The soul of Christ was now mixed with those names heralded in the masses. How could God countenance the burning of His people? Surely not all were lost souls?

Poncia grasped her arm, and Auda inhaled an inadvertent breath of the passing incense. She struggled to cough the smoke out. Eyes raised in alarm, she begged forgiveness of the souls whose essence she'd trapped.

Poncia's tone grew light. "I tried the recipe for a hot ale posset last night," she said. It was a draught their nurse Na Maria had made when Poncia was younger and her monthly period came irregularly, if at all.

"Guards against the suffocation of your womb," Na Maria had said to a blushing Poncia while Auda looked on with interest.

Her sister caressed her stomach. "You will have to tell me about that physicking book you made for me. It says lady's mantle is good for getting child, but I don't know how it's to be prepared. I've ordered two sacks, to arrive on the next boat."

Auda wrinkled her nose. The sermon would surely come now; Poncia had never been one to hide her emotions.

"You give good advice in that book, easy recipes you've written out with clarity. You should spend more time with that, maybe make draughts for those who can't afford a proper physician. Perhaps the *vicomtesse* can advise you. It's a proper trade for a woman, and steady work."

And there it was. Auda shook her head.

"You must be clever about these things," Poncia said. "The *vicomtesse* can help you, and you should make sure that she does. It's a far better future she can carve out for you than anything Papa can offer you."

Her sister had not yet forgiven their father. Or her. She might as well bring up the failed arrangement with the miller.

She leaned in closer so her sister could see her fingers. *Mar-*

riage. Not good. She forced herself not to think of the artist, whom she was meeting later today.

Poncia bit her lip. "Perhaps you are right. Not all men are meant to be married."

Auda watched her sister. Poncia was not usually so easy to sway. Something else was going on. She put her fingers on Poncia's cheek. *What's wrong?* Her sister's wimple moved out of place, revealing an ugly green bruise at her temple.

Auda stared in alarm. *Hurt? Who?*

Poncia's face grew distraught. "Nothing, Auda. It's nothing. I had too much on my mind, wasn't paying attention. It doesn't hurt much."

Poncia never did lie well.

Jehan? Problems? Perhaps it was the monks he'd been so worried over the night Auda was there. There was something off about those men. She remembered his terse words that evening, the grim look he wore after meeting them. And later one of the men had showed up at the Gypsy's tent.

About those men he met? Their secret?

Yet as she tried to ask her sister, Poncia grabbed both of her hands. "I told you not to speak of them again. Some things are best left unknown. You never did understand that. Papa either." She dropped Auda's hands and clapped hers together in prayer, closing her eyes. "God hears our prayers, I know He does. But He needs to believe our words. We need to make Him believe."

Auda wrinkled her forehead. Did He really hear? Or was He so disgusted by His children that He'd turned His face away? Was this why He let them hurt one another? Jehan had done something to her sister, she was sure of it. But what could she do? Many men beat their wives.

Poncia's blue gaze turned upon her, soft skin drawn taut under her eyes. "The archbishop would have said the masses himself for Maman today," she said in the softest of whispers. "He prays for me, you know, prays for our family, and for help in getting with babe. I've a tonic from the herbal woman, and the simples you wrote, but perhaps I need help from the Lord Himself." She tightened her grip on Auda's wrists. "You need His help too."

Why? Auda whipped her head to face her sister. Did the burnings mean something for her?

"You need help to stay under notice, away from suspicious eyes," Poncia continued.

No, it was only Poncia being her normal fearful self. Auda sighed. The lady, even the *vicomte* himself, had no love for the Inquisition. Auda was safer under their care than anywhere else in town. And her life now seemed so much more interesting, held so much more promise than when she'd lived at home. She was using her skills, working in a way no one could have predicted. She was as close to the workings of the town as Poncia was, in her own way. And the lady had even complimented her on her wits. For once she'd not been banished to the shadows.

Poncia looked up with wide eyes. "I've a favor to ask of you. The archbishop is coming to say a prayer at our house on Saturday. Will you come? You and Papa?"

Auda drew back. With all that still threatened the town, inquisitors and charges of heresy, her sister thought it was safe to seek out the archbishop himself?

Poncia's grip grew tighter. "He's a good man, the archbishop. He'll say naught against us. He knows us."

How? Auda asked, confused.

"I'll say no more. It will make a good surprise. For you and Papa."

Auda wrinkled her forehead in alarm.

"It's true, we've taught you to stay far from men of importance," her sister said, pulling her back. "But he'll not hurt you, I swear. He's a special man, you'll see. And he's asked to see Papa specifically. Please, Auda. For me."

Auda swallowed, trying not to react under her sister's watchful gaze. Perhaps she should go. Perhaps it was not so dangerous. Poncia, she knew, was trying to help her. She could do this one thing for her sister.

Chapter Nineteen

Auda left Poncia deep in prayer and headed outside. As soon as she pushed past the church door, she let out her breath. Shaking off the mantle of incense and judgment, Auda sought, for the first time that she could remember, the brightness of sunlight and crowds. Through her wimple, draped about her face, the summer warmed her cold skin. She felt anonymous in the crowd, safer in the masses than in the dreary church, even if the sun hurt her eyes.

She threaded her way through the fair toward the Gypsy's tables. Minstrels, jokesters, and jugglers were in full abundance. The Old Market had been expanded by four streets on each side to accommodate the additional crowds. At least fifty more tents and two dozen temporary stalls had been erected, mostly for the lower-class vendors who peddled here—the farmers and millers, the wine sellers and porters, and of course harlots on every street.

Activity from the fair spilled onto the roads, with Gypsies selling flowers and tokens while jongleurs sang their latest verse. Later the fairgoers would end up merrymaking in the local taverns, where they would be serenaded with songs about lusty women while sipping ale and throwing dice.

Auda breathed in and closed her eyes. The terror she'd felt in the palace, and again in the church, seemed faraway here.

In the market, the Gypsy Donino beamed when he saw her approach. He rummaged underneath the table and came up with a small device held on the palm of his hand. "Your piece is ready."

She took the wire contraption by its edges. The Gypsy had done fine work, rendering the bridge in seven fluid arcs with a tiny *M* that adorned the center pier. Her mouth curved into a smile. Her father would be touched.

"Ah, the lady is happy then?" Donino beamed. "I think you've paid two pennies?"

She nodded and fished out a handful of deniers. Counting out the three coins she owed, she added one extra.

Donino bowed with a flourish. "Many thanks, *domna*. Look around, see if anything else catches your splendid eye." He spread a hand over the table. "We have beads of every color and size, or perhaps the sweetest Spanish fragrance, fit for a houri, and in a fine stone bottle."

But she shook her head in apology. She wished she could stay to ask about the Gypsy's new paper, and the stranger from Jehan's house who had spoken to her here. But then she'd be late to meet Jaime, and in truth, she was not sure she could suffer any more revelations today.

Sidestepping a pair of donkeys, she nearly collided with the acrobats and dancers hurtling along the gutters. A band of dirty boys brushed against her—farmhands or petty thieves, she wasn't sure. The thud of hay bales and the din of hammered metal gave way to the chatter of haggling, followed by a racket of lows and brays. Even though the town had been cleaned from streets to shops, church to taverns for the fair, the stench of dung and garbage rose over the savory scents of the cookshops.

She arrived at a small chapel in the bourg just in time to see the priest pound on the door, a crowd of peasants surging around him. He rapped again on the heavy wood. Anticipating the third and last knock, representing the blessing of the clergy, mirthful laughter rang out.

"Ha ha!"

"*Oc!* Let's be started, Father. The beer's getting warm and my legs waren't fit for standing!" someone yelled out.

"Aye, your legs haven't been fit for much, except if you're counting the kicks you give your wife," another voice replied. More gales of laughter.

Auda watched in delight. She'd never been to a wedding before, other than Poncia's which had seemed more like a somber supper, rich in décor but restrained in warmth. She pushed away thoughts of her brutalized sister.

Most marriages among peasants and poor artisans took place by a tree or hedge, with a quick exchange of vows before the couple resumed the chores of their day. But she had heard of more cheery celebrations like this, where a whole quarter planned their weddings together, the vows, and, of course, the feast afterward.

She looked around for Jaime. He was standing to the side, his lean frame relaxed against the stone wall of the chandler's shop. The chandler himself stood beside him, holding a fat pillar candle as its tiny flame danced in the summer breeze. Jaime crossed his arms over his chest. His thin lips, stretched in an indulgent smile, curved upward even further when he spied her.

A thrill of desire shot through her.

"I was not sure you would come," he said, holding a hand out to her. When she took his hand, his dark eyes twinkled.

She blushed at his warmth, noting how different she felt when it was Jaime and not the *vicomte* who appraised her with desire.

"This is your girl then?" the chandler asked.

Auda ducked her head, uncomfortable under the stranger's gaze, but Jaime laughed.

"Ah, to be young again," the chandler said, gesturing with the blue candle at the ceremony by the church door.

The priest, dressed in a white surplice belted with rope over a long black gown, held his hands up for silence. He bowed his head, the locks of matted brown hair ringing his tonsure falling over his face. Saying a quiet prayer in front of the closed door, he crossed himself and addressed the crowd.

"Most worshipful friends, we are here under the gaze of the Father, the Son, and the Holy Spirit to combine these good souls in the unity of the sacrament of holy matrimony. Come, the men who would be husbands; come, the women who would be wives. Let all eyes be upon you as you seek the Lord's blessing."

Among the assembly of ladies in starched dresses, girls with flowers in their hair, and smiling men, the couples stood out, happy players in the ceremony. The grooms wore varying shades of blue and gray, some with tunics matched with dyed shoes, others in their work garb, wrinkled but clean.

The brides wore light blue dresses belted with flowers, matching crowns of ivy and hyacinths in their hair. Each clutched a bouquet of herbs and blossoms in both hands, and stared through a dark blue veil fluttering in the breeze. Auda sighted Na Maria's niece, Rubea, standing beside Jaime's painting partner from the stall.

Under the portico of the church, the priest held up a heavy, gilt-edged Bible and flipped to a marked page. Beside the wedding party, a cluster of jongleurs broke out in melody to the accompaniment of a harpist, piper, and drummer.

"And now the ceremony begins, ta-da ta-dum . . ."

Again, laughter rose among the crowd.

Frowning, the priest spoke in a loud, deep voice.

"O Eternal God, Creator and Preserver of mankind, send Thy blessings upon Thy servants, this man and this woman whom we bless in Thy name. May they surely perform and keep the vow and covenant betwixt them according to Thy laws. Let us pray."

The priest bent his head, his entire face except his beakish nose disappearing behind brown locks. A hush fell over the congregation, broken only by the scuffling of children underfoot. The priest cleared his throat, clasping his hands, and turned to the couples.

"Each of you seeking the Lord's blessing today, be honest in your words. Are you of an age?"

"An age to what?" came a voice from the back. "Marry or—?"

"Best it be marriage, else they're in trouble!"

Auda giggled. She'd never seen such an impudent crowd. It reminded her of a jongleur's verse, songs of unlikely heroes and interfering wives. Nothing at all like the lofty lyrics of a troubadour.

"Enough!" declared the priest as other responses piped up and laughter again ensued. Glaring, he repeated his question and the couples, still smirking, murmured their assent.

"Are you free to marry?"

"*Oc.*"

"Not bound by kinship?"

"No."

"Then it's time for the plighting of troth and exchange of

vows. Men, will you have your woman to be your wedded wife, to live together after God's ordinance in the holy estate of matrimony? Will you love her, comfort her, keep only unto her, so long as both of you live?"

"I will," came the mismatched chorus of deep voices.

"And women, will you have your man to be your wedded husband, to live together after God's ordinance in the holy estate of matrimony? Will you obey him, serve him, be bonny and buxom at bed and at board, keep only unto him, so long as both of you live?"

"I will." Rubea's crisp voice rang out above the others. Auda gave Jaime a sidelong glance, surprised to see a wistful smile playing over his lips.

A murmur rose up among the crowd as the ceremony came to an end. The priest joined each couple's right hands and selected a few family members to accompany them into the church.

"And that'll be that," the chandler said, winking out the candle between blackened fingertips. He unbolted the lock to his shop. "Pity I can't make the celebration. I hear they've been cooking for days."

As the crowd dispersed around them, Auda stared at the church door, which had shut behind the wedding party. Now the couples were receiving instruction and advice about marriage from the priest in the House of God. What would they hear? she wondered. Promises of love and fidelity, to keep each other safe, healthy, and whole? The thought of her sister, bruised and weary, saddened her.

"Shall we head to the house and await them?" Jaime asked. "All that's left to witness is the exchange of dowry. And to hear the wisdom *God* has given them." He rolled his eyes.

Auda pretended not to see, though she was a little shocked at his defiance.

The celebrations were already underway by the time they reached Na Maria's house. A gray sackcloth tent had been erected in the field behind the small wooden dwelling, with snippets of ribbon and dried herb bouquets screwed into the willow branch lattice protecting the house from wind and rain. New daub made of mud, cow dung, and reeds patched up holes from the winter storms.

Inside the tent, a long board held gifts for each of the newlyweds—mostly wooden tools and utensils they would need for their new life. Another board outside was laden with enough food to feed a small army. The feast centered around a sheep's head soused in ale and curds, surrounded by platters of lagoon mussels and sea crickets poached in beer, vinegar, and rosemary. At one end of the board sat a large bowl filled with a *sallat* of scallions, marigolds, and radish roots, dressed in an oil of parsley and pepper. On the other end stood a clay pot filled with a warm stew of leeks, nuts, and salt pork. Bread flavored with ale was passed around on trays. It seemed as though an entire village had cooked for this day, and it probably had. With each family bringing a colorful dish, soon a feast would be assembled to rival that of the *vicomte*'s own supper board.

In the yard, a circle of young girls surrounded a lone minstrel in a dance, laughing as he sang a love song to the tune of his psaltery. Behind them, a troupe of actors fussed with their costumes for a performance of the legend of St. George and the Dragon. St. George himself was clad in a gray tunic emblazoned with a red cross and equipped with a wooden helmet, sword, and shield, but the six playing the dragon seemed a more hapless bunch, entangled in shreds of green rags and topped by a large horned head streaming with green and black ribbon.

"The dragon I be!" boomed a hollow voice from inside the mask, and the four players comprising the dragon's body wobbled. The rear actor swung his wooden tail. Auda laughed at the awkward movement.

"What do you bring?" St. George replied, adjusting his helmet.

"Not peace," came the reply from some onlookers.

"Not love," chanted another.

"Not hope," someone else said.

The helmeted St. George tripped over his sword and fell into a sprawl on the ground, and the crowd lapsed into laughter.

Jaime sat on the covered ground beside Auda, holding a stiff trencher filled with pork meatballs crusted with nuts, fish pastries, and a shiny heap of *sallat*. He chuckled as the body of the dragon ran past its head.

"In the last wedding I was at, St. George was bested by the dragon and half the guests left in protest."

Auda covered her mouth, laughing. Jaime edged closer so that the trencher rested on both of their knees, until his warmth bled through his clothes into her skin. She picked up a handful of the *sallat* with trembling fingers. Sweet and peppery, still it was hard to swallow, and she coughed against the foreign texture.

"Here," Jaime said, handing her the mug at his side.

Auda took a deep swallow of the wine mixed with honey, egg, cinnamon, and clove burning her throat. She returned the drink and smiled at Jaime, wishing she could speak, even using her fingers, with him. Yet she could always share her happiness with a kiss. She pressed his fingers to her cheek, smelling charcoal and pigment. A contented sigh escaped her lips.

"Auda!" a voice rang out.

She dropped Jaime's hand and looked up. It was Na Maria, dressed in a long gown of grayish blue and purple flowers in her tight but frizzy braid, balancing a large wine jug on her ample hip.

"Girl," she said with a bright smile. "It's so good of you to come. Rubea is a cheery bride, don't you think? I meant to come by and tell you in person, but it all happened so fast. Has your father come too?"

Auda shook her head, shy.

Maria grinned at Jaime and winked. "No, of course. Sly girl, just like her Papa."

Reaching into a pocket under her belt, Auda pulled out a denier. It was a small gift, but all that she had left from the coins Martin had given her to spend at the fair. Maria's smile cut further into her doughy face.

"I'll see they get this," she said, tucking the penny in her bodice. "I've my own for them." She showed Auda two halves of a penny. It was a common gift; each half of the couple would carry one half of a coin that only had worth when joined together. "There wasn't coin for rings, so I found the best penny I had and traded a kiss to the blacksmith for some quick work."

Auda blushed, and Maria laughed again. An actor ran past them, chasing the dragon head with a torch blazing above his head.

"Pestilence and plague is what I bring," the dragon boomed.

"I don't care what you bring, but keep that fire from my house!" Maria yelled, joining in the awkward chase.

Auda looked up at Jaime, trading a smile, and he placed a light kiss on her lips. Auda drew in her breath. She looked around, self-conscious, but he only laughed and pulled away. He untied a roll of canvas from his belt. After spreading the small canvas across the blanketed ground, he took a charcoal from a pouch at his side, leaned forward, and began sketching. His nimble fingers drew dark lines that soon grew into the scene before them: the cursed dragon, separated now by head, body, and tail; and the more wretched St. George, prostrate upon the ground. In the background, he drew the newlywed Pietr and Rubea with matching laughter in their faces. Their joy was so unlike the complacent certainty with which Poncia had approached her own wedding.

Jaime wiped soot from his fingers onto the blanket and shrugged. "It's a start. A false memory of a brief moment, inadequately captured."

Auda tilted her head.

"Only an image," he said with a sigh. "And not nearly so glorious as life itself. The fate of all art, worth only the happiness it gives to someone else."

No, Auda wanted to protest. The worth of art could also lie in the happiness it brought its creator, no? Not a false memory, but a kernel of beauty captured forever. She thought of the verse stored in the palace. Though their authors were long forgotten, the words still compelled their readers. Words of love and loss. If Jaime knew her love for writing those words, would he understand? Would he approve?

Yes, she knew he would.

A shout rose up ahead of them: the newlyweds had arrived. The brides streamed to their families while the grooms stood around, congratulating each other.

"Aha," yelled one of the jugglers, lifting his wine-stained face from a cup tucked in his lady's breasts, snug in her bodice. "What kept you?"

"Instructions from the Father priest?"

"Or sweet messages to each other?"

"I say they didn't talk at all," another said, evoking raucous laughter.

"Time for music, time for the dance," Maria said, opening her arms to embrace her niece. She kissed a flushing Pietr. "Play something gay!"

The jongleurs struck up a lively beat and a round dance began not far from the feasting table.

"Join them?" Jaime said, tucking away his canvas roll.

Auda shook her head. *Fast.* She twirled her fingers of one hand in a complicated round until they twisted.

Jaime grinned. "You'll get the steps. I'll show you."

Auda looked at the crowd, reluctant, but before she could reply Pietr stepped to the table. "Attention all!" he cried, banging his hand on the board as he wobbled from side to side. "It's said a virtuous woman is a crown to her husband, that her price is far above rubies."

"Give me a ruby and I'll give you a virtuous woman," some woman in the crowd yelled.

"Your husband ought to beat you silent," Maria yelled. "I'll beat you myself if you don't silence your tongue!"

"Have you another use for it?" one of the jugglers asked with an impish grin.

"I am truly grateful," Pietr continued over the laughter, the wobble now in his throat and voice, "to have found a woman of such worth."

"Come, throw grain on the newlyweds to hearken their fertility," Maria yelled out. The crowd roared their approval and she rushed to pour handfuls of wheat into people's hands.

"Ah, but it's time for the marriage bed, no?" said one of the youths who'd been hanging about Rubea.

"Never you mind them!" Maria yelled, running after the laughing boys. "Let them have their night in peace." She hurried to the band, instructing the piper to play something festive.

Jaime entreated Auda to dance again, and this time she took his hand.

Another girl came up to her other side: Rubea. Spying Auda,

she faltered momentarily. But Auda forced herself to look past the fear in the girl's eyes. She took a deep breath and smiled at Rubea.

Rubea met her watery eyes, then shrugged and offered her hand. Auda took it without hesitation and they continued the dance. She traded grins with Jaime, enjoying the exhilaration of it all, and wondering, for the first time, if such a love could truly be hers.

Chapter Twenty

𝕵aime escorted her home after the wedding. They walked in silence. Auda glanced at him through her wimple, surprised to see the same soft smile that had touched his lips at the wedding. When they reached the crest of the hill that led down to her home, she stopped and faced him.

With a quick glance toward the small dwelling, she shook her head. No need to get her father involved, asking too many questions.

Jaime seemed to understand. He bowed over her wrist and placed a kiss on her pale skin.

Auda quivered at the thrilling touch.

"Will I see you again soon?" he asked.

Auda nodded, heart aching.

"Next week?" he said, pleading with his eyes.

She nodded again and put his hand to her cheek and lips. She'd find an excuse.

Her reward was a crooked smile. The artist kissed her hand once more, bowed, and headed in the opposite direction. Auda ran home, giddy and needing a reason for her flushed cheeks and labored breathing.

Her father, sitting in the hearth room cutting paper sheets to size, beamed when she walked through the door.

"*Ma filla!*" he said, jumping up to embrace her. "Come, sit. Tell me about your week." He stepped into the kitchen to fetch a drink. He'd bought a large earthenware pot of beer with his new funds and had parked it in front of Auda's old hiding spot built behind the kitchen wall.

Auda looked around the house, noting the loose dirt and withered rushes gathered in haphazard piles across the floor. The iron pot stood cold and empty over the missing fire, save for a few pigeon bones lingering in a cupful of greasy water. The house smelled old, forgotten.

She shouldn't have lingered so long at the wedding, she berated herself, should have come home and seen to her chores. Untying her wimple, she rolled her hair into a bun and started sweeping the dirty floor.

Martin walked in with two cups. "Let it be, Auda. You were at the church late. What news from your sister?"

Hiding a guilty look, Auda laid aside the broom and sat at the table. The meeting with her sister seemed like it had happened a lifetime ago.

She asked. You. Me. She shook her head. It was too difficult to convey her sister's request with gestures.

Martin passed her a tablet. "Here."

She chose precise words.

> *Poncia needs us at her house on Friday.*
> *It's a special prayer. The archbishop leads it.*
> *He asked for you, for me.*

She handed the tablet to him, watching cautiously for his reaction.

Martin read her words and threw the tablet across the table. "Will she never stop? What does she expect me to do, beg for a living? Not even the archbishop can gainsay my trade. No matter what she thinks!"

Auda shook her head. She didn't know what her sister was up to, but the bruise on Poncia's temple was still vivid in her mind.

Blessing, she signed, making a gesture of benediction. *For family*. It was a simple lie.

Martin wasn't convinced. "You trust too much, Auda. Especially when you should not." Struggling to recover his temper, he sat again at the table. "Tell me of other things. About your week."

What to tell him? Of the immensity of the palace? The wealth displayed so casually in every room? Maybe he'd like to know about the *vicomtesse* and her husband, their reputations and lofty words.

Instead, she told him of the verses that captivated her. She'd committed most to memory, and even now carried copies of her favorites to reread.

Martin was not as enchanted. "Bah," he said, pushing away a verse she'd copied on the exaltedness of distant love. "Simple concerns for simple times. We've no room for this frippery, with the way Narbonne is growing today. Why only this week, two papermakers passed through town along the fair. There's not work enough here for them yet, but soon. The world is changing, Auda. We can't go back to the simplicity of past times."

Auda turned her face away, stung. Maybe past times were simple but they were also honest. She'd made a careful study of the troubadours, not just in the documents she'd copied, but also in her questions to the *vicomtesse*. At first the lady had been impatient, curt with her. But when she saw Auda's interest was genuine, she told her what she knew of Narbonne's lyrical history.

"Our city once boasted the most proficient of musicians," the lady said, "under the patronage of our own Lady Ermengarde. She held whole courts full of music, and called them her Courts of Love."

"The custom began hundreds of years ago with discussions on whether love was mere bodily lust or a morally elevating spiritual experience. Highborn ladies gathered alongside their men to bandy words on what it meant to love, and whether a pure love could ever exist amidst the obligations of noble life.

"Eleanor of Aquitaine had held the most famous courts, and her daughter carried on the tradition in her own courts at Champagne. In those days, poets brought forth all manners of verse on the nature of real love, love based on noble actions and character rather than on birth and wealth. In the face of such love, they asked, does one give in to self-discipline or passion? An exalting love or debasement of the body? The transcendent or the physical?"

The questions seemed all the more reasonable after her time with Jaime.

In the last generations, apparently the Courts of Love had gone into decline. But still the beauty of the words, their rhythm and honesty, lingered. A man and a woman had to see each other honestly in love, had to value each other. Surely Poncia's marriage was proof, the lesson still had to be learned.

"Pay no mind to me," Martin sighed, softening at the hurt in her eyes. "I am an old man talking to a young girl at the height of her promise. Truly, Auda, you remind me of your own mother."

Auda blinked, starting at the mention of Elena. Her father rarely spoke of her, and not in many years.

Martin sipped his beer and sat back. "I remember it well, the day we moved here. It was winter, and cold as a crone's tit. We carried everything we owned on our backs. Your grandfather wanted to send us by horse and wagon, but we decided to save the money to start the studio instead."

He leaned forward. "The winds whipped straight off the ocean and settled in our bones. Your mother never got used to the salty smell in the air, the reek of the fishing boats. It was she who insisted we live along the river. It smelled as fresh as home, she used to say."

Auda put down her cup, which she hadn't touched. Her father's words entranced her.

"She never looked so beautiful as the day she birthed you," he whispered, his voice distant.

Auda sighed. This was more than he'd ever said about her mother, and now she understood why, if it made him so melancholy. Remembering the token she'd bought for him, she pulled the Gypsy's watermark, wrapped in a fine red cloth, from the purse on her belt.

Martin took the package. "What is this?" Unwrapping the bundle, he stared at the glittering piece of wire.

Watermark, Auda wrote on her tablet. She rose and went to the studio, returning with a mould screen to demonstrate how the device worked.

"A priceless gift," he said, turning the device over and over in his fingers. His voice grew rough with tears. "The finest gift your mother ever gave me was her belief we would make our fortune with my paper." He looked up. "How fitting that her daughter now does the same."

Smiling, Auda laid a kiss on his head, glad at least for the moment that everything between them was as it had always been.

Chapter Twenty-one

The next week, the *vicomtesse* surprised Auda and decided to hold her own Court of Love.

"Your questions set me to thinking. It won't be a Court of Love in the precise sense, but these verses are too rich not to share." She paced the study, inspecting the piles of boxes still unexplored. "Never mind the other documents for now. Search out whatever verse you can find. Make sure the originals are cared for, and make two copies on paper. In the meantime, I'll have my minstrels perform what you've already given me."

She allowed Auda to attend her court that week—as a maid, of course.

"Stay out of sight and don't make a fuss. It will be helpful for me if you see what this is about, what I am looking for. You've done a fine job so far."

Auda bowed, pleased by the compliment. The *vicomtesse* normally held court every week, inviting noble ladies in town to visit her. Auda had never attended before, of course, but she'd heard the maids talk about it in the servants' kitchen. The court sounded mostly like an afternoon of gossip and food, nothing like the vaunted discussions of passion and duty the Courts of Love were said to be.

On the day of the event, Auda arrived early so as not to be noticed. She had never been inside the lady's solar before. The room felt lush, not just in the cushioned chairs and benches that lined the walls, but in the sunlight spilling through each of the room's three glass windows, illuminated by eight candles besides. Two desks stood in one corner, and a large table in another. Rich red tapestries hung on the wall and a hearth fire, alive even in midsummer, warmed the stone floor.

The women began arriving down the hallway in small groups, soon totaling over two dozen. Their gossip grew loud, like a discordant symphony of bees. Their comments, when distinguishable, all hovered around the same topic: the Great Fair.

"The New Market is a disgrace with the fair here!" one woman said. "Rubbish and refuse everywhere!"

Another sniffed. "If the archbishop spent less time on riches and food, perhaps he would see what goes on beneath his own nose."

"He only takes his due," a younger voice answered, "seeing how much he's given to the town's prosperity. I've never seen a more honest priest."

"Ha! An honest priest." Several people laughed in agreement.

Auda took her place in the back corner of the room, standing beside one of the desks, and none of the ladies noticed her as they entered. Just to be sure, Auda turned her face away. She felt naked without her wimple—the lady disliked the extra cloth, said it looked too much like church garb—and had banned it in her presence. Perhaps it would have been best to have feigned illness and not come here today. Auda had no wish to draw the court's attention, to intrude on the day's discussion of poetry. Yet she couldn't stay away. Every time she read the verses, she felt her spirit soar. What would it feel like, she couldn't stop herself from wondering, if the verses the minstrel sung today were hers?

The ladies settled around the room, chattering in loud voices. Most had brought sewing to occupy their hands as they talked. One girl brought a rosary, which she twisted constantly.

The *vicomtesse* walked in a few minutes later. The younger women rose.

"We were just discussing the fair," an older lady said. The wrinkles around her mouth continued down her neck and disappeared under the high collar of her crimson gown.

"It's a crowded muck, of course," the young girl by her side said, her pleasant face and willowy body matching her youthful gaiety. She sat on a bench, adjusting the pink rosette in her hair and smoothing her skirts.

"I told Clarys it always was," a matronly woman answered. Behind her, a number of women murmured their assent.

"Have you been out to see it yet?" another woman inquired. She too wore a rose-red gown, though it shimmered russet brown in the sunlight. Gold winked from her ears and her hands, clasped over her pregnant belly.

The *vicomtesse* stood over the blush-dressed women, tall and slender in her green dress, cut simply but made of the shiniest emerald silk. Settling in her velvet-cushioned chair, she fingered her pearl necklace. "I have, but only to listen to the minstrels and see whom to invite to court," she said. "I heard some promising tunes. But nothing along the likes of what this court has seen in the past." She gave them a conspiratorial smile. "Before we dive headlong into our chatter, let's have a bit of music and some sweets."

Musicians entered the room to play some songs, and servants passed platters of candied fruits and pastries. The conversation soon grew louder than the music.

The lady rapped her knuckles against her desk. "Come now, let us listen to the songs. I have a new one to share with you today."

This was the moment. Auda strained forward, anxious.

A young man dressed in colorful clothes and a banded hat walked into the room, carrying a fiddle. Beardless with a boyish face, he seemed only a lad. But once he started plucking his instrument, his skill was indisputable. He played a simple tune of discordant notes, a song that was popular in the fair, but when he opened his mouth he sang a verse that the *vicomtesse* had chosen, one by the troubadour Bernart de Ventadorn.

> *My* Midons, *I love so much*
> *Cherish but fear to attend her much,*
> *I speak to her naught*
> *And ask her for naught so naught is what I send her.*
> *But she feels my sorrow and my pain*
> *And if it pleases her, she sends for me.*
> *To succor me, comfort me, honor me.*
> *I could make do with far less than she.*

Auda closed her eyes, entranced by the crescendoing rift. The minstrel repeated the melody and sang the verse again. When he finished, the ladies clapped with enthusiasm.

"Such beautiful words from a doting husband," the young girl, Clarys, said. "He sings with such honesty."

Next to her, an older lady, Esclarmonde, huffed. "Honest with what? Does your husband speak to you like this? If this man was even her husband. Frippery meant for song and dance."

"It should be like this," a middle-aged woman dressed in a russet gown replied, "simple and heartfelt. I tell you, my own husband had a tongue of honey before we married—"

"And you had a fine body before four children," Esclarmonde interrupted in a wry tone.

Appreciative laughter sounded around the room.

"More likely he sends her a signal of where to meet," Esclarmonde continued. "Play the song again, boy." She waved at the minstrel.

As the song resumed, the ladies paid rapt attention. Esclarmonde interrupted midverse.

"Yes, that's it. He wants succor and comfort, wants her to send for him. It's a missive for a tryst." She smiled in triumph.

"Or a declaration of love from afar," another woman said. "Simple and sweet without deeper intent."

"Can't it be both?" the *vicomtesse* weighed in. She templed her fingers and nodded at the minstrel. "Listen to another song by the same man."

The minstrel took up his fiddle again. This time, however, he plucked only a single succession of notes that he repeated for each line of the verse. It was a melancholy series, sharp and bleak.

> *With the tears I weep from my eyes*
> *I make ink to write a hundred letters*
> *And send them to the most beautiful love of mine,*
> *The courtliest, oh, my* Midons.
> *And afterwards, many a time*
> *I was reminded of her act when we parted.*
> *She covered her face in a sweet veil*
> *So not to say yes or no to my hail.*

The minstrel repeated the last line thrice before he finished, each time in a quieter voice. Auda blinked away a tear as the sad notes faded in the air.

"Ah, this is clear," the Lady Esclarmonde said right away. "He speaks of her act, and his hail—need I say more?"

The ladies tittered.

"No, *domna*," young Clarys protested again. "She may be an innocent, even a nun, hiding behind her veil."

A few voices rose in protest, and the talk between the ladies took a lively turn. Each woman spoke of her husband, trying to convince the others that she had ended with the worst catch, a man who'd gone from lofty words to lusty grabs and little else.

What was the point of such discussion? Auda wondered. Did the *vicomtesse* want to engage in a game of words? Or did she want to change things? Perhaps she had looked at her own marriage and seen a lack she wanted to right.

Auda pondered the troubadour verse as she slipped out of the back of the solar to the adjoining chamber leading to the hallway. Courtly love, at least honest love, seemed more like what Jaime offered when he kissed her, or smiled at her. Had Poncia felt the same way about Jehan? Maybe Jaime hid some agenda too.

The Church said the role of the woman was that of wife and mother. One of the verses in the lady's collection had even confirmed it. She'd found no author's name on the simple words, but they'd stayed with her all the same.

> *True virgin, like Maria*
> *True life and true faith*
> *My friend becomes lover*
> *Lover becomes wife*

Gives birth, passions sate.
My domna, *my mercy, my fate.*

All women began as virgins, to be wooed for a time, only for the purpose of bearing sons to start the cycle again. Her sister would say so, but surely courtly love offered more?

As she rounded the corner, Auda heard a pair of voices, one low, the other melodic. She stopped, seeing a man and a woman grappling with each other against the wall. The *vicomte*!

Rooted to her spot, Auda cast about for an escape. She couldn't be found here—not by this man doing this thing!

The lady laughed in a rich, throaty tone. Auda recognized her burnished copper hair from the larger group of women. The girl was young; her mother had escorted her to the palace and was still in the solar right next door. Yet now the girl leaned back and offered the *vicomte* her creamy white shoulders and her small, firm cleavage. Auda swallowed, shamefully curious. She squinted to see better. She'd never seen the act of sex before, only heard about it in jest and song. Was this what everyone clamored over?

The *vicomte* nuzzled his face against the girl's breasts, grasping at the two mounds through her silken dress. His fingers clawed against her skin as he clasped her close about her shoulders.

The girl whimpered, pushing his hands lower.

From somewhere within his cloak, he drew out his fat member, and curled the girl's fingers around it. Guiding her to her knees and keeping his hand on the crown of her head, he directed her toward his veined cock. She sank upon him, and took him in with her cheeks. He wobbled as her lips flapped against him, again and again. Finally he moved, a quick shudder before he collapsed against the wall. His seed spurted out in globs, spilling over her lips.

"Oh yes, God, I almost see Him." The *vicomte*'s voice sounded wondering.

Auda sucked in her breath, horrified and fascinated at once. She was not naïve enough to think the *vicomte* stayed true to his wife, but what of this girl, whose mother was in the next room? Did she think to win some favors, coins to pay the family debts, or to hook a wealthy man?

And what had the *vicomte* meant with his cryptic laudation?

The girl, adjusting her dress, didn't notice Auda, but the Vicomte did. His eyes tracked her in the shadows and his lips curved down.

"Ah, little bird," the *vicomte* said in a sad tone. He shifted to cover himself. "I suppose you were meant for finer things. But I'll wager you see."

The girl before him murmured a thank you, but Auda knew the words were meant for her.

Horrified, she dashed out of the room and ran down the hallway. She'd been wrong about the progression of women from virgins to lovers to mothers, so very wrong. There were many other choices—some of them entirely terrifying.

Chapter Twenty-two

The following week, Auda made a startling discovery: verses written by women. She'd found them sewn together in a folio and stored in a roll, by far the most preserved manuscripts she'd seen. Most were anonymous, yet a few bore authorship, among them Marie de France, Beatriz de Romans, and a slew of single names: Iselda, Alais, Carenza.

Unsure at first of what the verses were, Auda read through each one. Unlike the other poems, which held women in some mystical light as the gateway to happiness, these verses seemed more commonplace, lacking the romance of the male poets.

> *Good Friend, I want to know*
> *The truth of the love between us two*
> *So strong once, so tell me please*
> *Why you've given it away a-free?*

Another one read:

> *I have a friend of great repute*
> *Stands high over all men*

His heart to me is, unlike yours, so true
With him I know where I stand.

Not quite the vulgar verse that simple jongleurs sang, but more direct and interested in the practicality of love than the troubadours' breezy lyrics of enduring devotion and endearment. Here, the tributes to a beautiful *midons* whose mere existence made a man cry were replaced by the simple heartfelt sadness of not being loved enough.

Auda sought the *vicomtesse* in her solar. The lady sat at her writing desk, poring over a parchment roll bearing columns of numbers. She lifted a finger as Auda entered, but didn't look up. Auda waited.

The solar looked different now than it had during the audience with the ladies. It seemed darker, richer. A red velvet cloth had been laid over the table, its deep hue a perfect complement to the floral wall tapestries, and fewer candles cast their light across the room. Was it the lens of expectation that made this room seem so grand?

At last the lady put aside her scrolls and looked over her thin spectacles at Auda.

"Have you brought the next set of verses?"

Auda nodded, handing her the folio. The lady handled the collection with care, paging through each verse, reading some aloud.

"A magnificent find," she remarked when she was done. "Someone's preserved these with great care. Perhaps our own Lady Ermengarde. I'd heard of the lady troubadours before—*trobairitz*, they are called."

Auda looked at her in surprise.

"Yes." The lady nodded. "There *were* women poets, yet only in our Occitania and not in many years. I heard a song once in my travels to Italy that was said to be written by one of the *trobairitz*." Her voice wavered for a moment. "A sad tune, about a girl whose lover seemed aloof to her. She wondered what calamity distracted his mind that he could not gaze at her in love anymore."

The *vicomtesse* cleared her throat and straightened her back.

"Foolish notion, to wait for a man who will never love her. The girl would do better to be more practical."

Auda nodded, wondering if this was why the *vicomte* took other lovers, and if there was a reason the lady pushed him away.

Later that night, Auda copied out each of the *trobairitz* verses for herself in her room. The male troubadours all said that love was a spiritual quest, in which two lovers who may not even have had the occasion to touch found themselves bound together. It could culminate in a whisper, a caress or a kiss, a thing of beauty, and it was very fragile.

Thinking of her artist, Auda understood.

Yet the *trobairitz* had a different view.

> *My friend, I've been in a great sadness*
> *Over a knight I once called mine.*
> *And I want the world to know for all time*
> *How much I loved the man who was mine.*
> *Now I see I've been betrayed by him, my friend.*
> *Because I would not sleep naked with him.*
> *In bed and at day, when I'm dressed.*
> *Over my mistake, I'll never rest.*

Auda scowled. The more she'd read the verses of the *trobairitz*, the less she liked them. So unlike the troubadour verse, this song seemed flippant, the musings of a jilted girl saddened by the loss of her lover. Coarse sentiments, fit for no better than a drunk jongleur.

She read through a second verse, then a third. These were simply poor testaments to a love unrequited instead of a love fought for. Why could the women not sing lofty tunes like the men, pressing their suit with the passion they no doubt felt? The men used spiritual love to obtain the physical; the women used the physical to bemoan the loss of the spiritual. Surely there could be someone who appreciated both?

"True love cannot exist between a husband and wife," the *vicomtesse* had opined at the end of her last court. "For love there has to be competition, and jealousy, and such things have no place in a marriage." She tilted her head. "At least that's what earlier courts have concluded. We shall see."

Auda put away the verse and thought instead of what love she herself would want. An image of Jaime came to mind, the brightness in his eyes when he'd kissed her, when she kissed back. Her lips curved in a soft smile. If ever there were a sensitive soul, it had to be him.

What did he see when he looked at her? she wondered, not for the first time. She'd always been afraid to ask. She was no beauty, yet the way he kissed her, she thought that she might be the only girl in his world.

She fanned herself, suddenly hot under the summer heat. Her room had no window, no draft. Swinging her feet to the ground, she willed the coolness of the earth to rise into her limbs, but it was no use. The chill stopped at her ankles, leaving the rest of her feverish and edgy.

She closed her eyes and ran her hands over her damp face, skipping from her temples to her cheeks and along the sides of her neck. Stiff fingers pressed into the swollen knots of tension at her shoulders and continued downward. Her touch roved over her body, massaged the firmness of her breasts, the bulge of her hips, and finally the wetness between her legs. In her mind, Jaime smiled.

But in the next moment, the *vicomte*'s haunting memory washed over her. Visions of his searching call assaulted her. What was he looking for that seemed just out of his reach? She screwed her eyes shut. Still the images came at her, not of the *vicomte* this time, but of Jehan, raising his voice and his hand against her sister. The betrayal of love.

Auda let herself give in to her sobs. Competition didn't fuel love; maybe jealousy didn't either.

Maybe it was simply that some people weren't destined to love at all.

Chapter Twenty-three

That Friday, the lady allowed Auda to leave early to attend her sister's supper.

Martin met Auda at the palace and escorted her to Poncia's house, grumbling the entire way. "I still don't know why you've insisted I had to come along for this foolishness."

Auda tried to repeat her explanation with patient gestures. She didn't want to tell her father about Poncia's bruise. The evening was just a prayer for the family, she mimed instead. And since the archbishop had asked for him personally, they had no choice but to attend.

Martin glared at her but said nothing more.

They arrived early. Poncia was still readying the hearth room, and the floorboards above them creaked under the heavy movements of the cook and her servants. As they entered, Poncia started talking to them without preamble. "Do you think the room will stink of tallow if I don't open the window?" She rummaged through the basket of dried herbs on the step below the hearth. "It may be best if I burn something sweet over it."

Martin accepted a mug of ale from the maid and rolled up

the sleeves of his brown wool tunic. "Now that we're all here, perhaps you can tell us why you've brought the Church into our lives," he said. "And the archbishop, no less!"

Poncia avoided his glare. Smoothing her gray cap, she straightened the unlit candles that stood in the center of the table.

"Please, Papa," she said at last. "The archbishop has been ministering to me. I wanted to do something for the family, to help us all through these difficult times."

Martin laughed out loud. "Difficult times? What difficult times? Your sister works in the employ of the *vicomtesse* herself, and I have more orders than I can keep up with. This is the life we've always been waiting for!"

Poncia ran a hand over her tired eyes. "Yes, the life we have been waiting for. Please, Papa, I only want to feel closer to God."

Auda felt sad as she looked at her sister. What else had passed with Jehan? She knew she wouldn't get a chance to talk to Poncia alone this evening.

Martin waved Poncia's plea away. "God's will is done best when good men conduct their daily work, lead their good lives," he said, emptying his mug. "Too much prayer leads a man to be idle."

Poncia swiveled on her heel, her hands clenching a sheaf of dried lavender. "Better to pray than to spend a life selling your Moorish-born paper to the weak-minded and the Jews!"

Auda sucked in her breath. Martin turned red from his cheeks to his ears.

"You think it's well that someone wishes to make a coin off your paper," Poncia continued, her voice quiet but strong. "But tell me, do you tell your customers the danger you put them in? Do you tell them the Church has disallowed paper for any document of worth?"

"It was fine enough to feed and clothe you all these years," her father said, acid in his tone.

"Don't you see?" Poncia's voice turned pleading. "Maybe this is why God turns away from us, this impiety he sees."

Enough. Auda rapped her hand on the table.

"The Italians and the Spaniards have sold their broadsheets for years," her father said, glancing at Auda. "The Church has done nothing—"

"Because Her eyes are fixed on France."

"*Oc*, because France houses her pope, not because of any heresy!" His voice rose. "Even if paper brought cause for concern, that doesn't put me in the same barrel as witches and heretics."

Poncia rose to face him. "And if I say the heretics use paper for their words?"

Auda sucked in her breath. How could Poncia know this? Auda hadn't told her of the heretic paper their uncle had brought. She was sure their father hadn't either.

Martin stopped midstride and glared at his daughter. He exhaled explosively and sat, still watching her as a maidservant entered and laid five newly polished tin plates out on the table.

"I don't sell to heretics," he said after the girl left.

"But you sell to the Jews," Poncia replied. "It may be legal but will that save you against the immoral? Will that save any of us? God sees everything."

Auda shook her head, trying to understand this change in her sister. Poncia was trying to please God in exchange for His favor—like the girl with the *vicomte*. It worked on mortal men. Would it work on God?

Just then, the front door opened with the murmur of male voices. Poncia jumped up, surveying the room a final time.

"Throw the lavender on the fire," she said to Auda. "Papa,

can you douse those?" She nodded at the torches nearest to the flames.

Martin grumbled, but turned to labor over the wall sconces. Soon footsteps approached the hall, and Jehan led a large man through the doorway. Dressed in a simple brown robe with a matching cap over his round head, the archbishop radiated comfort and satisfaction in the rosy health of his cheeks. He glided across the room with practiced grace and raised his hand in a benediction.

The three knelt, Martin fidgeting between his daughters, and the archbishop stooped to kiss each of their hands. The maids streamed out of the room, their heads bowed.

"My children, you do me too much honor," the archbishop began, his voice soft and velvety. "There is no need for this."

"Your Excellency," Poncia said, rising.

Jehan pulled out a chair by the hearth and the archbishop lowered himself into the cushioned seat, plaiting his jeweled hands on the table. The scent of frankincense hung to his skin like a perfume. Though his eyes had gone blue and watery with age, a sharpness gleamed behind his wrinkled face.

"Please, please, it was you who opened your house to me," the old priest said. "Truly I am fortunate to warm my creaking bones by your hearth. Come, sit."

Poncia blushed. "It's only a simple meal I've had prepared, fish, bread, and wine."

"A meal fit for the Lord," the archbishop said. "Though a bit of that wine would not be amiss now."

"I'll see to it," Jehan said with a bow.

"And I'll check on the meal," Poncia added, following her husband.

As they left, the archbishop looked at Martin, seated across from him at the table. Trying to keep her face in the shadows, Auda stared at the two men in profile. Even dressed as a simple priest, the archbishop wore his piety like a rich mantle. Martin bowed his head, as though he were, in fact, some sort of penitent.

"You would be Poncia's father then," the archbishop said in an amiable tone. "She has spoken much of you."

"I'd not thought that an archbishop would have time to minister at the houses of his flock," Martin said. He met the archbishop's soft blue eyes for a moment, then added, "Your Excellency."

"It's true," the archbishop said, "normally the schedule of my office duties and prayers would not leave me time for this. But I have known Poncia since she was a child." His voice warmed. "I was her confessor once, at Maguelone."

"You were at Maguelone?" Martin repeated, his voice choked. Maguelone, Auda recognized, had been Elena's favored retreat. Poncia talked about it often.

The archbishop templed his fingers. "Before my time at Rouen. Yet even after they gave me the Holy See, I visited the place. It's truly a garden of God's own making." He nodded at Martin. "Poncia bears her mother's look about her, as if God Himself created her as her mother's own twin."

Martin only swallowed.

The archbishop turned to Auda. "And I knew your mother when she was pregnant with you."

Auda looked up into the archbishop's wrinkled face. This man was a stranger to her, yet he knew her mother—not just the young wife, but the mother she'd been to Poncia. And to her. What little things did he remember about her, things that were too painful for her father and sister to share? The thought tugged at her.

"She tended the gardens then, a simple life under God's peace. I always expected her to bring you back for a blessing, and was saddened when she did not. I am heartened to see her babe survived." His eyes flitted to the soft cap that covered her hair, then to her pale eyes.

Despite herself, Auda tilted her face toward the lilting of his voice. He spoke with a certain familiarity, his melodious words soothing the fear in her chest. Perhaps Poncia had been wise to trust this man. Anyone their mother had trusted could not be bad.

Her sister arrived at the doorway, carrying a candle with one hand and a large jug with the other. Approaching the table, she poured red wine into each of the wooden cups.

The archbishop nodded at her. "We were just speaking of the luck I have in being able to tend to good Christians as if I were but a parish priest." He laughed.

Poncia smiled and sat next to the archbishop, across from her sister. "The luck is ours. Had you not noticed me attending your sermon and remembered my face as Maman's . . ." She turned a soft smile upon their father. "I wanted to wait for an opportune moment to share such a fine discovery." Reaching for his hand, she squeezed his fingers, and Auda bit back a pang of jealousy at the memory they shared of Elena.

"It is God's grace I see in this," the archbishop said, watching Auda. "Who can help but be humbled before His magnificence?"

Bending her head, Auda braced for some words of sarcasm from her father. But none came, and when she glanced at him in her periphery, he seemed struck silent, gazing at Poncia.

The biting words, in fact, came from Jehan. "It is hard to master humility when the whole of town is burdened with taxes for new fortifications, new shops, even a new church."

"Jehan!" Poncia shook her head. "Your Excellency, I must apologize—"

"No, no," the archbishop said, holding up a hand.

"It's no church but a cathedral," Poncia said to her husband. "And the taxes are our duty."

"Say that to those dying of starvation even as Narbonne grows in prosperity," Jehan said, leaning both elbows on the table. "Ten more crushed last week under the crowds seeking alms at the gates of Fontfroide."

Poncia's eyes went wide. Auda turned a curious gaze on her brother-in-law.

"The bread for the poor has increased in number," the archbishop said, still smiling, "and though the cathedral was started under my predecessor's rule, still I say it is a shining star for Narbonne. Consider, if in the world of men, only the simpleminded take notice of half measures and lowly efforts, then how much grander it has to be to catch the gaze of the Lord?"

"A house such as has never been seen, where all the children of God can raise their voices in prayer." Martin's words were soft.

Poncia swiveled at the sound of her father's voice, tears suddenly gathering in her eyes to match his. "Mother used to say that about Maguelone. I remember."

Auda only stared at her father and sister, trying to push back another surge of jealousy. Why had they never talked about all of this, told her stories about her mother? The subject had always been discouraged at home, yet here they were, admitting a stranger into their quiet grief.

The archbishop sipped his wine. "Tell me, have you heard the story of the pelican's sacrifice?"

At Auda's sharp look, the archbishop turned his gaze on her.

"Her large beak, you see, is suited for gathering fish. In times of plentitude, her young feed well off fish collected fresh from the sea. But in times of leanness, the pelican pierces her own chest to feed her blood to her younglings. Even though it kills her, the pelican is happy to do this, just as our Lord Christ is happy to nourish us when none else can or will. So much like your own mother's sacrifice."

She swallowed against the lump in her throat. What did he mean, her mother's sacrifice?

Martin had always said her mother favored the pelican. Had she heard its story from this very man? What was her sacrifice?

"Jehan coughed. "It will take more than faith to fill starving bellies. This is where the heretics find their power. What sacrifice does the Church make, they ask, to nurture the souls of Her children?"

Auda widened her eyes, just as Poncia narrowed hers upon her husband. How did Jehan know all this? And to say it aloud so brazenly!

The archbishop fixed a stern stare upon Jehan. "I know of what they say."

"Everyone knows," Poncia agreed. "Their insidious words penetrate the market."

The archbishop spoke in a milder tone. "Yes, there are a few who labor to bring ruin to all. But we shall find them, and those who would support them. We will care for their souls. After all, by persuasion, not by violence, is faith to be won." The archbishop sipped from his cup slowly. "Be on guard against them. Even the ones who've repented and wear a cross to warn off all others may yet try to seduce you with their lies."

Auda blinked, drawing together disjointed fragments of her memory. Those men she'd seen speaking with Jehan in his house some time ago—they'd not been priests at all, but heretics! The cross the shorter one wore on his cloak was not a symbol of piety, it was the heretic's cross, a reminder to all that the man who wore it had strayed from God once, and could do so again. Auda closed her eyes. How could she not have realized?

The archbishop focused on Martin. "You are a bookmaker, no?"

"I make paper."

"For people to write upon."

Martin nodded under the old man's emotionless stare. "That is what it's for."

"But what they write—" Poncia said, stopping as Auda shot her a glare. Behind her, Jehan shifted. Auda willed her father to answer with care.

"Can be for good or evil, as the writer intends," Martin said without looking at her.

"Yes, that is so," the archbishop said, folding his hands on the table. "Even more reason why we must be on guard against false prophets, men who claim to know the word of God, to have read the word of God. If a man hears an evil idea, unless his mind is bent toward evil, he will not dwell on it, will forget it before long. But if that same idea is written, he will be drawn back to it, again and again. Evil has a temptation and man is bent toward it. It is born in him with his soul, writhes in ugliness against the light of God's word. In any case, I have heard there are heretics who look for cheap means of spreading their word, that they look for men to make them paper."

Martin spoke in a neutral voice, his face betraying no emotion. "Of course the heretics do. They look to whomever they can to spread their lies. I've heard they consort with jongleurs and town criers too."

The archbishop nodded. "Then you've not been approached by any such as these?"

"No," Martin answered.

"And if you were?"

Martin did not blink. "I would turn him away."

The archbishop smiled and nodded at Poncia, who looked relieved. "I am glad to hear it, my son. If one such as this does come your way, be sure you let me know. Tell me, in your trade, do you come across many books?"

Martin nodded. "As expected."

"Have you read any of the works by St. Thomas Aquinas, or better, by his inspiration, St. Augustine?" He looked into Martin's face without expression.

Martin did not flinch. "I am no learned man to make sense of such words."

The archbishop leaned forward, his voice silken. "Then let me educate you on his words. He says, 'Why should not the Church use force in compelling her lost sons to return, if the lost sons compelled others to their destruction?' And why not, I agree. For 'there *is* no salvation outside the Church.'"

The words hung in the air as servants entered with trays of fish and bread.

"To the beauty of God," the archbishop intoned at last, gracing each of them with a thin smile. "In God's eyes we are all beautiful. When we arrive at heaven's door, we too will share in His vision." His gaze ended on Auda. "Let us pray."

He bowed his head, clasping Poncia's hand on one side and Auda's on the other. The words he uttered held no meaning for Auda—she had thoughts only for her mother.

Later that night, when they had returned home, she turned to her father.

Mother? she signed. *Sacrifice?*

Martin shook his head. "He meant nothing by it, I'm sure—"

But this time Auda did not let the question go. Cupping his face with her hands, she forced him to look at her.

At last Martin sighed. "We knew the birth wouldn't be easy, early when she carried you. There was a risk, the midwife said." His voice grew rough. "She had to make a choice, to let them cut you out while she still lived, or let both of you die." He turned eyes gleaming with tears on her. "She made a choice, a sacrifice, for whom and what she loved."

"You."

Chapter Twenty-four

Auda sat before the hearth, eyes reddened and swollen with tears. Yet she couldn't shed a single one.

How could they have kept this from her, father and sister? Her mother had given her life for Auda, and she had never even known. They hadn't wanted her to bear the guilt, Martin said. Yet what about the burden of not knowing if her mother had ever loved her?

Auda had been saved for a purpose, just like her father had always said. She was not just a girl born badly, cursed, the death of her mother, but a girl her mother had loved, had saved. But for what?

Surely not to be chattel for a man like the miller. Nor to be trapped in a marriage with a man who beat his frustrations out on her. Nor to be cuckolded by her own husband. Auda could do, could imagine, could write so much more than that. She could bring back the poems of love, only her verses would tell a different story. Hers would tell the truth of love.

Her father walked down the stairs, staring at her for a moment. "She loved you," he said at last. "As I do." He handed her a sheaf of papers. "I made the first batch of paper with your new watermark. All of my new sheets will bear the mark now."

The pages looked beautiful, creamy sheets marked by the faintest of imprints. The bridge of Narbonne stared back at her, replete with the tiny M that made this paper her father's. Hers.

Auda turned teary eyes to her father and hugged him as hard as she could. She felt his own tears hot upon the back of her neck.

She pulled back abruptly. *Have to go.* She needed to talk to someone—but not her father. She needed to see Jaime.

The artist had told her he lived in a rented room above a certain brothel near the western edge of the extended market. She'd never been to such a place before and felt apprehensive the moment she walked in. The bar was crowded today, full of people who'd wanted a respite before either succumbing to the smoldering embrace of some half-dressed woman or heading back out to join the fair.

Auda threaded her way around sweaty customers trading bawdy jokes, curses, and laughter. A brawl erupted two tables from her, a man kicking back his stool and knocking over a cup of ale. The clay shattered on the ground.

"What'd you say? D'you take me for a lying Churchman?" he said, drawing out a dagger. The crowd roared in raucous encouragement. The other man took a swing.

Auda jumped back, hearing laughter behind her. She hurried up the stairs toward the back, into a dim hallway reeking of urine and ale. Four doors lined one side, three lined the other. The door nearest to Auda opened and a girl dressed in a transparent tan shift emerged. Auda gasped. It was Rubea, Na Maria's niece.

The brown-haired girl looked just as shocked, though she recovered in a moment. Her full lips opened into a laugh. Patting her ample hips, she ran a hand over her frizzy braid and winked.

"S'ma third week here. You?" The scent of old sex wafted about her.

Auda flushed and dashed past.

"You'll get used to it," the girl called out, her laughter mocking.

Desperate to get away, Auda scurried to Jaime's door, which would be the last one on the right. Luckily, he'd left it cracked open. She pushed inside and slammed it shut behind her. Only a short time as newlyweds. Had Rubea's husband already left her? Or was this a plan they'd hatched together to earn a little more wealth?

Jaime sat at the end of the small room behind an easel by the open window. He brightened as she entered.

"What are you doing here? Never mind. Have a seat, I'm almost done." He waved her near.

The room was functional, furnished with a thin straw pallet, a low table, two stools, and an easel. Canvases of all sizes were stacked along the walls, and a bag stuffed with clothes had been shoved in one corner. Pigments lay scattered in boxes and cups on the table, along with bottles of inks and clear liquids.

Auda forced herself to smile back and waved at him to keep working.

"No, I am finished," he said. Reaching for a multicolored rag, he wiped his charcoal-stained fingers. "It was not a bad day. I sold two drawings of Fontfroide's mill." He shrugged. "The man wanted one of the monks, even offered to pay me to paint one in portraiture." He gave her a dark look.

She made a cross with her fingers and looked pointedly toward his canvas. Not many people had the money to spend on art for their own tastes. Most likely he'd find his customers among the wealthy, those who favored religious subjects and wanted to display piety before God's suspicious Church.

His frown deepened into a look of disgust. "I know. They come, they look, they tsk, they leave. One man asked me if I'd pay him to sit as model for the Christ. Can you imagine, a dirty wooler as the face of the Lord?"

Auda moved closer. Peering around the side of his canvas, she caught her breath. Like most of his work, this one depicted a simple scene, a series of hills painted in vibrant shades of green and brown and a tan road snaking through. But in the foreground Jaime had drawn a naked boy lying across the road, his body pale, his lips and fingers a bloodless blue. The boy's eyes were closed, and his limbs twisted, each in a different direction. A small furrow creased the boy's brow before deepening down his body into a dark crevice that ended between his legs.

She breathed out. Anger drove this picture, anger and sadness. Jaime wanted to disturb with this scene. It was the first time she'd seen anything like this done by his hand. Who would buy such a cruel depiction, a marker of melancholy and doom?

This hadn't been drawn for any customer.

Jaime tossed a cloth over the canvas.

"My brother." He smoothed the fabric with trembling hands. She knew those hands, had grasped and kissed them—his callused palms that smelled of charcoal and paint, his bitten nails, his stiff fingers, curled as if around a brush. She had not expected they could create this.

"It seems in this world, there are things you can control, and things that control you." His voice was matter-of-fact. "That idiot who wanted me to paint him as Christ—him I could say no to, but this . . ." His voice wavered as he caressed his painting. "This won't let go of me."

Her mind conjured an image of her mother lying eviscerated on the floor. Yes, some things wouldn't let go of you, no
matter what the consequences.

Moving around the easel to face him, she tucked her hand
into his. He closed his eyes, face tightening and lips turning
down, but didn't pull away. Silent for a moment, he opened his
eyes and with a quick squeeze of her hand, spoke with false
interest.

"I'm glad you came to see me today."

Auda dropped his hand and plaited her fingers, then sat on
a stool in front of him.

Jaime reached out to touch her fingers. "Some days are more
difficult than others, aren't they?"

Auda let her head fall so low her chin almost touched her
chest. He understood; of course he did, even through the lack
of words.

She took a piece of paper from her pouch. It was another
verse about his fisherwoman. She had played with it for weeks,
but only this morning had the final meaning become clear.

> *Manna from Heav'n, fish from the sea*
> *Kettles and kettles a'full*
> *The fisherman's wife, she chops and she slice-s*
> *Three pennies for every fish that she kills.*
> *"Gather close. Oc, do come to me!"*
> *She says as her husband shivers and quivers.*
> *"Be ware what ye ask, what ye deem dear."*
> *"Be ware ye still want it when it's here."*
> *As fingers cramp and her body slumps*
> *She drops deadened blade to the dirt*
> *Grabs a live fish with both of her hands*
> *Hews and chews it thoroughly dead.*
> *Dark blood drips from her teeth and her lips*

Frightful sight of fear mixed with need
Not on her face, the ecstatic fisherwoman
But on the faces of her man, now drawn near.
"Be ware ye still want it when it's here."

Jaime's voice faltered as he read aloud. "Bleak words. Hardly befitting . . ." He stared at her hard. "Though perhaps not. Something bothers you. What?" His eyes looked troubled.

Auda pushed her wax tablet at him.

Come with me.

Auda's patched leather boots sank into the cemetery mud. It was a good day for the trip. The clouds formed a diaphanous curtain over the bright summer sun, tempering both heat and light. Pink and white almond blossoms sweetened the air, accented by the buzz of bumblebees and the twitter of robins and chaffinches. Auda let the folds of her wimple hang loose.

At the entrance to St. Paul's, budding poplars encircled the rusted gates and a choke of weeds concealed the pathway. Normally a place for quiet contemplation, today the grounds seemed burdened, forgotten. Blackbirds preened on a bare tree, the only movement against the sky.

Auda threaded her way through the cemetery to a simple plot, marked with a desiccated vine and a thick wooden cross. Laying down her basket, she sat beside the marker.

"M-Ma," she said, wincing at the thickness of her voice, and made the sign of the cross. She picked away the dead leaves from the creeper twisted around the grave marker.

Taking her tablet from her basket, she wrote into the wax.

I always wanted to know more about my mother.
Yesterday I learned she died so I could be born.

She didn't add the question she asked herself—was her mother's sacrifice worth it? A beautiful life given to a child born wrong. Unless Auda did something with the blood her mother had shed for her.

Jaime knelt beside her and took the tablet. Auda was surprised to see tears form in his eyes as he read.

Caressing the gravestone, he knit his brows. "You asked about my painting," he said in a soft voice. "I came here from the north. I always wanted to travel away from the town I grew up in." He handed her the tablet. "It was a small city, not far from Paris, just outside the abbey I ended up in.

Auda gasped. Jaime gave her his crooked smile.

"Surely you guessed I had a Church education. I was to be an illuminator. It's a rich profession."

His eyes took on a faraway look. "I was orphaned there. Bandits on the road overtook my parents' cart. I was young, my brother younger yet." His voice stayed flat. "They slit my parents' throats with gentle ease, I'll give them that. But the silver my parents had was meager, so they tied us, my brother and I, to the back of their horses and dragged us on the road near to a league. Lucky for me, I'd worn a leather jerkin that day. My brother's clothes were softer, just a thin tunic that shredded against the rocks and dirt like ribbons."

Auda stared without blinking.

"I think they tied his knots loosely, perhaps out of kindness to a young child, for his rope broke first. It was a fading humor for them anyway, watching us scream. When my rope snapped, a few hills past, they laughed as I ran away. My brother was just pulp and blood when I found him. The skin on his back and legs had rubbed away. He'd died with his eyes screwed shut."

Auda let out a soft cry, staring at Jaime as though seeing him again for the first time. How did one so young put aside

such cruelty and sadness? She knew the answer firsthand—
you couldn't.

"I wrapped him in my jerkin and carried him to the abbey.
They took me in but said it was too dangerous to go back
for my parents, that the bandits ruled the road. I dreamt that
night that the buzzards picked their bones clean." His lips
were pressed flat.

"A caravan of Jews brought their bodies back a few days
later, wanting them to have a proper burial."

Auda breathed out. She laid a hand on his arm, feeling the
warmth of his flesh under her cold fingers. He didn't move,
not to flinch, not to face her.

"We live our lives the best we can, the way we can. I believe
that's what God asks of us, whatever His damned Church
says." He closed his eyes and smoothed the lines on his forehead. "I came here searching for peace from my life." He
paused, opening his eyes, and reached for her cheek. "And I
think I've found it."

Chapter Twenty-five

Auda sat against the wall in Jaime's room with a wax tablet balanced on her knees. She pulled at a lock of her hair and nibbled on the end, pondering the different verses she'd copied for the *vicomtesse* so far. There were many more to go through, and some essays too, written in Latin and French and other languages she didn't understand. Even written Occitan was difficult for her to follow, took time for her to sound out the words, though she was getting better.

One essay in particular had caught her notice. It was a treatise that talked of how men were to speak to women, and women back to men. Without a doubt the author had been a nobleman. He'd written, "Through time there have been only four grades of love. First is the arousal of hope; then the offering of kisses; next come pleasure in intimate embrace; all leading to abandonment to each other, the body and the soul."

A perfect philosophy—if only the author hadn't written that such a love could only exist among the nobility, and even then only for the pleasure of men. "Women are base creatures," the author continued, "but for noble blood, can be beaten and raped, and sometimes even then."

She shuddered. There had to be a better way, where men like that had no power. Gripping her stylus, she wrote,

Quiet lass, silent lass
Laughs as dawn rides past.
Reach's for his rays, bright 'n' gay,
No longer alone, the outcast.

Drivel. She knocked her head against the wall and concentrated on an imagination of her mother's face. The plan to write new verse that sang of the true beauty and challenge of love had come easily enough. So why not the words?

Jaime, sitting at his easel by the window, gave her a kind look. "It's not always so easy is it, finding the vein of thrill that lives inside you?" He'd been nothing but supportive since she'd told him her plan, agreeing that the *vicomtesse* might well be intrigued by a new type of song, smart and witty with something daring to say.

If only Auda knew what that was.

She breathed out through her nose, frustrated. That 'vein of thrill,' as he called it, was the force that drove him to sketch that first line on a blank canvas, to blend it into a curve and give it shape. Her vein had never been so dry. The words had always come before, insistent with something to say.

Jaime wiped his hands on an old cloth and picked up her tablet. He held it outside the window in the sunlight until the wax became soft. Smoothing the surface out with the edge of his knife, he knelt and handed it back. He placed a kiss on the edge of her temple, his touch light and warm.

Auda breathed in, smelling the familiar odors of charcoal and paint on his skin, the faint fragrance of the outdoors, the vestiges of watered beer on his lips. She turned her face toward him and he kissed her again, this time with more pressure. His hands cupped her face, then slid to her shoulders. She leant into his embrace, urgent. The arousal of hope, kisses and embrace indeed. How could she not want what came next—the abandonment to physical love, though the thought seemed frightening and heady at once. She moved her lips against his, hungry and demanding. He could ask anything he wanted of her in this moment, take anything he dared. She would not refuse.

Then he broke away and leaned back. Eyes closed, he struggled to recover his breath. She gulped—had she done something wrong? But then he opened his eyes and gave her his crooked smile.

"So hard, sometimes, to stop. My apologies." He bobbed his head even as she shook hers in protest. Then he winked. "To you and not your virtue."

"Still maybe now you have some motivation." He dropped a light kiss on her lips.

With a cat's grace, he leapt back onto his stool and picked up his charcoal stub. Auda watched, amazed yet again at her fortune. Not even a year past, she was hiding in her father's house, afraid to be seen by anyone who was not family and trading happiness for security in marriage to a stranger whose dreams, if he had them, were foreign to her. She hadn't even known what true happiness was.

If all wishes were possible, this is what she would have chosen. This life with this man who saw her with more clarity than anyone else in the world, including her father.

And then it came to her. She picked up her stylus and began writing the words.

Auda met with the *vicomtesse* a few weeks later. Instead of the usual selection of folios and verse, she handed the lady a single sheet of paper. The page bore her father's watermark, faint under her words. It had taken her a week to perfect the verse. Jaime had taken a week more, to add his own touch.

"We should make it something beautiful," he'd said. "Something people will want to own."

The result was a paper tract folded into three panels. The first panel bore the title of her verse, *A Girl's Lament*, written in looping brown letters.

The lady gave her a quizzical look and opened the tract to the next panel. A racket of colors greeted her. Jaime had drawn small but precise figures across the panel, miniature animals—cats and chickens, goats and sheep frolicking among the words of her verse. The predators—jackals, lions, and a lone griffin—lurked on the borders, mostly inked in red and yellow, though some bore a hint of green. An intricate design adorned the back, a pattern of interlocking flowers worthy of the carpet pages in a noble's Bible.

The lady fingered the page.

"What is this?" She scanned the panel. "Where did you find this? These drawings are fresh and on paper. Surely you did not create this?"

Auda steeled her shoulders. Anticipating the lady's questions, she had written her thoughts on her wax tablet in preparation. For many hours she'd debated how to tell the *vicomtesse* what she proposed.

She passed the wax tablet to the lady.

> *The old verses never let women decide,*
> *choose what to want.*
> *They are always victims of man's choice.*
> *I wrote something different.*

Bowing her head, she held her breath and waited for the *vicomtesse* to speak. Jaime was waiting outside the door—was he, too, anxious to hear the lady's decision?

"Such a curious thing," the lady said at last. Was this bemusement in her voice, or approval? "Who penned these drawings for you?"

Auda went to the doorway and rapped against the frame. Jaime walked inside from the corridor, and bowed.

The lady sat in her pillowed chair, drumming her thin fingers against the wooden desk. Her cheeks were pale and tight against the pull of her hair, gathered into a bun. "As usual," she said to Auda without quieting her restless fingers, "you are full of surprises." She turned her head a fraction toward the artist. "So then, tell me what you will of yourself."

Jaime bowed again. "What would you have me say?"

"Have you a story?" she said.

"A story?"

"Yes, is that not what she does?" the *vicomtesse* said, jerking her head toward Auda. "Are you not the inspiration behind her verse? The hero with a tale? I'd first thought you were one like her, perhaps a deaf minstrel or a blind scribe, some sort of repentant sinner."

His words were wry. "You credit me with much."

"Not you," she said. "Her." She tapped a long, bejeweled finger against her nose. "Have you read this?" she asked, pushing the soft paper toward him. "Can you read?" She twitched her mouth. "Of course, you must. What do you think of it?"

Jaime rocked on his feet, his gaze flickering from the page to the *vicomtesse*. "I think . . . well, I think it's beautiful."

The lady flattened her lips and tapped her fingers in a staccato beat against the table.

She gestured at Auda.

"Well, girl. What is this mystery you've brought before me?"

Auda met the lady's gaze. She pulled a sheet of paper and a charcoal stub from her basket and walked toward the pair on shaky legs.

Jaime bowed and took the items from Auda. Turning to the lady, he said, "*Domna*, if you would propose a scene . . ."

"What?"

"A person or a place."

The lady bit her upper lip. Her eyes darted from side to side and her fingers resumed drumming. The skin around her eyes tightened when she spoke.

"A girl," she said at last. "Young. Scared. Commanded to marry a man much older than she."

Jaime gripped the charcoal. His fingers moved across the page, swift lines creating a simple scene. When he was done, he put the stub down and turned the drawing around for the *vicomtesse*.

He had sketched a child clad in a jeweled dress, fragile like a costly figurine. There were smudges on the girl's face and hands and a skinned knee poked out from the laced hem of her dress. The girl's eyes were turned down but her lips were firm and thin. Behind her lay a discarded doll; behind it stood a stern lady in a gown that matched the girl's dirtied dress.

The lady caressed the edge of the paper for a moment.

"Yes," she said in a trembling voice. She turned to Auda and nodded, the corners of her eyes crinkling. "Yes, I see. You can tell a story worth hearing, I'm sure. Be certain that you do." She held onto the tract with a firm grip.

Auda bowed as low as she could, so the *vicomtesse* would not see the tears of joy that pricked in her eyes.

The next day, the *vicomtesse* bade her to buy more paper from her father and scribe two dozen copies of the verse, simply, without illustration. The following week, the lady summoned Auda back to another Court of Love.

Auda stood again in a corner of the solar, hidden from all but still able to see everyone's face. Trembling, she wiped her clammy palms against her linen dress and hid them in the pleats of the tan cloth. The ladies ambled in, their voices loud with chatter about family and matters of the fair. As before, they were dressed in silken gowns and bright jewels, though Auda paid scant attention to the details. The room seemed foreign today, the ladies mingled in slow movement, gossiping without purpose. She chafed to move on, anxious and expectant. Finally the *vicomtesse* convened her court.

"Today, ladies," she said, "I have a different treasure to share with you, a new type of verse. The less I say about it the better. Let us see what you think." Opening the plain brown box before her, she unfolded a layer of cloth and drew out the paper tract. She held the front up to the women, who exclaimed their appreciation of the vivid illumination.

"Such colors! What is it?"

Auda blinked to see better. In her dreams she could never have imagined such a thrill, even if the rich ladies clustered together in the solar knew nothing of the story's author. Was this how learned men felt, releasing their writing into the world? Did they wonder who would read their words, what places their works would reach?

A nervous shiver ran down her spine, her gaze darting between the ladies. The *vicomtesse* signaled to the minstrel.

Auda felt another thrill of worry. What if the minstrel fouled her words? He seemed so young.

But he nodded with confidence and bowed, and picked up his fiddle. He started with a simple tune, not one Auda had heard still merry and light. When he sang, his voice bore an edge of mischief.

> *Here's the tale of sweet Marg'ry*
> *Who all day works in the fields.*
> *She's bosoms like pears on a tree,*
> *And a bottom fit to be teased.*

A de-vour-esse to be sure
With the sweet tongue of a lamb
The scent of her 'ginity sears,
Calls far 'n' wide to come near.

White knight on white horse approaches
"Come lass, the tall grass invites.
A gift for you's a gift for me,
My girl, lay with me, and see."

A priest on the road halts their talk,
Says, "Girl, sweet-as-Mary, so pure."
"List'n to me, we'll pray together,
Right here, let's kneel in the heather."

Just then the Count of the land chances by
His lance firm at the ready.
"She's my chatt'l, my field to plough
Bear me sons, girl, let us start now."

"Gallant sirs," the poor lady says
"Your suits all have much merit.
Yet I am one, you are three,
I can't split 'mong you all, you see."

Duel of arms! Pray'r to God! B'gone curse!
They clamor at once. She smiles.
"Nay, wait, it is not meet," says she
"To fight, pray or rape for me."

"Let wit be our guide, good sirs,
Tell your tales one after 'nother
We'll see who's fit for the apple
The lion, griffin, or jackal."

The minstrel ran through the melody once more with quick fingers, then bowed. Auda blinked, her eyes dry. She'd forgotten to look around. Her verse had sounded so real, just like all the others. And yet, what would everyone think? What did the lady think? If the women hated the verse, dismissed it as drivel, would the lady take her fury out on Auda?

Yet instead, she only heard the ladies clapping around her.

"Quite the tale, my lady," Clarys-with-the-rosette said. "Has it an ending?"

The *vicomtesse* looked up, her gray eyes twinkling. "All stories do." She gave Auda a surreptitious glance.

Auda flushed. She had written a score of other verses, trying to decide where the story would head next. At first, she had only meant to wonder what would happen if many men vied for the same girl. What would the girl choose, if the choice were hers? What would she value in the man who garnered her love, and could she even find that in these men? A lecherous *vicomte*? A man married to God who betrayed his vows? Or a knight who thought only of his needs? None of them seemed the right match.

"It's a tease of a verse," one woman complained. "Surely there is more you can read to us now."

The lady shook her head. "There is plenty here to discuss. Whose suit bears the most merit? Whom would you choose, if you could? Come closer, have a look."

Chatter hummed around the room. One woman rose and examined the tract, inviting the others to marvel at it.

"Where did you find this?" a pregnant woman dressed in earthy brown asked.

"I've not seen anything like it in all my years," Esclarmonde said, peering through thin spectacles at the page. "A jongleur's verse illuminated like a book." She shook her head. "Such expense."

"But it's not, my dear Lady Esclarmonde," the *vicomtesse* said, leaning her head in toward her elder. "This is written on paper, a new type of parchment."

"Paper, you say?"

"Cloth parchment, if you like," the lady explained. "It's the fashion all over Italy, these little tales. Some have quite a collection of them."

Was that true? Auda wondered. Her father had spoken of Italian masters whose works were captured on paper, but he'd never mentioned they were anything other than serious tomes like the ones rented from Tomas. The thought excited her, that there might be others who were interested in tales such as hers.

"There are copies here for you," the lady announced, "illustrated, though not like mine, of course. Consider it a gift, to keep your attention."

The *vicomtesse* passed the copies out to her ladies. A few read through the words at once; others struggled to sound out syllables.

"I don't read well," Clarys complained. "Will your minstrel not perform it again?"

The other ladies nodded in enthusiasm and the *vicomtesse* obliged them. Auda watched with more care, soaking in the audience's anticipation, the audible moments of appreciation.

"But what is the story?" Clarys persisted. "Is it a tale of battle and prowess, or the enchantment of love?"

"It is, of course, of love." The soft voice, so familiar, came from a newcomer who'd arrived just as the minstrel finished. "Or rather, the search for it."

The ladies looked behind them at a small woman dressed in a pale blue kirtle that seemed out of place over the plain gray gown underneath. She entered the room. Her gaze flitted to Auda, standing in the back.

Clarys plaited her fingers. "My lady Poncia, you must see a

lot of novelties with your husband's business. But how do you know what this girl's story is?"

Auda forced herself to keep still. She hadn't expected her sister to be present. Poncia had never mentioned the invitation, though there had been no time after the archbishop's supper, especially with their father pushing Auda out the door at evening's end. In truth, Auda had not wanted to see her sister. There were too many questions about the strange heretics that had visited Jehan, and Poncia's knowledge that the heretics used paper to spread their words.

There was also the fact that since that evening, Poncia had not sought *her* out.

"It's not a story but a lament," Poncia remarked, "and what else would a girl know to lament over but affairs with men?" Her voice bore a brittle edge.

The ladies laughed in appreciation.

Auda tried to search out her sister's gaze, but a quick blink from the *vicomtesse* froze her movement.

"Well, it's no courtly love, I'll swear," one woman said.

Poncia tilted her face. Looking straight at the *vicomtesse*, she spoke in a quiet but firm voice. "Not all love is, I daresay. Some love even transcends the earth, though I doubt this verse has much to do with the heavens."

The *vicomtesse* met Poncia's stare. "You did not say, my lady," she said, "what you thought of the work."

Auda watched the two women in her periphery, breath caught in her throat. What would Poncia say?

"It is . . . a curiosity." Her sister's voice stayed level.

Auda let out her breath, aware that all of the other women had grown silent.

Eventually a conversation was struck up, but Auda had eyes only for her sister. Poncia met her gaze with disdain and Auda knew that her sister understood the verse was hers.

Chapter Twenty-six

Auda returned home that afternoon straight after court. The *vicomtesse*, pleased with the day's success, had let her go early.

"I'm giving you an extra day and a half as reward. Be sure you use the time wisely," the lady said, glancing at the tract that she'd replaced in its case.

Auda bowed as low as she could and raced home. Martin would not yet be back from Tomas's stall; that would give her hours to work on the next verse. She flung open the door and came to an abrupt halt. Poncia was waiting inside. Her sister was dressed plainly in a gray dress of homespun cloth that hung limply on her and matched the poor quality of her cheap leather shoes and rough wimple. Around her neck she wore a small wooden cross hanging from a leather cord; a similar cross strung with prayer beads was sewn into her skirt at the waist.

Poncia met her gaze with eyes shot through with red. Her face was set into a rigid mask, except for the tic that pulsed at her jaw.

Auda hung back, unsure what to say. Poncia spoke first.

"What are you doing, Auda? Do you even know?" Her voice quivered at the last.

Auda hung back. The tone of her sister's voice was a mixture of suspicion, anger, and regret. *It's good*, she signed after a moment. *The vicomtesse*—she made the sign of a crown—*thinks so.*

Poncia spoke as if to herself. "You are in such danger, I wonder if you understand." She shook her head. "How could you, Auda? That verse, those disgusting words of a priest courting a girl . . ."

Thought you would not want to know. The truth, however simple it sounded.

Poncia's face hardened. "At least you're honest about it. Unfortunate that you weren't that forthright before you let me sit in that woman's solar while she paraded your words." Her lips curled up. "The things you wrote, disgusting things about a holy priest chasing a girl with such lust. Oh yes," she said to Auda's expression of surprise. "I've seen what else you wrote." She picked up one of the wax tablets scattered on the table.

"Lion, you call me," he preened,
And looked with a saucy grin.
Opened his cloak to draw her in,
"Sweet girl, you'll see it's no sin."

Poncia tossed aside the first tablet and read from the second.

Dark knight points to ants, bees, and birds;
They do it too, God's will, to be sure.

Auda had fought with herself before putting pen to the page to say this. A woman could certainly want a handsome knight or a powerful lord. Could she also tempt a priest away from

God? Many had. It was a common complaint she'd heard in the market, how the servants of God were no better than men in a brothel. Why would a woman try to compete with the Lord? Did she do it to see if she had the ultimate power over a man's fate? The thought shocked even Auda, and she'd almost melted the words smooth. Instead, she'd showed them to the *vicomtesse.*

"Delicious," the lady had said, licking her top lip. "I don't suppose you'll tell me how it ends."

Auda stared before smiling.

And the lady had actually laughed.

Poncia's voice grew loud. "Did you think I wouldn't recognize your sly words and clever jokes? Did you truly think me that naïve?"

The words stung. She hadn't known that Poncia would be there. Never had her sister called her sly, pronounced her clever with that sneer of judgment. Auda didn't have to keep the bit about the priest, but surely Poncia could see some good in the rest of the tale. *Didn't know, you—*

Poncia clenched her hands. "How did it feel to be the lady's favored pet?"

Auda sucked in her breath. Was it not possible that Auda possessed a skill that had caught the lady's notice?

Poncia came toward in a rush, grabbing Auda by the shoulders. "You think she helps you? Out of what, kindness? Pity? It's a trifle to her."

Auda broke out of her sister's grip. *Important to her, me also.*

"And when the Church takes notice of what you've written, will she help you then?"

Auda clenched her jaw. *Everyone sings. Of church and priests.*

"But you've written it down," Poncia cried. "In your hand! For all to read. Can you not see the difference?" Her words were a harsh whisper. "Do you think any of those ladies, your admirers who clutch your words within their sweaty grasp, care one mote of dust for you? What do you think they'd do if the Church came for you? What would they sacrifice to preserve your words? Would they argue for you when you were thrown in the dungeon? Storm the platform when you were set afire?" Her eyes narrowed. "No, they'll show up to cheer and jeer. And then they'll forget you."

Auda raised her hands to retort but then dropped them, unsure what to say. Her sister was right. They would never come to help her. Even so, did that matter? Were these not questions that needed to be asked? Everyone searched for love, and it didn't seem anyone outside of their lonely father and dead mother had found it. Elena would not have wondered why her daughter asked these questions now. Auda was certain of it.

"You tread dangerous ground, Auda, and I fear your soul will burn for it." A muted cry slipped through Poncia's lips. "They've burned people for less. Much less."

Auda remembered the spring months, the frenzied fear of the town, and the hands that had grabbed and tore at her in Carcassonne. She shuddered. They'd thought her a witch, a heretic. Like those friends of Jehan.

Her sister welcomed heretics in her home and then castigated Auda for words?

What of the men who met with Jehan? Heretics. She made the sign of an upside-down cross.

Poncia nodded in resignation. "I knew you would not let that go. Yes, they are heretics, like his wretched parents. Half the money we made went for bribes to hide them. Jehan was too weak to right their wrongs. We argued over it incessantly. For them he would do anything, then come home to beat me when I told him what a fool he was."

Auda stared, confused.

Poncia sniffled once. Auda reached for her sister with ink-stained fingers, unsurprised to see the cuts and bruises on Poncia's hands. She pulled back, opening Poncia's fist and turning it over to look at her sister's swollen knuckles, the pools of blood darkening under the skin.

Poncia wobbled on her feet, closing her eyes against Auda's frenetic fingers.

Jehan? Did something? Tell me! She pulled at Poncia's wimple, tied under her chin, and gasped. The right side of Poncia's face was swollen and discolored. She'd been hit, several times, and the blows had split her skin. Poncia pushed her off.

Auda slapped her hand against the wall. *Come, tell Papa.*

"No, Auda." Her voice firmed. "No."

Why? Papa? Me? Auda's eyes widened. What had this savage beat her sister for?

"No. No, Auda." Poncia bowed her head, her voice teary. She seemed deflated. "All men beat their wives. Good men too. It's hard to be married, hard to . . ." She stuttered. "He didn't mean to. He brought the best doctor in town to treat me."

Auda spat to the side. Was this what it meant to marry, to trust one's future to another person's whim? So much for declarations of love and promise if this was how it ended. She stood and turned toward the door.

Find Papa.

"*No!*" Poncia ran to face Auda. "You don't understand, you never have. Life isn't the silly tales you make of it. Marriage is no fine thing built in perfection. If you had accepted the miller, you would have seen that."

Auda shook her head. Was that tremble in her sister's voice caused by Auda's poor choice, or Poncia's?

Why marry then? It seemed a losing proposition.

"There is good and there is bad." Poncia's voice was gentle.

Auda shook her head. *What good, this?* She jutted her chin at Poncia's bruises.

The skin around her sister's eyes tightened. "He did the best he could, and so did I. I used his remorse, his regret for beating me, to help you, to help Papa, and yes to help myself. It is the sacrifice you make, to get what you want."

Auda felt saddened. Some choices shouldn't require sacrifice.

Poncia fixed her red eyes on Auda. "Come with me. I'm going to Maguelone on pilgrimage. The cart has been hired; I leave in an hour. Come, let us find solace together. If you won't do it for yourself, do it for me."

Auda wiped away nascent tears against the back of her hand. Maguelone was a place of fantasy to her. She'd heard that her mother had traveled there every year after the dawn of spring to give thanks for and cherish the birth of new life. And yet how could she leave? What would she tell the *vicomtesse*? Would the lady take her displeasure out on their father?

"It's a beautiful place, rich soils for growing food, and waters filled with fish," Poncia told Auda. Poncia had gone on pilgrimage once with their mother as a child, and often regaled Auda with lush descriptions of the church grounds.

One day, Auda had sworn, she would see the place for herself.

"Nothing touches the place. The waters are so clean and blue. Not even the birds dare disturb it. They hide in the pines and sing praise of our Lord."

Now her gaze focused on Auda. "You would like it there. The church is small and bare, with only a few statues to adorn it, not even a bench to pray at. Even the windows are plain, just rippled pieces of glass. Nothing like the greens and blues and reds of our own church windows. But so beautiful, you'll see."

"On a summer day, you can almost hear the bees buzz from flower to flower, just over the waves on the beach. The rector holds morning and afternoon Mass; otherwise, there's naught to do but ponder God's beauty on earth and think to one's self. Come, Auda. We'll find our answers together."

It was so tempting—to visit her mother's retreat, to walk the paths she had walked on, to ruminate over the same patch of ocean, tend the same roses, sit under the same trees. And yet, she could not leave. Not her father, not Jaime. Not her writing.

She looked around the room, at the table with her half-written verse, and the quires of papers her father had left on the stool to be smoothed. His paper, her words, their mark. Hadn't she always dreamed about this?

And then there was Jaime. For the first time, she'd found someone who looked past her ruined body, tried to speak with her instead of at her. Someone who thought her ideas had merit, wanted to help them come to fruition. She had finally stepped out of her hiding place, had found a way to express her voice. How could she leave that?

She looked again at Poncia, her poor bloodied sister who had trusted in marriage, and for what? Did she bear more bruises under her dress, in her heart? Maybe Auda could be her salvation, instead of the other way around. She reached for her sister.

But Poncia wrenched herself from Auda's grasp, stepping back. "Promise me. Promise me you'll come with me."

Auda dropped her arms, staring at the gap between them that was only growing larger. She shook her head sadly. *Can't. Want. Can't.*

A quiver flickered across Poncia's forehead. Her speech, when she spoke, was clipped. "We gave you too much, coddled too much. You never lacked anything you cared for, never had to sacrifice anything to have the life you wanted. It was a mistake."

Auda let out a soft cry, but Poncia only reached into her bodice and drew out a small trifolded square.

"Here are the godforsaken answers you want. Maybe now you will see." She threw the square at her sister and swept out of the house, leaving Auda blinking away tears.

She picked up the folded wad that had fallen to the ground. It was a piece of paper. Not their father's. This paper was smoother and more uniform in color. Like the Gypsy's paper.

The front panel was empty. Auda moved to the fire in the hearth and held the paper up against it. The page bore a watermark! It was a crude design, of a ladder leading up to a star, not nearly as fine as the design she'd bought for her father.

With trembling fingers, she flipped to the next panel. It was covered with elegant script, and by habit she turned it over to see the back. The ink had not bled through, not even in an isolated spot or line.

> *Hold the faith of the Lord Jesus Christ and his gospel*
> *as the apostles taught.*
> *Do not swear, or lie, or speak evil of others.*
> *Do not kill any man or animal, nor anything having the breath of*
> *life.*
> *Abstain from eating meat, milk, eggs*
> *and cheese, for these are all sins of the flesh.*
> *Aspire to chastity.*

She skimmed the rest of the panel, disappointed; it read like the rules from a sermon. What did Poncia wish her to see? A declaration that fish was the food of Jesus and that disease was rot of the soul, to be treated through spiritual means? What was it that had frightened Poncia? Her eyes idled over the neat writing scripted on the other two panels of the tract. It wasn't until the end that a surge of fear returned.

Women are no lesser than men, men no more than women. It is the spirit that God has given. The body is but a shell of Satan.

Auda stumbled over the words.

Educate and be educated. Rely not on the word of man's church but on the Church of God as written by Him.
God is Good. God is the Spirit. God created His Son as an angel, never in body, never on earth. The visible world is all of Satan. To follow Christ unto his Father, we must shake the yoke of flesh and ascend into the Spirit.

Dear God. This *was* a heretic's tract—it had to be.

Be baptized in spirit and fire and you will see———"The Father is greater than I."
Work is prayer. We are the Good Christians.

Auda stared until her eyes stung. The phrases mesmerized, speaking to her as if they had their own voice, silky and unctuous. Women are no lesser than men. The thought resonated in her mind and in her verses.

She'd written the very thing that heretics believed.

Chapter Twenty-seven

Auda knew she should consign the tract to the flames. She built the hearth fire up, watched the flames rise. But she could not bear to see the tract burn. The words would not leave her.

> *Women are no lesser than men, men no more than women. It is the spirit that God has given. The body is but a shell of Satan.*

She wrote the simple lines on a piece of paper and stared until the words were a blur.

A knock sounded on the door. Had Poncia returned? Auda ran to her pallet and stowed the tract along with her papers and tablets. She'd have to burn the heretics' words later. What would she do with her own?

Piling two blankets over the bed, she swung open the door. Not her sister at all, but Jaime. It was the first time he'd come to the house.

"I have something for you," he said. "Here, you must see!"

It was a copy of her first verse. She'd scripted an extra one to keep for herself. But he had made it something magical, with drawings even more fanciful that the ones on the lady's copy.

She caressed the tract with trembling hands. To see her words so beautifully scripted, illustrated like fine writing with such color and precision. Jaime didn't think her words venom, treated them with the same care he treated his own work. Would he still, if he knew what she now did? Her eyes teared.

Jaime misunderstood. "I know you wanted to show your work to your father. Now you can show him a worthy expression of your gifts."

She froze. Would her father have the same reaction as Poncia, see nothing but danger in her words? Was her sister right?

Jaime tilted his head. "You've not told him, have you?"

She gave him an uncertain look. She hadn't told Martin what they were up to. It would be best to tell him only if it were a success, she'd reasoned. In truth, she'd been afraid to share her verse, afraid he'd dismiss it as frippery. Now, after Poncia's words, she was afraid he'd read it as something worse.

Jaime swallowed. "I'll stay with you then. I need to speak to him anyway."

Auda flashed him an anxious look. What would Jaime have to say to her father? The realization dawned upon her. He'd want to speak of marriage.

Was that not what she'd wanted, what he'd wanted in pursuing her? Poncia would say so, but look how her marriage had gone. The troubadours and *trobairitz* would say something different, but they didn't speak of men like Jaime. Did they?

Poncia's advice sounded in her head. She should take this

chance. She would be happy with Jaime. And it would be safe. She could leave the *vicomtesse*'s employ, go from virgin to wife, maybe even to mother. Even as the thoughts tumbled through her head, she knew she could not give up writing what she had to say. No matter if it brought her danger.

But she could not consign Jaime to the same fate. He had to choose on his own. And now was not the time for that decision.

Not now, she signed to Jaime. She wrote the words on her tablet to make sure he understood.

Wrong time. Father's new order keeps him busy.

It was a poor lie, one that Jaime saw through. His lips tightened.

"The time has come, long since," he said. "I won't sneak about anymore."

Dragging a chair toward the open door, he sat in silence, regarding her with flat stubbornness.

Auda held his determined look for a moment and looked away. She set a thin pottage of beef broth and bone to bubble and waited for her father to return home. Whatever he said today, she'd soon have to tell him the truth of what she learned.

Heavy footsteps at the door alerted her to her father's arrival.

"Auda, I've bought pigments for the water to flatten the uneven color in the paper," Martin said, bursting in. "Umber and rouge!" His gaze turned to Jaime. "Who is this?"

Auda curled and uncurled her fingers as she rushed to meet him. *Artist. Poncia's stall, met.* Her gestures tumbled over each other.

"I'm called Jaime," the artist said, dipping his head.

"What is this? Who is he?" Martin pressed a cloth to his florid forehead and blinked at his daughter.

"*Monsen*, my name is—"

Martin shook his head, watching Auda sign.

Brought this. Auda thrust the tract in his face. Martin stepped back, taking the sheet. He rubbed the paper between his thumb and forefinger, scrutinizing the page. "You've given him my paper?"

No.

"Sold it then? He is a minstrel?"

Auda frowned, impatience masking her nervousness. It was the first time she'd shown him her verse, the first time he would see what she wrote. *Read.*

Martin squinted at the page, bringing it closer to the fire to see. "I don't understand. It's a jongleur's verse. They sing tales like this all throughout the fair."

Auda flushed. *Mine. I wrote.*

Martin's frown deepened. "Yours?"

Tale mine. Words mine.

"The lady *vicomtesse* has seen it, *monsen*," Jaime said, stepping up. "She thinks great things of your daughter." He lowered his head. "As do I."

"You? Why you? What is all this?" Martin folded his arms over his chest and stared at his daughter, his voice betraying no emotion.

Auda swallowed her fear. *He said.* She gestured at Jaime.

"The *vicomtesse* has taken a liking to Auda's verse," Jaime explained. "The lady has a minstrel sing them in her court. I am fortunate your daughter asked me to illustrate her words."

Martin looked at Jaime now. "These are your sketches then? You have skill."

"My deepest thanks, *monsen*."

"We will talk, soon. But for now, I must speak to my daughter."

Flashing Auda the hint of a triumphant smile, Jaime bowed low and left.

"What is this about?"

Auda hesitated at her father's rough voice. *Saw my stories, Lady. Liked. Sang aloud at court.* She summarized her meeting with the *vicomtesse*, fingers feeling thick and awkward. Just this morning her verses had been the star of the *vicomtesse*'s court. And now? How had things gotten so muddled?

"This painter?" Martin turned his back on her, rubbing his hands at the fire. "Who is he to know so much about you? That you would sit alone with him?"

From his flat tone, she could not tell what he wanted to say. Joining him by the flames, Auda put her hand on her father's chest and pulled at his tunic until he faced her.

"You've fine sense," he said, voice thoughtful. "You've a knack for the sly tale. People will notice you."

Auda swallowed hard against the lump in her throat. There was that word again: sly.

"And you've found someone to share your vision with." He stoked the fire with the poker.

"Perhaps if this succeeds, you can pull together your tracts into a booklet. Then we'll speak of sewing pages, and putting together cover boards. I have the suppliers in place."

Auda laid a cool hand on his cheek and met his gaze. *What do you think?* She waited for his condemnation, his horror that her words sounded like those of the dreaded heretics. But it didn't come.

Instead, he looked pensive. "I've thought many years on how to best make a book of paper. It's been the focus of many of my dreams, our dreams, what book our people will see first, a philosophical work on the equality of all men and our duties in the mortal world, or perhaps a Book of Hours commissioned for minor nobility."

His voice grew warm. "So many worry over what heresies will be committed to the page and here you assuage them, with nothing more lofty than tales of power, lust, and sex." He broke into a smile.

"Maybe you've found a way to make the people see after all."

Chapter Twenty-eight

Later that day, Martin prepared to go back to the stall.

"I told Shmuel I would meet his customer there," he said to Auda. "It's an easier place for him to pick up his ten folios. I finished them last week, did you see?"

Auda nodded. She had inspected the folios that morning. They looked nearly perfect, with her father's watermark on every sheet, the pages smooth and cleanly cut.

"Come with me," Martin suggested. "We'll see what kind of man has ordered the first folios with our mark." Auda was torn between wanting to accompany him for his big sale and staying at home to burn the heretic's tract. She hurried away from her pallet, where she hid them, and nodded.

Father and daughter headed for the market. Traffic was slower on the streets now. It was the doldrums of midsummer, when the fair had lasted long enough to lose its initial allure but still drummed up enough regular business from ladies stocking their households and artisans ferreting out bargains.

On Parchmenter's Lane, Martin pushed open the door to the stationer's and called out. "Tomas! I left a few items in the stall. I'll only be a few moments." He spoke to Auda in a lower voice. "He should be here soon. The fifth bells are near to ring."

Auda sat in the back of the shop next to the curtain. The words to her next verse ran through her head:

> *Oiled skin, sweat-shined sinews*
> *He flexes and grins. Flexes, then grins.*
> *He holds pose, looks one eye t'other*
> *So sweet Marg'ry can a'flutter.*

She heard voices beyond the curtain: her father's customer had arrived.

A man spoke. "The ten books are ready then?" He sounded familiar.

"Yes, yes, all packaged up for you," her father replied. "Here, have a look, make sure the work is to your liking."

"No need." Auda heard the sound of jangling coins. "Here, the ten silvers we agreed on."

Ten silvers! It was a pittance for parchment folios, which would go for twenty times that amount, but it was more than they had ever earned before. What good fortune it was to find this customer! And if he came back for more . . . Yet who could he be?

Auda peeked around the curtain. Her father was packing up the folios in a small box, while his customer stood tall in front of him. She squinted against the sunlight to see better. She couldn't make out the full details of his face, but he looked familiar. Memory of the man who'd spoken to her at the Gypsy's tables came to mind. Yes, it was him, the man from Jehan's house, who knew about heretics' paper. A heretic himself who wore the cross on his back.

She opened her mouth to cry out, but before she could make

a sound, Tomas pulled her away from the curtain. "Have I not told you never to interfere with the stall?" He scolded her in a loud voice.

Auda squirmed out of his grasp and raced out of the shop. She shaded her eyes from the light. The customer was nowhere in sight. Was it truly him? Had Martin sold his folios to a heretic? She could hear her father calling out to her but she couldn't stop. She had to be sure.

She ran through the dazzling sunlight, clutching her wimple tight over her face and ran toward the road where the Gypsies had camped. A flurry of activity surrounded their tables. A trio of dark-skinned men roved in and out of the large dirty tent, each picking up various wonders from the tables and trying to attract passersby with loud, honeyed invitations.

"A look, just a look!"

"Make me an offer. One sou, two sous—something for all!"

Around them, the women barked out orders, directing children carrying crates from the tent out onto the cobblestone road. Where was Donino?

An old man with dark wrinkles had set up across from the sprawl. Sitting cross-legged on a tattered piece of old red cloth, he strummed a trapezoidal psaltery and sang a song of war and betrayal. It wasn't a typical tune, but rather a meandering of sharp notes picked on the gut strings. The soft-skinned man crooned along in ululated tones.

"We took up the cross and beat them back; they drank our blood and became stronger."

Auda sidestepped him. Other men rushed around her with hands full of trinkets—glass baubles, clay bricks with foreign symbols, a suit of white feathers—but she shook her head and strode to the entrance of the tent, bumping straight into Donino.

"Ah, *domna*." His expansive words were underscored by a brittle anxiety. "You liked your watermark and have come, perhaps, for another?"

Fidgeting, she looked past him for the heretic she'd seen here the last time. She mimed the motion of writing. This time the gypsy brought her a wax tablet.

Man, here, who spoke of paper?

Donino moved back. He pushed her away with his palms held up. "No, no. I thought you were going to draw me a design, not words I cannot read. Take anything you like," he said. "I'll make you a good price. We have to leave, other business. It is your last chance." His smile was tight.

No, she had to know of the heretic. Had he come back? Had he come here? She shook her head and pointed at the tablet, knowing from their long association that the Gypsy could read.

"There is no time for this." Donino shed his smile. He gathered the glass baubles in front of him into a pile.

She pointed again at the tablet, and moved around the table toward the large tent. Donino leaned forward and gripped her thin shoulder.

"There's no one there, little girl. Understand?" With a final frown, Donino disappeared into the tent.

"Pay him no mind," the old singer said beside her. "He is uneasy. Trouble in the city."

She raised her eyebrows.

"Heresy, they say." He shrugged, plucking a few notes. "Always heresy." He jerked his head toward the main fair, where a crowd surrounded a lone crier.

A sudden fear seized her. The crier was being pushed back

into the message post. A creamy cut of parchment bearing the archbishop's seal had been nailed high above.

"*Oyez! Oyez!* Safety from sin! Inspections to begin this day."

"He's just hiding his tail behind fancy words, that one," someone said in an angry mutter. Voices next to him chimed in agreement.

"Too bad he don't run away to his uncle for help."

"That fancy-fucking-French pope."

Auda craned her neck toward the parchment.

Narbonne is to be on guard against preachers of Sin and Satan. She shall not fall into the clutches that imperil other cities, where the faithless burn by the hundreds. Inspectors will make certain we are all safe from the devils of heresy and temptation.

Auda sucked in her breath. Inspectors? Inquisitors? Had he released more of his infernal manuscript on heretics and witches?

Narbonne had always resisted the local inquisitors by allowing the Jacobins to hold courts on Church justice when necessary. They'd come to town during the rains, but she had not seen them since then. They'd never caused the town any real trouble before . . . Had Poncia been right after all?

People collected, pushing and surging around her. "Devils and heretics? We ain't got any."

"More so the woe for the innocent then. Someone's got to burn."

"Just look at them all up in Carcassonne."

Carcassonne. Where the inquisitor had planned to go. Where the heretics now burned.

Auda shoved her way out of the crowd and rushed back to

their house. They had to leave, both of them, before the inquisitors found the heretic and traced him back to her father. But first she had to prepare. Bursting through the front door, she ran for her papers on the table; the basket she had left was missing. She rushed to her pallet and reached under the hay. Her fingers felt around, but nothing was there. She began tearing the mattress. Damn her soul, where were her pages? She hunted through each of her discarded pages. Her illustrated verse—the one Jaime had made for her specially—was gone. So were her newer snippets.

Along with the heretic's tract.

Chapter Twenty-nine

Martin arrived home minutes later.

"Where did you go?" he demanded. "Tomas said you ran out of his shop like you'd seen a ghost. I've been a-worry, running after you."

Auda shook her head and held up her hands, but her father didn't stop.

"The archbishop—he's closed the market. In all the chaos, I worried . . ."

Auda had to tell him about the tract. "Ba-pa!" she said aloud.

He stopped, staring. She rarely spoke aloud.

Things taken, she signed, but he didn't understand. She scratched a few words into her wax tablet.

I had a heretic's tract.
It's stolen. We are in danger.

She didn't tell him his customer was a heretic. He might not believe that, but this he would fear. And he would do anything to keep them both from harm.

Martin glared at her. "A heretic's tract? One from your uncle? We burned that nonsense!"

She shook her head, already melting the tablet. *Not from Uncle.*

Her father didn't stop his questions. "Where did you get it from? Who took it? Who took it? Never mind." He grabbed her by the hand. "Come."

Where? she started to sign.

Her father's voice was curt. "We'll go to your sister's. Where you'll be safe. Come!" But when they stepped out the door, they saw a crowd gathering at the crest of the hill, down where the road to their house began. Sounds of the mob grew louder as the group surged toward the gate. Soon the inspectors and their retinue rounded the hill down to their house. Auda recognized their neighbors thronging among the rabble.

"Who's next?"

"The fool of a papermaker."

"*Oc,* of course!"

The wine seller and the milk woman headed the crowd, followed by the old lady who stopped twice monthly to see if there was washing to be done. The family duMartier who lived on the other side of the hill had also come, anxiety etched on the faces of both husband and wife.

"Ba-pa," she cried again.

Martin gasped at the black-robed inquisitor who headed the crowd. Eyes flinty, he pulled Auda back into the house, wrenching the door shut behind them. He dragged her into the kitchen. "Remember what we told you, remember how we planned. The time is now."

He pushed away the large earthenware pot that stood in front of the hiding place Martin had built into the house. He pulled out two slats that led to a crawl space in the wall. It had been meant for Auda as a child, in case she was in danger and alone. The spot was barely big enough for one adult, no chance for two.

"N-no," Auda cried out.

She pushed against him but he was too strong. He carried her up in his arms as if she were a babe and fit her into the small space. His breath caressed her cheek. "Stay quiet. Stay safe." He gave her a gentle shove and replaced the slats, then slid the pot back into place.

Auda sobbed in silence. Through a small crack in the slat, she saw her father open the door.

The inquisitor marched inside. He was a tall man with blond hair and a stern face, wearing a black *cappa* over his white habit. The white cross emblazoned on his dark cloak was stark. Four red-and-blue-garbed church guards followed him as he entered the house, while the rest of the crowd remained outside.

"Who here is the man Martin du papier d'Espagne?" the inquisitor began in an elegiac tone as his bright brown eyes roved around the house.

Martin stepped forward. "I am."

The inquisitor pulled a parchment roll from his belt and cracked the red seal. "You are accused of consorting with heretics. I have a writ to bring you in for questioning, commissioned by His Eminence, Bernard de Farges, Archbishop of Narbonne." Waving the roll near Martin, he nodded at the guards. "Bind the prisoner."

No! Auda sucked in her breath. They couldn't take him. It was she they should be after, not Papa. He knew nothing about what he was accused of doing. Unlike her.

Martin submitted to a guard who bound his hands behind his back.

"Heretic!" someone outside yelled.

Tears streamed down Auda's face. Martin looked in her direction, his fingers moving at his side. For the first time, he used her own sign language to talk to her. *Sister. Go.*

And then he was gone.

Chapter Thirty

𝕬𝖚𝖉𝖆 𝖍𝖚𝖉𝖉𝖑𝖊𝖉 𝖎𝖓𝖙𝖔 herself, limbs folded and cramped, and cried. She pushed against the slats that kept her hidden, but the large pot of beer blocking the exit was too heavy for her to move. Where were they taking her father? What would they do to him? She had to help him.

She hit her shoulder against the slats, again and again, but it was no use. The pot would not budge. Through the uneven pieces of wood, she saw someone entering the house. Jaime! He was frantic, searching for her.

"Aaaah!" she cried out as loud as she could.

He swiveled around and cocked his head. She yelled again, and another time, until he found her. He shoved aside the pot with ease and yanked at the slats.

"Auda," he cried in relief, and, cradling her in his arms, lifted her out.

"Ba-pa," she said, not caring what she sounded like.

He pressed his lips to her head. "I know. Word's all over the market about your father. I didn't stop to think, I was so worried about you. Damn self-righteous priests."

But she had no patience for his hatred of the Church today. She struggled against his chest.

"Best to go to your sister," Jaime said. He put her down but kept his hand on her shoulder. "She can keep vigil with you, and her husband may have resources we can use. Or you'll have to take refuge in the palace. Maybe the best thing to do would be to just leave town, at least till we know they're not coming after you too."

"N-no," she said in her thick voice, struggling to push the sound out. She would not leave her father. And she had to send a message to Poncia, make her return home.

Jaime nodded.

They headed into the city together using the side roads. Jaime stayed by her side, shielding her from the occasional glance of others on the street, until they reached her sister's house.

Auda pounded on the door, and a young boy answered, peering through the open doorway with guarded eyes. Auda wedged her foot in the crack of the door.

"She wants her sister, the lady Poncia," Jaime said. "The lady of the house. We've a message for her."

"Ain't here," the boy said and tried to close the door again. Jaime slapped his hand against it.

"Your master then."

The boy shifted. "He's away s'well, gone off with hims parents to the country. There ain't none to see you." He glared at Jaime.

The artist removed his hand from the door. "We need to get a message to them." He rummaged in his belt pouch and drew out a piece of charcoal. The boy looked at Auda's foot, but she refused to move it, even as she retrieved a wad of paper remnants from her bodice. Holding the pages against the stone wall of the house, Jaime scribbled out two messages.

"Here," he said, handing the folded notes to the boy. "Send one to your master, the other to your mistress." He pulled out two deniers from his purse. "This is the first half for the messengering," he said, dropping the coins in the boy's expectant hand. "Return to me when the deliveries are complete and you'll get the rest. Ask for Jaime the artist, in the Old Market."

The boy nodded eagerly.

Auda removed her foot as the door slammed shut. She looked at Jaime with tear-filled eyes. *Father.* She hiccupped over a sob.

"We'll do what we can," he said, gathering her close to him.

What now? Why hadn't she ever taught him her signs?

Jaime stared at her hands and heaved out a sigh. "I don't know what you want to do, Auda. It's not safe to be out. Not for you."

She gestured toward the city center. *Father, go see.* She had to know what was happening to him.

Jaime looked in the direction she was pointing. "No, no." He shook his head. "We don't even know who has him, where he's being held, except that a Jacobin guards him. We need more news." He held up a hand. "I promise, I'll go myself to find out what I can, when I know you're safe."

Auda clenched her jaw and nodded, letting Jaime escort her back to his room through the outskirts of town. "Lock the door," he said when she was inside. "Stay away from the window and don't open the door for anyone but me."

Auda paced in the growing darkness, neither lighting a torch nor venturing near the window. Unfamiliar sounds made her start at every turn: the crack of a floorboard, a laugh, a whisper in the hallway. Jaime returned after what felt like hours.

What?

He faced her without blinking. "Your father's in the archbishop's care. He's been arrested for selling to heretics. They have proof he knows their words. I think they mean to make an example of him."

Proof, what proof? Auda's body crumpled. It was no less than she'd expected. But what evidence had they against him? So he sold folios to some man—they were blank! The heretic's tract, if they had it, was troublesome, but she could explain. If only Poncia were here to talk to the archbishop. They could tell him about the strange customer, search for him instead.

"It will be best for you if you return to the palace," Jaime said.

She shook her head but he held out his hand. "I'll escort you myself. But first, you must eat."

Closing the door behind him, he went downstairs to the bar, returning with two cups of wine and a slab of brown bread with cheese.

Yet Auda couldn't manage a single morsel. The very smell of the wine nauseated her. After Jaime ate, she lay on his pallet and closed her eyes, inviting the tired fog that tugged at her thoughts take over her mind. When she awoke, the evening had already grown into night.

Jaime was sleeping, slumped in the small chair by the window, his chest rising and falling in slow rhythm, his breath a gentle wheeze. Deep asleep, he looked defenseless. His eyes were shut and shrouded by long lashes, his hands crossed over his chest. He woke and, blinking, reached for her.

"We will save him," he murmured, pulling her against him. "We will."

She wished she could believe.

They walked toward the palace hand-in-hand, strolling in leisure like a young couple in love. Auda strained against their slow pace. She wanted to run to the *vicomtesse*, beg her help.

But Jaime was right, it was best not to draw any attention to themselves.

At this time of night, the bourg was quiet and empty. Merchants and customers had retreated into their homes, as if after emptying their vitriol on the papermaker's arrest they now needed to immerse themselves in the righteous love of family.

They arrived at the palace. Jaime placed a kiss on her forehead. "I won't be far. Go now."

She walked to the front gate, noticing a single light flickering in a window on the top floor. With one last look at Jaime, she entered the palace. Rushing up the stairs, Auda made her way to the drawing room, then the lady's solar, and finally the lady's bedchamber. The room with the flickering light. She had never been here before.

The *vicomtesse*'s personal maid was not standing by the door, which was cracked open. The *vicomte*'s words were loud with anger. "It was you who brought this scourge into my palace." Auda heard the smack of a palm against a wooden surface. "Never forget that!"

"We've done nothing to yell over," the lady replied in a frosty voice. "It is the archbishop you're to blame. If he hadn't blundered and let the inquisitor overrule him—"

"It was one thing to use this paper to copy old documents and something else entirely to tell tales upon it. You think I haven't read them, watched you and your clever scribe? We'll all be implicated now."

Auda gulped at his rough voice.

The lady sniffed. "Surely you don't think our womanly gatherings are going to draw the ire of the archbishop. He has more important worries, now that the inquisitors control his domain."

"And if these tales written for your gatherings come out?"

The *vicomtesse*'s answer was immediate. "Courtly games for bored women."

Auda could bear no more. She shoved the door open and stepped inside. The couple stopped mid-argument, turning to stare at her.

"Auda!" The *vicomtesse* sounded confused and anxious at once. "What in the world are you doing here?"

"Returned to the scene of the crime, I should say." The *vicomte* stared at her with a mixture of anger and naked desire.

She looked down, glad when he turned, and handed the lady a wax tablet bearing the words she'd written in Jaime's home.

My father arrested. Help him.
Talk to the archbishop. Please.

The lady read her note and looked up with pity. "Yes, dear, we know."

"Of course we know," the *vicomte* cut in. "It's his own fault your father is in the inquisitor's clutches. Selling to heretics and then pleading ignorance. Such idiocy!"

The *vicomtesse* shot him an icy glare. "Leave her be. She worries over her father." She turned back to Auda. "I will ask my maid to see if there's any news. Wait here."

Placing Auda's message on the desk, the *vicomtesse* lifted her skirts and hurried out of the room.

Auda fidgeted. She didn't want to be left alone with the *vicomte*. But neither could she leave without word of her father.

The lord shook his head at her. "I warned you, little bird. I told you not to court trouble."

She looked him in the eyes and shook her head.

He curled his hands into fists. "Oh yes. You are innocent,

your father is innocent, the whole damned town is innocent."
He turned away, his voice resigned. "A whole town in danger
of burning, all for one man and his fragile daughter."

Auda stepped back, struck. It was true. The whole town
would be in danger. If one heretic was found, they would not
stop till they found more. It did not matter who was innocent,
did not matter what was written on her father's condemned
papers. People would burn. Just like in Carcassonne.

But the *vicomte* could not give up now. She couldn't let
him.

She scurried around him. With shaking hands, she reached
for him, not knowing where to grasp. Images of the girl she'd
caught him with outside the lady's solar flashed through her
head. Yes, Auda too could trade for what she wanted, what
she needed. She stood on the tips of her toes and put her lips
to his.

His eyes widened and his arms came around her, drawing
her near.

She struggled not to squirm under his touch. His breath
came hot and fast, on her lips, her face, her throat. She felt
cheap and dirty, his kisses degrading instead of glorifying.
Only weeks before she'd be willing to give her entire self to
Jaime—if only she had, so she would have known real love
before she learned this. But it was too late for regrets.

She kissed him once more, and led his hands to her breasts.
He fondled her curves, flicked his fingers over her nipples.

And then he pulled away. Auda moved closer, confused.
Denial merged with betrayed arousal in her veins. She could
not let him refuse her.

"No," he shook his head. "It's not right. Not like this." He
looked over her head.

Auda reached for him again, stopping as she saw the lady,
waiting at the door. How long had she been watching?

A mixture of anger, loathing, and regret shined from the lady's eyes. She had been watching long enough.

"Get out." The *vicomtesse*'s voice was a hash whisper.

Auda ran out the door, down the hallway and outside, heading toward the river. She hurried out the back gates and headed toward the river. Its roar felt like a sympathetic caress; she longed for its coolness, its cleanliness. She glided, like a ghost, toward the water, her bare feet sinking into warm mud, and let the river wash her tears away.

The heretics affirm that all visible and material things were not created by God the heavenly Father, whom they call the good god, but by the devil, Satan, the evil, malevolent god, as they say, the god and prince of this world. Thus they distinguish two creators, God and the devil, one of things unseen and non-material and the other of visible and material things.

—Bernardo Gui,
Practica inquisitionis heretice pravitatis

Part III

Midsummer 1320

Chapter Thirty-one

Auda returned to Jaime's room, telling him only that she was no longer welcome in the palace. He seemed shocked to see her, outraged that the *vicomtesse* had let her leave without even an escort to protect her.

"So much for Christian charity and the divine right to rule," he muttered, even when she shook her head against his dark words.

She could not bear to tell him any more, could not lie either. Instead she retreated into the silence that kept her alone. For three days she hid, waiting for Jaime to come back to her with news. Each day the verdict grew bleaker.

"The public sentiment turns against the Jacobins." He crumpled his lean frame into a chair beside her. "The Church has threatened to bring in more inquisitors if the demonstrations don't settle. They'll come anyway."

She recoiled and turned her face, trying to recall at what point it had all gone so wrong. She was the only one who knew it all—the heretics, their writing, even what she'd tried to do with the *vicomte*. She and God.

Jaime sighed. "There've been riots in other cities—Toulouse and Aix—and the people have had enough of the burnings in Carcassonne. People talk in whispers here. They won't see Narbonne burn. Narbonne is different, they say. But they do nothing."

Of course. The people were fickle. With their acceptance and their anger.

Jaime motioned for her to pour him a cup of wine as he reached for a pear on the table. "I have seen your father."

Auda stared at him.

"You have Jehan to thank for it, I think. He's spoken to people in the Church and the Guild. And the *vicomte* himself has taken up your father's cause, but unless something is done soon . . ."

She flinched at the mention of the *vicomte*.

"Auda," Jaime started, then paused. "If the *vicomte* works to save your father, why then won't he keep you from harm in his palace?"

What could she possibly tell him? She made gestures he wouldn't understand, shaking her head as he searched for her tablet. *Vicomte will save whom he can.*

Sighing, he cut a section of the pear and handed it to her. Its sweet scent felt cloying. What did her father eat in his prison cell? Did they feed him at all?

Someone rapped on the door. Jaime traded a tense look with her.

"Who goes?" he called out.

A soft voice answered. "It's me, Poncia."

Auda leapt from her chair and ran to the door. She swung it open and fell into her sister's arms, sobbing. The scent of frankincense and apple blossoms swirled around her. Auda pulled back, breathing in her own sour odor of deceit and despair. Her sister's smile seemed too bright to look at.

The older girl led her to Jaime's bed and they sat. "Auda, I've thought only about you and Papa since I got your message." She hugged Auda about her shoulders. "It was hard, so hard."

Auda nodded, swallowing a lump in her throat, and lay her head in her sister's lap. Poncia caressed her hair.

"Papa will be home soon, Jehan says. He's worked long for it, all the hours of the daylight and sometimes into the night."

Auda sat up and stared. Memories came to her in slow movements. Poncia confronting her. Revealing Jehan's heretic friends. Throwing the tract at her. How could Poncia trust that man to help their father?

Her sister looked past her. "I thank you for watching her, for keeping her hidden. It's not safe for anyone right now, much less so for her."

Jaime nodded. "They'll come looking for her soon, once someone tells the inquisitor of the papermaker's too-pale daughter. I've heard no rumors yet, but we'll have to move her soon."

Why? Auda asked. If the inquisitor took her, maybe he would release her father.

Poncia sighed, turning back to Auda. "The Church has sent in an inquisitor, Auda. He holds court in the palace with the Jacobins as the city riots outside their doors." She shook her head. "A fool's folly."

Jaime passed a hand over his weary eyes. "I suspected as

much. Talk in the streets speaks of the death of the Church. Priests in other towns have been crushed to a pulp by the mob. The inquisitors all hide, or flee. Bishops too."

"Not here," Poncia insisted. "Our town will never do that, especially with our archbishop appealing for peace. He speaks from his balcony, importunes and prays. The Church will never fall, not with men like him about."

Yet the soft-spoken old churchman was the one who'd sent the guards. A display, to make an example of what happens to those who challenged his authority. If the *vicomte*'s words held any truth, this archbishop was a cunning man. But then why not target a stranger? Why hunt a man while claiming to minister to his family?

"At least the river recedes; it's a good sign," Poncia added.

Jaime shook his head. "Branches and logs dam it up in the mountains. It will burst soon and the Church can preach another week of sermons on it." He ignored Poncia's frown. "Ills of the Church will mean penance for us all. And an inquisitor does nothing if not signal illness."

"Yes," her sister agreed. "But we've no appeal except for the archbishop."

A pair of ants appeared on the table, skirting the trail of pear juice. They moved in and then back, to the side. Auda closed her eyes.

"They say the cross needs cleansing by new blood," Jaime was saying, his voice soft. "But not by the blood of innocents."

Poncia's brightness fell away. "Not everyone is an innocent."

Realization dawned on Auda. None of the people working to free her father believed in his innocence. Not the *vicomte*, not Jehan, not even Poncia.

None of them were innocent, so how could he be?

Chapter Thirty-two

The next day, Auda asked Jaime to go to her father's house and bring back sheets of paper.

"The ones with the watermark," she wrote on her tablet.

Jaime looked at her with suspicion. "We have tablets. Why do you want the paper?"

Auda didn't want to say. But she had to do something to save her father, and there was only one path she could take.

Jaime relented and after a half hour he brought her back a small stack. Auda held one of the pages to the fire and looked sadly at the silhouette of the bridge that shone through.

That night, she started writing her confession.

> *It was I who sought out the heretic.*
> *My father knew nothing of it.*
> *It began when I first saw a watermark.*

Jaime looked over her shoulder and gasped. He knocked the inkpot and dark black ink ran over her words.

Throwing the page into the hearth fire, Jaime turned to her in horror. "What are you doing?"

Auda shook her head. The only way to save her father was to give the Inquisition someone else to blame. Surely he could see that.

"I know you want to do something—we all want to do something," he continued. "Should you not go to the *vicomtesse*? Maybe she will reconsider?"

Auda shuddered. The *vicomtesse* would not want to see her again—that life was past. Auda had to look to herself from now on.

Voices sounded at the door, along with a scuffle. Motioning for Auda to stay quiet, Jaime put his ear to the door. A familiar woman's voice rose above the rest.

"Let me in," her sister said. "I've come for Auda. We have to go."

Jaime unbolted the door. Poncia strode in and pulled Auda up. "Come. We have to leave."

What? Where? Why?

"Auda, listen." Her sister cupped her chin and forced her to stay still. "The inquisitor has released another page of his treatise." She brandished a small scrap of parchment.

The Mark of the Devil

They walk among us, as brothers and sisters,
Feigning good deeds and spreading good word.
But they say nothing of their true nature until it is too late.
And the city of God has gone to the Devil.
You may not know them by looks alone.
They clothe the school of the Devil in an appearance of goodness.
But still you can find them for they cannot hide
The Mark of the Devil upon them.

Auda sat with a thud, gripping the parchment with both hands.

"Where did you get this?" Jaime breathed.

Poncia kept her eyes on Auda. "They are looking for you, if not now, then soon. They will find you."

And Poncia. And Jaime. And how many others she knew?

Her sister nodded. "Already they have taken the stationer to be questioned. And they look for the Gypsies."

Auda let out a low cry. Tomas had been arrested too?

Jaime spoke with authority. "We'll leave now. I have thought long about where we can go. I have some ideas."

Poncia shook her head. "No, it's already done." She opened the door and let in two men wearing dark brown robes. One of them pulled back his hood to reveal a sallow face.

Auda gasped. It was the man from Jehan's house, not the heretic who'd sold to her father but the other one, shorter and stout. The one who'd worn the yellow crosses.

Jaime flashed her a confused glance and moved closer toward her.

"I brought them with me, Auda," Poncia said with a hint of reluctance. "They are here to help."

"I am René," the tall man began. "This is my brother, Ucs." His gentle tone seemed not to fit the impassive mask of his face.

Auda only glared at him. Was he the one who'd written the words on that damned tract Poncia had given her? How could she bring him here?

"We are not your enemies," the man said.

Auda flashed him an angry look. Was he not the reason her father was imprisoned, him and his partner? She raised her hands to speak to Poncia.

How could you?

"Who are you then? What have you to do with all of this?" Jaime demanded.

Poncia's voice was a whisper. "Jehan sent them. They are helping to free Papa."

Auda shook her head.

"We can help you," the heretic, René, said, "but we must move fast. They will soon be upon you."

Jaime turned on him with angry eyes. "And how do we know to trust you? Who are you to take her away?"

Who would know better how to hide than a heretic?

René spoke in a lower tone, eyes fixed on Auda's face. "We have much to talk about. This will give us time."

Auda regarded him, and nodded. Yes, she had to learn what she could of these men, anything that she could use to save her father. She turned to face Jaime.

"No," he said, seeing her determined face. "You need not go with them. We can leave town ourselves. Tonight."

And go where? How far, with her father still languishing in the dungeon?

Poncia crouched beside her. "Listen to René," she said. "Jehan works hard to bring Papa home. We will take care of him. You trust me, don't you?" Her voice trembled, and Auda dropped her head, nodding.

Jaime leaned in close. Hot tears from her eyes fell upon his hand.

"If this is what you choose, I will wait. As long as it takes, I will wait," he said.

Auda collapsed against her sister, allowing Poncia to wrap her in a dark cloak. "A Kiss of Peace," Poncia said and touched her lips to Auda's forehead. "You will be safe with these people, I promise you."

"Where are you taking her?" Jaime asked as Poncia led Auda to the door.

René answered. "It's best if you don't know."

Chapter Thirty-three

In the darkness, René and Ucs shepherded her along an ill-marked path around the walled city, wending eastward into the fields surrounding town. A full moon silhouetted the mossy stone blocks of the old abandoned amphitheater. Something moved out here tonight. Shadows flowed in and out of other shadows, and muffled whispers mingled with the rustle of mice and birds in the garigue.

Auda stopped to catch her breath. The Roman theater was a cavity, ravaged and decayed among the tall weeds. It sagged in the dirt as the ghosts of the ancients, gladiators, and actors danced in forgotten splendor.

What was she doing here, alone with these heretics? Somewhere in the city, her father waited for her.

She let René and Ucs guide her around the stone structure, through a splintered wooden door and into an underground maze.

"We can hide you here for a time," René said. "There are others here but they'll leave. It's the best hiding place we know of."

Auda stopped. Bring her where? Who were these people

meeting in the middle of the night in a desolate ruined building? More heretics, of course.

She shook her head.

"It's as dangerous for us as it is for you," René pointed out. "Now that you have seen our faces, you can turn any of us in. But you won't, any more than we would you."

They arrived at a small room filled with people. Pastilles of rosewood burned on a low table along one wall. A dozen people knelt on the dirt floor in silence, while brown-robed men placed lit torches in brackets around the room. In the front, two people garbed in black robes were whispering to each other.

Someone clapped in the back and everyone bowed heads. Kneeling, Auda bowed too, trying to peek out through her lashes.

A black-robed man came forward, tall and thin, with a slightly bent back. He looked to be about her father's age but his face was old and gaunt, his skin sagging on his bones. In his right hand, he held a dark-colored book. An old lady stood by his side.

"He's the Perfectus Pierre," René murmured to Auda. "The other is the lady Beatrice."

Auda shook her head, frowning. She didn't want to hear any more explanation of this cursed ritual.

The *perfectus* raised the thick book high, his hand faltering. The lady Beatrice knelt, and he placed the book on her head.

"*Benedicite, Benedicite, Domine Deus, Pater bonorum spirituum, adjuva nos in ommibus quae facere voluerimus,*" he said in a mellifluous voice, every word rich and loud.

"*Benedicite,*" the woman replied, clasping her hands in front of her. She rose and bowed to the *perfectus*. He handed the book to an acolyte at his side. "*Benedicite,*" she said again, kneeling before she rose and bowed again, and then a third time.

Auda fidgeted. What was this ceremony, this dark ritual

they'd forced her to attend? She would not be turned into a heretic, not after everything that had passed. She pulled on René's cloak, but he only shook his head.

"Why do you come here, Beatrice?" the *perfectus* said.

The woman bowed her head further. "I come to seek forgiveness. I come willingly, with goodness in my heart, to seek the blessing of God, to pray to Him for worthiness, and that He shall lead the Good Christians to a good end."

The *perfectus* took the book and laid it again upon the lady's head, a small trickle of sweat dripping down his jawline. "Receive blessings from God, then. Is it your intent to take the *consolamentum*, to undergo baptism of the spirit under the Friends of God and His Church?"

Flames from an overhead torch flickered. Under their orange glow, the lady's face was sallow and wrinkled, an old lady weakened by the burdens of life. Yet when she spoke, her voice was firm.

"It is."

"Understand then, these vows you make come to us from the time of Jesus Christ and his apostles, that they are preserved by the Friends of God and His Church for all days. A Good Woman carries the Holy Spirit within her. If it be her will, she can help worthy souls free their imprisonment and sins to meet their Ultimate Creator. Do you wish to take up this responsibility?"

"I do."

As the *perfectus* recited the Lord's Prayer, Auda shifted on her knees and looked around. Every member of the congregation watched, rapt as they knelt on the uneven ground. Even René didn't move, his attention fixed on the performance before them. Like the sheep in her own church, Auda thought bitterly. All someone had to do was speak with authority, and there was always a fool who would listen.

And yet part of her longed to hear more about this faith that allowed women to stand beside men, to make the same choices with the same consequences. Was that not what she had sought all along? She tried to calm her nerves and listen.

An acolyte handed Beatrice a paper tract. It wasn't her father's paper, she hoped—it couldn't be. He did not sell to heretics, not if he knew they were heretics. He had been trapped. She was *la fadata* who'd been duped by so many. Maybe she should ask to see the tract, to use it as evidence. But how?

The *perfectus* asked Beatrice to adhere to the tenets of being a Good Woman: not to eat flesh, sin with flesh, kill flesh, honor flesh.

"Only the spirit matters. Whether man or woman, crone or child, the spirit is always the same." The *perfectus* raised his hand in benediction. "May God keep you in a good life, and from a bad death."

The congregation murmured their approval and Beatrice rose. Two acolytes came beside her and tied a black thread around her waist, then garbed her in a robe of coarse black cloth. She stood while the *perfectus* finished his homily.

"Keep the commandments of God and hate this world," he concluded. "If you continue well to the end, your soul shall have life eternal and nevermore be condemned to walk this earth. Ours is not to bring new evil in the world, but to help others shed their mortal coils until all souls are free of Satan and live together with our Lord." He gave her the Kiss of Peace. "I welcome you into the Church of God."

The congregation rose, dissolving into a mass of tears and hugs. Auda tried to breathe, but the air was heavy with the mingled odors of sweat, unwashed bodies, and incense. The events of the last day overwhelmed her. When the crowd broke, she collapsed against the wall, relieved to be alone.

* * *

A plain meal of fish and boiled carrots was served alongside pitchers of water. When the plates were cleared, the congregation split into groups of threes and fours. Pamphlets and books were handed to some, tablets and styluses to others.

Auda sat apart from the rest, watching. Some read to each other in quiet voices while others struggled to sound out simple words. Had it been so long ago that her father had taught her to read and write? Now, watching humble men and women taught to read by leaders of their own faith, she felt a shiver of excitement down her spine and fingers.

"Have you never seen the *consolamentum* given before?" René asked, sitting beside her.

Of course not. She'd read about it once, that it was some sort of baptism. That was more information than she needed right now. She shook her head, her eyes fixed on the pair in front of her. Curiosity and longing warred with good sense; she knew she should show no interest in these cursed folk, but she could not help but watch. An old man was straining to copy a row of letters written on a tablet held up for him by a young boy. What did they read? What were they allowed to read?

"It was a simple ceremony, no?" René said. "Simple and beautiful. A confirmation, if you like. Beatrice is a *perfecta* now; she has been perfected in our beliefs and practices. She can liberate the souls of those who believe."

Much as she sympathized with things they had to say, of equality between men and women, and the need to be educated, still these were heretics.

"Man is a living contradiction," René sighed, spreading his arms wide. "Look at this world we live in. It's filled with such beauty and we corrupt it. Why is that?" He caught her gaze.

"Have you not felt it? That joy that suffuses? There is a beauty inside all of us, a wide, expansive beauty that wants to rejoin its Creator and fill the skies with love.

"We bear the gift of God within us, but only within a rotten body that decays and rots and weakens the resolve. It is filled with ill smells and fluids, an ether that reeks of bad digestion and disease." He gestured at her hair, still covered under her tight coif, her eyes, and then her lips. "The body is just a shell that means nothing to those who believe."

Auda sat unmoving, though something tight, something painful she'd thought shuttered away, eased inside her.

René nodded. "We brought you here specially, and for good cause."

She looked up in alarm.

"The Good Men and Women, we look after our own. We show others the path but do not force anyone along it. We educate our own. We hold school, when we can. When we won't be discovered."

Auda shook her head. She was not one of them. She didn't need to be looked after, not by a band of heretics. Neither did her father.

"It is fitting you are here to see our school," René continued, "to see plain people reading the word of God. It was for this, after all, that your father has given his sacrifice."

Chapter Thirty-four

Auda stared at René in confusion. Her father had been imprisoned wrongly. He didn't know he was selling to heretics. But René was shaking his head.

"We'd searched for so long for one such as him, who would help spread our message. Papermakers are rare in this area. And with the rains, we could not get a steady supply from afar to make more books."

Auda shook her head. What was the man talking about? Her father was no heretic. He only cared for his paper, his folios, not for what was written upon them.

"We went to the Jews," René explained, "to see where they got their supplies for their school. They sent us to your father. We weren't sure he was one of us, at first, even when we first approached him. But then he delivered the folios, and we saw his watermark."

Auda gaped at him. The watermark. Was it really like Tomas had said, a means of communication? A way for heretics to identify one another? She slumped back. This was her fault! She'd bought the watermark for her father. Ignoring the advice from the stationer against Gypsies, not asking any questions. It was her fault alone.

Women are no lesser than men, men no more than women.
In spirit, in thought—even in blame.

They installed her in a larger room with a blanket, a pitcher of water, and two small bags of dried fish. It was not safe for them to meet at the same location on a regular schedule and they would not take her along. Trust, it seemed, only went so far.

Yet René stayed with her.

"It will only be for a few days," he said, "before we find something more permanent."

He left her to get more food, and news from the city. At first there was none. But on the third day, he returned with a gentle smile.

"Your father's release is almost bought. He will be home soon."

She stared at René, willing him to tell her more. Out of habit, she used her hands to speak, though she knew he could not understand her.

Family safe?

"Your sister is beside herself, you know. She doesn't trust us." He winked a heavy-lidded eye at her. "Like you, she has much anger in her. She's demanded, a dozen times over, to see you. In a few weeks, perhaps, when things have quieted, we will arrange it."

He switched to town matters: the Church had arrested near a dozen more people on the orders of the visiting inquisitor. Auda wanted to ask for details, but he seemed reluctant to linger on the topic. Were his friends among those captured? The public outrage that had erupted with such vehemence against the inquisitors had now died down. Auda had been right about their fickleness.

"People move about town with eyes firm on the ground and ears closed except to rumors and gossip," René said. "Like how the crops and grain harvests were low this year, and the fish in the oceans are turning up sick. Twenty, thirty fish in one catch, but they all flop about rotten. People say it is a sign from God."

He took out a small piece of hard cheese and brown bread from his tattered bag, along with soft pears and a stack of tracts for her to read. "It can be lonely," he said in an apologetic tone. "I know."

She raised her eyebrows. Minutes passed like hours here. She'd explored the small amphitheater a dozen times, not just the single circular tunnel underneath the ruins but the paths that led to the surface. Such victories these rocks and dirt must have seen. Bloody defeats also. She tried to compose a verse about it when she came out at night, but no words came to mind.

She rifled through the tracts—they all seemed the same and spoke of the ways of the Friends of God. At first she was ravenous to look at the different watermarks—hearts and crosses and fish atop other patterns. There was no commonality between them. How did heretics know who to approach?

Or were watermarks reserved for heretics alone?

She asked Rene, writing the words out on her tablet and he looked at her with surprise.

"It's easy to tell who is one of us. All you have to do is look for a path to the heavens. A ladder. A star. In your case, a bridge."

Auda dropped her head, cheeks burning. She put the tablet aside and asked no more questions.

When René left, she went back to the tracts, studying them.

She observed other details: the smoothness of the paper and the uniform color of the ink on the page, and of course the watermarks. The most common was a dove, although the rough sketch of a unicorn with pointed horn also appeared frequently. There was another with a dove above the Lady Virgin (she thought), and one of a hand with its fingers split into a V, from which a heart emerged. Ladders and stairs abounded.

Auda closed her eyes. At every turn she seemed to step into heresy, dragging her poor father with her.

"Someday I will also take the *consolamentum*," René said one day in a tone laced with wistfulness and frustration.

"Why?" she wrote.

He seemed surprised. "It's a simple life, closer to God. In the end of things, He is all we have. Bah," he said, puffing his cheeks as he looked at the ground. "I want to take my vows this winter. They say I am not ready yet, that I am not yet wise in the ways of the world."

Auda thought of his simple words, his simple dreams.

What would you sacrifice for this? she signed to his back. He turned, giving her a sad smile, and she was glad that he could not understand her.

Her gaze fell to the book René was studying, a thick paper tome.

He noticed her interest. "It is the Gospel," he said in a shy voice. "We are lucky to have a copy." He held the book close and read aloud.

Lo, I am with you always, even unto the end of the world.

Auda rose, restless. Perhaps He *was* with them at all times, but for what? To lie, cheat, deceive, and kill? To hurt and be hurt?

What had Jaime told her, that God expected them to live

their lives the best they could? Was the best she could do to hide and let others bear the consequences for her choices?

Women are no lesser than men, men no more than women

It became clear, what she had to do.

She left René reading, tiptoeing away until she was outside in the ruins of the theater. Then she broke into a run, leaping over fallen branches and old stones. She headed straight for the city, seeking the first set of church guards she could find. Sighting a trio of red-clothed guards, she threw herself before them and whipped off her wimple. Her bone-white hair swirled around her. She met the eyes of one and bared her teeth.

Someone yelled, another screamed. She felt hands grabbing her around her waist and her shoulders, tossing her to the ground. The ropes stung as they bound her hands behind her back.

They started beating her and then she blacked out.

It must also be noted that if anyone speaks openly and manifestly against the faith, relying on the heretics' usual arguments and authorities, educated and faithful churchmen will easily be able to convict him of heresy simply from his trying to defend the error.

—Bernardo Gui,
Practica inquisitionis heretice pravitatis

Part IV
Fall 1320

Chapter Thirty-five

When Auda regained consciousness, she found herself slung over the shoulder of one of the guards. She squeezed her eyes against the sun. Her wimple had been taken, her headcap torn. The brightness burned past her eyes straight into her skin. She must be in hell. Nothing so pure and bright could be born of heaven. No, heaven lay in fleeting moments: the warmth of working in the studio on a summer day. Her father's smile of approval. The scratch of quill on paper. And the feel of her fingers on Jaime's face.

The townspeople watched as the guards carried her along the river to the prison, past the grand domiciles of both the *vicomte* and the archbishop. Her captor dropped her in front of the keep of Giles Aycelin de Montaigu, named and constructed for an earlier archbishop. With its rough masonry, battlements, and turrets, this tall building seemed less like a holy place and more like military barracks.

She cried out against the brightness of the sunlight. Only hell could tempt like this, with something so alluring, a light that drew you in until you discovered its flames would incinerate your soul.

Would this be the day she burned in the flames?

The guard prodded her with his club, leading her into a courtyard near the unfinished cathedral. A cool breeze blew the scent of apples and warm bread past her. He herded her on toward a separate tower at the northern corner of the keep, up three sets of stairs. Pushing her into an empty room, he locked the door.

Auda hurried to the window. Through the iron bars, the sun-drenched riverbank beckoned. The colors—the faded green of the grass, the yellowing of leaves still fluttering on their trees, the blues and grays of the river—hurt to see.

The room itself was plain, with a wooden crucifix on the wall, a table with a basin filled with water, two chairs, and a pallet of hay in the corner. She hesitated, then washed her beaten face in the basin. The water darkened with dirt and blood from her skin.

Without a sign, the door opened and the archbishop walked in, dressed in rich finery. He wore all the accessories of his office—a soft white robe trimmed in gold, a matching oval hat, a ruby cross around his neck, rings on his fingers shining with jewels.

Auda breathed in relief to see him, but he seemed not to notice. He grimaced at the basin, and a servant rushed to take away the dirty water, while another brought in a roll of parchment, several quills, a pot of ink, and two cushioned chairs.

The archbishop sat, crossing himself. He mouthed a prayer

and looked up. "There is much to talk about, my child," he said.

Auda shivered as he smiled and motioned for a clergyman to sit beside him. She stared at him. He sat back and regarded her with soft eyes. Old eyes, blue and fringed with wrinkled skin.

"Will you swear an oath that the answers you give to my questions are the truth?" His voice sounded tired.

Should she trust him? Poncia did. She nodded.

"What do you know of those who call themselves the Good Men and Women?" He said the words offhand, not looking at her as he spoke.

Auda shook her head, her heart thumping.

He glanced at her, lips turned down with reproach. "You should not be afraid to admit it, child," he said in a voice that was eerily soft.

"We are but mortals, children of God," the archbishop continued, "who do wrong, stray from goodness. God forgives those who recognize their sins. It's not you we seek to punish but those who spread their lies without thought for their malice."

Auda closed her eyes, unable to tell what was the truth anymore. She didn't care who believed what, hardly remembered what had brought her to this moment. All she knew was the pain in her head and limbs and the ache in her heart bearing her father's name.

The archbishop templed his fingers. "We will protect you, as far as we can, from the lies that have filled your head. Your punishment will be light; we seek merely to show you the truth. This heresy your father courts is a false truth. Come, child, answer my questions with honesty and you'll have nothing to fear. Tell me, how long has he known the heretics?"

She snapped back and shook her head. Her father knew no heretics.

"Tell me, then, when was the last time you and your father went to church? Did you go willingly? What was the sermon? Who saw you there?"

She shook her head again, and he frowned.

"Quick, my child, your father's soul falters. If you don't answer any of my questions, I must assume you are either dumb as a beast or clever as a fox. Which would you have it be?"

She nodded, again and again. He knew she couldn't speak. How was she to answer? She was a good daughter of the Church, her father a good son. If he but gave her a chance, she would tell him the truth of it. She mimed the motion of writing.

"*Oc, oc,*" the archbishop said. He slid a trimmed section of parchment and an inked quill across the table. "Write for me your confession, and God will forgive you."

Confession? An image of her father, his face bruised and body broken, stirred in her mind. Yes, God would forgive them all, but who would forgive Him?

Her fingers curled around the quill and she wrote in quick strokes.

Father did not know he was selling to a heretic.

The archbishop shook his head in disapproval. "Child, this is no time for deceit. We have proof of your father's guilt, proof of his heresy. But he tells us nothing, will not repent to save his soul. Help me help him. Who duped him with words of deceit against our Lord? Write down names, and places."

She gripped the shaft of the quill in a grasp that was too tight. Why would he not believe her? She wrote again.

It was all a mistake. He knows nothing.

The archbishop pursed his lips into a tight line. "Don't test my patience, child," he said in a louder tone. "I give you a chance many others would not." He looked her up and down.

She put down her quill. The archbishop narrowed his eyes. "Pick it up, child, and write. God will guide your words."

She grasped the shaft of the feather and inked it again, then wrote block letters across the creamy parchment.

My family is good, pure.

The nib broke in the middle of her line.

"Child! If you don't do it for yourself, at least think of the family you say you love," the archbishop said, sweeping a hand across the table. The parchment and quill flew to the ground. "They will be next!"

Auda shook her head. Tears fell from her cheeks onto the table.

"I seek to help you and you spit at my feet. Spit upon the feet of God! Is this how you repay your sister for all of her concern?" He pulled a piece of paper from underneath his parchment, a single page folded in three.

Through her tears she couldn't see what he held. He read aloud:

"'God is Good. God is the Spirit. God created His Son as an angel, never in body, never on earth. The visible world is all of Satan. To follow Christ unto his Father, we must shake the yoke of flesh and ascend into the Spirit.'"

She blinked. The heretic's tract she'd saved from her sister? Who had given him that? She brightened for a moment. The matter was easily cleared then. She could show him the water-mark on the tract was not the same as what they used.

Oblivious to her smile, the archbishop kept reading, his tone derisive.

" 'Educated. Rely not on the word of man's church but on the Church of God as written by Him.' "

Auda scribbled on the parchment.

Not our words. Not our paper.

The archbishop read her words and growled. "Do you think me a fool?" He brandished another stack of papers—her papers with her verse written all over them.

"Silly tales, the lot of them," he said, "except for this." He held up a page that bore her writing.

Women are no lesser than men, men no more than women. It is the spirit that God has given. The body is but a shell of Satan.

Auda slumped back as if hit. Her words. Her father's paper. Once it had been their dream. He had been the only one to believe in her. And she had failed him.

"Who taught you this filth?" the archbishop asked in a dangerous tone. "No, no hands, speak his name! Was it a Good Christian who taught you such sins?" Rage throbbed in a vein at his temple. "A Friend of God?" he sneered.

"Nohh."

He inhaled, once, then again, breathing out of his nostrils. His voice, when he spoke, wavered. "Perhaps you know them by a different name. The Good Men, the *Bonhommes*, the *Parfaits. Les Innocents.* No, don't shake your head."

He shot a hand out. Cupping her chin, he forced her closer until his face was inches from hers.

"Where did you get this?" he said. "Tell me now and I will have mercy on your sentence. Can you name any people who have previously been hereticated? Have you had relations and intimacy with the heretics Pierre and Jacques, the words of the brothers Authié, or others? Do you worship them, give them comfort, or send them anything whatsoever?"

She could not move in the face of his fury.

He let go of her chin, snatching his fingers back. "You may say the words don't belong to you. Prove it then. Where and whence did this come from? If you know, you will tell me. Tell me, now! Have you believed and do you believe still that which they told you concerning the Good Christians, concerning the sin of the spirits in the sky and the reincarnation of spirits? No, don't shrug at me! Write your answer!"

No, no, no. She didn't need to write to tell him she knew nothing.

His thin lips flattened. "Tell me then, if these words are not your father's, whose are they?"

Hers. All hers. A certain giddiness took over her. She would tell them the truth, her truth. It would lead nowhere but herself, end nowhere but with her. She wrote a single word on the parchment.

Mine.

She pointed to her verses.

> *Their cases a-pled, words a-spoke*
> *They bargained now with each other.*
> *"I'll buy her life!" "Her soul from God!"*

"I'll buy both," the Count a-told.
"God made us, God loves us, you know."
"And tells us to Love one anoth'r."
The Priest shuddered and said, "No sin."
"Only through you can I speak to Him."

She picked up the quill again.

I wrote these tales. To spread the word. She chooses, not the men.

Women are no lesser than men, men no lesser than women.

She held her head high and looked at him straight on, daring him to disbelieve.

Chapter Thirty-six

A week passed. Unsure what to believe, the archbishop imprisoned her in some sort of underground cell, swearing time and hunger would break her to the truth. The place was dark and reeked with the stench of sweat and feces.

In good moments, she thought of Jaime's stall, where he was surrounded by paintings of cows and sheep and the boys who tended them, or of fruit vendors in the market, and little girls who helped their mothers tie up the produce. From time to time, her thoughts skittered over memories of his fisherwoman.

In other moments, her mind turned toward her father. Daydreams showed Poncia and Jehan taking him to safety; Jaime waiting for her to return so they too could steal away.

"Do the Good Men wait for you?" the archbishop demanded in another interrogation. "Do they keep vigil?"

No, no, no.

Auda gave up her tally of days imprisoned and instead counted the number of times she'd been taken for interrogation.

Visit One: the archbishop questioned her with gentle words.

"You poor wretched child."

Visit Two: he had asked after her, then said, "The dungeon chill must be ill for your health." He started again with the questions.

No, was all she could say.

Visit Three: this time, he began without preamble.

"What are the words of the *Bonhommes*? The *Parfaits*? Do you know them? Do you swear by them?"

She shook her head against him without pause. The stories were hers, the songs were hers. She said nothing more. Who could she name anyway? Who could she give up? René? The Gypsy? Her brother-in-law? Where would it lead, except back to her? Where would it end?

Visit Four: they led her to a lower chamber in the tower, where the scent of fresh air was replaced by the murderous stench of a charnel house. The guards herded her into a small, barren room and shackled her to the wall. One set of heavy chains clamped her hands together; another imprisoned her feet. She could not move but to rest the burden of her manacles on another aching muscle or bone.

"Mamaaaaaaan!" the scream came from the next room.

Auda trembled, a deep shake that rattled her bones. Would she die here, chained to the wall? Would her body decay without a proper burial, a warning to others?

Fettered to the wall so that she could not move, she spent hours hearing curdling cries and screams. Most were men, though sometimes she thought she heard a woman's wail.

Her father had likely borne this same torture, on account of her. If he could survive it, so could she.

When they released her from her chains, many hours later, Auda collapsed in the corridor. Her flesh was pulled taut over her bones and ached even to touch. Through a feverish haze, she remembered being pulled to her feet by her injured arms.

She didn't know if she cried out then, but later she sobbed in the cell as a woman dabbed at her wounds with a moistened cloth.

Visit Five: she quivered before the archbishop, but her answers were still the same.

"Where did you meet the devil-worshipers you made paper for? Did they teach you to write those words? Do you believe their heresies that Jesus never lived on this earth?"

No, no, no!

The archbishop shook his head with a sad look.

"I don't want to send you underground again. I *am* trying to help you. I've no wish to lose your soul. But I can only help you if you confess and repent. I don't know how else to make you see."

Yet still she would not say the lies he wanted to hear. She no longer even knew what she wanted, only that she would not sacrifice someone else to save herself. Her eyes traveled to the paper tract he held in front of him. Was it hers? She could see flashes of color on the inside. Which one was it? It didn't matter.

She wrote with a shaky hand on the parchment he'd provided.

Who gave you this?

His blue eyes narrowed. "If you answer my questions, I will tell you. Only three questions, you have my word."

She nodded without pause.

"Have you seen this tract before?"

Her eyes roved over *The Priest's Vice.* Yes, it was hers. She gave a quick nod.

"Do you know what's written upon it?"

Another nod.

"Will you tell me who commanded you to write such ugly tales? You say your tales carry the message—who then taught you thus?"

She looked him full in the face. Frowning, she placed her hand to her own chest.

He stood abruptly, snatching the tract from the table, and walked toward the door. Auda cried out and he turned around.

"This was given to me by someone who is concerned for you. If you want to know more, you must stop lying. You won't have many more chances. Even now the inquisitor demands you for himself!"

Someone concerned. Who else could it be but her sister? The revelation should have shaken her to the bone. But Auda thought of her father and felt nothing but sadness. Had her sister thought, as Auda did, that the verses would bring him freedom? It was a good trade, her life for his.

Visit Six: the guards took her to the underground prison. Her contusions, only partially healed, stung with pain as she was shackled to the wall again.

"She'll not survive this," one guard said, fastening a metal collar around her neck.

Auda lifted her head and girded herself. Maybe today would be the day she died. At least she would die without succumbing, without betraying herself or anyone else further.

The other guard shrugged. "The Devil's Fork won't pierce her heart or her core." The device looked like a double-ended fork fastened under a metal collar that held her head straight. One end poked against her upper chest, the other against her chin. The guard put his hand on her head and pushed down hard. The fork rammed into her flesh at both ends.

Auda screamed. Beyond the guards, beyond the pain, Elena

danced across her vision. She reached toward her mother with shackled hands.

Warm blood dripped onto her dress. Clamping her lips together, she screwed her eyes near shut. A black haze encroached her eyesight. The poppy scent of Elena's hair tickled her nose.

The guard gouged the fork in deeper. Auda sobbed, a wave of pain and nausea overtaking her. She struggled to open her eyes, to see her mother's ghostly face smiling upon her.

"Thumb up to say you recant," the guard said.

"Recant and give us names," the second whispered, "and we can release you."

Elena's voice was also a whisper.

Smile, daughter, and their pain will never touch you.

She kept her fists clenched, her body rigid.

When she awoke, she found herself back in the upper room of the tower, curled on a coarse bed of hay. Blood clotted where the fork had pierced her chin and chest. The wounds, packed with herbs and coated in a balm, still burned. The drafts of bitter wind from the window were her only distraction.

Someone came each day, with food, which she did not crave, and water, which she did. A nun, garbed from head to feet in white linen, inspected her wounds, cleaning them and packing more herbs into them. She came several times, speaking only to say prayers.

Days or weeks later, a guard entered with a bucket of water. Auda opened her parched mouth to drink in the cool liquid as he dumped it over her body. Someone else had brought dried bread and moldy cheese, but she could not see through her swollen eyes who pushed the food into her mouth.

Eventually she regained some of her strength, could sit

up on the floor, even look around. Her next visitor, when he came, was the tall blond man who had arrested her father. Dressed in a dark black robe and matching skullcap, he crouched beside her.

"Do you know who I am?" He did not wait for a reply. "I am an inquisitor, *your* inquisitor. It was by my decree that you were sent to the Chamber. It was not my intent that the torture go this far. Only that you should use the pain to clarify your thoughts."

Auda couldn't see his face through her dim vision, but she imagined a skeletal frame, haunted eyes deep in their sockets, an eerie paleness to his skin. A devil, sent to frighten the children.

His voice was deep and somber. "So you are the White Witch. I have heard much about you, have sought those like you. I should tell you that the last prisoner under the fork was your father. His blood is mingled with yours. As it should be."

A sob bubbled within her throat. Was this the man who wrote a book on witches and demons? It had to be. Good. It would end with her.

The inquisitor nodded. "We will talk now. I will learn some things from you." Opening a roll of parchment, he began, "You are accused as a heretic, that you have been taught, and teach others, beliefs against those of the Holy Church. Are you guilty of this?"

She shook her head once, crying out against the pain in her neck.

He looked again at the parchment. "Have you heard of faiths other than those of our Mother Church?"

She paused, then nodded, careful to keep her head rigid.

"Have you listened to their words?"

She swayed.

"Do you believe as they teach?"

She shook her head under a wave of pain. Straightening, she shook it again. She'd burn if that's what was in store for her, but never would she condemn anyone else to this terror.

His voice rose as he let the parchment roll up. "Your archbishop believes you, he says in his notes. He says you are a fool, a *bête*, but innocent."

Auda nodded with emphasis, crying out again. The pain stabbed into her like a knife.

"Perhaps." The inquisitor sat back with a puzzled frown. "But then where did these words come from? That you can read and write, you've already admitted to. That your soul is in peril," he gestured at her hair and her eyes, "it is plain to see. Admit who taught you to write this and we will cleanse the heresy you have wrought!"

She closed her eyes, tears staining her dirty cheeks, and reached out. The words were hers alone. Why would no one believe her?

"Answer me this," the inquisitor demanded. "Do you believe in the Holy Trinity, the Father, Son, and the Holy Ghost? Do you believe Jesus came to us in body and spirit, to save us from our sins? Do you believe in His Church, your Holy Mother?"

She nodded, collapsing into a fit of tears.

"Why then do your words speak of heresy? Why do you write your lies that malign the Church and demonize the Lord?"

She closed her eyes and let him speak.

"Even if the archbishop does not see the heresy in your words, I do. You speak against physical love, lusty and carnal, and for love of the spirit. Is this not what the heretics have taught you? *Love God, hate the world.*" His lips twisted into a sneer.

Faced with a world like this, it was easy to love God. And her family, and Jaime—anyone who had thought to love her. Love, be it carnal or spiritual, earthly or heavenly, was a far better answer than the fear and hate this man brought.

Peace washed over her as Jaime's words ran through her head—God only expected them to live their lives the best they could. And so she was.

The inquisitor bent to cup her chin and pull her face upward. "Your own words condemn you. It is your script, your mark on the page. All that remains is for you to name your accomplices, your teachers in this madness."

Her, only her. She looked back at him defiantly.

He turned back to the guards. "Block the window. I won't have her sending messages to her cohorts."

They covered the small window slit with two layers of oil-cloth until the room was shrouded in shadows.

The inquisitor glared at her. "You'll never leave this cell to spread your heresies anymore. I'll burn you in front of the very town that protected you. And then your father and your sister too!"

She forced herself to stare at him without buckling. They couldn't think Poncia had anything to do with her verse, nor her father. It had to end with her.

She made the motion of writing.

The inquisitor narrowed his eyes at her. He snapped his fingers and the guards brought an inked quill and parchment. Sitting at the table, she fumbled with the nib. Her fingers moved in stiff awkwardness.

"If you have something to say, be quick with it."

Auda firmed her back and scratched her words out, letter

by letter, line by line. The effort left a thin film of sweat on her forehead. Finally, she laid the quill down, and the inquisitor snatched the parchment and read aloud.

> *It is no truth I was taught, but learned on my own.*
> *Women are no less than men. Men no less than God.*
> *We are all things of beauty.*
> *And we all make our own choices.*

If that didn't convince him of her heresy, nothing else would.

The inquisitor snarled, dropping the parchment. Clutching her with the strength of Colossus, picking her up by the shoulders and dangling her as a doll. She didn't resist, her head lolling to one side. He'd acted just as she'd predicted, taking her words as a challenge to break her instead of hunting elsewhere.

"No matter. I will get what I want in the end." He sucked in his breath and strode out the door.

Fever overtook Auda. Her mother came to her in her dreams, black eyes staring from the face of Jaime's fisherwoman.

Just as dawn broke and the room grew lighter, she sat up and crawled to her bed of hay. Searching through the dried straw, her fingers curled around a thin stick. She pulled it out. It was only a twig, but it would have to do. Careful not to snap the callow branch, she sharpened it against the wall.

She dipped the pen in the water, murky now with blood and dirt. The mark she made was thin and uneven, but it would suffice.

She wrote her words on the reverse side of the parchment the inquisitor had left on the ground. There would be no chance to make corrections. She thought of her verse. Which suitor would the girl choose? Auda no longer cared. This verse was meant for her alone. She squinted, steadying her hand.

It took her an hour to write the simple lines.

> *Dark hearts masked by strong deeds, words, 'n' coin,*
> *Hold no candle to the one I want.*
> *Neither Lion, nor Griffin nor Jackal shall I choose,*
> *But my Own Love, the Beauty in my heart.*

Chapter Thirty-seven

Regaining strength from her resolve, Auda hobbled around her filthy cell, still shrouded in darkness. She poked two tiny holes in the layers of cloth covering her window and struggled to line the holes up.

She swore, leaning her head further to the side. The wounds in her neck throbbed in pain. She inched the top layer of the window covering into a bunch until the holes were aligned, and peered through.

She couldn't discern much in the harsh sunlight. Someone was imprisoned in the main square, probably in stocks or a pillory. It was a woman, from the sound of the screams. Auda imagined the wooden stocks were stained with the woman's blood; each time a passing boy threw something—a rock or dead rat—at her, the wretch wailed.

"I heard no heresy, I swear!"

Above her, a lone falcon shrieked.

Carts bearing the bones of the dead and the partial bodies of the wounded rolled through the streets. Auda craned her neck to hear. These were the warriors from the Shepherd's Crusade, the town crier declared, fallen soldiers from a war against France's own Jews that neither king nor pope had sanctioned. Denied the true targets of their vengeful folly, the warriors had fallen upon each other, the crier in the square said. Blood, it seemed, was the nourishment of the day. As each cart bearing the fallen rolled by, Auda imagined she could see their vacant faces. They all bore the visage of her poor father.

Some time later, the door to the room swung open and the guard kicked in another prisoner, a hunched figure cloaked in dirty brown. The creature collapsed on the ground as the guard slammed the door shut and locked it.

"Help me," he whispered reedily, clutching at the cloak that was drawn too tight around its neck.

Auda limped to the hooded prisoner. Her fingers fumbling over the thick knots of the cloak's drawstrings, she unbuttoned it along the front and peeled the tattered cloth from his body.

Her eyes fell to the brown cloak, cast off like dead skin. She moved closer, picked it up and turned it in her hands. A cross of yellow cloth was sewn onto the poor material. Broad and bright, for everyone to see.

The cross of the heretic.

She gasped and moved to the man, ripping off his hood. It was René. A fresh contusion swelled on his right temple. One of his eyes had exploded, was flat and crusted in blood. Red scratches ringed the other. His skin was pale gray, hanging in folds around his eyes and the ridges of his head.

Auda pushed away her revulsion. Even after everything she had been through, the sight of her bruised friend sickened her to nausea.

She put a hand to his forehead. It was hot and sweaty.

He jerked back. "Don't touch me," he said in a hoarse voice. "It is not meet—"

Auda murmured a muffled sound.

"Auda?" he said, leaning closer. A faint smile managed to cross his lips. "I'd not thought to see you again."

She propped his head in her lap, despite his protests, wishing she still had water. Even a befouled bucket of piss water such as the last one they'd brought would be welcome now.

René's lips were parched, but he tried to speak. "I saw you when they found you. I tried to reach you, but I was too late. Someone saw me, I am sure of it. They followed me, but I got away. I went to the market a few days later, to speak to your artist. They grabbed me then. They knew to look for me. I wasn't brought here right away, but I am glad they brought me so I could see you."

Her cheeks burned in shame, but she made no sound. Another innocent caught because of her. And René *was* an innocent. Yes, he believed things the Church decried, but this man had never hurt another, never would. He would not lie or pretend to be something other than who he was.

His voice grew somber. "I think I have little time left on this earth. No, don't fear for me," he insisted when she let out a soft cry. "I go to a better place, to be in the arms of God." A glaze came over his open eye. He blinked, then frowned.

"I must take the *consolamentum*. Please, Auda, you must help me."

She shook her head. How could she help him?

"Please. I need an object. Something important. Something I can imbue the Spirit with."

She cast about the room for something, anything. Her eyes fell upon the plain wooden crucifix on the wall, adorned by a simple carving of Jesus. Shifting René's weight to the wall, she climbed on the table to retrieve it.

When he saw what she had in her hands, he shook his head. "It's sacrilege, Auda. Jesus was not a God born on this earth."

Puckering her lips, she twisted the carving until it came apart and threw the figure aside. She twisted a splinter off the cross and handed it to him.

René clutched the wood to his chest. "It's the Spirit I venerate," he said and held it closer. He moaned. "This is not right. I need the *perfecti* to give me the *consolamentum*."

God will understand, she thought furiously.

René jerked as if he'd heard. He closed his eyes and whispered.

"Benedicite. Benedicite. Benedicite."

His voice grew distinct as he chanted the Lord's Prayer. He could barely shape the words between his bruised, swollen lips. And yet the prayer was loud and clear. He said it again and again until his voice was a croak.

"I promise never to kill, to lust, after the body or material things. I promise never to glorify the flesh, not the body of Christ on the cross, who came to this earth only in Spirit. Neither meat nor cheese nor milk nor eggs shall pass my lips henceforth. Neither shall water nor fish. Forgive my trespasses and lead me to a good end. Dear God, lead me to a good end."

René's voice became a whisper. It wasn't until he grew silent that Auda turned and noticed the inquisitor watching from a shutter in the door.

Chapter Thirty-eight

The guards ushered René and Auda out of the room, each in a separate direction. She stretched out a hand toward René, but the guard slapped her back. Where were they taking him?

The guard prodded her outside toward the holding cell. Daylight, though filtered through the shroud of heavy rain clouds, pierced her eyes.

The sores on her neck broke and bled. A thick paste covered the welts, but still she cried when the guard shoved her into an open prison crammed with people. The cell was above ground, in the main square, near the Giles keep. Normally only half filled with petty criminals and the poor who hadn't paid their tenant fees and tithes, the cell was now full to burst. Prisoners teemed toward the bars separating them from freedom, sticking their hands out to grasp what could be theirs, pleading with family and friends to pay their release.

Auda crawled to the front and knelt in the shade to see outside. From the cell she could see the whole of the square. It had been a woman held prisoner in the square. They'd nailed her by her ears to a pillory, no doubt for repeating ill words she'd

heard somewhere. A crowd had gathered, quiet and apprehensive. Their words were hushed, their movements muted.
Where was René?

The clang of chains caught her attention. A procession of
men and some women walked across the stage, led by three
pairs of guards, each armed with a halberd. Some of the prisoners tripped, while others lagged against the rusty chains
binding their arms and legs. The clink sounded like bones rattling against each other. Auda shuddered.

The guards stopped the condemned midway across the stage
and the archbishop stepped onto the dais, flanked by clergymen, dressed all in white, and the inquisitor, all in black. The
archbishop was the first to speak.

"For crimes of heresy and thoughts against our Church,"
he began, "the condemned who have repented are forthwith
instructed to wear the yellow cross of the heretic upon their
clothes at all times, so all may know their crimes and trust
or mistrust their words and deeds as is just. The cross must
never be taken off or punishment of trial by fire. The Lord
will be watching." He brandished a parchment roll and read
off names followed by crimes in his sonorous voice. Relief
rose in cries after each name.

Auda watched the archbishop's mouth move. More than
ever, he seemed like a puppet. Did he truly believe all these
people guilty? Or had he condemned them because the inquisitor expected it? Were they all puppets of some grander
scheme, players with no choice?

"For more grievous sins, the Church condemns the following to life imprisoned." Again he read a list of names and
crimes, and this time there was no relief in the moans.

"Guillaume Martis, guilty of housing two heretics, giving
them food and comfort. Simon de Montbleu, guilty of errone-

ous thought and desecration of the Mass. Tibout d'Orion—"
The list seemed endless.

Finally the archbishop finished. He seemed to droop, as
though his bones grew waxen and melted. Yet perhaps it was
a trick of the light, for when he spoke, it was in the same rich
voice.

"Bring the prisoner."

The guards who had herded in the chained procession now
ushered them out quickly. They returned with a single man,
shackled at the ankles and wrists. A thick, coarse sack covered
his face.

A guard ripped the cloth from the prisoner's head, revealing a bruised face, an eye that squinted against the diffuse afternoon light, lips that quivered without sound. He tripped,
nearly falling. The crowd jeered in unison.

"René Lacis, you are brought here for thoughts and deeds
of heresy, for schooling others against our Holy Church and
the teachings of God and His Son," the archbishop said. "Evidence against you has been heard by a jury of law experts
and judges, consuls of the *vicomte*, noblemen, myself, and the
inquisitor of Carcassonne. For the last time, do you repent
your sins?"

The crowd was hushed, but René said nothing. Of course
he wouldn't. Auda's heart sank.

The archbishop sighed. "The Church has no recourse but
to declare you a heretic, and relax you to the secular arm. May
God have mercy on your soul."

The *vicomte*, looking like a stranger in a strange scene,
rose to the dais in jerky movements. His voice shook when he
spoke. "For the sin of heresy, René Lacis is sentenced to death
by burning."

Auda sagged against the wall. She closed her eyes and lifted her face to heaven. The heretics had it right after all—people did bear a duality, but it was not in their spirits and bodies. It was all in their psyches, the push between competing wills. The *vicomte* with his love of his town that lived alongside his debauchery; the archbishop with his love for his flock's souls that blinded him to the truth; even the inquisitor, who saw things only in terms of good and evil, never in nuances or mistakes.

And Auda, who never believed she was truly in danger, but who had brought danger to everyone around her.

The crowd rustled in anticipation. Auda blinked, unable to see clearly. But she couldn't look away.

The guards bound her friend's torso and legs to the pole with thick ropes, and his head and neck with a chain. Some-one pulled on the chain until he choked. Auda cried out over the jeers that filled the air.

Other guards on the platform piled dry faggots around him, until the wood was heaped nearly to his chin. Still René did nothing. Auda pushed against the prisoners in the cell who were crowding her so they could see better. She screamed at them all until, frightened, they moved aside.

At last, two executioners came forward and lit the dry wood. The blaze caught immediately. René coughed on the swirls of smoke. His eyes were too far away to read.

The smell of the burning flesh hit her before René's screams. It was an oily stench that roiled out of the flames in black columns of smoke, thick and greasy under the acrid reek of burned hair. Her throat grew hoarse as she cried for her friend, her keening rising as his shrieks faded. Long after his screams stopped and his slumped head was shrouded in haze, her lament hung on the fat-soaked air.

Chapter Thirty-nine

𝕬𝖚𝖉𝖆 𝖘𝖕𝖔𝖙𝖙𝖊𝖉 𝕻𝖔𝖓𝖈𝖎𝖆 through tear-stained eyes just as the older girl saw her. Poncia rushed to the metal bars, reaching for her. Auda sidled to the far end of the cell, where fewer prisoners crowded the gate. Her sister looked well, dressed in warm finery.

Poncia drew in her breath in horror. "What have they done to you?" Her fingers trailed over the scars under Auda's chin and along her neck.

Auda shrugged, willing away her own tears just as they spilled from her sister's eyes. After so much scorn and abuse, Poncia's gentleness hurt to bear.

Poncia's hands caressed Auda's dirtied face, fluttered over her greasy hair and swollen lips. She rubbed her own face against Auda's rough palms.

"I can't believe I've found you. I've been looking for you each day! They've told us nothing about you. Someone said on burning days, they bring the prisoners out here. It's God's will that I found you."

Auda's fingers stumbled over themselves? *Papa? Jaime?* She had to be certain they were safe.

But Poncia rushed on to other things.

"What do you need? What can I give to you? Wait—" She looked around, noting the guard patrolling the road in front of the prison. The other prisoners stared at them with fear. When the guard looked away, she handed Auda a linen bag.

"Tuck it under your skirt," she whispered, glaring at the nearby prisoners. "Just things from the market—a round of cheese, a mince pie, some nuts and dried fruit."

Hiding the treasures in the dirty folds of her dress, Auda reached for her sister's warm hands again. Poncia drew Auda's fingers into the warmth of her coat, resting them on her belly.

"Auda, I—"

Auda interrupted. *Papa. Tell me. Well?*

"Papa. Auda—" Poncia's blue eyes brimmed again.

What? Tell! Her fingers felt clumsy.

"Heaven will keep him for us."

Auda reeled back. No, her sister had to be mistaken. So many people had been working for his release. What had happened?

A fat tear rolled down her cheek. *How? When?*

"He was sick, so ill with fever and infection. I wish—" Poncia hiccupped on a sob. "I didn't mean for it to happen this way. It was an accident."

What? What had her sister said?

Poncia didn't look up. "The tract, Auda. Why did you keep it?"

Auda's hands froze in the middle of repeating her question.

"Why?" Poncia's words were halted, edged with sobs. "I gave it to you to see the error of your ways, so you'd know firsthand the danger you courted. Why did you not just burn it?"

Auda stared at her. So she had been right. But why had Poncia done it, given the archbishop her writings?

Poncia's face paled, twisting away from Auda's glare. "I didn't mean to. I took those things from the house to save you! I meant to burn them as soon as I was alone. But Jehan surprised me. He wanted to make amends for beating me. He came with the archbishop." Her voice broke.

"The archbishop saw that I was reading and asked to see what captivated my attention so. When he realized," again her voice skipped, "it was too late. I had to tell him. I could have told them the truth, that I had gotten the tract from Jehan's parents and the rest was the rubbish of a wild imagination. But I was so scared. There was too much evidence that could be found against Jehan and his family. And me. And Father had nothing to blacken his name. I thought they would just release him." She pleaded with her eyes for Auda to understand.

Auda wanted to spit at her sister's feet but she could not make herself move.

"I asked the archbishop to help Papa, help you. Papa was an innocent, I know. The archbishop knew it too. But then the inquisitor came." Poncia trembled as her hands caressed her belly. "God saw my efforts to save you, at least."

Auda closed her eyes. They had all stumbled into danger, their father, Auda, her sister. Poncia was the only one so quick to absolve herself.

"Papa is gone," Poncia repeated in a quivering voice. "But at least his soul is safe, at peace now. He is with Maman."

Sucking in her breath, Auda slashed at her sister's perfect face with ragged nails.

Poncia stumbled backward, bringing her own hand up to the three thin scratches in her cheek that slowly welled with blood.

Behind her, Jehan moved closer to caress his wife's shoulders, whispering to her. "Auda—" Jehan started.

Auda glared at him. She dropped Poncia's sack of food, moving away so other prisoners could fight over it. The restless crowd was dispersing now that the burning was over. It could have been her father up there. Or her. It still could be.

Jehan shook his head. "She didn't want darkness to touch her family," he mumbled. "She didn't see what I did in the Church, didn't see its rotting core. And I did too little to help. Oh, I didn't turn the Good Men to your father but they found him anyway. I should have warned him." His shoulders sagged. "Have pity on her. It has been difficult, hiding my parents, and seeing you and your father on the same road. She thought with her heart."

Auda turned away, her breath wavering. The anger welling in her chest had nowhere to go.

"Please, Auda. Can you not show her any mercy?" He turned an anguished gaze toward the crowd where Poncia was waiting, still wracked with sobs. "She is with child. She is your family. And you are all the family she has left. She loves you."

Auda stared at her sister. Reaching into her bodice, she pulled out the verse she'd written and pressed it into Jehan's hands, jerking her chin at her sister. Whether he gave the verse to Poncia or not, whether her sister even read it or understood, didn't matter anymore.

Chapter Forty

𝔖ometime in the middle of the night, the bolt on the door of the cell unlatched. Auda opened her eyes into the brightness of moonlight. Putting up a hand against its incandescence, she struggled to sit up. A shadow crept into the room and, before she could scream, clamped a hand tight over her mouth.

Struggling, she bit into fingers rough with calluses. The grip around her tightened.

"Shhh! I won't hurt you!" a whisper hissed out.

She knew that voice, how could she not? Rising above the damp odor of the cell, the familiar scent of charcoal and paint danced in the air. She relaxed.

Jaime released her, turning her around to face him. Removing a dark scarf from around his face, he reached out a finger to stroke her dirty cheek.

He was tall, too tall for her to see without moving her injured head. She held a hand to the bruises in her neck and stared at him, wide-eyed. What was he doing here?

"They've hurt you," he said in a gruff voice, crouching beside her. "Shhh." He followed her eyes to the door and shook his head. "It's not safe to leave. Not yet. The signal will come, we must wait for it."

Auda trembled. Drawing her arms around her chest, she stared at this phantom man who stood before her. Her memories of him seemed like they belonged to someone else, in another lifetime.

Jaime cocked his head toward the door. "We've planned a distraction. The city's a mess. The river has flooded and the town is awash. This is the time. Rubea is watching—it was her idea to gain entry as a girl of the night. I didn't know how else to get to you."

His forehead, which she could see only in profile, furrowed. "I've searched every day for you, for any bit of news. The town's been rioting. The archbishop has been put aside. The inquisitor is in charge now."

Auda watched through swollen eyes, understanding little of what he said. She focused instead on his voice, the warmth of his familiar tone. She wished she could envelop herself in it.

Jaime crouched beside her, stroking her face. "I've failed you," he said, his voice cracking. "But I will never forsake you. Listen. There is a plan. We'll sneak out of here to a meeting point by the new scriptorium. I have a cart waiting for us."

Auda struggled to follow the conversation. When she was gone, who would they go after next? Poncia?

Sister? she signed. But before he could answer, a thin scream split the air. Jaime stood and ran into the corridor.

"The river!" someone yelled.

He came back for her. "Come, we have to leave!"

Auda hesitated only for a second. Her father was dead. She thought of her sister, of the babe within her, praying Jehan would keep them safe.

Entwining her hand in his, Jaime led her along a long corridor and down a dark flight of stairs. In the hallway, they rushed toward a group of guards and priests, jostling about the narrow passage. Auda turned her face, her heartbeat so loud she wondered it didn't eclipse the commotion. But they didn't look at her, didn't even notice her. They were too concerned with getting out.

"The river's silted up," someone said behind her.

"It's the mountains, they've overflowed!"

"No, it's the dam, she's broke—"

"God fails us!"

Jaime plunged through the gaps in the crowd, dragging her with him. They squeezed into gaps in the crowd and made their way toward the door.

Outside, amid the thronging crowd, the air smelled fresh, wet with rain and fury. Lightning cracked overhead. Its thunder roared, like the voice of God.

They waded into the road among the others milling outside the keep with nowhere to go. The river had flooded and now it seemed to be washing the town away. Water rose to Auda's knees, her waist, threatening to wash her away also.

The water surged with power. Another wave engulfed her and she lost Jaime's grip. She flailed as her head went under the water. Kicking desperately, she pushed with her arms and sought anything that would propel her to air. She hit something and grabbed on to it. It was the platform upon which René had burned. The wooden legs of the dais were already buckling under the weight of the people clinging to it.

Auda's feet slipped as she fought to push herself upright. Bodies of the young and elderly floated among the rats in the water. In each corpse, she saw the face of her father. She coughed, throat and eyes burning. She was surrounded by stragglers, but where was Jaime? She couldn't see anything clearly.

"Help!" a man's voice rang out, familiar and strange all at once.

Auda turned to see someone perched on a precarious wooden slat at the far end of the platform. The inquisitor. A rough current rushed past him. She squinted to see better. If she climbed the palace steps from higher ground, she could reach him. But should she save him?

Jaime surfaced, not far from her. "Auda!" he yelled, reaching out.

She turned back to the inquisitor. She had to help him. It had to end somewhere.

Pointing at the struggling man, she turned her back on Jaime and started moving toward the palace steps.

"No, Auda!" She could hear the telltale hatred and desperation in Jaime's voice as he understood whom she was going to help.

A sudden wave surged, dragging Auda into its waters. The current threw the inquisitor from his raft. She saw his black cloak swirling on the surface.

Feeling herself sink, she tried to clutch at what remained of the podium. Her lungs burned to breathe. The river was violent, its fury raging and rushing, grabbing at her. *We know you*, the waters sang to Auda. *We've tasted you before.*

She pushed hard, at the voices and the bodies around her. Even in the darkness she could tell she was being carried under and downstream. She struggled to keep her pace.

With a final gasp for air, she clenched her muscles and brought her knees to her chest. She searched for the surface but couldn't tell which way to swim. Her hand brushed against skin, another person searching for leverage. Arms grabbed at her, pushing her under.

The chill of the water melted into her skin, so cold. Her limbs failed. *Sleep with us*, the river tempted her. It would be so easy to let go, to be carried into a blissful slumber here and end her misery. A heavy weight pulled at her. But this time Auda pushed back. Back, ahead, arms and legs, she pulled herself forward.

Crawling on top of stone blocks breaking the water, she scrabbled toward shore. She spotted the inquisitor, still hanging on, and yelled at him. He looked up and saw her. His lips curled in revulsion but he reached out.

She stretched her arm and grasped him. They locked hands. She strained to pull him toward her. Just then Jaime appeared beside her and joined his grasp with hers. With one heave, they dragged the man to the steps. Auda spared him a moment's look and then Jaime tugged her away.

She looked at him in gratitude.

"Not for him, but for you," he said, putting a finger to her lips. "Always for you."

In the darkness, strangers helped them find their footing. Auda pointed toward the city heights. They headed into the residential streets, where the water level dropped, a slow climb up the gentle hill. Over her shoulder, Auda saw the gray waters run down the way they had come, leaving behind only muddy dregs. Yes, this was the best choice. There were more people in the streets now, others with the same idea.

"The river's changed course," someone said behind them.

"The town has drowned!"

"We need to find the scriptorium," Jaime said. He cast about. "I've a cart waiting."

Auda looked at him, startled. That's right, there had been a plan. Looking at the city once more, she saw torches moving in erratic paths against the ebb and sway of the river.

Somewhere out there were Poncia and Jehan. But not her father.

She turned her back on the lights, forging further up the hill.

The scriptorium. But the whole bourg seemed underwater. She had no idea where it was being built, which direction to even look.

As she vacillated in the wind, something caught her eye: a pelican flying overhead. Determined to keep it in sight, she tugged at Jaime's hand and followed its path to an arch above the door of a small church. Moving closer, she could see intricate incisions chiseled into the marble crescent, a manticore, a basilisk. Etched on the door was a quill and bottle of ink.

Half finished and with no roof, it stood pummeled by the rain. She dropped Jaime's hand and rushed toward it. On the other side, a small hill rested under a short break in the clouds. A gray silhouette stood in the waning light. The cart.

She turned her face up to the sky and in the dim light caught sight of the pelican, flying away. Half laughing, half crying, she tracked its flight until it disappeared.

Then Jaime came up beside her, laughing too as he drew her into his arms, and she was alone no more.

Here the Inquisitors show mercy, enjoin penances and impose sentences according to the merits or demerits of the persons.

—Bernardo Gui,
Practica inquisitionis heretice pravitatis

Part V
Winter 1322

Chapter Forty-one

They settled in a small town inhabited mostly by simple monks.

Auda sat by the open window in their one-room cottage, penning the last line of her verse on a smooth sheet of paper. She scrawled her name on the bottom with a flourish, laid the quill on her workbench, then blew on the page to dry the ink. Her father's watermark peeked out in the early morning light. She smiled.

"Such zeal," Jaime said, laughing. He winked at her from his easel, where he sketched a scene of two boys fighting with wooden swords. His fingers, blackened with charcoal, worked quickly over the paper canvas.

Looking at the new drawing over his shoulder, Auda snorted. But the drawing delighted her. It had taken some time for Jaime to start sketching happier scenes like this one. His melancholy still lingered, right under the surface, in the sadness of his eyes or the tender way he looked at her sometimes, as if she would break. But it dominated him less and less each day.

Setting down his charcoal, Jaime rubbed his hands in a cloth moistened with sage oil. "Are you ready?"

Auda nodded. As he went outside to wash up in a barrel of rainwater, she looked out their window. They had been lucky to find this small village, tucked between the limestone gorges. In the days after Narbonne's flood, she and Jaime had journeyed uphill, hauling only the donkey-led cart that carried their few possessions—his paints and what sketches he grabbed from his room, and Martin's favored mould and deckle, their watermark still attached to it.

"It was a simple funeral, but fitting," Jaime told her the only time they spoke of it.

Providence had brought them here, Brother Calvet said. Certainly Jaime had not planned to stop in this tiny town. Wherever they might be headed, it certainly was not a town steeped in monastic life. Auda was, however, feverish from infection and tossing in the back of the empty cart. When she began to cough up blood, Jaime had no choice. It was already well into the night when the cart creaked into the meager village of St. Chinian in the Hérault district.

The watch guard had sent for Brother Calvet, who looked once at Auda's writhing body and went for the monastery's healer, Brother Jaufres. Jaime paced the halls that night and the next, until finally the healer announced that she'd passed out of danger.

"There's room enough here for a couple wearied of life's cruelties," Brother Calvet said a few days later, when Jaime inquired about payment. "We have need of a gardener to tend to the vegetables and herbs for our daily meals," he said to Jaime, who was worrying over Auda's wounds. "If you and your wife would like the work, we will give you lodging and food."

He asked nothing about the state they'd arrived in, who had inflicted Auda's wounds and why. But when he smiled at her, there was a knowing sadness in his eyes.

"Till our debt is paid and she's fit for travel," Jaime agreed, not telling him he and Auda weren't married. Not in any traditional way.

"Work is prayer," the priest said.

Later, that night, Jaime and Auda made a pledge to each other. If the Inquisition found them, if they were still looking for her, they agreed, they'd flee before the Church ravaged this secluded town. Each single deed, they knew, had its own consequence, its own reward—she'd learned that from René. And from the inquisitor.

That had been over a year ago. Though neither admitted it, they had grown comfortable in this simple town of priests who, when not at prayer, worked the vineyards that lay around their monastery. Herdsmen drove their sheep across the green fields that covered the foothills beyond town, selling their wool for fair prices in the town's marketplace. At night, Jaime sometimes regaled the town's children with Auda's stories while she looked on in amusement.

Soon word of their arrival spread, and other monks came bearing paints for Jaime and, when they learned of her skill, old rags for Auda. The cloths sat unused in a corner of their cottage. A few months later, the pope in Avignon sent word to his churches that he needed large quantities of "cloth parchment."

No, was Auda's only word on the subject. To Jaime. To Brother Calvet. She had no desire to use what her father taught

her to help the men who'd killed him. But when Brother Jaufres entreated, she frowned over the valerian root she was
planting in the church garden.

"We had a papermaker once, but he's long since passed
away," the monk explained. "The monies the pope offers will
go toward feeding the poor in the next town. And to fix our
leaky roof." He watched her hands. Intrigued by her gestures,
he'd learned to recognize a few words.

Sighing, Auda nodded. *For you.*

With the Brother's help, it took her only a few weeks to get
her workshop started. Someday, she thought she might build
a barn to act as her studio, where she could keep a larger vat
and more barrels for linens. She made a new watermark for
the effort, an image of a fish in memory of René, his religion,
and the lessons she had learned from them. No ladders. No
bridges.

Now Auda moved from the window to her workbench and
unwrapped a square of brown cloth, counting out fifty small
slips of paper from the latest batch. She'd bleached them in the
sun until they were a pure white, then cut them to size with a
sharp blade. The script on the pages was all the same:

Indulgentia a Culpa et a Poena

Underneath was a line for the penitent's name, and for his
list of sins. The thin trace of the piscine watermark was barely
visible.

She searched under her pallet, where a signed and sealed
indulgence was stored in an oilskin parcel. She'd thought to
burn it when it arrived, unasked for, as payment for the town's
papermaker who'd made such fine wares. Auda snorted,
wondering what the pope would say if he knew whom he'd

absolved. She'd resolved to burn the worthless scrap, yet somehow, the time for burning had never seemed to come.

Drawing out a wooden box, she stacked her new batch of indulgences inside and nailed the lid shut. Putting it in a linen sack that she slung over her shoulder, she joined Jaime outside.

"The decorations are well done this year," he said as they strolled down the cobblestone path to the monastery. Holly, laurel, and ivy bedecked the town, while simple carols from the monastery choir broke through the thin mountain air. Stalls along the main road sold strong drinks made of honey, ale, and spices, along with humble pies made of venison.

Every morning Jaime bought her faerie floss, spun colored sugar that hung like gossamer on a wooden straw. When she laughed, he only said, "Two weeks more of this indulgence, and then it's onto the new year."

Leading their way into the main hall of the monastery, Auda left the box with Brother Calvet, who would send it to the pope. Then they wandered to outside the rear of the building, along a rivulet that further downhill joined the great Hérault River.

It was a favorite path of theirs, a dirt road that followed the creek down through town and ended at the threshold of their small cottage. Birds chirped unseen from the bushes and trees along the path.

"The trade routes no longer go through Narbonne," Jaime remarked, his voice nonchalant.

Auda stopped. She knew he had sent messages asking for word of the area, what had happened after the flood. He'd never talked to her about it before, and she'd never asked.

"The flood ruined the town's commerce. The port has silted up and the river has changed its course." He shrugged and pulled at her hand to keep walking. "The old Narbonne is gone."

Auda swallowed, nodding. They hadn't spoken of what had happened in the months between her father's arrest and the flood. What he knew, he did not share; what she knew, she would not. She wondered what had happened to the inquisitor, whether he had survived the flood. She even felt a twinge of pity for the *vicomte*, who'd looked so broken the day he had condemned René to burn, and the *vicomtesse*, whom Auda had so easily betrayed. But that life seemed so far away now, nothing to do with her.

Jaime slowed his pace, eyes straight on their path. "Your sister raises a boy," he said after a moment. "He's healthy and hale. They've named him Martin Aude."

Auda bit back tears at the sound of her father's name. Strange that she only felt mercy for her sister, a sad compassion for the life she'd chosen. They'd made mistakes, all of them—Poncia's were just nearer to the surface. Someday perhaps Auda would go back to see her, to hold her nephew and teach him his letters. But for now it was better that Poncia thought her gone, drowned or killed. Safer, for both of them.

Tugging Jaime off the path, she turned toward the creek. The river had been with her all her life, a giver and taker of life. Now it somehow just seemed like an old friend.

"Are you ready?" Jaime repeated, a smile curving the edges of his lips.

With an eager smile, she reached into her sack and pulled out a bottle, into which she'd stuffed her latest verse. *The Crow's Delight*, written for the innocence of a child and scribed on one of her remaining pages with her father's watermark. An identical copy of the tale lay in her chest, illustrated with Jaime's drawings. She kept a copy of everything she wrote, to be sewn into a book later. The time for her brand of song had not yet come, but when it did, her verses would be ready.

Jaime bowed with a flourish and, without another moment's hesitation, she dropped the bottle into the water. The package bobbed with the current, maneuvering around fallen branches and jutting rocks until it disappeared into the distance.

Who will find it? The words were part of their ritual.

"A lonely girl with three spiteful sisters and a biting chicken," he said this time, "desperate for a smile and a tale." She laughed, suddenly feeling effervescent, full of beauty, full of life.

Jaime's crooked smile was the only reply she needed. He took her hand in his and, with a light kiss to her fingers, they followed the water home.

Acknowledgments

Watermark was a story in my head long before it ever saw life on the page. I have many people to thank for their support over the years, starting with my family and friends. First and foremost, I thank my sister, Sujatha, who started this journey with me. I also want to thank Laurence, whose patience with a tortuous, and often obscure, path cannot be measured. I thank my parents, Shankar and Bhanu, and Aunt Betty for their faith in me; Ejner Fulsang and Annette for their thoughtful comments and discussion; and John, for turning whimsy into reality. I must also thank Tom and Alandra, as well as the cast and crew of Project Watermark, for bringing my characters literally to life, and Audra and Kelly for their precise, polished work.

I would also like to express my gratitude to the many readers, primarily at Antioch University, on Greytalk and on NovelPro, with a special shoutout to J. R. Lankford, who have given me their valuable feedback at different stages of the writing proces. Your kind words and honest criticism are much appreciated.

My sincere thanks to Lucia Macro and Esi Sogah at Avon Books and, lastly, to my agent Marly Rusoff, without whose dedicated efforts Auda's story would have stayed silent forever.

Author's Note

𝕿𝖍𝖊 𝖒𝖊𝖉𝖎𝖊𝖛𝖆𝖑 𝖊𝖗𝖆 is one that has garnered much interest, as is evidenced by the plethora of books, both fictive and not, that concern this time period. For me, the Middle Ages have always seemed a delicious bundle of contradictions—a time of mystery, deep convictions, and yet also expansive social change. Whether through open or private (often heretical) discussions, such weighty topics as women's equality, the role of the Church with respect to daily life and one's soul, even the possibility of sex bringing one closer to God, were discussed. Right alongside derogatory comments about the Church's excesses were heretical sects studying God's word and inquisitors actively seeking to stamp out their efforts.

My personal interest in the era is best exemplified by the development and spread of papermaking from Moorish to Christian Spain and through the rest of Europe, as well as the subsequent growth and rebellion of an educated middle class. Most of this novel is based on nuggets of historical fact, although I have manipulated people, time, and place in the interest of spinning what I hope is a gripping tale.

The details of papermaking are accurate. Although there is no direct evidence that papermaking flourished in Narbonne, there are some who believe papermaking was significantly advanced by heretical sects who needed cheap writing materials for their secret studies. I chose Narbonne as the setting for this story for several reasons:

It bore great commercial promise in medieval times;

It was a remarkable haven from heresy, even while surrounded by the Inquisition;

It was also a great patron of troubadour poetry and discussions of courtly love;

It was a cosmopolitan society, with various Christian influences (Hospitallers, Benedictines, Cistercians, Franciscans, and Dominicans), the largest Jewish population in southern France, and the regular presence of Gypsies and Moorish influences.

Additionally, the flooding of the Aude did occur in 1320, which added considerable drama to my tale. The flood eventually changed the course of the river Aude, and rendered the once-lofty Narbonne a literal backwater.

Catharism, or the religion of the Good Men, is a poorly documented heretical religion that permeated much of south France during the eleventh through fourteenth centuries. The Archbishop Bernard de Farges, the *Vicomte* Amaury, and *Vicomtesse* Jeanne were historical personages; however, all aspects of their lives and personalities are fictional. The remaining characters, and the story in general, are works of fiction.

Finally, any errors, whether in history or ideology, are my fault alone.

Glossary

armarius: director of a scriptorium
A la vòstra: To your health. (Occ.)
amé notz: with nuts (*Occ.*)
Au va!: Are you kidding? Come on! (*Cat.*)
Baiser la veuve: Fuck the widow. (*Fr.*)
banderii: local guards (*Fr.*)
Bonhommes: the Good Men; *les Innocents* (*Fr.*)
canonical hours: the liturgical hours, loosely given as

Matins	(sunrise)
Lauds	(6 A.M.)
Prime	(9 A.M.)
Terce	(noon)
Sext	(3 P.M.)
Nones	(6 P.M.)
Vespers	(sunset)
Complies	(bedtime/nighttime)

cappa: robe
cers: northwesterly wind
consolamentum: baptismal sacrament of the Good Men
denier: medieval penny

domna/dominus: formal title—lady/lord

donjon: prison/vault (dungeon)

du cabre: of a goat (*Occ.*)

fin d'amour: fine love (*Fr.*)

garigue: brush and shrubs (*Fr.*)

houri: fair woman of paradise (*Ar.*)

jongleur: medieval entertainer (*Fr.*)

kirtle: woman's gown or outer coat

la fadata: fey girl (*Occ.*)

la Vierge: the Virgin

ma filla: my daughter (*Cat.*)

Mare: Mother (*Cat.*)

marin: warm marine wind

masco: witch (*Occ.*)

Michaelmas: a feast signaling that start of autumn; a holy day of obligation

midons: my lord—code name for my lady (*Occ.*)

monsen: sir (*Occ.*)

Na: Madame, honorific (*Occ.*)

oc: yes (*Occ.*)

oyez: hear; listen (*Occ.*)

pariage: sum paid to the king for protection (*Fr.*)

pelardon: sheep's cheese (*Occ.*)

perfectus/perfecta/perfecti: perfected Good Man/Woman (priest)

rioja: red table wine (*Sp.*)

roumèque: a fantastic creature that frightens children (*Occ.*)

scriptorium: room where manuscripts are read, stored, and copied

simple: a medicine, often taken as a draught or tonic

sou: medieval silver coin

toft: plot of land attached to back of house

trobairitz: female troubadours (*Occ.*)

troubadour: singer and composer of love songs, especially in
  medieval Languedoc
trencher: stale or dry bread used as a plate
una mica: a little (*Cat.*)
verjuice: acidic (fruit) juice used as a condiment

Cat.   Catalan
Fr.   French
Ar.   Arabic
Occ.   Occitan
Sp.   Spanish

Chronology

Date	Event
1085	Papermaking in Xativa, Spain
1209	Pope Innocent III launches Albigensian crusade in southern France; Narbonne fortifies defenses
1215	Fourth Lateran Council pronounces sweeping Church reforms; has little effect
1221	Holy Roman Emperor Frederick II declares all official documents written on paper invalid
1231	Dominican convent in Narbonne established
1234–1237	Inquisition in Narbonne
1235	Heretics arrested in Narbonne
1238	James I of Aragon gains control of Muslim paper mills in Xativa; paper mill starts in Capellades, Catalonia
1248–1250	Inquisitors probe Narbonne
1249	Cistercian/Benedictine abbey of Fontfroide acquires milling rights in Narbonne
1250	Italy becomes major paper producer

1261	Fontfroide starts keeping house in bourg of Narbonne
1272	First stone of Cathedrale de St. Juste is blessed and laid
1276	Watermark invented in Fabriano mills in Tuscany; first paper mill in Italy
1278	Mirror invented
1280	Spectacles invented
1285–1314	Philip IV (the Fair) rules with absolute arrogance; controls papacy
1288	Fontfroide has land dispute with consuls in bourg of Narbonne; woman associated with Beguines sees visions and is accused of heresy
1289	Fontfroide charges Narbonne citizens to cut wood; block printing begins in Ravenna
1290	Franciscan Church in St. Felix starts construction
1294–1303	Boniface VIII becomes pope; defies Philip IV
1295–1306	Donjon (part of Cathedrale de St. Juste) built in Narbonne
1296	Fontfroide takes over one-fourth of Narbonne's grain-measuring rights
1298–1315	Spirituals dominate Narbonne's Franciscan Church *Vicomte* Amauri II (who is at odds with Narbonne's archbishop) rules; loses power to the king from 1309–1322
1305	Clement V becomes pope
1306	Expulsion of Jews from France (they go mostly to Barcelona and Toledo)
1307–1323	Bernard Gui is inquisitor in Toulouse, writes *The Conduct of Inquiry Concerning Heretical Depravity*

1309–1378	Avignon papacy (moved to Avignon by Clement V)
1311	Pierre Authiè—the "Last Cathar"—is burned at the stake
1312	Thirteen guilds in Narbonne appeal to the king claiming consuls are unfairly held by rich families; reforms never take effect
1314	Philip IV dies; succeeded by three sons
1314–1315	Dante's *Inferno* is complete; he writes *Purgatorio* and begins *Paradiso*
1315–mid-1800s	The "little ice age"
1315	Bad weather; crop failure in northwest Europe
1315–1317	Beguines burn for heresy in Narbonne
1317–1343	Friars of Narbonne summoned to Avignon to defend themselves for being Spirituals; two burn at stake; Franciscan Church is excommunicated but is appealed by consuls
1320	Flooding of Aude in Narbonne; port silts up
1322	Poor of Narbonne crushed at Fontfroide's gates by Church's negligence; twenty-one Beguines burn
1328	Forty-nine people (mostly artisans) accused of heresy in Narbonne
1332	First service in Cathedrale de St. Juste
1337–1453	One Hundred Years' War
1338	Oldest known paper mill begins in France
1348	Black Plague; Great Schism for control of papacy between Rome and Avignon
1387–1400	Geoffrey Chaucer writes *The Canterbury Tales*
1388–1470	French monks produce paper for holy texts
1400	Paper for low-grade textbooks, volumes of sermon, popular tracts, and papal indulgences

1450   Gutenberg invents printing press; paper becomes popular

1517   Martin Luther's *Ninety-five Theses;* Galileo's incarceration

1648   Peace of Westphalia

Selected Bibliography

The following bibliography is presented for the reader who wishes to read more about the factual history and influences behind this novel.

Anonymous. *Aymeri of Narbonne: A French Epic Romance.* Edited and translated by Michael A. H. Newth (2005). New York: Italica Press.

Barber, M. (2000). *The Cathars.* Harlow, UK; New York: Pearson Education.

Bayley, H. (1967). *A New Light on the Renaissance, Displayed in Contemporary Emblems.* New York: Benjamin Blom.

Bogin, M. (1980). *The Women Troubadours.* New York: Norton.

Caille, J. (2005). *Medieval Narbonne: A City at the Heart of the Troubadour World.* Hampshire, UK: Ashgate Publishing.

Cantor, N. F. (1999). *The Encyclopedia of the Middle Ages.* New York: Viking.

Cheyette, F. L. (2001). *Ermengard of Narbonne and the World of the Troubadours.* Ithaca: Cornell University Press.

Duby, G. (1991). *France in the Middle Ages 987–1460: From Hugh Capet to Joan of Arc.* Oxford, UK; Cambridge, MA: Wiley-Blackwell.

Emery, R. W. (1967). *Heresy and Inquisition in Narbonne.* New York: AMS Press.

Gies, F., and J. Gies (1999). *Daily Life in Medieval Times: A Vivid, Detailed Account of Birth, Marriage, and Death; Food, Clothing, and Housing; Love and Labor, in the Middle Ages.* New York: Black Dog & Leventhal Publishers.

Gui, B. (2006). *The Inquisitor's Guide: A Medieval Manual on Heretics.* Translated by J. Shirley. Welwyn Garden City, UK: Ravenhall Books.

Halsall, Paul, ed. *Internet Medieval Sourcebook.* http://www.fordham.edu/halsall/sbook.html

Hunter, D. (1943). *Papermaking : The History and Technique of an Ancient Craft.* New York: Knopf.

Lindberg, D. C. (1992). *The Beginnings of Western Science: The European Scientific Tradition in Philosophical, Religious, and Institutional Context, 600 B.C. to A.D. 1450.* Chicago: University of Chicago Press.

McEvedy, C., and C. McEvedy (1992). *The New Penguin Atlas of Medieval History.* London; New York: Penguin.

Ong, Walter J. (2002). *Orality and Literacy: The Technologizing of the Word.* 2nd ed. London: Routledge.

Scully, T. (1995). *The Art of Cookery in the Middle Ages.* Woodbridge, Suffolk, UK; Rochester, NY: Boydell Press.

Siraisi, N. G. (1990). *Medieval & Early Renaissance Medicine: An Introduction to Knowledge and Practice.* Chicago: University of Chicago Press.

A+
AUTHOR
INSIGHTS,
EXTRAS &
MORE...

FROM

**VANITHA
SANKARAN**

AND

AVON A

The Story Behind the Book

When I decided to write my first novel, I knew right away it would be about papermaking. Paper has always fascinated me. As a child, I was forever asking for a clean sheet; in old photographs, I'm often clutching that empty page. Sometimes I actually wrote on the paper, but most times, just holding it gave me a sense of comfort.

My search for the story behind papermaking focused primarily on the craft's spread during the Middle Ages. I've long thought that, if not for the plague, the Middle Ages would have blossomed into the frenzy of thought, reason, and discovery that characterized the Renaissance. The later part of the medieval era was ripe with change; it was teeming with growing tensions between the burgeoning middle class, the corrupt Church, and a nobility worried about its own power, which makes the perfect backdrop for a compelling story. How would paper, an invention brought to Europe by the Moors and deeply distrusted by the Church, have fared in such a chaotic environment?

In order to pick the right location to host my tale, I looked at small towns along the prominent trade routes that led from Spain—where the Moors built some of Europe's first paper mills—to France, Italy, and England. Today, each of these towns, a gold mine of history, still proudly boasts to history-savvy travelers of surviving the turmoil and destruction. I chose a French town, Narbonne, as my setting. Situated in the heart of heretical France, where alternate religious philosophies often thrived alongside the Church, Narbonne remained a haven for heretics, Jews, and other undesirables, even during the Inquisition. Compared to the thousands who were consigned to the flames in neighboring cities, very few people burned in Narbonne. And the town has a colorful cultural story of its own: its rise as a prominent trading town and its surprising demise, brought about by the flooding of its river.

Much of medieval Narbonne exists today. Though the *vicomte*'s palace has been lost to time, the archbishop's palace, which went through centuries of construction, remains an impressive edifice. The donjon has also been preserved with eerily little degradation. St. Paul's, in the bourg, looks little different than it would have in Auda's time. Her namesake, the river Aude, still flows through the city. So much of the medieval flavor has been preserved in Narbonne that when I walked down the old cobbled Via Domitia, sniffing the smells of myrrh and incense in St. Paul's, I almost felt my characters come to life. I felt their excitement at introducing the new craft of paper making into their world as if it were my own.

Developing Auda as a character to love and admire was not as easy a task. I didn't want to write another historical novel with a heroine whose sensibility is taken from modern times, a feminist who believed men and women are equal and set out to prove it. Nor could Auda be one of the illiterate commoners, with a convenient faith in this incipient art of paper. Her ability to read and write, and her love of paper, had to be born of need as well as desire. Through several incarnations, Auda appeared as an orphan, a cripple, even a healer. Eventually, she emerged as someone who didn't recognize her own limits, someone who had every reason to use paper, for nothing less than to find her own self.

People often ask me why I write historical fiction, where these characters and themes come from. I was never a particularly good history student in school; dates and names often elude me. The best answer I can give is that historical fiction appeals to both sides of my brain. I love the empiricism of historical research and the creativity of writing. It is a good balance between the real and the imagined, a duality not unlike the one at the heart of Auda's story itself.

My research for the novel began with a practical experiment trying to recreate paper production from the Middle Ages. For two months, I kept a bucket of molding linens on my balcony, judiciously adding bird droppings, lye made from ashes, and rainwater to help the cloth break down. Each day, I noted the color, consistency, and pH of the mixture in my notebook. Then I would inhale the sharp scents, press the slick material between my fingers, and capture every detail in paragraphs of description. I'm not sure where the scientific explanation stopped and artistic expression began, but I do know that much of what I learned in this experiment made it into my novel.

In many cases, researching the past made the history feel more modern than I ever expected. People of the medieval era seem to me every bit as curious about the world as we are today. Nobles debated the meaning of love in their courts. Learned clergymen discussed heady subjects like whether sex brought one closer to God. Dissidents questioned the feudal system and the meaning of freedom. There were even people wondering what role the written word could have in a culture weaned on oral news and entertainment. And Auda encounters all of these dilemmas, in varying degrees, throughout the story.

My goal in writing this novel was not to write a story that probably did happen, but one that possibly could have. The narrative of history, for me, is just like fiction with some immutable facts thrown in. All I had to do was stretch my imagination and let the story come to life. I hope you will do the same.

Papermaking: A History

The history of humankind is intricately intertwined with our desire to create a record of our thoughts, hopes, and imaginations. Written communication can be traced back to cave drawings and symbols etched into wood and stone; historically, the form it took was manifested in a myriad of ways depending on the resources that were readily available. For example, on one continent you might find papyrus, constructed from the stems of water plants, while on another, rice paper would be the written surface of choice, made not of rice at all, nor pressed out like paper, but cut from the pith of a shrub.

Throughout time, we have gone through an amazing range of writing surfaces, from bark to rock, metal to ceramic to animal skin. Paper is unlike these natural sources in that it is a man-made invention, defined as a thin sheet manufactured from a fibrous pulp made of straw, bark, or old cloth. The fibrous pulp is first macerated until each filament is separated. The filaments are then mixed in water so they can intermingle, or felt. The interwoven fibers are sieved through a screen, dried and smoothed, then sized so as to better accept pigments and ink.

We believe that papermaking began sometime between 100 BC and 100 AD when the Chinese sought a surface with which to capture and perfect their delicate art of calligraphy. The Chinese empire took to paper wholeheartedly, using it not just for handwriting and record keeping but also for ornamental purposes. Although the first papers of China were likely made from disintegrated cloth, cheap and plentiful vegetable materials soon became the preferred source. It was this bark-based paper that passed from China through Korea into Japan that not only made the first paper printings but also encouraged the establishment numerous paper mills, as well as a guild, to support the emperor's needs. China, Korea, and Japan elevated not just paper but the papermaking process to an art form. These arts exist to this day.

From China, paper also made its way into central Asia, India, and Persia through well-known trade routes and, from there, spread to Samarkand, Baghdad, and Damascus, then into Egypt and Morocco. It took nearly five centuries for papermaking to find Europe, via either Spain or Italy. Although Europe initially regarded paper as an inferior writing material, more fragile than parchment and "invented" by distrusted Jews and Moors, slowly paper became an accepted Western commodity.

The papers of early Europe were made differently than those of Asia. Rather than using vegetable matter, Europeans preferred old rag scraps that had no other use and made hardy pulp. The cloths were macerated into fibers, dried into sheets, and then dipped in gelatin to change the porosity. The result was a material more adaptable to quill and ink than the delicate vegetable-based papers suited for slow calligraphy. This strong rag-based paper was also well suited to the rigors of Gutenberg's printing press and its use of movable type. As printed books became commonplace and literacy spread throughout Europe, so did paper, a much cheaper and more plentiful commodity than either parchment or vellum. After just a few decades of books printed with movable type, paper not only became an acceptable form of communication, it became the preferred one.

The spread of paper throughout the world also had a profound impact on how people communicated, not just in correspondence and literature, but also in the way that they spoke. People no longer had to devise long oral narratives that relied on rhyming and rhythm to stay fresh in their listeners' minds. Now they could be short and precise, or clever and sly; they could even ramble without end because one no longer needed to rely on memory alone to keep track of words. One could now go back and read them.

Society today is experiencing an information upheaval not unlike the one that happened with papermaking and printed books of hundreds of years ago. These days we have an explosion of media that is conveyed digitally; and these audio, visual, and even written communications have given a new twist to how we are able to communicate and share those communications with the world around us. Much like in our medieval past, there is a frenzy of excitement about the leveling of the playing field. Anyone who has access to a computer can now reach out to a worldwide audience. And as the reader, we now have a world full of voices clamoring for our attention. As in times past, we now have to look at the criteria we use to judge the worth of a communication, whether we accept it as truth or distrust the message and the messenger.

It's not so different from the days of medieval paper after all.

Papermaking: A Simple Recipe

Making paper at home is a fun way to get a feel for how old-time papermakers would have worked in their studios. Paper is such an integral part of our lives today and has such a long history. As a scientist accustomed to research, I wanted to get a feel for the kind of work Martin and Auda would have done in their own studio. How much work was it to make paper pulp? What did the rotting linens feel like? Smell like? Would the finished product bear any resemblance to the paper we use today?

Methods and materials have come a long way since the Middle Ages; however, although there are a number of subtleties that can affect the look and feel of paper, the process is essentially a simple one. In this recipe, we are going to use recycled paper as our starting material so that we don't have to worry about boiling or macerating our fibers, and about sizing the finished product. As you get more experienced at papermaking, these are some alternatives you might want to experiment with.

Materials Needed

Fiber source (one cup loosely packed scrap or recycled paper)
Kitchen blender
Wood frame (any size will do)
Metal-wire mesh (such as window screening)
Vat or tub large enough to accommodate a horizontally submerged frame
Two pieces of wool felt slightly larger than frame
Laundry line and clothespins

Step 1

We'll begin by assembling all of the necessary materials.

First, tear the scrap paper into one-inch squares and gather into a pile. You might want to try different types of scrap paper to experiment with color, consistency, and smoothness. Keep in mind that long fibers intermingle better than shorter fibers and thus create a stronger sheet of paper. You can check fiber length by tearing a piece of your scrap paper. Does it tear smoothly (short fibers) or leave a raggedy edge (long fibers)?

Next, cut a section of the window screening and stretch it over the wooden frame. Staple the screening into place. Make sure this screen is flat and clean—the quality of your paper depends on it.

Fill the vat or tub halfway full with water and set aside. Next to it, spread out one of the wool felt pieces.

Step 2

Mix the paper squares you've torn with water and pour into a blender, adding four parts of water to one part paper. For smoother pulp, you may want to boil the paper–water mixture for a couple hours ahead of time, or soak the paper overnight. Blend the mixture until the pulp becomes creamy and smooth.

Step 3

Holding the frame over the vat, pour the pulp onto the screen and shake laterally until the screen is covered. Slowly lower the frame into the vat of water and continue shaking laterally until the pulp is dispersed evenly over the screen. Raise the horizontal frame up and out of the tub and let the water drip out.

Step 4

Turn the frame over on top of the wool felt piece next to the vat. The sheet of pulp should fall out of the frame easily; if it doesn't, tap the frame gently until the pulp falls onto the felt. Cover the pulp sheet with the other piece of felt and push gently on the pile to squeeze out the excess water. Be careful to push evenly. You may want to use a rolling pin or handpress to get out as much water as you can.

Step 5

Press out as much water as you can, then carefully remove the top piece of wool felt. Take two corners of the paper and slowly roll the paper off the other piece of felt. Clip the sheet to a laundry line with two clothespins and let dry in a warm area shielded from any wind.

Drying time can take anywhere from three hours to a day, depending on the thickness of the sheet and the amount of sunlight.

Other Ideas

As you can see, the basic steps to making paper are quite simple. From here, you can experiment with different types of fibers and other additives, such as flowers, glitter, and dyes, which can be mixed with the pulp—just add white glue or startch as you blend the pulp with the additives. If you want to use vegetable matter as your fiber source, be sure not to skip step 2, where you boil the pulp. You may also want to add some white glue or other starch to the pulp to help bind the fibers together. And if you are feeling adventurous, you may even want to give your screen some texture—shape it into a person's face, for example, and make a paper mask. The possibilities are endless!

Questions About *Watermark*

1. Elena, Auda's mother, is often talked about in terms of her sacrifice. How did this sacrifice affect Auda? How is this sacrifice similar and different from the story of the pelican told by the archbishop?

2. Auda suffered two traumas at birth—her albinism and the loss of her tongue. Which experience shaped her more?

3. How does Auda use her other senses and abilities to make up for her lack of voice?

4. Paper is discussed as a way to share knowledge among all people, thus equalizing everyone. Do you agree with this premise? Why or why not?

5. How is writing different from speech, both in terms of what and how something is communicated? Is there an inherent danger in the act or products of writing, and in making the ability accessible to people of all backgrounds? Would the inquisitors' manual be more or less fearsome if it were transmitted by the spoken rather than the written word?

6. What about the Good Men's philosophy scares the Church? How do piety and fear work against each other?

7. Why does Martin give the scribing job to Auda? What are his hopes for her?

8. Medieval beauty and love were spoken in terms of both body and spirit. How do these concepts apply to Auda and Poncia? How do they apply to women today?

9. Watermarks were thought to be a way for heretics and infidels to communicate with each other. How do you think people might have used watermarks, and their designs, to communicate? Why is this different than a baker's mark or a guild's symbol?

10. Medieval women often married for security rather than for love. Did Auda make the right choice in rejecting Edouard? How might her life have been different had she married him?

11. How does the *vicomtesse* become a mother figure to Auda? Is she the type of mother Auda wished for? How does she displace or augment Poncia as a caretaker?

12. As Auda finds new freedom in her job as a scribe, Poncia retreats into her marriage and her faith. What events in Poncia's life cause this retreat? How is Poncia's shuttered life similar and different than Auda's childhood?

13. What does the *vicomte* see in Auda? What does Jaime? How do the attentions of these men compare? Do they fall into the category of courtly love?

14. How is life at the palace different from Auda's previous life? Was it a wise decision to send her to a place of such prominence?

15. Both Auda and Jaime seem to view the world differently than most others. How do they view each other?

16. The transition between the spoken and written word also brought with it ideas of single authorship, accountability, and plagiarism. How does storytelling written by one author compare with the traditions of oral storytelling by multiple performers?

17. Courtly love seems to have different definitions according to men versus women. What are these differences? How do they compare to modern-day attitudes from both genders?

18. It is easy to see why cheap paper may have had appeal for heretics wishing to share their ideas with many. Who else might have been attracted by paper? How could the Church have used paper to its benefit?

19. In the story, sacrifice is touted as a method of asking for something one wants. What sacrifices have each of the characters made and for what?

20. Auda's verses portray men of different stations, including those of the Church, as villains and predators. How are these views supported by her own experiences? How much of an influence does Jaime's past have on her?

21. What significance does Auda's gift of a watermark to her father have?

22. When Auda decides to trade her body for the *vicomte*'s help, whom does she betray the most—the *vicomte*, the *vicomtesse*, her imprisoned father, Jaime, or herself?

23. René appears to have a deep effect on Auda. How do his actions impact her choices later?

24. The death of Martin and Auda's torture can be blamed on many people. How did each character's actions get them to this point? Are any of them truly guilty or truly innocent?

25. How does Auda learn that men and women can be equal? How does she use this philosophy?

26. Both the archbishop and the *vicomte* find themselves doing the unthinkable in favor of a larger good. Does the inquisitor fit into this category as well? Why or why not?

27. The relationship between Auda and Poncia is close throughout the book. What did each sister expect of the other? How were these expectations met or disregarded?

28. Given Jaime's hatred for the Church and Auda's traumatic experience with the inquisitor, was it a surprise the couple ended up at a monastery? Does this mark a new life and change in attitudes for them?

29. Watermarks, and being marked by water, are discussed throughout the book. How do these concepts apply to each character?

30. What is the nature of true love? Do any of these characters find it?

VANITHA SANKARAN holds a Ph.D. in biomedical engineering from Northwestern University and an M.F.A. in creative writing from Antioch University. Her stories have been published in various print and online journals; in addition, she is a founding editor for the literary journal *flashquake*. She is at work on her second novel, which is about printmaking in Renaissance Venice.

CPSIA information can be obtained
at www.ICGtesting.com
Printed in the USA
LVOW08s1959240118
563591LV00004B/75/P